CLIVE CUSSLER
THE
HEIST

TITLES BY CLIVE CUSSLER

DIRK PITT ADVENTURES®

Clive Cussler The Corsican Shadow
  (by Dirk Cussler)
Clive Cussler's The Devil's Sea
  (by Dirk Cussler)
Celtic Empire (with Dirk Cussler)
Odessa Sea (with Dirk Cussler)
Havana Storm (with Dirk Cussler)
Poseidon's Arrow (with Dirk Cussler)
Crescent Dawn (with Dirk Cussler)
Arctic Drift (with Dirk Cussler)
Treasure of Khan (with Dirk Cussler)
Black Wind (with Dirk Cussler)
Trojan Odyssey
Valhalla Rising
Atlantis Found
Flood Tide
Shock Wave
Inca Gold
Sahara
Dragon
Treasure
Cyclops
Deep Six
Pacific Vortex!
Night Probe!
Vixen 03
Raise the Titanic!
Iceberg
The Mediterranean Caper

SAM AND REMI FARGO ADVENTURES®

Wrath of Poseidon (with Robin Burcell)
The Oracle (with Robin Burcell)
The Gray Ghost (with Robin Burcell)
The Romanov Ransom (with Robin Burcell)
Pirate (with Robin Burcell)
The Solomon Curse (with Russell Blake)
The Eye of Heaven (with Russell Blake)
The Mayan Secrets (with Thomas Perry)
The Tombs (with Thomas Perry)
The Kingdom (with Grant Blackwood)
Lost Empire (with Grant Blackwood)
Spartan Gold (with Grant Blackwood)

ISAAC BELL ADVENTURES®

Clive Cussler The Heist (by Jack Du Brul)
Clive Cussler The Sea Wolves
  (by Jack Du Brul)
The Saboteurs (with Jack Du Brul)
The Titanic Secret (with Jack Du Brul)
The Cutthroat (with Justin Scott)
The Gangster (with Justin Scott)
The Assassin (with Justin Scott)
The Bootlegger (with Justin Scott)
The Striker (with Justin Scott)
The Thief (with Justin Scott)
The Race (with Justin Scott)
The Spy (with Justin Scott)
The Wrecker (with Justin Scott)
The Chase

CLIVE CUSSLER
THE HEIST

An Isaac Bell Adventure®

※

JACK DU BRUL

G. P. PUTNAM'S SONS
NEW YORK

PUTNAM
— EST. 1838 —

G. P. PUTNAM'S SONS
Publishers Since 1838
An imprint of Penguin Random House LLC
penguinrandomhouse.com

Library of Congress Cataloging-in-Publication Data

Names: Du Brul, Jack B., author. | Cussler, Clive.
Title: The heist / Jack Du Brul.
Other titles: At head of title: Clive Cussler
Description: New York : G. P. Putnam's Sons, 2024. |
Identifiers: LCCN 2024000529 (print) | LCCN 2024000530 (ebook) |
ISBN 9780593713587 (hardcover) | ISBN 9780593713594 (e-pub)
Subjects: LCGFT: Detective and mystery fiction. | Novels.
Classification: LCC PS3554.U223 H45 2024 (print) |
LCC PS3554.U223 (ebook) | DDC 813/.54—dc23/eng/20240117
LC record available at https://lccn.loc.gov/2024000529
LC ebook record available at https://lccn.loc.gov/2024000530

Printed in the United States of America
1st Printing

Title page photograph by Vladimir Mulder/Shutterstock.com

CAST OF CHARACTERS

THE AGENTS

JOSEPH VAN DORN Legendary founder of the Van Dorn Detective Agency

ISAAC BELL Chief investigator of the Van Dorn Agency

ARCHIBALD ABBOTT Van Dorn detective and Bell's best friend and frequent partner

JAMES DASHWOOD Van Dorn detective and Bell's former protégé

CLINT SLOCOMB Van Dorn detective in the Philadelphia office

TELFORD JONES Van Dorn detective in the Baltimore office

BERNARD ARSENEAUX Van Dorn detective in the New Orleans office

OTHERS

MARION BELL Isaac's wife and a filmmaker

EBENEZER BELL Boston banker and Isaac's father

LILLIAN ABBOTT Archie's wife and best friend to Marion

CHRISTOFF TAMERLANE Marion's go-to assistant

WILLIAM McADOO Secretary of the Treasury

REX SMITH Aircraft owner in Maryland

TONY JANNUS Aircraft pilot

CHARLEY BRIGGS Contractor on the Bureau of Engraving and Printing building

HARVEY WANAMAKER Philadelphia locksmith

REGGIE HAUSER Railroad executive

C. FREDERICK LAWSON Head of security at the Bureau of Engraving and Printing building

PHILIP FINDLEY Head of the Atlanta Reserve bank

VIC CARVER Treasury agent

PAUL HAYGARTH Treasury agent

JACKSON PICKETT Newport, Rhode Island, socialite

FEDORA SCARSWORTH-PICKETT Wife of Jackson Pickett

ISIDOR STEINEM Pickett's attorney

THOMAS LASSITER Newport police detective

RAY BURNS Newport police detective and Lassiter's protégé

FLYNN AND SEAN O'CONNER Leaders of a Baltimore harbor gang

MICHALEEN RIORDAN Irish assassin

JOSE Louisiana boatman

CLIVE CUSSLER

THE
HEIST

1

Washington, D.C.

August 1914

WHEN WOODROW WILSON ENTERED THE LAVISH DINING room aboard the presidential yacht, *Mayflower*, the men seated around the conference table got to their feet and turned to him in silent reverence. The slender President was dressed in a fashionable mocha-colored lounge suit that seemed to add to his tall stature. He had a long, some said horsey, face, while his stance and expression were that of a stern schoolmaster. But when his lips parted, a velvety voice laced with humility and intelligence enraptured all within earshot.

"Gentlemen, please take a seat before a Potomac River cross-current forces the issue."

A ripple of laughter reverberated through the room as the men visibly relaxed and retook their seats with the President. A white-gloved steward closed the doors behind the chief executive while two Secret Service agents took up station just outside the room.

"Thank you all for joining me today," Wilson said as he settled at the head of the table. "The captain informed me that we will cast off shortly. We will head down river to our planned lunch at Mount Vernon, although I'm sure there are some in this town who would prefer that we keep on sailing, all the way to South America," he added, to a flourish of grins. "While this would be a prime opportunity for a few hands of poker and a good cigar among new friends, we do have a bit of business to conduct." He tilted his head a moment, then turned to the steward. "On second thought, there's no reason we can't enjoy a smoke and a drink in the process."

Wilson was relatively new to politics, having won the White House only two years after being elected the governor of New Jersey, but he'd been a college dean for many years prior and knew how to lead. And having garnered nearly fifty percent of the popular vote in a three-candidate race, he enjoyed a strong mandate to do so.

The twenty-eighth President of the United States was given a rosewood box of cigars and he handed it to the man on his left. As the cigars were passed around the room, the steward returned with a tray of shot glasses and a bottle of amber liquid with a label so old it was peeling away.

"This is our first meeting together and it must be one of celebration. This bottle of scotch was a congratulatory gift from H. H. Asquith, England's prime minister, upon my inauguration. I'm told it was aged in a barrel for fifty years and has been in this bottle another fifty."

Shots were poured and the room was soon wreathed in aromatic smoke. The consensus was the whiskey was the finest any had ever enjoyed. "I might just be compelled to run for reelection if Asquith will promise another bottle for a second inauguration," Wilson said to more laughter.

The meeting on the yacht was the culmination of years of work and careful negotiations across party lines and involving all three branches of the government. The President, knowing he had his audience, began his speech.

"If I were to claim the absolute brain trust of American banking was assembled before me today, there wouldn't be a dissenting voice in all the nation. Each of you have dozens of years of experience running some of our most successful banks and now each of you has agreed to head one of the twelve newly created Federal Reserve Banks and finally give the country the centralized monetary system it needs as we forge ahead."

"I need not tell this august group that the United States is growing or that the budding twentieth century will be our time to shine among the nations of the world. But in order for us to reach our fullest potential, we must come together in a more centralized fashion."

He was greeted by murmurs of agreement.

"We saw less than twenty-five years ago how the states and even individual counties set their own time standards. Efficient railroad scheduling was nigh impossible as a result, and fatal accidents occurred with regularity. It took all the railroad owners coming together to codify the system of regulated time zones we use today.

"That is but one example of how our nation's needs have outstripped our ability to meet them at a state or local level. The devastating bank runs we endure on a cyclical basis are another example of how America is falling behind the rest of the civilized world. The Panic of 1907 nearly ruined many of us and left countless businesses and individuals destroyed in its wake. I imagine each of you had at least one acquaintance or close friend end his life because of his ruination."

Heads nodded around the table.

"The individual states will maintain all of the rights laid out in our Constitution, but the federal government must take a stronger leadership role and that begins with a private, centralized banking system overseen by the board I have appointed."

The men in the room hung on Wilson's every word. All but one man. Peering out a side porthole in boredom, Isaac Bell, lead detective for the Van Dorn Agency, found few topics less appealing than banking.

"And this, gentlemen, shall be our new banner." Wilson opened a slim leather case he'd just been given by the man seated next to him and withdrew a neat stack of green paper cut in a rectangular shape about the size of an invitation envelope. In a somewhat theatrical display, he shoved the notes down the table so they fanned out enough for the men to get a couple for themselves. "This is the freshly minted Federal Reserve hundred-dollar bill."

Bell had been standing by the wall with some of the aides, and his disinterest vanished as he reached over an unknown banker's shoulder for one of the bills. He felt the motor yacht begin to pull away from the dock at the Washington Navy Yard and into the lazy current of the Anacostia River just north of where it joined the Potomac. Outside the bank of beveled glass windows and beyond the motor yacht's rail, the massive brick buildings of one of the nation's premier military shipyards slid past in silent majesty.

Bell turned his attention to the hundred-dollar bill, which represented an average worker's monthly pay, give or take. The bill was done in dark green ink and ornately styled. It took him a moment to recognize that the profile figure in the center of the note was none other than Benjamin Franklin, perhaps the cleverest and most forward thinking of the Founding Fathers. To the right of the portrait was a red fleurette surrounded by a Latin phrase Bell's schoolboy tutoring translated roughly as the "Seal of the Treasury of North America." The back of the note was printed in a lighter green and showed five robed figures out of Greek or Roman mythology. The paper and ink had a curious texture unlike anything Bell had felt before. Very tactile, he thought.

A few of the bankers asked their neighbors if they understood the tableau on the back of the bill and Wilson read the room perfectly. "I'm told those characters are Labor, Commerce, Plenty, and Peace. The figure in the middle represents America. A little fancy for my taste, but what's a President's opinion really worth?"

Wilson got some chuckles. The man immediately to Wilson's right was William McAdoo, the secretary of the treasury, and as of earlier this year, the President's son-in-law. He was a tall, lean man with a face that resembled a beardless Abraham Lincoln. There had been some scandal, as he was twice Eleanor Wilson's age and a senior member of the administration, but it had now passed. McAdoo said, "I must ask for all the bills to be returned to me. Some notes have already shipped, but we're trying to keep the design a secret until they go into full circulation."

The mostly gray-bearded bankers passed the notes up the table for McAdoo to place back into the satchel.

Bell used sleight of hand to replace the note he'd examined with a similarly sized Manhattan Bank hundred-dollar bill that he sandwiched between two of the new bills being passed from hand to hand to the treasury secretary. He hid the new hundred in his wallet.

There was a reason for his mild thievery. He planned to distribute hand-drawn facsimiles of the new currency to all active Van Dorn agents. He wanted them as familiar as possible with the new notes because soon after their release, clever counterfeiters would no doubt try to pass fakes on to inexperienced bank tellers and store clerks. Bell anticipated a lucrative trade weeding out phony bills from the real ones until people were accustomed to the new currency.

He watched as the hidden Manhattan Bank note was passed up the table, and just as McAdoo was about to receive it, Bell faked a loud sneeze. The secretary looked up at the disturbance while his hand continued to slip the notes into his bag. He'd not seen the switch and Bell smiled to himself. This made him the first person to pull off a successful heist of the new Federal Reserve Bank. He made his way back to his spot leaning against a bulkhead.

As McAdoo sat down and placed the leather bag on the floor, a white-jacketed steward entered the dining room. Bell thought the aide was there to take the case away, but instead he stood nervously for a moment and then pulled McAdoo aside for a private word. Bell saw McAdoo's face turn pale as he glanced toward Wilson. He took a deep breath and approached the President, whispering something in his ear.

Wilson closed his eyes in a pained look that told of both long-suffering and resignation. He balled his hands into tight fists as if the gesture could hold his emotions in check. After a long pause, he turned and nodded to the steward and the man fled the room.

Wilson glanced around the table, making eye contact with most of the men assembled at his beckoning. "Gentlemen, I have to apologize," he said, his smooth voice turning hoarse. "In a few minutes we're going to divert to the Washington Arsenal, and I will disembark. I . . ." He hesitated, gauging how much he should share, and decided his distinguished company deserved the truth. "Most of you are unaware that my wife is gravely ill. It's her kidneys and there's nothing the doctors can do. When I left for the Navy Yard a short time ago, she was in good spirits and feeling reasonably well. Her attending physician sent a radio telegram just now. She's taken a sudden turn and he requests . . ." Wilson fought through the last few words. ". . . that I be at her bedside."

Bell locked eyes with his father, Ebenezer, who sat at the far end of the table across the room. The senior Bell would head the Reserve Bank of Boston, where the family had been successful lenders for generations. Although it had been years since Isaac's mother had passed away, he and Ebenezer felt the anguish in the President's final sentence as if they had only just left her graveside.

The yacht heeled to starboard as it changed course for the unscheduled stop and increased speed to get the President on his way back to his wife as soon as possible.

Wilson regained his composure quickly enough. As the First Lady had been ill for some time, he had to have grown accustomed, though never desensitized, to grief. He said, "Since you've come from all corners of the country to be here, there is no point to canceling this opportunity to talk. Secretary McAdoo will act as host in my stead, and to be perfectly frank, he speaks your language far better than I do. I only pray I'll understand his report on your discussion's progress."

He strode quickly from the room and vanished down the hallway beyond the glass doors, his armed guards in tow. Though the engines continued to drive the ship, and water sluiced along her hull in a steady whisper, the men in the dining room would maintain a full minute of silence following the President's sad news and abrupt departure.

Secretary McAdoo eventually got to his feet and unnecessarily straightened his tie. He paused, cleared his throat, and finally said, "I know that came as an unwelcome surprise, but my mother-in-law insists her illness be a private, family-only matter. As you can imagine, the President is deeply worried about her well-being, and yet remains fully committed to the launch of the Federal Reserve Bank. He understands that this is an historic moment, and he doesn't want it to slip through our fingers. So, let's refrain a few minutes while President Wilson steps off at the armory, and then we will get down to brass tacks."

While they waited for the luxury yacht to maneuver close to the dock at the Washington Arsenal, the chief steward and an assistant poured fresh coffee from silver carafes and set down plates heaped with pastries dripping with sweet icing or honey.

A few polite conversations were started. Each man at the table owned or ran a successful bank in their district, but because of how the Board was organized none were in competition with any of the others. Bell imagined the banker from Minneapolis, James Rich, according to the placard in front of his plate, had never heard of, or much less met, the man next to him, Atlanta banker Weldon Burdett.

Bell's father had confided in him on the train ride down to D.C. that the choice of Atlanta as home to a Federal Reserve Bank had been quite surprising to many of the others. It was well understood that the most important city in the Deep South in terms of its economy was New Orleans and yet Atlanta had been chosen. There had been some mild grumbling that both President Wilson and his treasury secretary had deep Georgia roots and a little favoritism had been in play.

The *Mayflower* came to a brief stop in the shadow of one of the many buildings along the shore of the armory and pulled away again, backing down the Washington Channel with the current out of the Tidal Basin before turning around near Greenleaf Point. Behind them was Long Bridge, which connected Washington to Alexandria, Virginia. The beat of the engine changed as steam built in the boilers and the sleek craft began picking up speed southward for Mount Vernon.

The conversation around the table soon intensified as each man put forth their vision of how the Federal Reserve should work. The basic framework had been dictated by an act of Congress, but there were many details to work out.

Isaac Bell had only agreed to accompany his father to the conference for the opportunity to meet the President. Bell himself had no interest in politics or politicians, but Joseph Van Dorn was a canny boss who sought opportunity wherever it could be found. It wouldn't hurt to remind the President that the son of one of his new Federal Reserve directors was the lead investigator of the nation's foremost detective agency.

With the President now gone on his sorrowful business and no chance to make his acquaintance, Bell's eyes began to gloss over and his mind to wander as the men discussed the details of discount rates, check fees, revenue sharing, and all manner of financial minutia. He slowly made his way toward the door. His father had noted him shuffling ever closer to escape, and frowned, but none of the others seemed to care.

Ten minutes after reaching the double doors, one finally opened. A steward stepped into the dining room as cautiously as a cat in order to check on the President's guests. Bell took his shot and eased around the doorjamb with even more feline grace. He backed up against the hallway wall and let out a breath. Never had he been more grateful for deciding to not follow in his father's footsteps into the family business than at this moment.

He understood the challenges of high finance and he was even more detail-oriented than most people, but it was all just so boring and the payoff of the work was both uninteresting and far too delayed. Bell liked money as much as anyone, or at least the freedom that having it gave, but amassing more and more for money's sake alone didn't seem a worthy goal.

Picking a winning company or person to invest in took talent and intuition, to be sure, but a banker doesn't know for years if they made the right call. Henry Ford's backers had to wait half a decade and watch him build twenty unsellable prototype cars starting with a model dubbed A until he reached success with the Model T.

In Bell's line of work, the stakes were usually life-and-death and a case rarely lasted more than a week. That suited his temperament far more than sitting in a boardroom talking percentages and shares until his eyes rolled into his skull and he passed out from boredom.

It was a beautiful day. Washington's notorious humidity had broken early this year, and the air was made comfortable by the cool sweet river water. Bell made his way to the open deck to watch the lush banks of the Potomac River slide by. Already Alexandria was far behind them. It used to be that there were a lot more boats heading to Mount Vernon, but a new tramline from the city was faster and cheaper and had poached much of the lucrative tourist trade.

They did pass one such boat and Bell waved back to the children waving enthusiastically at him. He doubted even the pleasure boat's captain knew he was chugging upriver past the presidential yacht. But then he caught sight of the man in the pudgy boat's open wheelhouse snap a crisp salute. Bell turned to look up at the *Mayflower*'s bridge to see her captain salute back just as smartly.

Forty lazy minutes passed, Bell lulled to a state of near-sleep standing at the rail by the gentle breeze, the thrum of the engines, and the dazzle of sunlight that danced across the river's gentle waves. He was just coming to the decision to disembark at Mount Vernon and take the trolley back into the city when he caught a new noise tickling his semiconscious state. His blue eyes flashed open, and his senses were fully aware a second later. He perceived no immediate danger, but something about the idyllic scene had changed.

A noise drew closer. He quickly realized it was an approaching airplane. He looked up, his hat shading his eyes, but the plane was approaching from the east and so it had the sun to its back. Against the brassy glare, it looked like an indistinct dark speck.

Bell considered himself a man of the modern age. He embraced all the changes going on around him, societal as well as technological. Seeing a woman in trousers or an integrated club didn't arouse even a curious glance on his part. But aircraft made his pulse quicken. He had piloted a good many planes and never refused the opportunity to fly.

He kept his attention on the plane, and as it grew closer still, he quickly made his way aft so as not to look directly at the sun to see the approaching craft.

It was a type of plane Bell had never seen before, but that came as little surprise. It seemed each week a new aeronautical engineer or even an established manufacturer was testing a design and pushing the boundaries of performance and endurance. This particular kite had a pilot sitting just ahead of the bi-wings, with a passenger in a seat up at the plane's nose. A large pusher-style engine was mounted just aft of the wings and the prop was a blur behind it. The craft had a twin-boom tail with a broad horizontal stabilizer slung between and normal-looking rudders atop. The motor looked big enough to give the plane impressive velocity, but it appeared to him that they were loafing along at just above stall speed.

There was something very wrong about what Bell was seeing. He knew pilots. He knew how they thought and acted. None would fly low and slow unless they had a reason, and he could think of no innocent ones at the moment.

The aircraft was no more than two hundred feet above the tree line along the river's edge, and as it crossed over the water, the plane sank farther still. It looked as though it were going to fly directly over the presidential yacht at less than fifty feet altitude.

Bell was alone on the fantail with no one around to warn. On reflex he pulled his Browning 9-millimeter automatic from its shoulder rig. And braced for whatever was to come.

2

THE NOISE OF THE PLANE'S ENGINE WAS REACHING A THUN-
derous crescendo as it barreled at the *Mayflower*, but in fact
was bumping along with just enough speed to remain aloft. Bell
didn't raise his pistol just yet, though the urge to defend himself
against an unknowable threat was huge. An instant before the
pusher plane flashed overhead, the passenger leaned over the
rounded nose of his forward compartment and hurled an object at
the steamer. The aircraft immediately went into a climbing left
turn that looped it back over the Virginia countryside.

Bell was too disciplined to shoot indiscriminately. For all he
knew this was some stunt President Wilson had planned for his
guests.

The object hit the *Mayflower* amidships on the port side and
thankfully only a few feet above the waterline. It was an incendiary bomb that smashed against the boat's flank and erupted into
a fireball that quickly boiled up higher than her masts. Bell threw

himself to the deck and covered his head as the overflash of heat hit like he was at the threshold of a potter's kiln. The fire clung to the side of the ship and spread in a gelatinous mass atop the water, breaking up into smaller and smaller islands of flame as the *Mayflower* surged past the site of the attack.

Fire continued to burn along the ship's flank. Bell jumped to his feet and ignored the nearby roaring inferno. The range was more than extreme, but he raised the Browning anyway and fired as fast as he could pull the trigger, anger focusing his concentration to a pinpoint spot. A nearby scream pulled his attention from the fleeing aircraft. A sailor had been splattered with the incendiary fluid and burned like a Roman candle. He performed a macabre dance of unknowable agony.

A crewmate ignored his own safety and crashed into the burning figure with enough force to send them both over the rail. The water doused the fire in a spurt of steam and both men surfaced in the *Mayflower*'s wake. A third sailor grabbed up a pair of cork life rings and leapt over the rail to rescue his comrades.

More sailors started swarming the deck. Bell turned his attention back to the sky, searching for the plane, as it appeared to be circling around. The men were unaware that their aerial attacker was coming back on another bombing run. If the bombardier's aim was better, the men looking to fight the fire with portable extinguishers would be immolated where they stood.

Bell knew his pistol was a tall order against the plane. The engine appeared too robust, and the pilot and passenger were simply too small of a target on an aircraft doing better than sixty knots. It's why bird hunters used shotguns. He needed a way to fill the sky with lead.

He watched for a second and saw the plane was almost through its turn. He had a minute at best before it was in position to release another bomb. When boarding earlier he had passed a closet marked ARMS CABINET in a neat stencil. He rushed there now even as more men reached the deck, one uncurling a fire hose attached to a pump deep within the hull.

Bell swapped out the Browning's spent magazine as he ran.

The metal door mounted flush with the wall was as he remembered it. There was a handle with a lock for which he had no time to find a master-at-arms with the key. He turned his body sideways, aimed, and shot the lock twice, blowing the handle clean off.

That's the moment a wall of smoke erupted from the entry to the dining room, where he'd left his father and the others minutes earlier. With it came the gut-wrenching sound of men in pain and beginning to panic.

Bell ignored the arms locker for a second. Safety was the priority of any ship's crew, but it was doubly important when the principal passenger was the President of the United States. Between where he stood and the dining room was another cabinet, with a glass door outlined in red metal. Inside was a hose hooked up to the ship's pressurized fire prevention system. Bell tore open the cabinet, snapped down on the bronze nozzle to unreel a sufficient amount of canvas hose, and twisted open the platter-sized wheel.

Water erupted from the nozzle with more force than he'd anticipated and he almost lost his footing. He braced his feet, leaned forward as much as necessary, and lurched for the dining room.

Windows were shattered and flames danced in the empty frames while smoke curled and coiled across the ceiling. The fire hadn't taken root inside the ship, but it was a matter of time. Many of the bankers were sitting or lying on the floor, faces and hands covered with blood from the hail of broken glass that must have scattered across the room like grapeshot from a cannon.

"Father?" Bell shouted into the din. "Father!"

He marched across the room, mindful of the injured, but so focused he did step on one man's outstretched arm. The stream of water battled the jellied accelerant, washing it off the window frames more than extinguishing the fire. With each passing second, more of the flames were suppressed or sluiced into the river. Also, Bell knew that each passing second brought the plane that much closer.

A hand grasped his shoulder and he turned to see the familiar face of his father. He didn't look like he'd been injured in the blast.

"Father, take the hose," Bell said. "The attack isn't over."

He passed the bronze nozzle, making certain his father had a proper grip and body angle to keep from being bowled over. He needn't have worried because almost immediately another of the bankers rushed to Ebenezer's side and, together, they manhandled the pulsing jet of water to best effect.

Bell ran back into the hallway to the arms locker and yanked open the door. Inside were several rifles, antiquated boarding cutlasses, and pistols on a shelf with boxes of ammunition. What immediately caught Bell's attention was the light machine gun propped up against the back of the shallow cabinet. It was a Hotchkiss M1909. The French-designed weapon was normally chambered in 8 millimeter, but when they sold licensing rights to the United States the gun was reconfigured to fire standard .30-caliber rounds off a twenty-four-round feed strip that fed right to left.

Bell snatched up the nearly thirty-pound weapon and a box of loaded feed strips. Usually fitted to a bipod or small tripod, this Hotchkiss had a flimsy metal rod on an articulated gimbal where the traditional mounts were attached. He guessed the rod would fit into holes or loops around the yacht's rail to give the weapon stability.

Back on deck, he saw the fire had been extinguished and the men were now watching the airplane as it began another run. They didn't seem to understand the danger.

"Take cover," Bell roared as he raced to the rail and found a piece of pipe welded in place that was perfectly sized to hold the Hotchkiss's monopod. He settled the gun into the pipe, one eye on the plane as it roared along the river's glassy surface. It looked to be making its attack straight over the bow.

Bell reached into the ammo box for one of the stiff strips. He was familiar enough with this type of weapon to know how to charge it and open the receiver to slot the ammo strip home. The angry roar of the approaching bomber's engine grew louder, becoming almost overwhelming. The air vibrated and it felt like the plane was already overhead, but Bell didn't let it distract him. He flipped the gun to full auto before pressing his shoulder against the stock and slid his finger along the trigger guard. He then looked up, crouching slightly so that he could raise the gun's barrel and center the hard iron sight on the fast-approaching plane.

The pilot opened fire on the ship with a pistol clutched in his left hand while his right stayed on the controls. The boat was too big of a target to miss even if he couldn't take aim at individual sailors. Bullets pinged off metal and whizzed past the men like angry hornets, forcing them to hide behind what cover they could.

Bell stood as still as a statue and finally loosened a ten-round burst just as the bombardier at the plane's bow reached up to toss another explosive at the yacht. The galvanizing sound of auto-fire made the cowering sailors cheer. The pilot yanked hard over on the stick just as the bomb left his partner's hand, and while it missed the yacht, it still exploded when it smacked into the river.

A geyser of water shot into the air as though the luxury steamer had been torpedoed, and when it crashed down on the deck it hit like the rain from a tropical cyclone. Bell had lost his hat running for the weapons locker, so he had to wipe at the water dripping down from his sodden hair. His suit was soaked through to his skin. He ignored the discomfort and swung the Hotchkiss around, aiming off the yacht's aft quarter as the odd two-man plane tried to escape.

The pilot should have kept straight on over the length of the boat and could have vanished upriver without exposing himself unnecessarily. But he'd been spooked by the shots that clearly hit his plane and he banked to head due east, presumably for home. The range was growing extreme, but he'd unknowingly presented the side of his plane as a juicy target.

Bell led the biplane like a hunter leading a bird on the wing and fired where the plane would be in the microseconds it took the fusillade to cover the distance. He'd emptied the strip, but didn't hear it auto-eject and fall to the deck. His ears had been hammered by the explosion and the staccato whipcrack of twenty-four .30-caliber bullets cooking off inches from his face.

Out over the Maryland side of the river, the string of bullets punched through the plane's canvas skin, shredding wood and flesh alike. The pilot took hits in his legs, abdomen, and high through his chest. He wasn't killed outright, but was soon coughing up so much blood from his punctured lungs that he wouldn't last long.

The passenger hadn't been hit at all. Bell had been shooting for the engine and pilot and had fired to near-perfect effect.

The bombardier looked back to see if the pilot had also been miraculously saved and saw his partner's mouth gushing strings of scarlet blood into the slipstream. Just as alarming was the wisp of smoke issuing from the engine that suddenly turned to a greasy black streak.

There was no way short of crawling over the outside of the hull to reach the cockpit and even if he could manage it, the bomb thrower had no idea how to fly the plane. He looked back in growing horror as the light slowly faded from the pilot's goggled eyes. He remained upright, pressed back in his seat by the wind, but his hand slipped from the stick. For several minutes, the aerodynamic forces acting on the plane maintained an equilibrium. The craft remained steady and even gained some altitude, soaring over fields and unspoiled forests as it continued away from the Potomac.

But then it hit an air pocket, like an invisible pothole in the sky, and all at once the plane rolled sharply to starboard and its tail pitched up as the big engine began powering the plane in an uncontrolled dive. Even above the throaty rasp of the six-cylinder engine and the growing shriek of the wind over the canvas and wooden wings and through the quivering metal bracing wires, the lone survivor's scream of total terror rang supreme. He closed his eyes in the last few moments, not wanting to witness the plane crashing through a couple of trees and slamming into the ground hard enough to rip the engine from its mount and crush his already lifeless corpse.

The motor tumbled far enough from the plane for its heat and burning oil not to touch off the gasoline spilling from the ruptured tank. Seconds after the crash the forest went quiet again.

BELL KNEW HE'D HIT THE PLANE AS SOON AS HE'D FIRED AND kept watch as it flew away from the river. The sailors had all gotten to their feet and watched with him as the makeshift bomber made its escape seemingly unscathed. And then, as it was just about to vanish, a thin wisp of smoke began to leave a trace of the flight path in the otherwise cloudless sky. The men roared with joy when the gray slash turned into a billowing black stain that showed their attackers weren't going to escape after all.

Bell stood still with his arm draped over the Hotchkiss's hot receiver, his eyes squinting into the east where the plane had finally vanished. He didn't know that part of Maryland, but he knew by the time he found the wreckage he'd likely be an expert.

He acknowledged the applause and back slaps from the young sailors. The jubilant air of survivors celebrating their very lives was quickly quashed when the *Mayflower*'s captain appeared at the rail next to Bell. The ship was already slowing to affect a rescue of the three sailors who'd gone over the side.

"Under other circumstances," he said after introducing himself, "I'd have you taken up on charges of interfering with the operation of a government vessel, but since you saved my ship, my crew, and my guests, I'll just say thank you and be done with it."

"Situations like this usually make me act without giving much thought to the consequences."

The captain nodded. "You have the look about you of someone who finds himself in situations like this far more than the average man."

Bell gave a little chuckle. "You have no idea."

They shook hands and the captain went off with his first officer to assess the damage the firebombing had inflicted on his pride and joy.

Bell waited a minute for the adrenaline to dissolve out of his bloodstream before making his way below to the dining room. The uninjured bankers milled about aimlessly or offered what succor they could to their wounded comrades laid out on the floor. For the most part all the injuries appeared superficial. Bell was little surprised to see his father had stationed himself near the door in a protective position.

Bell might not have his father's affinity for banking, but both men shared common traits of natural leadership and a strong sense of duty.

"Isaac," the elder Bell called when he saw his son enter the dining room. "Are you all right? What happened?"

"I'm fine," he replied and poured himself some water from a glass pitcher. He gulped it down and poured another. "We were attacked by an airplane. They tossed two bombs, one an incendiary that hit us a glancing blow and started the fire in here. The other was a high explosive that just missed the ship."

"We heard gunfire," one of the new Fed bankers said, posing it like a question.

"That was me. I grabbed a machine gun from the weapons locker down the hall. The plane was trailing smoke as it flew east over Maryland, so I winged him at the least. If he did go down, I want to find the crash site."

"To think someone would go to such lengths to kill President Wilson," Secretary McAdoo said breathlessly.

"It's like Buffalo all over again," another remarked, alluding to the assassination of William McKinley thirteen years prior.

"And coming on the heels of the assassination in Europe of the

Habsburg heir, Ferdinand," a third man noted. "Do you think there's a connection? As I recall, the king of Italy was killed by an anarchist a short time before McKinley was shot at the Pan-American Exposition."

Ebenezer pulled his son aside to talk in private. "I'm wondering the same thing," he said in a low voice. "Could this be the Germans or someone sympathetic to their cause?"

"I guess it can't be discounted. As much as we're maintaining our neutrality, the Germans must know our commitment would go to the democracies of England and France. I really don't think they'd want to push us in that direction any sooner than necessary."

"You're probably right. Thank goodness the President wasn't aboard. I just can't think of who else would want to see him dead."

Bell shrugged while the wheels were churning inside his head. There was something about the attack that didn't feel right in his gut, but the moment was too close at hand to view with any clarity. Somehow, he couldn't help thinking there were easier and more surefire ways to assassinate the chief executive, if that was the intent.

The *Mayflower*'s captain appeared in the room just then, his summer white uniform smudged and sweat-stained. "Gentlemen, if I may have your attention. As you likely know by now, we were attacked from the air. Two bombs were thrown at us, and it appeared they did little beyond some cosmetic damage thanks to my fire-control team and Mr. Bell here, who seemingly knows his way around a Hotchkiss gun.

"The ship's in good enough repair to return to the Navy Yard under its own power rather than wait for a tow. It'll be much faster and will get our wounded the medical attention they require. Also,

I'm sure the President's security detail will launch an investigation and will need to interview witnesses as quickly as possible."

Bell's experience told him that it would be hours before the Secret Service interviewed the sailors and he doubted by then that the ones who saw the attack would correctly recall the plane's size, color, or configuration. Eyewitness testimony was often contradictory in situations like this, he found.

He also knew none of that mattered.

An hour and a half later, the *Mayflower* returned to its slip at the Navy Yard in Southeast D.C. The captain had radioed ahead and so there were ambulances with attending corpsmen, as well as four grim-looking men sweating in the afternoon sun. The Secret Service investigators. Two looked competent enough, Bell thought, and the other two looked like pure muscle. He guessed that was doctrine for them. Have some bright men guarding the President who could identify threats early, and a couple of bruisers on hand to handle whatever needed to be handled.

Sound practice to save a man's life, a lousy way to run an investigation. Bell decided he wanted no part of the dog and pony show. The agents already knew the bankers and their respective entourages had been belowdecks and had nothing to report and that their valuable time need not be wasted.

The injured sailor was carried on a stretcher down to the dock and was quickly swarmed by the medicos. In just moments he was aboard one of the ambulances and on his way to a hospital and a long painful recovery. The other ambulances were soon loaded with the more lightly injured victims and they, too, took off.

The four agents boarded the boat as the ambulance pulled away and gave scant interest to the clutch of old bankers and their young aides waiting to disembark. The T-men immediately started talking with Secretary McAdoo, who was their ultimate boss, and with the captain. Bell made certain he had plenty of bodies between himself and their little confab and trooped down the gangway at his father's side.

"Father, catch a ride with one of the others," Bell said when they reached the dock. "I need to hustle off the base ASAP. Once the captain realizes I didn't wait around to be interrogated he might lock this place down."

"Sure thing, son."

Bell accelerated away from the crowd of bankers, who were moving at a snail's pace thanks to several needing canes and others claiming weakness for not yet having lunch. The cars were parked a quarter mile from the pier. Bell had driven a Van Dorn pool car, a Model T painted in anonymous black, although under its bland interior the car had undergone significant improvement. He performed the preignition rituals by rote and cranked the high-performance engine to life. He got behind the wheel, wincing as the black leather seat discharged several hours' worth of accumulated Virginia heat into the backs of his thighs.

He reached the main gates a few minutes later. There was a small guardhouse and a guard checking in a delivery truck. The gate to leave the base was wide open. As Bell drove through and out onto M Street, he heard the faint jangling of a telephone in the guard shack.

Too late, Captain, he thought and motored past the wedding cake–like Latrobe Gate, the Navy Yard's ceremonial entrance.

Bell in hot pursuit

B ELL CROSSED THE ANACOSTIA RIVER AT THE NEARBY 11TH Street Bridge and drove beyond the sleepy town that lay along the east bank of the river and was soon motoring through rich farmland. His destination was only about ten miles away and the route was mostly direct. The town of College Park was recently rocked with tragedy when all but a few buildings of the University of Maryland burned to the ground. In the two years since, much had been reconstructed, but some students still lived with volunteer families in the area.

Not far from the campus was one of the first dedicated airfields built in the United States. It was here that Wilbur Wright himself taught flying on a Wright Model A to a pair of Army signal officers and thus created the nation's first flying corps.

Bell hadn't ever flown in or out of the airfield and so only knew the general area where it had been constructed. He was forced to stop and ask for directions twice before pulling up to the grass strip. There were two hangars along the near edge, one painted white with the words REX SMITH AEROPLANE COMPANY in large block letters on the roof. The other was more utilitarian, and he guessed it had been built for the Army. The airstrip itself was plenty long, with some woods running along the far border.

Near the open door of Rex Smith's hangar sat a portable water tank painted red with brass fittings that had been mounted on two spoked wooden wheels. It was fitted with two long poles, so men could pull it across the field, and a hose for spraying water on a burning plane. Bell was very aware of the dangers of a fire following a crash and knew that an unconscious pilot would have burned alive by the time the firemen maneuvered their water bowser into position.

Inside the hangar was a pusher-style biplane sitting on the wood floor. The aircraft was much like the early Wright planes, with wings that warped rather than proper ailerons and no wind protection for the pilot or the passenger sitting beside him.

A man in mechanic overalls spotted him and came over. "Help you, fella?"

"You wouldn't be Mr. Smith, would you?"

"No." The mechanic pointed to where three men were standing outside the hangar's office. Two were civilians and one had on an Army uniform. "That's him there."

After flying, the things pilots loved most in life was talking about flying, and judging by the hand movements and body language, the trio was discussing their aerial exploits.

Bell started over and called Smith's name. The older of the three held up a finger to his companions and met Bell halfway between the plane and his office. "What can I do for you, Mr. . . . ."

"Bell. Isaac Bell." They shook hands.

The soldier heard Bell introduce himself. He shouted Isaac's name and rushed over.

Bell recognized him immediately. "Lieutenant Henry Arnold. Dear God, Hap, it's great to see you."

They shook hands with the sheer pleasure of men who'd thought their paths wouldn't likely cross again but wished they would.

"Rex, this here's Isaac Bell. Ace detective, crackerjack flyer, and all-around good man."

"I thought you were overseas," Bell said to the young soldier.

"I'm back with my boss. He made a presentation to the War Department about the situation in the Philippines yesterday. We head back to California on tonight's train. I had some time, so I came out to my old stomping grounds."

"Are you back in the air?"

"'Fraid not."

"I understand," Bell said. He knew a number of pilots who'd given up flying out of fear, usually following a harrowing crash or witnessing the death of a friend. In Arnold's case it was both. "I gotta tell you, though, Hap, aviation is going to be an important part of our military's future, as critical as the Navy, and it needs leaders like you who understand that fundamentally."

"I know it will."

"Get back into the cockpit."

"I'll think about it," the West Pointer said as a hedge.

"How do you two know each other?" Rex Smith asked.

Bell said, "Couple of years ago, Hap did the flying stunts for a movie my wife worked on called . . . Damn, what was it?"

The Military Air-Scout," Hap Arnold replied. "Pretty

forgettable, but Isaac and I had a lot of fun with that Wright Model B. Say, what brings you out to College Park?"

"Yes, Mr. Bell, how can I help you?" Smith was an attorney by trade and had a lawyer's sense of smell for money. The aviation business was a new sideline.

"About three hours ago there was an attack from the air against the presidential yacht, *Mayflower*." That got their attention, and after the initial shock wore off, Bell continued. "President Wilson wasn't on board, and only one man was injured, but it could have been devastating. I managed to shoot the plane and it was trailing a lot of smoke by the time I lost sight of it over the Maryland countryside."

"You want to go find the wreckage," Arnold said.

Bell nodded. "Be a lot easier spotting it from the air than driving back and forth across farmers' fields."

"You really are a flyer?" Smith asked.

From his wallet, Bell showed him his certificate from the Fédération Aéronautique Internationale, the globe-spanning licensing body for the sport of flying. "I was hoping there was a plane out here I could rent or hire."

The third member of the trio had been there for the full conversation but hadn't said anything.

Rex turned to him. "How about it, Tony? You up for a flight?"

He was young, slightly built, with inky dark hair and a broad chin. He held out a hand to Bell. "Tony Jannus."

"Isaac Bell," he said automatically and then he realized whom he was speaking with. "Wait, I know that name. You flew that St. Pete to Tampa flight, right?"

The young pilot smiled. "Yup. The first scheduled passenger flight in the United States. Maybe the world."

"It is my pleasure to meet you," Bell told him.

"It's nothing. Anyway, you got a rough idea where they went down?"

"I know the starting point of their flight away from the river and the course they flew, but don't know how long they stayed in the air."

Jannus rubbed his chin. "With two of us aboard, we can stay aloft in Rex's kite for about an hour and a half." He pointed to the plane across the cavernous hangar. "She was built three years ago, but this spring Rex splurged on a more powerful motor and a larger fuel tank."

"It looks like a Glenn Curtiss design," Bell remarked.

"You know your planes," Smith said. "Glenn helped me put it together. You know him?"

"Our group of New York aviators is a tight little community."

"How about it, Rex, are you going to let him go?" Hap Arnold asked.

"Are you going to pay?" Smith asked Bell.

"Tell you what, write out an invoice for double what you think is fair and I'll have a treasury check to you by this time tomorrow."

Smith smiled and shot out his hand. "Deal."

"Before we go," Bell said, "I want to ask about the other plane."

Bell described it in detail, but neither the pilot nor business owner recognized it.

"I think the French have a plane like you describe," Tony Jannus said, "but I'm not sure. I know I haven't seen anything like it."

"Hopefully there will be some clues aboard when we find it."

While Rex Smith went to find Bell a spare flying jacket, helmet, and goggles, the other three wheeled the plane out of the hangar.

It looked as delicate as a dragonfly, but Jannus kept up a running monologue on just how robust and maneuverable the plane was. He admitted that Rex had been unable to interest the Army into buying it, even after the upgrades, and he feared the business would soon close.

"Hopefully, this will inject some life into the company," Bell said.

Ten minutes later, with Tony Jannus at the wheel and Bell strapped into a makeshift jump seat next to him, the pilot advanced the throttles, the engine roared, and the wooden propeller beat the air in a deafening whirlwind. The plane started moving, bumping over the grass strip, and picking up speed as the broad wings began generating lift. They bounced and jumped until the plane hit one high spot on the field, took to the air, and didn't touch ground again.

They quickly gained both airspeed and altitude, though not as quickly as some of the newer-model planes Bell had flown in. Rex Smith's design, though only a couple of years old, was already hopelessly out-of-date, new engine or not.

The sky was clear, apart from a few puffy clouds drifting miles above the landscape, and the air was incredibly still, something Bell wouldn't have noticed from the *Mayflower*'s deck as she motored south toward Mount Vernon.

Jannus leveled out at a comfortable thousand feet and soon had them over the Anacostia River and up to about sixty knots. With the goggles in place and his ears protected by the leather flying helmet, Bell only had to deal with the wind against his cheeks and chin. It was a sunny day, so he didn't feel too chilled, just slightly scoured by the wind.

Within a few minutes into the flight, they flew past the District of Columbia. The Washington Monument was by far the most prominent feature, but the Capitol Dome also loomed large and the White House was clearly visible. At the far end of the Mall was the gaping hole for the foundation of the Lincoln Memorial.

The Anacostia joined the Potomac just south of the Navy Yard, and Jannus kept the plane centered above this much larger waterway. They were low enough to see people on one of the passenger ferries chugging back to Washington waving up to them. Jannus waggled the plane's wings in reply.

In what the *Mayflower* needed an hour to cover, the Smith Flyer covered in a fraction of the time.

"We're close," Bell shouted over the tremendous racket of prop, motor, and wind. Jannus nodded.

Watching for the landmarks he'd committed to memory, Bell felt they were over the exact spot the bomber had fled to after the presidential yacht attack, and he tapped the young pilot's shoulder. He pointed in the direction the other plane had retreated and Jannus banked the Smith Flyer over. He pulled out of the turn a tad early and so Bell had him adjust his course until it matched the flight path of the damaged biplane.

With no idea how long it had remained aloft, Bell began searching the ground below. It was mostly farmland and meadows with a few small, scattered forests. He knew their trip might be totally fruitless. The plane could have altered course as soon as he'd lost sight of it or could have flown on to a makeshift airstrip the men had used to launch their attack and it was now hidden in a nearby barn.

Long odds, indeed, but then, long odds tended to be Bell's specialty.

Ten minutes after leaving the river Bell's attention was on the ground just ahead of the plane, so he didn't notice what Tony Jannus had just seen. The pilot tapped Bell's shoulder and pointed to a spot several miles ahead but only a couple of compass points off their exact heading.

A column of black smoke was rising out of a small clutch of trees. As there was so little breeze it went straight into the air, almost like an accusatory finger pointing to their target.

"It just started to burn," Jannus shouted.

Bell grasped the meaning. The plane hadn't caught fire when it crashed, which meant someone had just torched the wreckage, someone who knew its significance and wanted the evidence turned to ash.

Bell pumped his arm as if on a cavalry charge and Jannus tweaked the throttle for a little more speed and lowered the plane's nose. "After the fox," he said with a devilish grin.

They came out of the dive at around four hundred feet, and a half mile shy of the sooty shaft of smoke. It was clear to see where the plane had struck several thin branches of a small copse of trees by the naked white wounds of torn limbs. The plane had come down just past the last of the trees. The wreckage was engulfed in flames, so it was difficult to see how badly it had been damaged in the crash. Or learn the fate of its occupants. One piece of evidence as to the severity of the impact, though, was that the motor had sheered from its mounts and lay several yards from the pyre.

Just then an open-back truck pulled out from under a canopy of thick leaves and struck out across a field left fallow for the season meadow. Dust kicked up from its tires as it made a break for it. They were still several miles from any road, but Bell knew once they hit pavement, the truck would be lost forever. He pantomimed for Jannus to get lower and closer.

They came in at the truck with barely fifteen feet separating the ground from the plane's bicycle-style wheels. They thundered close enough that the driver was spooked by the noise and sudden appearance of a plane diving at him. He cranked the wheel in a panicked response and the front of the truck dug deep furrows into the ground. But then he straightened out and continued on, pressing the accelerator with everything he had.

Bell felt bitter disappointment. He'd hoped at such speed that the sharp turn would have snapped the truck's front wheel's spokes. The wheel held and now the element of surprise was gone.

Jannus tried the trick again a moment later, but rather than jerk away, the driver tried to slam his heavy-duty truck into the plane's delicate wings. Jannus pulled them up in a hasty climb that left Bell's stomach down by his knees and the wires that warped the wings singing with tension. Jannus slowed the plane to match the speed of the truck jouncing along below them and looked to Bell for ideas.

The truck's passenger suddenly appeared out of his window and raised a sawed-off double-barrel shotgun. He fired both chambers at a close-enough distance to see ragged holes appear in the biplane's fabric wings and at least one pellet ping off the engine block.

Bell immediately pulled his pistol and returned fire. His was a much steadier platform than the truck hurtling across the bumpy field and scored several hits against the hood and fenders. One bullet punched a hole through the cab's small rear window, shattering it entirely.

He needed to change out the empty magazine, so he was ready to fire again if the passenger reappeared. He popped the spent mag from the gun and let it tumble away. As he pulled the final spare from his shoulder rig, it snagged against an inside pocket of his unfamiliar flying jacket and slipped from his grasp. Just like that it was gone, dropping past his boots in a flash of black metal.

He cursed loud enough for Tony to hear and look over. Bell holstered the Browning to show he was effectively unarmed.

"What do you want to do?" Jannus yelled.

Bell's mind spun through a number of options, none particularly good. He came to a crazy solution. "Are you as good a pilot as your reputation?"

"Yes," Jannus said without false modesty.

Bell started untying his safety strap. "Get me low enough so I can jump."

"Are you nuts?"

"Bad enough they could have killed the President," he shouted over the wind, "they could have killed me."

Without another word, Bell grabbed on to one of the wooden bracing struts that held the two wings in position and pulled himself from his jump seat. Tony had throttled back so the wind force was only forty or so knots, but it took strength and balance to lean into it and try to reach for the next stanchion. Bell also had to contort around cabling and guy wires that were thin enough to cut to the bone if he slipped and needed to clutch one.

Jannus kept one eye on the truck and the other on his passenger, who was edging out closer and closer to the Flyer's wing. As the plane's center of gravity shifted with each shuffling step, he had to adjust the controls in tiny incremental movements in order to keep them level.

Bell always had a head for heights, but this was unlike anything he had ever tried before. The press of the wind wanted to spin him around whenever he took his foot off the wing, while the wooden braces vibrated painfully against his hands because of the engine and prop. He kept glancing at the truck. Unless Tony Jannus had the reflexes of a cat, he was a dead man if the shooter popped his head out now.

He was halfway to the wingtip and moving well. Jannus started crabbing the plane closer to the truck while losing more altitude. The driver saw him coming closer and swerved in toward the plane. Jannus let the truck slide right under the biplane's landing gear. Bell moved out to the last pair of wooden uprights near the wingtip, his coat flaring around his waist like the torn sail of a sloop caught in a typhoon. The driver corrected the direction of the truck as he had done before. Jannus had anticipated the maneuver and dropped the plane those last couple of feet with the wing extending directly above the truck's open rear bed.

Bell not so much as leapt for the hurtling truck but let himself tumble so as to minimize his body's wind resistance. He landed on his feet, but crouched low so that he could roll to shed his momentum. Jannus pulled ahead of the truck and started veering away. The gunman saw he had the perfect shot. He thrust his torso out of his window with the shotgun hard to his shoulder and aimed.

He didn't realize the last big rattle they'd felt wasn't from the bumpy field and so he had no idea there was a man standing right behind him. With a hard yank, Bell pulled on the collar of the shooter's jacket and unceremoniously tossed him to the ground. He pinwheeled for three full revolutions before coming to a stop.

Bell didn't wait to see if he got up again. He got down on the running board just behind the cab and whipped open the passenger door. He lunged onto the bench seat and fired a straight right into the driver's jaw. The man's head barely moved and that's when Bell realized the guy was a gorilla in a cheap suit. The gorilla threw out a backhander with his right fist and Bell felt like he'd taken a hit with a sledgehammer.

He pulled out his gun before the guy could hit him again. The sight of the weapon made no difference. The driver tried to crush Bell's head against the back of the seat with his elbow and just barely missed. He kept throwing the elbow, forcing Bell to keep close to the passenger-side door in the tight space.

The guy then did something Bell hadn't expected. He took his left hand off the wheel and lunged across the cab to strangle Bell where he sat. The guy was too big to move quickly and that gave Bell the fraction of a second he needed to slam the butt of his pistol against the driver's forehead. The blow cut his scalp and blood welled up in a crimson slick. The man blinked away the pain and whatever fuzziness he might have experienced and again went to get his hands around Bell's throat.

Bell couldn't get much power behind his strikes, but he hit the lug three more times in the exact same spot. The guy finally retreated to his side of the truck, his eyes glassy and his lips rubbery. Without wasting a second, Bell slammed his body into the man while his left hand popped open the door's handle. The driver's torso tipped out of the cab, but his legs were jammed under the dash and he started fighting back, clutching the running board with one hand, and swinging the other with his ham-sized fist.

With his foot off the gas the truck had been slowing and careening wildly without anyone controlling the wheel. That gave Bell inspiration. He elbowed the guy in the groin at the same time he yanked the wheel hard to the right. The pain and sudden shift in centrifugal force did the trick. The gorilla lost his grip and tumbled into the dusty field.

Bell jammed his foot on the accelerator and steadied the truck's crazy route. He was about to turn and hit the guy with the truck's fender hard enough to incapacitate him when the goon opened fire with a pistol Bell didn't know he'd been carrying. He ducked down as low as he could when a couple of shots hit the truck. One bullet passed through the missing rear window and spider-webbed the windshield. Bell knew he'd gain nothing by sticking around and so put on some speed and raced along a narrow tract between two empty fields.

The path through led to a hard-packed dirt road that funneled between a small farmhouse and a swaybacked barn. Beyond was an unpaved county road. Bell's sense of direction told him to turn left. The lane remained barely two lanes wide while he passed several other farms. There were no utility poles, no electricity out here or phone service. He continued on but didn't come to a town for a solid thirty minutes. The place was little more than a handful of businesses ringing a park with a statue of some bearded soldier in the middle.

He parked and killed the engine, giving himself a minute. He checked the truck's glove compartment and found it empty except for a couple of screwdrivers. He assumed the vehicle had been stolen and the paperwork dumped. There was nothing in the footwells, but there was space behind the seat. He fished around and came out with a sturdy canvas bag with a loop that fit around one's shoulder.

He opened it and let out an involuntary whistle. The satchel contained wads of cash bound with rubber bands. Judging by the size, he'd guess a few thousand easily.

Bell considered the most likely scenario. The guys in the truck worked with the flyers, possibly supplying the bombs. They knew the pilot and bombardier had been paid in cash to attack the

President's yacht. They had split up somewhere near that farm with the aircrew taking their money with the intention of landing somewhere else, likely in the direction of their home airfield. When the raid went bad and the pilot couldn't fly to his intended destination, he went back to land from where he'd taken off.

It made sense, he thought. The goon and shooter saw or heard the plane returning and headed out across the farm to find out what had happened. They located the plane. Pilot and passenger were doubtlessly dead and so they took back the payment and torched the evidence.

As Bell looked at the money in his lap, another realization hit like a thunderbolt. He pulled out his wallet and removed the hundred-dollar bill he'd purloined at the morning meeting. Already knowing the truth, he nonetheless compared the two. The flyer's bills were twenties, not hundreds like his, and the portrait was of Grover Cleveland rather than Ben Franklin, but the style, font, size, paper, ink, all of it was the exact same. These weren't yet in circulation.

It confirmed what his gut was trying to tell him earlier. The attack on the *Mayflower* wasn't meant for the President. It was the new Federal Reserve banking heads, gathered together for the very first time, who were the real target of the attack.

Bell just didn't have any idea why.

4

BELL ATE AT A DINER AFTER MAKING A CALL TO THE WASHington branch of the Van Dorn Agency. It would be simpler for agents with local knowledge to reach out to contacts in the Treasury Department to investigate the crash site and obtain Bell's eyewitness account of what had happened since he snuck off the *Mayflower.* He was on a third cup of coffee, and enduring the glare of a waitress who wanted his table back, when two of the four agents who'd met the yacht came into the restaurant accompanied by the sound of a tinny brass bell attached to the door. It was one of the competent-looking agents and one bruiser.

They took a pause at the door to survey the five-booth establishment and determine who they were here to meet. "Two coffees," the bruiser said to the waitress as they crossed to Bell's booth.

"Bell?" asked the big guy.

"Yes."

"I'm Vic Carver. This is my partner, Paul Haygarth. You really with Van Dorn?"

Bell gave him a business card, which Carver glanced at, then pocketed. He said, "New York office, huh? Why were you on the President's yacht this morning and why didn't you stick around the Navy Yard when she docked?"

"My father is going to be the first head of the Federal Bank in Boston," Bell explained. "I asked to tag along so I could meet the President. Didn't work out as I planned, obviously. I left the Navy Yard when we returned because I didn't want to waste the time it took to be interviewed while the plane was somewhere out here in the Maryland countryside. Have you guys begun organizing a search?"

Carver looked a little uncomfortable. Haygarth, who Bell originally thought looked like the guy in charge, sat with a blank expression on his face. He'd misread the two men when they'd come up the *Mayflower*'s gangplank. "It . . . Ah. We are going to start first thing in the morning."

"I like to do things on the jump." Bell pulled up the satchel he'd found behind the truck's seat. "You might as well take this now."

Carver reached a long arm across the table and took the satchel. He set it between himself and Haygarth and looked inside. Haygarth gave a low whistle.

"You recognize them?"

Carver had obviously been around the new Federal Reserve notes for some time because seeing them didn't really get a response. He looked around the diner and remembered that the customers weren't allowed to see the new bills. He quickly closed the bag. "Where did you get this?"

"Behind the seat of the truck the two guys had. I believe this money was actually paid to the pilot and his bomb-throwing friend. After they crashed, their partners in the truck found the plane, took the money, and torched the evidence."

The waitress brought the coffees while Bell got to his feet. "We have time to get out there now."

Bell turned to the waitress and said, "We need to take those with us. I'll pay for the cups." He placed enough money on the table to cover the coffee and cups, his camping out there for the better part of two hours, and then some.

Back in the truck, Bell retraced his route from the farm with Carver and Haygarth following in a Treasury-issued sedan. This time there was another car pulled up to the side of the farmhouse. As he and the agents got out of their vehicles the front door opened and a bearded man wearing a pair of black pants and a clean white shirt stepped out onto the covered porch.

"Help you?"

Carver made the introductions and Bell explained about the crashed plane on his property.

"I was at a funeral for most of the day," the man confided. "Don't know anything about what you're saying."

"I saw the wreck with my own eyes," Bell assured him. "As for the man I tossed from the truck, I'm not sure of his fate."

"I'm afraid that this connects to a larger crime," Carver told the farmer. "We're going to do a quick check of the wreckage today and be back tomorrow with a larger team with the intention of taking the wreckage away with us."

"Mind if I ride out with you?" the farmer asked. "I'd like to see the damage myself."

Expecting the T-men to be overly protective of the crash site, and knowing they'd get more cooperation if they gave a little, Bell quickly answered. "Not a problem at all. Hop in."

Though he maneuvered across the farmer's fields as if he recognized every landmark and fence, Bell had some doubts about finding the location quickly. The fire had long burned itself out, so there was no telltale smoke column, and he'd been concentrating on wing walking rather than the geography. His anxiety began as a little tingle in the back of his mind, but then vanished when he spotted the birds.

They were black, large, and ungainly, and circling in the sky about a thousand yards to Bell's left. The plane could wait. The body couldn't. He pointed them out to the farmer. "Something's dead out there, for sure."

A few buzzards were on the ground near the corpse of the man Bell had yanked from the pickup. They flew off on great ebony wings as Bell braked next to the body. The carrion eaters only went so far as the nearest tree limbs, where they sulked as their meal was being seized.

The birds had already done a number on the guy's face and hands, but hadn't yet worked their way through his clothing. The T-men rolled up and stepped from their vehicle. Vic Carver hunched down close to the body, studying it for a long moment. He'd left his hat in the car, so the wind pushed wisps of his sandy hair across his brow. From the unnatural angle of the dead man's head, it was obvious his neck was broken. Death would have been instantaneous.

"We can't leave him out here," Carver said, straightening up and wiping imaginary dust from his pants. He looked to Paul Haygarth. "Grab the blanket from the trunk."

It took just a minute to roll the body into the blanket and for it to be placed in the pickup's cargo bed. The blanket wasn't long enough to cover the lower legs and feet, so if someone gave the truck a casual glance, they were in for a shock.

They all got back in their vehicles. Inspired, Bell described the physical features around where the plane went down, and the farmer said he knew the spot, and less than ten minutes later they arrived at the accident scene.

There was nothing left of the plane except some lengths of wire and the mechanical linkages that controlled its flying surfaces. Everything else had been reduced to ashes, which were already being scattered by the breeze. The engine was a short distance from the charred remains and looked as though it could be salvaged. The bodies of the pilot and bombardier had been placed amid the wreckage before it was drenched in the fuel remaining in the tank and torched. The fire had burned long enough that all that remained were their fire-blackened bones and the metal bits from their clothing, like snaps and buckles.

"No extra bombs," Bell said at last.

"Huh?"

"They threw two bombs at the *Mayflower* before I shot them up. There are no bombs here, ergo they had finished their attack. I figured there would be additional explosives for a longer, more sustained assault."

"Don't know," Carver said.

Bell then amended his statement. "The guy could have thrown them overboard to lighten the plane. If the bombs weren't armed, they might not have exploded when they hit the ground."

"I'll have a team make a sweep from here to the river."

"That's better than fifteen miles," the farmer told him. "Some thick woods, too."

"Didn't say it was going to be easy," Carver said a little testily. Bell suspected that his resources were limited and the scope of the investigation was far wider than he'd anticipated. "There's nothing more we can do here. Let's head back to Washington."

After dropping the farmer back at his house, Bell asked that either Carver or Haygarth ride with him in the pickup. "If for some reason law enforcement sees our gnawed-on friend back there, I'd rather not spend the night in custody explaining my way out of a murder charge."

"Makes sense," Carver agreed. "Paul, ride with Mr. Bell and take the body to the Georgetown medical school."

"H Street, right?"

"Yep."

"Perfect," said Bell. "You can drop me at the Willard on the way."

"What about the truck?"

"I suspect it's stolen, but God alone knows from where. Replace the broken glass, patch the bullet holes, and add it to the Secret Service fleet."

New York City

Bell arrived back in New York's Penn Station three days later. He'd mostly cooled his heels in Washington waiting to be questioned and eventually telling and retelling the same story to no less than ten different agents. He'd offered to draw the plane as best he could, but no one seemed interested. In all, it was a frustrating waste of time. The Treasury Department was one of the oldest bureaucracies in America and its culture of caution and ponderous decision-making had also deeply infected the Secret Service and its new roll of presidential protection.

The train wheezed to a halt at precisely noon and Bell got to his feet.

He worked his way through the crowds disembarking from the train's first-class compartment and headed for the stairs up to street level. He was just about to start climbing when he felt someone sidle up next to him and thrust a slender arm through his.

"I usually like to pick up conductors or train engineers, but today a random passenger will have to do." She was blond, tall, very pretty, and also happened to be his wife.

Without missing a beat, he said, "I always suspected this was where you went when you said you were having lunch with friends."

She steered him away from the exit stairs. "Actually, I'm here to rescue you."

"Didn't know I needed rescuing."

"Archie told Lillian that Joseph has an all-points bulletin out for you. With you in Washington, he felt he had to stay here and he's been missing some golf event in Georgia. He wants to brief you on pending cases pronto so he can go play with his sticks and balls."

"Clubs."

"Whatever. It's a ridiculous game and if you ever take it up, I shall divorce you. Anyway, there's a pair of Van Dorns staking in the main concourse to meet you and two more posted in the Knickerbocker lobby in case these guys miss you and you make it home."

"And naturally Lilly warned you."

"Of course. She tells me everything."

"Everything?" he said with a wry smile.

"I know things about your best friend that you'll never know."

His smile faded. "I do hope you show some discretion."

"Darling, among women there is no such thing as discretion. We reserve that for talking to men."

A station employee stood next to a metal door. He opened it as the couple approached. Marion availed him with one of her most charming smiles and discretely slipped him ten dollars.

He tipped his cap. "Ma'am."

They exited the massive building via an employee entrance and outside Marion already had a taxi waiting. A well-thought-out rescue indeed, Bell thought.

The cabbie held the door for her. "Still going to the Waldorf, ma'am?"

"Please."

"This is better planned than most prison breaks," Bell said. "You do know that when I'm a no-show at the office, Joseph Van Dorn will suspect you intercepted me en route. The Waldorf-Astoria is the first place he'll look."

He settled into the back seat and Marion immediately tucked in under his arm as though she were burrowing into a den. "All true," she answered. "That's why we're registered under Marty McHale's name."

"The Yankees' pitcher?"

"He's also a heck of a singer. He's seeing one of my regular actresses. She's doing us this favor."

"Devious."

"Aren't I, though?" she said wolfishly. He turned his wrist in order to read the face of the watch she'd gifted him. "We have twenty-one uninterrupted hours until you have to report in at the office tomorrow."

"And you have plans for us?"

She gave him a carnal smile, her voice suddenly husky. "Oh, I have plans, all right."

THE FOLLOWING MORNING, LONG BEFORE DAWN, BELL LEFT Marion asleep with a romantic note on his pillow. As he hadn't planned on staying in Washington for more than twenty-four hours, he had no luggage and had tossed away his soiled clothes and bought new ones, although his suit wasn't faring too well after four days of continuous wear and tear. He kept spare clothes at his gym and hoped he could get in a bit of a workout.

Alberto Cicchetti's, one of the last gyms in New York to adopt padded gloves, was his destination. Boxing had gone mainstream following the Corbett/Sullivan fight two decades ago, but guys like Cicchetti were slow to change their ways. The canvas in the main ring hadn't been replaced in years and there was a swirl of blood and sweat stains patterned like a hunter's winter camouflage. Bell was in luck, as there were several men already at the gym and looking to spar.

He was in the third round with a thick-necked fighter who came down from Harlem. Berto ran a black and tan gym and had high hopes the kid would be the next Jack Johnson. That's when an intern from the Van Dorn office at the Knickerbocker Hotel in Times Square found him.

"Mr. Bell," the intern's voice practically cracked.

Bell was annoyed at being interrupted, but didn't let it show.

"Where's the emergency, kid?" He hadn't bothered to learn the lad's name; he was a summer hire following his first year at Columbia Law and would be gone soon enough. "The old man really this keen to get to his golf buddies?"

"Um." He was clearly overwhelmed speaking directly to the legendary Isaac Bell and probably put off by his surroundings. The first few minutes in a place like Cicchetti's made you think you were breathing through a hobo's old sock. It was not only the smell but also the humidity, which tasted salty on the back of the throat.

"Out with it."

"There's been a shooting," he managed to say between breaths, "in Newport. Your presence is requested by an attorney named Isidor Steinem on behalf of his unnamed client. Mr. Van Dorn said it's priority one and sent out every intern in the office to look for you."

Bell knew of Steinem. His was an exclusive New York firm with satellite branches wherever the rich and famous vacationed. Apparently, he'd shifted to Rhode Island for the season. Most of what the firm did was legitimate—wills, trusts, and the like—but there were times he'd been used as a fixer of delicate problems, usually getting the wayward sons of society scions out of legal jams, or paying off the used-up mistresses of those boys' fathers.

He'd never met the lawyer, but he'd heard him described as slick without being oily.

"Newport, huh?" Bell said rhetorically.

"Yes, Mr. Bell. There will be a car and driver waiting for you once you arrive at the station. They want you there as soon as possible."

He found it interesting that the message said shooting and not murder. A shooting was very open-ended. It could be anything. Murder, on the other hand, was a very definitive act. There was no reason to call in a Van Dorn agent if there hadn't been a murder, likely the wife or husband of whoever Steinem represented. Bell thought Steinem was being intentionally cagey with the language he used. This led him to believe that the attorney was already laying the groundwork for his client's defense.

"All right," Bell said. "Head back to the office and let Mr. Van Dorn know I've gotten the message and that I'm on my way." He turned to the young man he'd been sparring against. He held out his gloves and they bumped fists. "Sorry, Clyde. Duty calls."

The fighter grinned. "You just saved yourself from another beating."

"Not a chance," Bell said with a wry smile. "You're still telegraphing that left hook like the night manager at a Marconi office."

He showered at the gym and dressed in a spare suit he kept in his locker. He used Berto's phone to call the Waldorf and left a message for Marion that he probably wasn't going to be home tonight. Any other husband who pulled a stunt like that after being gone for four days would likely get an earful, but Marion Bell was used to her husband's chaotic schedule and had a forgiving heart.

He knew he was the luckiest husband alive.

5

———— ❧ ————

Newport, Rhode Island

T HE HOUSE WAS LAUGHABLY BIG. ITS CENTRAL DOMED SECTION
was as large as a municipal public library, and it had a pair
of three-story wings that stretched from it for fifty yards per side.
There was no porte cochere to protect passengers exiting their
vehicles from the elements, but rather a wide ascending staircase
and a terrace with enough columns to support the roof of the
Acropolis. The building's stone facade appeared as pure as a
mound of sugar cubes.

A staff of a hundred would need to work overtime to maintain
such a property. The grounds were expansive, and this was only
one building of many. There was the pool house, the seaside pavil-
ion, the stables, garage, and servants' quarters for those not resid-
ing in the rooms tucked under the house's eave, plus the private
power plant.

The family that owned the estate occupied it only twelve weeks
out of the year, or not at all if they summered in Europe or roughed

it in the twelve-thousand-square-foot "cabin" they had on Upper St. Regis Lake in upstate New York. Some in the Gilded Age were far more gilded than others.

Four vehicles were pulled up to the house on the crushed-stone drive, including two sedans and a car converted to carry bodies for the medical examiner's office. Just discernible under it was a puddle of water from the melting blocks of ice to keep the body cold. The sedans were black Model Ts identical to half the automobiles on America's roads, but they still somehow looked like cars that belonged to cops.

The fourth vehicle would never be mistaken for a patrol car. It was a long tourer with an open cockpit for the driver and a comfortable enclosed compartment behind him that would still be roomy for six. The fabled Flying Lady, officially known as the Spirit of Ecstasy, graced the radiator cap above the car's large grille.

Isaac Bell wasn't familiar with this model of Rolls-Royce. It was something brand-new. As an admirer of all things mechanical and especially those that go fast, he couldn't help but let out a low whistle when he turned his attention to the cherry-red car that seemed to glow.

"That's Mr. Steinem's car," said the middle-aged driver who'd picked him up at the station.

"The attorney?"

"Yes."

"Do you also work for the firm?" Bell asked. The answer would tell him a great deal about what to expect inside. If Bell had to guess judging by the man's age, he was an ex-cop working as an investigator for the prestigious law practice.

"Yes, I'm the senior associate."

Bell gave nothing away, merely opened the door when the car

rolled to a stop at the base of the stairs. But he was stunned. It was expected that a high-powered attorney like Steinem would be here making a concerned and lawyerly house call. After all, a very rich client was involved in a potential homicide. But using his senior associate as a taxi driver told him that Steinem thought his client was likely guilty and wanted to keep this whole thing a secret for as long as possible.

Bell climbed the stairs, purging his mind of any biases his suspicions would have on his investigation. He needed to remain neutral and focus only on what he saw and not on what others considered relevant.

"Well well well, if it isn't the great detective Isaac Bell. This story gets better and better."

Bell knew the voice. It belonged to a reporter named Abel Loohey, a bottom-feeding muckraker of the first order. Archie Abbott said of him once that "his journalism is yellower than the snow around a fire hydrant after a pack of dogs has passed by." There was always a grain of truth in his stories, but the embellishments and innuendo he buried them in was overwhelming. The even sadder truth of his deceptions and exaggerations is that the people ate it up. His byline was read by half the people in New York.

He'd tried to smear Bell a couple of times about cases that took time to crack, suggesting Bell was stymied and intimating that Bell would never catch a particular criminal because the fiend was too smart. In the end, Loohey had been forced to write retractions or corrections, but those didn't really reduce the sting of being publicly humiliated. Bell straightened the curl of disgust from his lip and turned.

Loohey wore a shiny suit and kept a press card in his hatband.

He was short, a little pudgy, and not all that attractive. There was a disquieting eagerness about him, as if he were too impatient to ever listen and his brain was already on to the next thing.

"Got a statement, Detective?"

Bell said nothing.

Loohey gave a toothy smile, one that never touched his eyes. "My sources tell me there isn't much blood, but I think I'm going to write it up as if there was. Better lede, you know."

Bell shook his head and continued on to the big house.

The mansion's doors were eight feet tall and ornately carved. One eased open on well-oiled hinges as he approached. A servant in black tie greeted him. Bell handed him his calling card. He noted a personalized receiving dish on the side table that let guests know this was the home of Jackson Pickett and his wife, Fedora Scarsworth-Pickett. He wasn't familiar with the names, but the city's wealthiest families weren't high on his agenda.

The butler led Bell through the house.

The place felt even grander and more ornate on the inside. The ceilings towered up to the underside of the dome and the plaster-work had been adorned with all manner of friezes and murals. The furniture he glimpsed in an adjoining sitting room was dark and looked heavier than the Rolls parked in the driveway. Rugs were all thick and richly patterned, and the drapes looked to be thirty pounds of fabric hanging like frozen scarlet waterfalls. To his taste, the interior of the house was oppressive and even more funereal than the outside.

Their footfalls echoed no matter how lightly Bell tried to tread.

As they neared the back of the house, Bell could just hear muted voices. Men talking in the half whisper he'd heard at a hundred crime scenes when the body hadn't yet been removed. By the Cartier on his wrist, the decedent had been dead for roughly nine hours.

The butler led him into a tall wrought-iron and glass solarium with twenty-foot ceilings and a small forest of potted trees trimmed into meticulous balls. The far wall looked out over a sprawling lawn dotted with more marble buildings that looked like confectionery. Beyond that were rolling waves of the Atlantic that broke against a sandy beach.

There were five men standing about the room: two plainclothes cops, no doubt Newport's senior detective and what appeared to be a much younger protégé; an iron-haired uniformed officer who had to be the department's most experienced sergeant; and two men in blue coveralls—the meat wagon attendants. This group was standing a little ways off from the central cluster of the solarium's couches and chairs, where two additional men were seated.

The detectives didn't try to hide their contempt for Bell's presence at their crime scene. The orderlies were indifferent, and the gruff old sergeant appeared curious. The cops and the orderlies had been the ones doing the talking. The two seated men on one of the long velvet-upholstered couches were tight-lipped, one out of grief and one because he had been trained by Harvard Law to say nothing around the police.

The air in the room was thick with cigarette smoke despite some open windows. Tension hung even thicker.

Obviously, it was Mrs. Scarsworth-Pickett, her husband's surname tacked on as an afterthought or a compromise, that was dead. Bell studied Jackson Pickett, the home's owner and now accused murderer.

He was a little older than Bell's mid-thirties, with dark hair slicked back and held in place by gel. He didn't have a mustache but wore his sideburns long. His slacks were well tailored and his shirt custom-made and had been expensive before being covered in blood. Pickett was movie star handsome even with the thousand-yard stare that was doubtlessly stuck on the singular vision of his dead wife's body. Whether he had been an active participant in making her that way was likely why Bell had been called out on this auspicious morning.

"Mr. Isaac Bell," the butler read off the calling card, "chief investigator for the Van Dorn Detective Agency."

"About damned time!" the older of the two detectives rasped, grounding out his cigarette in an overflowing ashtray.

Bell ignored him and crossed to the lawyer as the man levered himself off the sofa next to his bereft client.

Isidor Steinem was about sixty, with gray but thick hair, a scholar's broad forehead, and quick, intelligent eyes. He had a presence about him, a calmness that likely couldn't be ruffled in any situation. He was softening in the middle as he aged, but his handshake was firm, and his voice steady. "Isidor Steinem, Mr. Bell. Thank you for coming on such short notice. Joseph and I go back many years, and when I called him, he said he'd get his best man out here as quickly as possible."

Joseph was, of course, Joseph Van Dorn. He did find it telling that Steinem felt the need to drop his employer's name in such a blatant fashion. To a lawyer, all conversation was negotiation. They never stopped working the angles. Steinem had juice, as they called it, and he wanted Bell to know how much.

The lead Newport detective shouldered his way into the conversation, as subtle as an ox. He was tall and big and doughy with small eyes and a drinker's florid complexion. "What's your name? Bell?"

Isaac ignored the cop's belligerent tone and replied evenly, "That's right, Detective. My name is Isaac Bell. And just so we're clear, I have no idea why I was called up here from New York."

"It's because these fools think I killed my wife," Jackson Pickett said from the couch. He had the honeyed accent of New Orleans's upper class.

"Not another word," Steinem admonished with a snap.

To Bell's ear, Pickett spoke with the studied indifference of one confident in his innocence, but still with the dullness of a man in grief. Entitled but vulnerable, Bell thought.

The lawyer spoke so all could hear. "Detective Lassiter, as I said before, I do not mean to impugn your abilities or those on your force, but I am very concerned on behalf of my client that the police can have a bias in situations like this and investigate accordingly. I am not accusing you specifically of any malfeasance in your preliminary conclusions. However, I believe my client deserves an, ah, second opinion of the facts as they are presented."

Lassiter practically snarled. "It's only the call from the governor to my chief that gets you your . . ." He again looked at Bell. ". . . second opinion."

Bell had read the room correctly when he'd entered. Steinem had used Pickett's vast wealth as a leverage with Rhode Island's governor to intercede on his behalf. Detective Lassiter was rightly upset to have politicians trample over both his autonomy and authority.

"Be that as it may, Detective," Steinem went on, "our request to have Mr. Bell inspect the body and scene has been granted and your cooperation is expected."

Bell held out his hand to the Newport cop as a peace offering. "All I ask is a little professional courtesy. I have no expectations of you liking this situation."

The detective considered the offer for a second and relented. "Thomas Lassiter."

"Isaac Bell. Sorry about stepping on your toes."

"I guess it ain't your fault."

The other detective ambled over. "Ray Burns."

Bell shook his hand as well. "Would have enjoyed meeting you both over a beer rather than a body, but let's make the best of this." Bell then said to the room in general, "I'm not sure if you know, but the press is already here in the form of Abel Loohey. If you're not familiar with him, suffice it to say he cares little for facts and everything about headlines."

Steinem uttered a couple of curses that would have made a sailor blush. His voice low and compelling, he said, "This came from a leak in your office, Lassiter. This will hit the evening edition of the *New York Globe* and be top of the fold on every paper by morning. They are going to savage my client, ruin him no matter what. This is a travesty, I tell you. And I will see you are held accountable for whatever libel Mr. Pickett endures."

"Easy, counselor. The leak could have just as easily come from the governor's office. You woke him up in the middle of the night, no doubt he's going to call a chief of staff or something."

"Gentlemen, please," Bell said, raising his hands and getting instant cooperation. "Whatever the source, it hardly matters now. We're under the gun, so to speak. Most evening papers go to print by three-thirty. That leaves us . . ." He checked his watch. "A little over six hours before it's too late to stop Loohey from writing whatever he wants. Let's get cracking."

"You want to hear what we think?" Burns, Lassiter's protégé, offered. He was much younger than Lassiter and not quite worn down to a cynical nub as his partner.

"Thanks, but I like my own first impressions. I would like to understand the timeline."

Lassiter pulled a greasy leather notebook from his suit pocket and flipped through some pages. "Call came in to our shop at six thirty-seven. We arrived at six fifty. The suspect was in this room wearing the clothing he has on and with his lawyer present."

"Did he give you a statement?"

"He did through his attorney. He claimed—"

Bell cut him off with a gesture. "Not yet. I want to hear it after I've studied the scene. What then?"

"At five after seven the house phone rings. It's our chief telling us to cool our heels here until another investigator arrives from New York. And that's it. We been smoking butts and drinking Pickett's coffee ever since."

As a courtesy, Bell should have told them that Steinem's call to the Van Dorn office had been logged at four-fifteen, but Pickett was his client, and it was the Newport Police Department's job to burn up some shoe leather if they wanted to make a case. He said, "Okay. I think I'm up to speed. I'd like to see the body now."

6

THE VETERAN SERGEANT STAYED IN THE SOLARIUM WITH Pickett, Steinem, and the two coroner employees. Lassiter led the way with Burns lagging a few paces back, leaving Bell effectively bracketed between them. Burns was just far enough back that Bell couldn't turn and attack, but close enough to prevent Bell from going after his partner. It was a classic police technique done on instinct rather than necessity. The two men weren't complete incompetents.

They snaked back through the open atrium and off to the east wing of the house and up a back set of stairs. The hallway they reached was dimly lit and seemed to stretch forever. There was a set of double doors at the very end of the corridor that would likely be the master suite. They stopped at the final door on the right side of the hall. The room beyond would overlook the ocean.

The door had been kicked in. The trim around the latch was

splintered and very white compared to the rest of the stained woodwork.

The space beyond was bright with every lamp lit and light turned on, and airy because of the twelve-foot ceilings trimmed with moldings covered in hammered gold leaf. There were built-in benches under the three bay windows, their cushions upholstered in pale pink silk. Most of the polished hardwood floor was covered in an intricate Oriental rug so tightly knotted it barely gave under the weight of Bell's shoes. At one end of the room was an ashy fireplace with an elaborate mantel. Above it was the John Singer Sargent portrait of a then eighteen-year-old Fedora Scarsworth that she had sat for while she and her family were summering in Europe.

The fabled portraitist had been as kind as artistic license would allow, but Miss Scarsworth had not been a pretty woman in life.

Or death.

At the other end of the room was a set of couches, a few delicate side tables, and a writer's desk opened to show the dozens of little pigeonholes and drawers for storing supplies of ink and stamps and scented envelopes that were expected of a woman of her station. On the chair, slumped into a position only a corpse could achieve, was Fedora Scarsworth-Pickett.

Bell's immediate impression was that she'd had too much to drink and had passed out draped partially over the chair's wooden arm. There was no blood to be seen (despite Loohey's claim) and no overt signs of violence. And yet he knew she was dead, knew it in the ancient part of his brain that recognized violence and its aftermath. She was utterly still and what skin he could see was pale and waxy except around her exposed ankles. They were liverish purple and swollen with the blood that had pooled in her lower extremities.

One hand was on her lap, the other trailed almost to the carpet. She wore a simple cream dress.

"Don't touch nothing," Detective Lassiter warned as they slowly crossed to the corpse.

The windows were open, so Bell couldn't detect the scent of gunpowder in the air. Thankfully, it was far too soon for the body to give off the inevitable aromas of death. He had no idea how many bodies he'd seen, how many murders he'd investigated. He would never become numb to it. Lassiter and, to a degree, Burns plastered indifference to their faces and slouched around as nonchalantly as they could, as if being this close to mortality had no effect. They might be able to fool themselves, but Bell wasn't buying it. Even the most sangfroid mortician gets the willies every once in a while.

When he drew closer, he smelled the blood, and then he saw it. The way she was slumped over, her head hid most of her lap and it was there that blood had pooled in little puddles and delicate connecting rivulets. Bell watched where he stepped. The spray of blood was easy to see on the lighter parts of the ornate rug but all but invisible on the darker spaces. She had blond hair, and the back of her head had a matted spot of dark coppery blood as thick as tar. The entry wound.

He glanced at Lassiter so he recognized Bell was going to approach even closer but would follow the dictate of "not touching nothing." Bell settled onto his haunches just to her side and craned his head so he could see her face through the golden curtain of her fallen hair.

The bullet had exited just below her right eye. It hadn't been a large-caliber weapon. The damage, though unsightly and tragic, wasn't particularly gruesome now that all the blood had drained away. It was just a hole, rimmed in dark red with just a tiny shard of white bone showing through.

Bell stood and moved around so he could closely examine the entry wound. It was almost perfectly centered at the back of her skull and appeared to be at a slightly downward angle from a spot closer to the top of the occipital lobe. On Fedora Scarsworth-Pickett's writing desk sat an ornate cup containing fountain pens and a single ivory-handled magnifying glass. He pointed it out to Lassiter. "May I?"

"Yeah, go ahead," the detective replied.

Bell plucked the remarkably heavy glass from the cup and stooped over the entry wound. Here he could smell the distinctive chemical signature of gunpowder and see visible flakes of charred powder in her hair and embedded into the wound. Sooting around a wound meant only very fine particles of gunshot residue reached a victim, indicating the gun was farther away. What Bell was looking at through magnification was known as stippling and usually meant the mouth of the barrel was very close to or in direct contact with the victim when the gun was fired.

Close contact at the back of the head was usually not the calling card of a mere murder. This had all the hallmarks of a targeted assassination.

Bell noted a little bloodless nick on the back of her head next to and slightly above the bullet's entry point. He had no explanation for it.

He straightened and returned the magnifier to the cup. He bent low again to examine the hand trailing down toward the floor, leaning in close enough to smell it, much to the discomfort of the two cops. He ran his hand over the carpet below the body.

"We already found the bullet," Detective Burns said helpfully. "It had lost all its energy when it exited the skull and was just lying on her lap. It's a .32 caliber."

Bell didn't reply. He systematically moved around the room, sometimes taking in entire walls with a glance and at others pressing so close his nose nearly touched the plasterwork or a piece of trim. He swept his hand across other sections of carpet and used a small single-cell flashlight to provide additional illumination as needed. He studied the ceiling for a long while. In all, Lassiter gave him fifteen minutes in the writing room before becoming fed up.

"Enough already, Bell."

"Was a weapon recovered?"

"Yeah. We found a .32 revolver in a bag at the bottom of a trash can," Lassiter said, pointing to the can sitting next to the writing desk. "It had been fired once. Recently. And the butler fella identified it as the pistol Pickett keeps in his bedside table."

"That's a meaningless identification," Bell pointed out. "Nearly every manufacturer's version of the .32 revolver looks about the same."

"This one has a gold monogram on the barrel. *JDP.* Jackson Davis Pickett, in case you're wondering. It also has bespoke grips that we already fitted to Pickett's hand, and before his lawyer could shut him up, he asked where we found it because he hadn't seen it in, well, that's when counsel clamped down on him."

"Any staff on last night besides the butler answering the door?"

"Couple maids in the attic area in the other wing. They didn't hear anything, but this is a big damn house. Butler says he didn't hear anything prior to Pickett yelling his head off to call for an ambulance early this morning."

"What has Mr. Pickett told you besides recognizing the pistol?"

"Him? Nothing. His mouthpiece says Pickett was out with friends at a club following some charity thing. He got home at midnight or there abouts. Searches for his wife. Can't find her, but finds the door to her *salle de rédaction*, as he called it, locked. He tried talking to her through the door for a bit and then went to bed. Woke up early this morning. The missus is still locked away in here. He gets concerned and pounds on the door a minute and then breaks in and finds her dead."

"Did he say why he didn't have a key?"

"Lawyer says the deceased carries the only copy of the key around her neck."

"Did you . . . ?"

Lassiter dug a handkerchief from his jacket pocket and unfolded it very carefully. Inside was a standard brass key on a slender ribbon of lilac silk. "I looked for prints using that same magnifier you used, but didn't see any. We got some guys back at the station who are pretty good with the science stuff."

"Not to sound immodest, but I am an expert on the 'science stuff.' Mind if I have a go at it?"

"No chance," Lassiter said, his eyes squinting as he held a flaring match to another cigarette and led them from the room. "Can't risk you having a case of butterfingers and wiping the key clean."

Bell smirked. "Don't trust me, Detective?"

"It ain't personal, but no."

"Given the circumstances, I can't say I blame you."

Lassiter closed the writing room door and plucked one of the hairs from his head. He used saliva to adhere it between the door and the frame. "Can't have you tampering with the scene in case the coroner needs to see anything."

"You are calling for a full autopsy?"

"For a case this big, you bet. I phoned him earlier. He's waiting at the morgue and told us if you weren't here by noon to take the body to him and arrest the lawyer for obstruction if he so much as cleared his throat in protest."

"Very reasonable of him, actually. I appreciate the cooperation."

"And the governor is gonna appreciate whatever help Pickett gives him after he leaves office next year."

"What do they call it?" Burns asked rhetorically. "Squid pro quo?"

"Quid, dummy," Lassiter said.

"Oops. Right. Quid."

"I am through with the deceased," Bell informed them. "I don't really want to be present at the autopsy, but I would like to talk to the doctor when he is finished."

"Our guy is thorough. But I'll do you the solid to have him hurry it along so you can give the reporter the facts rather than his version of the crime."

"I appreciate that. Thanks."

"I don't much like reporters, either."

The three men paused outside the solarium. Lassiter caught the eye of one of the orderlies and the two men soon passed by on their grim errand. Bell shook Lassiter's hand. "I'll see you back here with the coroner and his report as soon as he's done."

"Are you forgetting something, Bell?" Lassiter asked with a knowing smirk.

"No, I don't think so."

"We're arresting Pickett for the murder of his wife."

"Based on what?"

"The big three—motive, means, and opportunity," Lassiter said as if to a dullard. "Motive: hey, rich married couple must have all kinds of problems guys like me will never know. Means: he owns a gun that looks to match the bullet recovered on the victim's body. Opportunity: it's his house and she lives here, he's got opportunity aplenty."

"All circumstantial," Bell countered. "For all you know they had a loving marriage that was the envy of all their friends. He said his pistol was missing, so it could have been stolen by the real murderer, and as for opportunity, I don't think you noticed the black wooden chair in the corner of the solarium. The coat of arms on the back is for Tulane University. Do you really think a graduate of such a fine school would be stupid enough to commit murder without first giving himself an ironclad alibi?"

Bell steamrolled over whatever response Lassiter was about to give. "This wasn't a spontaneous crime of passion like he'd just found her in bed with a neighbor. She was shot in the room she felt safest by someone meticulous and calculating. Sure, husbands use that MO all the time, but in each and every case they also have their exit strategy just as well-thought-out.

"Be honest with yourself, Lassiter, you think it's him because you want it to be him. It's easy and could fit. It means your case is wrapped up in a few hours and the boys back at the station house buy your drinks on Friday and maybe there's a bonus in your check at the end of the month."

Bell could see the indecision on the detective's face. This case was far from open-and-shut and he knew it, and there was the political element with the governor getting involved. Hauling Pickett down to the precinct in cuffs could land him in water so hot it would melt the St. Michael medal Lassiter doubtlessly had in his pocket.

Bell added, "Mr. Pickett was here when you arrived, correct?"

Lassiter drew on his cigarette and nodded.

"On the advice of his attorney, Mr. Steinem?"

"Allegedly," Burns answered.

"Presumably," Lassiter corrected with a shake of his head.

"Do you think his legal advice to his client is going to change in the next couple of hours when the circumstances have not?"

"Probably not."

"Then Mr. Pickett will be here this afternoon for you to arrest if the facts of the case indicate that he is, in fact, the murderer."

"I don't . . ."

Bell pushed through into the solarium, whipping a pair of handcuffs from his outside jacket pocket. He strode across the room and clamped one around Jackson Pickett's wrist before anyone knew what was happening and locked the other through the arm of the sofa he was seated on. He finished with a flourish by tossing the key to Lassiter in an underhand lob.

"Unless he's going on the lam attached to a three-hundred-pound mahogany davenport, your suspect isn't leaving your jurisdiction today. Satisfied?"

Steinem opened his mouth to protest, but Bell waved him back with his hand.

"I asked if this is to your satisfaction, Detective?"

Lassiter didn't look happy about it, but he was a man standing in a minefield and Bell had just shown him a way out. "Fine, but Desk Sergeant Cross is going to be in his car right outside the front door until we get back from the morgue."

"I'll see he gets coffee and something to eat," Bell said affably.

Lassiter wasn't done. He still had to prove this was his investigation. "Make no mistake, Bell, if the coroner doesn't come up with anything I haven't already seen, your boy is headed to the iron-bar motel and that reporter will have the story of the year."

Bell smiled. "Suits me. I would ask one favor. Two actually. Ask the medical examiner about the scrape adjacent to the entry wound on her skull and ask if there was a substance of any kind on either of her hands."

"Substance? Like what?"

"If I knew I wouldn't be asking, now would I?"

7

As soon as Bell was satisfied they had the house to themselves, he produced a second handcuff key and freed Jackson Pickett. The socialite shot to his feet and rubbed his wrist. This action must've been theatrical, because Bell had left the cuff as loose as possible.

"Masterful performance, Mr. Bell," said Isidor Steinem. "But I expect no less from Joseph Van Dorn's lead man."

Bell made an impatient gesture. "Flattery aside, counselor, what exactly do you expect of me?"

"Reasonable doubt, Mr. Bell. You prevented Jackson from being charged with murder this morning, but that charge will definitely come this afternoon."

"What?" Jackson Pickett cried. "But I didn't—"

"Your protestations of innocence are all well and good, but they do nothing to counter the facts of this situation. You will be charged with Fedora's murder, and you will stand trial in front of twelve of your peers. Twelve peers, I might add, who collectively don't have even the smallest fraction of your wealth and are likely filled with petty jealousies and resentments. With luck, and Mr. Bell's help, I hope to get you a bail hearing so you aren't jailed between now and your murder trial."

"But I didn't—"

"At this point, Jackson, it really doesn't matter," Steinem said with a touch of exasperation. "You will be charged and there will be a trial. Its outcome depends on Mr. Bell here being able to present an alternative version of the crime, something I can get the jury to believe. That's reasonable doubt and all but guarantees your acquittal."

He turned his full attention on Bell. "How about it? Do you have an alternative version of the crime?"

"I need to ask a few questions before answering that. Also, I could use a glass of water."

"Something stronger, perhaps?"

"Water's fine," Bell said.

Steinem summoned the butler, ordered water for Bell and scotches for he and Pickett. "Now that we're done with the police," he said to his client, as if to a child, "you can have a drink, but only one. You need to be sharp for when Lassiter comes back."

"What happened last night and this morning?" Bell asked.

"It's exactly like I told Lassiter," Pickett said. "I went to a charity auction yesterday afternoon and then had dinner and drinks with friends at a club here in town. I got home around midnight."

"Why wasn't your wife with you?"

Pickett looked to his attorney for guidance.

"Don't filter your answers through your lawyer," Bell said. "Think of me as your priest or your doctor. Don't lie to me and don't hold anything back. A detail you think is trivial could be the fulcrum that swings a trial your way. Are we clear?"

Pickett was still reeling from the events of the past several hours and Bell needed him focused. With every passing hour, his recollection would degrade, subtleties would be lost, and his testimony would become unsure and vague.

"Are we clear?" Bell repeated.

"Yes." Pickett gave a small smile. "We're clear, Mr. Bell. Thank you."

"Why wasn't your wife with you last night?"

He glanced at a photograph on the wall of Fedora dressed in a flowing taffetta ball gown. His eyes were gauzy with unshed tears. "We've been married eight years. Eight pretty good years. Her father didn't approve of me, of course. I come from a good New Orleans family, you see, but like most good New Orleans families, my ancestors squandered our wealth. My parents were forced to live their lives on credit and the generosity of distant relatives. I only attended Tulane because I was a good-enough quarterback to regularly beat LSU.

"Fedora's father, Bill Scarsworth, thought I was only after his daughter for her money, and he only consented to the marriage after I agreed that in the event of divorce or death, I would forfeit all rights to her estate except for a one-time payment of ten thousand dollars."

"Is this something you drafted?" Bell asked Steinem.

"No. William Scarsworth uses another firm in the city. However, I have read their prenuptial agreement. It's ironclad."

"At Fedora's death, you lose everything?"

Pickett nodded. "I have a month to vacate the premises and

Bill's lawyers will be here to make sure I didn't stuff the family silver in my suitcase."

"That puts a hell of a dent in Lassiter's case," Bell said. "But you still haven't answered my question."

"I'm getting to it," Pickett said and took a sip from the scotch his butler had brought him. "We got along okay, Dora and me. We understood each other. I wanted to live the high life and she wanted a handsome husband who was at least discrete when he went catting about. We rarely fought and I was always there for her for whatever event she wanted to attend."

"Do you have children?"

"We tried in the beginning, but that part of our relationship slowly faded to nothing."

"Pardon me for being blunt," Bell said, "but it was a loveless marriage of convenience, yes?"

"It was. It was comfortable, you know? We did like each other and care for each other." Pickett went silent for a moment, his eyes out of focus. "It all changed six weeks ago."

Bell's interest was piqued. "What changed?"

"Dora. You see, she had a riding accident. She took a nasty tumble from a horse we had just bought. It had spooked and reared, and she hit her head on a rock when she landed."

"Were you with her at the time?"

"No, I was here. She was riding with a friend, Lauren Gardner, and our head groomsman."

"They were here on the estate?"

"They were actually in the woods owned by our neighbors. We all have verbal agreements about riding on each other's property."

"So, what happened?"

"They told me later that Dora was unconscious for just a couple of minutes and insisted on riding home. Of course, we had a doctor come out to examine her right away. She hadn't broken any bones in her skull, but she definitely had what he called a concussion. Apparently, it's when—"

"I'm familiar with concussions, Mr. Pickett."

"Oh, okay. The doctor told me she might have some side effects: headache, memory problems, mood swings, that sort of thing. But he told me they would be temporary."

The way Pickett said the final statement made Bell think they hadn't been temporary at all. "Her symptoms persisted?"

"They grew worse," he said bitterly. "She would fly into rages over the littlest thing, or sob uncontrollably over nothing at all. She would forget servants' names, servants she'd known since childhood."

"Did you take her back to the doctor?"

"She refused. I even brought the doctor to the house when her symptoms got worse, but she wouldn't allow him to see her. She became paranoid and thought I was trying to have her committed to a sanatorium. Dora is an only child, and her mother has been dead for many years. I had no choice but to reach out to her father. He came. He saw what she was like. He told me it was my problem and left with a reminder that if anything happened to his daughter I was out on my ear."

"Is this about the time your gun went missing?" Bell asked.

"Near enough," Pickett replied. "I asked Dora about it. She said she hadn't seen it, and I believed her. She rather liked the idea that I would arm myself on occasion. She said I reminded her of a Mississippi riverboat gambler. For herself, though, she was deathly afraid of the pistol. She never touched it. I tore the house apart looking for it. Ask Charles, our butler. He helped."

"Didn't find it?"

"No. About this same time, Dora's chambermaid was visited by a brother. I never met the fellow, however staff members tell me he looked, ah, unsavory. He had access to parts of the house far beyond what he should, and I believed he stole my gun."

"I'll need to track him down."

"Of course."

"Were there any signs that your wife's symptoms were abating?"

"None. She grew worse. We quarreled often. She talked about wanting a divorce. She constantly berated the staff and belittled me. She took to drinking alcohol, something she'd never done before. I consulted with more doctors. Some believed her symptoms could be explained by bleeding inside her head and wanted to perform exploratory surgery. Others said we should wait. I didn't know what to do."

"And in the meantime," Isidor Steinem interjected, "poor Jackson had to maintain a facade of normalcy as best he could."

"Right," he agreed readily. "I couldn't keep ignoring invitations. It's Newport during the end of the summer season, after all. I went to the auction and explained that Dora was still recovering from her fall and that she had an especially bad headache."

Pickett slumped and buried his face in his hands when he realized how gruesomely prophetic the excuse he'd used had turned out to be. "Oh, Dora!"

Bell said nothing, but his mind worked furiously. What Pickett described was someone becoming pathological and manic on account of the accident, but that didn't help him build an alternate-theory case. Given the clues at the scene, he had no theory other than Pickett being the murderer.

He asked, "Had her condition affected others in her life? A sibling or close friend who would be so hurt by something Fedora had said or done?"

"No. Dora was an only child and since her fall she hasn't had any visitors. She hadn't felt up for it."

"What does her father do for work?" Bell asked because he had nothing else.

"He's an inventor. He owns a company that manufactures some of the things he thought up. Most of his ideas pertain to mechanical hoists and cranes. I'm not too sure of the details."

"So, no real enemies there, either? No business partner he swindled or bankers he owes too much to?"

"None that I can imagine. You'd have to ask him."

"How about you?"

"Me?"

"Let's not be coy, Mr. Pickett. People trapped in loveless marriages usually look outside the marital bed for affection. Any jealous lovers or vengeful husbands I should know about?"

He glanced away, as if he were about to lie, but then turned back and held Bell's eye. "In years past there would be a long list of potentials, I admit. However, for the past six months I've been exclusive with a widow in the city. She understands my circumstances and is perfectly content with it."

Bell felt he might have something here. "She wouldn't want your wife out of the picture?"

"I assure you she would not."

"Why's that?"

"Because if she remarries, she loses the bulk of her trust fund to her younger sister. And my buyout from Bill Scarsworth wouldn't cover more than a couple of weeks of her expenses."

Bell's spark of hope that there could be another suspect flickered and died. "I still need to talk to her."

"I'd rather keep her out of this," Pickett replied.

His lawyer jumped in. "Is her reputation worth more than your freedom?"

Pickett hesitated again, and then said, "Gloria. Her name is Gloria Peterborough. She lives at the Waldorf-Astoria."

The name sounded vaguely familiar to Bell. He bet Marion would know her, or at least know of her. Marion herself wasn't much of a gossip. For one, she was often absent from the city to work on her latest motion picture, but her best friend was Lillian Abbott, and she was plugged into every social circle in Manhattan and many more beyond.

Steinem pulled a half hunter from his waistcoat and checked the time. "Lassiter will be back in a few hours. Jackson, I recommend you try to sleep. I need to go back to my office to prepare for your arrest later in the day. Mr. Bell, would you be willing to stay?"

"Of course," Bell said quickly.

Pickett summoned the butler, Charles, by pulling a silk-sheathed rope attached to the mansion's extensive electric bell system. The man appeared seconds later. Jackson Pickett shook hands with his attorney and his newly hired investigator and allowed Charles to lead him up to his suite.

Bell walked with Steinem to the front door. The lawyer said, "I've done a handful of murder trials in my day, so I defer to your expertise in these situations, as I'm certain you've seen more than your share of homicides."

"My share, your share, and a whole lot of other people's shares," Bell agreed.

"What do you think his chances are?"

"You'll get him out on bail until the trial. You can argue that this was a domestic dispute that escalated out of control and that Pickett isn't a danger to society at large. That said, unless I can find a plausible alternative suspect, he's going down for this no matter how vehemently he pleads his innocence."

The lawyer grunted. Clearly, he didn't feel optimistic for his client's future, either.

STEINEM'S CHAUFFER LEAPT FROM THE ROLLS-ROYCE AS HIS employer descended the steps and had the rear door open and waiting for the attorney to slide onto the buttery-soft leather seat. The car was equipped with an electric starter. The engine was so smooth Bell hadn't heard it fire up and only knew it was running because the driver slipped it into gear and the stately car began to glide down the driveway.

Bell ambled over to the last car left in front of the mansion. Bell's driver had left as soon as he'd dropped him off. The hearse had left a large puddle on the cobbles that would soon dry in the morning sun. He rapped his knuckles on the glass of the police sedan that had been left behind like a lonely sentry. To his credit, Desk Sergeant Cross was a light sleeper.

"Eh, what's the big idea?"

"I believe Detective Lassiter's intention was that you make sure Mr. Pickett doesn't escape like a thief in the night."

He said gruffly, "I never let another man's intentions get in the way of my sleep."

Bell smiled. "I like your style. Listen, Lassiter made a big scene of sealing up the writing room. I need to get back in there and I don't want a beef with him. I'm afraid you have to play chaperone."

"What did I just tell you about other people's intentions and my sleep?"

"Come on, Sergeant. There's a sofa in there and I got you a nice blanket and pillow. I suppose I can even arrange some warm milk as well."

The veteran cop levered open the door and stepped to the ground. He sloshed a half-full flask under Bell's chin. "Already got that covered."

Bell looked around but there was no sign of Abel Loohey. He'd have to call Loohey's editor. No doubt the reporter would check throughout the day. Bell needed him here when Lassiter returned so as to make his story as factual as possible. He felt the press of time weighing him down and he had little to leverage it off.

8

IT WAS NEARLY TWO-THIRTY WHEN LASSITER AND HIS PARTNER,
Ray Burns, arrived at the Pickett estate. Bell amended that
thought. It was the Scarsworth estate, or would be within the
month. William Scarsworth was on a business trip in Colorado
and wasn't expected back for several days. His lawyers, however,
had shown up promptly at noon and began inventorying the contents of the house. Pickett was told that their Manhattan town-
house had been sealed, but he would be allowed an hour at his
convenience to remove his personal items, limited to clothing and
such objects that he could prove were gifts from his deceased wife.

Pickett looked like he'd been unable to sleep. He remained haggard and defeated and his eyes red-rimmed and bloodshot. The
solarium had become the default waiting room. Pickett took to
one of the couches, alternating between sitting up or lying flat with
the occasional frustrated walk around the brightly lit room.

Bell had nothing to do. He had concluded his investigation not long after Lassiter had left and could only wait for the police and coroner and their findings. He had taken a couple of books from the adjacent library, but couldn't concentrate. He kept replaying the aerial attack on the President's yacht through his mind and the significance of the newly printed money being in the pilot's possession. The Secret Service made it more than clear that this wasn't his case, which made Bell think about it all the more.

Inside, though, he was concerned about the current deadline. Loohey would crucify Jackson Pickett in the press and right now there was nothing he could do about it. Everything came down to how fast the coroner could perform his duties and Lassiter could get him back here. He could almost feel the tiny movements of his watch hand as the seconds ticked by.

Isidor Steinem had arrived at two, with another attorney who would accompany Pickett to the jail when Lassiter took him away. Steinem himself would go straight to the courts to petition for an immediate bail hearing.

A different butler was on duty, a man called Hammond. He seemed to have some sway with Jackson Pickett, as he got his master to eat a couple of coddled eggs on toast just before the police cruiser and the coroner's county-provided Ford came up the curving drive and braked at the foot of the great stairs. Bell had been able to reach Loohey's editor and secured a promise that his star reporter would come to the house for a statement before his story went to press.

Hammond met them at the door. Along with Lassiter and Burns was another beat cop in uniform, who'd relieved Sergeant Cross at noon. Hammond announced the party as if they were honored guests. The coroner's name was Jim Trask. He was tall and stooped and looked exhausted, but behind wire-framed glasses, his gray eyes remained sharp and quick.

"This is going to be short and sweet," Lassiter announced. He hadn't bothered removing his hat. "Upon a preliminary examination of the deceased, Doc Trask didn't find anything to lead him to believe this was anything but an execution-style murder. Mr. Pickett was found by the staff with the body of the deceased. The gun was in the trash can not five feet from the accused. No one else was at home and the room was locked from the inside."

Those statements hung in the air, utterly indisputable.

"Open and shut," Ray Burns said unnecessarily.

Lassiter nodded to the uniformed officer, who pulled a pair of cuffs from a leather pouch attached to his Sam Browne belt. "Jackson Pickett," he said formally, "I am placing you under arrest for the murder of your wife, Fedora Scarsworth-Pickett."

Pickett remained seated on the couch, his mouth open as he sucked air past his teeth. His eyes were as vacant as a corpse's. The cop tugged gently on his arm and Pickett slowly rose to his feet, as meekly as a lamb to slaughter.

"One moment, please," Bell said. He, too, hadn't risen from his seat when the police arrived. "Dr. Trask, do you know who I am?"

"I suspect you're the investigator Mr. Steinem hired." His voice was thick with fatigue, and even without a lab coat over his thin worsted suit, Bell sensed an air of learned academia about him.

"That's correct. My name is Isaac Bell. This morning I asked Detective Lassiter to mention two areas of interest. Did he relay my queries?"

"You want to know about the scrape to her skull next to the entry wound."

"Yes, and if there was any substance present on her right hand." Bell turned to look at Jackson Pickett. "Are you okay? I can speak with Dr. Trask in private."

"I'm all right, I guess," Pickett said, the cop still holding him by the upper arm, the cuffs still clutched in his other hand.

"There had been some material on her hand, traces of it remained in the creases of skin at the knuckle, but I couldn't tell what it was. The sample was just too small. Some sort of lotion or jelly if I had to venture a guess. It didn't seem germane."

"And the scrape?"

"I'm not certain what made it, something metallic, I would venture, given the nature of the wound. There was no bleeding of note, so I would say it occurred on or about the time of death or shortly thereafter."

"Did you find evidence of prior intracranial hematoma?"

"Of what?" Pickett asked.

"Bleeding inside her head near her brain."

"I did, yes, and it was rather extensive. I suspect she would have been very symptomatic. Headaches, confusion, drowsiness, and irritability, perhaps. I'm afraid it likely would have been terminal over the next weeks or months had she not met her fate last night."

"Is it consistent with a fall from a horse?"

"Consistent, yes, but I can't say for certain. Any bruising on her skin had long since healed."

"Thank you, Doctor," Bell said and swung his gaze to Lassiter. "I must tell you that arresting Mr. Pickett is a gross miscarriage of justice. He didn't kill his wife. She committed suicide."

Lassiter snorted and his tone dripped sarcasm. "And the gun happened to end up in an intact paper bag in a garbage can five feet from the stiff."

Pickett winced and Lassiter quickly apologized to him. "Sorry, the deceased."

Trask then added with indignation, "Are you impugning my skills as a pathologist?"

"No, sir, but you were given a cleverly laid false trail."

"I don't see how. The angle of the bullet's path is clearly one of homicide. A suicide could never fire a gun with that trajectory. The limitations to movement of the human arm wouldn't allow it."

"It wasn't a gun," Bell said. "Not in the traditional sense. Doctor, other than trajectory were you able to deduce any ballistic characteristics of the bullet recovered with the body?"

"Just that it was a .32 caliber of approximately fifty grains weight."

"I did some snooping since the body was taken away," Bell said and pulled a small box from his pocket. It was ammunition from the Remington Arms company. The box was neatly labeled .32 CALIBER FULL METAL JACKET BULLETS -71 GRAINS. It rattled when he shook it. "This was in the back of the drawer where Mr. Pickett kept his revolver. There are six rounds missing from this box of fifty and your guys who you told me are good with the science stuff will match them with the five unspent rounds in the pistol you took as evidence."

Lassiter said nothing, his face a little pinched.

Bell went on. "If I was a dishonest investigator Mr. Steinem could have discovered what kind of ammunition his client used to murder his wife and had me bring a partially used box with a different bullet weight."

"That didn't happen," Lassiter admitted. "When Pickett told me he kept a gun in his bedside table I looked for myself. That box was in the back of the drawer. I remember seeing it was seventy-one grain. I didn't notice the bullet we recovered from the deceased was one-third lighter."

"I have no doubt that you would have corrected that mistake as your investigation unfolded," Bell said, though he was clearly thinking Lassiter could have easily ditched the inconvenient box of ammo in order to make his case. The chip on the detective's shoulder was that deep and sharp.

"This ain't exactly proof of a suicide, Bell."

"But it raises the prospect of reasonable doubt," Isidor Steinem said quickly.

"I'm saving the best for last," Bell said. "Would you gentlemen please follow me upstairs to Mrs. Scarsworth-Pickett's writing room? And, Jackson, if you're not up for this we all certainly understand."

"No, I . . ." He paused, gathering his thoughts. "Dora had been acting so different since the accident. I told you this morning after everyone left. She became spiteful and was keen on a divorce. She would sometimes gloat about leaving me penniless. That seemed to make her happy. I never saw her being suicidal, though."

"The pressure of blood in her brain could have made her act in any number of unpredictable ways," Dr. Trask said as they trooped up the stairs.

"Keep in mind," Bell said when they reached the second floor, "how you said your wife had grown vindictive."

Lassiter pulled ahead to check if his security hair was still in place. It had been replaced with an iron-gray hair from Sergeant Cross. He wheeled around when he saw it, his eyes hard and accusatory. "What's the big idea, Bell?"

Bell held up his hands in a placating gesture. "Sergeant Cross will attest that your hair was in place when we breached this room together and that he remained with me until I completed my investigation. He resealed the room himself."

Bell opened the door. The space looked as it had before, except brighter with the afternoon sun streaming through the windows. One detail that was different was the presence of a wooden stepladder borrowed from a utility closet in the basement that the butler had found for Bell.

Although her body was gone, the men still felt Fedora's presence.

Bell motioned to the chair next to the writing desk. "Detective Burns, would you do me the honors of sitting as Mrs. Scarsworth-Pickett must have been in the moments before her death?"

The Newport cop nodded and took his place, his expression a little uncomfortable at taking the seat of a dead woman. Bell moved behind him. "The deceased had a gunshot wound to the back of her head at a slight downward angle, leading you to believe that the perpetrator was standing behind her and held a pistol to her head."

Bell mimicked that action with his fingers held in the shape of a gun. "Such a scenario doesn't explain the scrape found on her skull an inch from the entry wound. It wasn't caused by the gun's recoil or any other natural action one would expect of a murderer."

Bell then nearly rested his arm on Burns's head and pointed his finger as if following the path of something that struck Fedora and continued across the room. "As you can see, the trajectory lines up with the fireplace almost exactly. I note this because I saw some ash in the grate when we were in this room earlier and I thought it odd. There has been no autumn chill yet this year and I seriously doubt the hearth has been left dirty all summer long. A house with this much domestic help wouldn't have ashes lying around in fireplaces."

Bell looked at Jackson Pickett and asked, "Was this room warm when you discovered her body?"

"Yes. It was very warm."

"I felt it, too, when I arrived," Isidor Steinem confirmed. "I opened the windows, in fact."

"And as we all recall, last night was rather warm. Having a fire going on a warm summer evening is an anomaly. When I returned to this room with Sergeant Cross, I checked the grate. The ashes were still warm hours later and I noted a chemical scent similar to kerosene, which makes me think an accelerant was used."

"But why?" Pickett asked, his voice pained as he tried to come to grips with his wife's final moments.

"She needed the room hot so that the substance she'd coated her right hand with would melt away rather quickly."

"What substance?" Lassiter asked.

"Your coroner couldn't identify it, and neither could I, but if you take a moment to get down on the floor under the chair, there is a dark stain, nearly imperceptible against the Oriental rug's pattern, but discernable, nevertheless. It smells faintly of perfume, but also of burned gunpowder."

Lassiter made a gesture to his partner and Detective Burns slid off the chair and onto his knees. He bent and began sniffing the carpet. He found the spot quickly enough. "Yeah," he said. "Smells sweet, but also like a freshly fired gun."

Bell nodded. "It's my contention that she smeared her right hand and forearm with some kind of cold cream so that she wouldn't get any powder residue on her hands. The bits of powder stuck to the cream and not her skin. She'd raised the temperature in the room enough for the cream to drip from her hand and onto the carpet, leaving behind only an indeterminate trace that you, Detective Lassiter, missed, and you, Dr. Trask, dismissed."

Bell let his gaze sweep his audience. He could see that none of them knew what to make of the evidence he was presenting. Lassiter and Burns had thought they had an airtight case of murder in the first degree and now they didn't know if they even had a case.

He forged ahead. "So now we have a suspect without gunshot residue on his hands and a victim who does. Curious, no?"

"He had more than enough time to wash his hands," Lassiter said.

"They were bloodstained when I arrived," Steinem clarified. "I was the one who told him to wash up. The butler and the two maids who'd come down by that time can corroborate."

"Doesn't matter. There would be evidence on his shirt and jacket, which Detective Lassiter admitted wasn't present when he inspected them."

"Powders and creams," Pickett said in frustration. "How does any of this make you think my wife killed herself?"

"Because I found the weapon she used to do it," Bell told him.

"Only weapon in the room was the .32 in a bag in the trash can," Detective Burns said before his senior partner could drive home that fact.

"Never said it was in the room." Bell put on a pair of thin white cotton gloves he'd borrowed from the butler. He positioned the painter's ladder in a spot midway between the chair where Fedora Scarsworth-Pickett had died and the fireplace and climbed up.

In the ceiling above the ladder was an ornate metal grate hiding one of the metal trunk lines for the house's central heating and air-conditioning system. Normally it was held in place with metal clips, but this one had been modified so it hinged open facing the desk and chair. Elastic bands had been installed to keep the grate closed, so Bell had to hold on to it tightly. He then unfolded a little spring-loaded pin that had been mounted inside the ductwork. The pin was designed to hold the grate open, but then fold up and vanish when the grate snapped closed.

He reached his other hand into the void and pulled out a metal object also tethered to the inside of the duct with another, much longer, piece of elastic. He descended the ladder, pulling the mysterious object from where it had been hidden, all the while stretching the elastic ever tighter.

"What is that?" Lassiter asked as the men huddled around him.

Bell held it flat so that they could all see. It was a single-shot pistol that had its trigger guard crudely sawn off and an odd-shaped flange attached to the actual trigger. He sniffed it and recoiled at the strong smell of burnt powder. Lassiter also gave it a whiff and worked his jaw back and forth as he contemplated the meaning of this new evidence.

A button under the barrel allowed Bell to slide the two-inch barrel from the receiver and reveal a single shiny brass cartridge. "Detective?"

Distracted, Lassiter didn't catch Bell's meaning right away, but then caught on. He used the tip of his pen to extract the spent shell casing. There was a partial fingerprint visible on the bright yellow metal.

"Did you fingerprint the deceased?" Bell asked the coroner, Trask.

"I did. Yes."

"Ten will get you twenty it's a match, Detective."

Lassiter slid the empty cartridge into a small evidence envelope, careful to not smudge the print.

Bell closed the pistol and pulled it all the way to the chair. It was taut, but he could still hold it steady. "By removing the trigger guard and adding the flange she could fire the pistol at an angle to make it look like she was shot from above."

He held the gun at the approximate spot above the chair where her head would have been. "Once she pulled the trigger . . ."

He let go of the pistol as if it had fallen from Fedora's dead fingers. The elastic rebounded almost faster than the eye could track. When the gun flew up into the duct, it knocked the little pin loose and the grate closed up behind it. No trace of what had just happened remained.

"The gun hit the back of her head when it returned to the air vent," Trask whispered as if to himself and added more loudly, "That explains the mysterious scrape."

"It does."

And that's when the full horror of what his wife had done to him hit Jackson Pickett like he'd been poleaxed. He bent over as if to retch up the little food he'd eaten and staggered in a rough circle, his breathing accelerating until he was hyperventilating in choking half sobs.

She had not only taken her own life, she'd done it in a way to frame her husband for murder. Bell understood the psychology of crime and criminals. It was his stock-in-trade, but he'd never come upon a situation quite like this. He'd seen fake kidnappings and disappearances made to look like the spouse was a murderer, but never someone staging a suicide to look like a homicide.

He could only imagine the pained emotional tides that washed through Fedora Scarsworth-Pickett's hemorrhage-ravaged brain to feel that escaping her life wasn't enough. She had to punish her husband as well.

Pickett had talked about being someone who could be discrete with his affairs, but surely she knew. And no woman would so meekly accept that her fate was being forever jilted by her husband. Bell imagined it grew worse in her eyes when he stopped meaningless trysts that were purely physical concessions and had become exclusive these past months with Gloria Peterborough. Her rage must have festered deep, and when she had such a traumatic brain injury, that rage turned into something far worse. She was despondent, but also so bent on revenge that taking her own life and pinning the blame on her husband became a rational course of action.

This had been meticulously planned and executed. It wasn't the impulsive act of one suddenly overcome with anger and grief. She saw taking her own life as worth it if it meant her husband spent the rest of his in jail. Because of the bleeding in her brain, this was all coldly rational and necessary.

Steinem was trying to console his client by repeating that it wasn't Fedora who had done this to him, it was the brain damage. She wasn't herself, he said, and Pickett must remember her as she was before the fall from the horse.

Bell didn't know if Pickett would ever be able to see past this cruelest of betrayals. He thought of his own marriage and wondered how he'd react if Marion's personality suddenly changed. He truly didn't know and silently hoped that he would never have to face such a situation.

Detective Lassiter ambled over and made to shake Bell's hand. "I admit I never saw that coming."

"I nearly didn't, either," Bell told him. "It wasn't until I came back with Sergeant Cross and really tore this room apart that it came together."

"What was it that made you come back in the first place?" Lassiter seemed to have lost his hostility about being second-guessed by another investigator.

"The ash in the fireplace," Bell said. "It was an anomaly that I needed an answer to. That opened up everything else, the cream on her hand and the scrape on her head."

Lassiter nodded, clearly impressed. "Going forward, I'm gonna spend more time at crime scenes just looking around."

"It can't hurt. The other thing I had going for me is I needed to find an alternative to your investigation. That's what Steinem really wanted from me. The case you had was a good one based on circumstantial evidence. You would have gotten your conviction. It made me desperate, and desperate people tend to be highly motivated people."

"Listen, Bell, I'm still going to come out of this smelling like a rose because, at the end of the day, the governor's buddy didn't get charged. If you ever need a favor in Newport or really anywhere in Rhode Island, go ahead and drop a nickel."

"Same in New York for you, Detective."

Everyone went back down the stairs. Standing in the foyer was Abel Loohey. He'd talked his way into the mansion, but there was no way the butler was going to let him upstairs. His expression was smug, and Bell relished watching it get wiped off his face.

"It was suicide," Bell told him. "A real tragedy brought on by a brain bleed she suffered following a horse-riding accident."

Isidor Steinem said, "And if you print anything other than that, I will sue you and your paper into insolvency."

"Bull feathers," Loohey blurted out. "I see what's going on here. You're all part of a cover-up."

"Do you know who I am?" Lassiter asked in his best cop voice.

Loohey had been on the Newport seasonal beat long enough to recognize the town's chief detective. "Yeah," he finally admitted.

"Are you accusing me of covering up a crime?"

"I . . ."

"I didn't think so. Mrs. Scarsworth-Pickett tragically took her own life. Now scram before I arrest you for trespassing."

The reporter skulked away exactly like a dog with his tail tucked between its legs.

Bell and Lassiter shook hands again. He and Burns said a few words to Pickett and his attorney and saw themselves out with Dr. Trask in tow.

Bell addressed the two remaining men. "Mr. Pickett, you have my sincerest sympathies for the anguish you've been through. I am sorry about your wife, and I can only imagine how this will derail the life you'd imagined living."

"No matter what my future holds, Mr. Bell, I won't be spending it in Howard Prison, thanks to you."

"Mr. Bell," Isidor Steinem intoned as he pumped Bell's hand like a politician trolling for votes. "I asked you for an alternative theory to Fedora's death so I could present some reasonable doubt in a long-shot defense, and you turn around and prove in one day that no crime was even committed. A remarkable feat, sir. Truly remarkable. Joe Van Dorn's faith in you is certainly well-earned."

"I learned by watching him," Bell deflected in modesty. "Listen, I need to get back to the city or my wife is going to—" He almost said "kill me," but caught himself before making a ghoulish gaff. "Be upset if I ruin our dinner plans. I could use a ride to the station."

Pickett pulled the lanyard to summon his butler. "I'll get my chauffer to take you to Providence. It'll be quicker than leaving from here."

"Thank you. Then I shall take my leave. Good luck, Mr. Pickett. Mr. Steinem, expect an invoice by mail in the next day or two."

Like all of his cases before, Bell had this one filed away and well behind him even before the chauffer pulled up in an open-topped Cadillac tourer for his ride to the station.

Little did he know that this case was only getting started.

9

Baltimore, Maryland
Some months later

T HEY THREW CHARLEY BRIGGS INTO A SPINDLY CHAIR AND
yanked the pillowcase off his head. His hands remained tied
behind his back. They had brought the rope. The pillowcase had
come from the linen closet of the Washington, D.C., home Charley
shared with his wife. She'd been out with her Bible study group
when the three men broke in and grabbed him. He knew who they
were and why they were there. Their response to his pleas of mercy
was to have his mouth stuffed with a stale dishrag from the kitchen
and his head covered by the cotton sack.

He continued to hyperventilate through his nose and his heart
rate spiked once again. His sweat was that of terror and so he gave
off a rancid odor. It had taken all his will to maintain control of
his bladder. His eyes darted like those of a cornered rat as he took
in his surroundings, desperate for a means of escape he knew
wouldn't be there.

The lighting was poor, and the space filled with murk and

shadow. It smelled of raw wood, the salt tang of the sea, and the rot of seaweed left onshore. As his eyes adjusted, Charley saw that he was in a small office and past the open door was an enormous warehouse filled with wooden packing crates stacked twenty or more feet tall.

He knew where he was. Baltimore.

And he recognized two of the three men standing around the office. One was an enforcer, a big guy in an ill-fitting suit with the butt of a gun sticking out of his waistband. There was weeks-old bruising on his forehead that looked like he'd been struck with a lead pipe. He was the personal bodyguard and chauffeur of the other man he had seen before. His name was Flynn O'Conner, and he ran the bootlegging and cargo-hijacking operations for the Port of Baltimore, as well as a large number of other illicit enterprises.

This was his city. He had enough bribe money going out the door to control the politicians, who in turn controlled the cops, who were given explicit orders not to touch Flynn's operation. Charley Briggs knew Flynn O'Conner because they'd done some business together and he'd stupidly tried to extort money from the vicious gangster. On the desk behind him was the small valise in which Briggs had stashed the money he'd already been paid. The goons had found it when they tossed his house during the abduction.

The third man in the office was an elfin figure no more than five feet tall with severely bowed legs, bright red hair and beard, and a long clay pipe held in place by tiny white teeth. He wore a dark green suit and sported a traditional Irish flat cap.

The men who'd kidnapped Briggs were on their way out of the office and closed the door behind them. The enforcer strode over and pulled the gag from Charley's mouth with a violent tug. He gasped and gagged for fifteen long seconds before he could find his voice. His words came in a tumbling rush.

"Mr. O'Conner, I'm sorry. I didn't mean it. It was a mistake. I'll tell you everything. I swear. I am really sorry. It was a dumb thing to do. I respect you too much to try and welsh on our deal."

"Shut up," O'Conner said with casual indifference to the absolute terror he was causing.

Briggs went silent for a second, but such was his fear he was soon babbling again. "I did it, though. I really did. It's there just like I promised."

O'Conner smiled a dark, wry smile. "Oh, I know you're not so stupid as to disobey."

"Yeah. I didn't disobey you. I weakened one spot on the roof like you asked me to. It'd take no time to break through and get inside the building."

"You were paid for that," O'Conner reminded the man. "And you were paid to tell me exactly where that weak spot is on the Engraving and Printing building. But you didn't do that, did you Charley boy?"

The building contractor said nothing.

"You took my money, Charley, and then you made it be known that you wanted more. You wanted enough to disappear with that hot little number you keep stashed in an apartment on Dupont Circle."

Charley Briggs's eyes went wide. Charley had been the lead contractor on that apartment building's construction and had installed a secret entrance in the back disguised as a service panel. He had rented the unit for Cathleen even before the building was complete, knowing it would be the perfect love nest for them once she moved out of her boardinghouse. They'd been very careful, he thought, and yet this man knew his dirty little secret.

"I'm not going to hurt her." Flynn O'Conner said it in such a way as to imply he could without any hesitation. "I just wanna make sure you understand the stakes."

"I do. Yes, of course, Mr. O'Conner. The weakened section of roof is on the southern interior projection twenty feet from the northwest corner where it meets the rest of the building. Measure twenty feet from the north edge and twenty feet from the west seam. It puts you right above a storage room in the attic spaces. The weakened area itself is three feet by three feet, just like you required."

"With that, Mr. O'Conner, our contract is complete," said the dapper little man in the Irish cap. His accent was full of pure County Cork lilt. "Thank you much for the assistance. The Marquess will be well pleased."

O'Conner smiled at the trussed foreman. "Was that so hard, Charley? Had you told me this when you promised you would, my bodyguard wouldn't have to work you over with a tire iron today."

Charley Briggs lost all control and started sobbing.

The ginger-haired Irishman was trying to write down the location of the weak spot in the roof of the government's brand-new Bureau of Engraving and Printing building, but his pen wasn't co-operating. He turned to the bodyguard, who was removing his jacket in preparation for the promised beating.

"Any chance you have a—" That's all he needed to say as he closed in on the hulking chauffer. The pistol was a .32 automatic, made for the smaller hands of a woman and thus it fit him perfectly. The report wasn't loud because he'd jammed the barrel into the slab of muscle under his victim's arm and angled the gun to shred his heart with a single round.

O'Conner froze as he processed what had just happened. He was quick, feral, but not fast enough. The little hit man pivoted away from the collapsing driver, raised the pistol, and fired a round through the gangster's forehead. The range was close enough for the lightweight bullet to pass all the way through his skull and lodge against the inside of his occipital bulge.

O'Conner fell back against a desk and lay motionless in a position so odd-looking it appeared he was made of rubber.

Charley Briggs had stopped crying and looked at the impish gunman in utter confusion. He was a smart man, well-versed in mathematics and engineering, as well as a physically capable man who'd first apprenticed as a mason in his teens. He didn't know what to make of the situation. Was the assassin a friend, a savior, or something else?

"My name is Michaleen Riordan," the man said in his bright Irish lilt. "They took away my O at Ellis Island, don't you know."

"Huh?"

"Lad, I was born Michaleen O'Riordan, but the sod at Ellis Island didn't right down the O on my form and now I'm just Riordan."

"Who are you?"

"Are you deaf, boyo? I just told you. Michaleen Riordan."

"Why did you . . ."

"Shoot O'Conner and his goon?" Riordan finished Briggs's question for him. "Housecleaning, you could say. Often done after a job is complete, but this time beforehand, I'm afraid. Ya see, there really is no honor among us thieves."

Briggs came to his senses finally and jumped to his feet. He was a foot and a half taller than Riordan and outweighed him by more than a hundred pounds. He ran as best he could with his arms tied behind his back and made it halfway to the little man before Riordan casually raised the pistol and shot him through the right eye. Briggs's corpse skidded for a foot, when it collapsed to the floor.

Riordan put his pistol away and finally plucked the clay pipe from the corner of his ruby-lipped mouth. He settled it in a form-fitting tin carrying case designed to protect the brittle stem and slid that into an inside jacket pocket.

"'Twas nothing personal," he said to the three dead men. "Just so's ya know."

He untied the rope that had bound Charley Briggs's hands and placed it on the floor behind the chair. He then pulled the big pistol out of O'Conner's driver's waistband. It was huge in his hands, making him look like a child playing with a gun, but he was no stranger to big heavy revolvers. He knew to brace his wrist with his other hand. He wouldn't have much time once he fired the gun, so he pulled Flynn O'Conner off the desk and propped him up just so. Then he rolled the bodyguard onto his side, grunting at the effort of moving so much literal dead weight.

He aimed the revolver at the tiny entrance wound made by his .32 and fired a big .44-caliber round down the wound path, obliterating all traces that the driver had been shot with anything other than his own weapon. He stayed hunched down on his heels, turned, steadied the weapon against the pain now radiating from his wrists, and fired again. This bullet struck O'Conner's head in the same spot as the first bullet, but did massive damage to the late gangster's skull. The splatter against the office wall would convince anyone that he'd been standing when he was shot.

Michaleen tossed the big pistol in the vague direction of Charley Briggs, grabbed up the bag of cash Briggs had been paid to sabotage one of the most secure buildings on the planet, and waited. Less than twenty seconds later, the three members of O'Conner's crew who'd snatched Briggs burst into the office from the warehouse floor. So hurried was their rush, the door's glass panel shattered when it slammed against the wall. The diminutive Irishman threw up his hands in the universal signal of surrender.

One of the men had a pistol in hand. He pointed it accusingly at Riordan as his dull mind spun in low gear, trying to comprehend what he was seeing.

"The rope," Michaleen said. "It wasn't as secure as ya thought. See it on the floor there? The feller shucked it off when the driver got close to him and took his gun. Shot the man first and then turned the pistol on Mr. O'Conner. That gave me the time to draw my own gat and take the feller down."

The leader of the three-man team slowly lowered his pistol and looked at the scene more critically, eyeing the blood spatter on the wall and the pool of crimson under the driver's body. He didn't look too carefully at what remained of his boss. The damage was sickening.

"Someone's gotta tell Sean O'Conner that his brother is dead," one of the other men said.

His partner said, "Don't you mean someone's gotta tell him he's the boss now?"

"Who tied the damn rope?" the armed gangster asked.

"I did. And it was as tight as I could make it," the smaller of the other two hoods said.

Michaleen knew that once they started throwing blame, they would inevitably begin to question the narrative as he'd laid it out.

Despite their common Irish ancestry, these weren't his people. He'd leveraged their shared background to get a meeting, but they were hired muscle. He was an unknown to them, and sooner rather than later they would turn on him.

"Gentlemen, if I may," he said with a cherub's disarming smile. "The rope was tighter than the bowline on Noah's Ark. Of that I have no doubt. But you see, the feller did something with his shoulder like the way those escape artists do."

"I saw Harry Houdini at the Palace Theatre once," one of the men offered.

"Aye," said Michaleen. "Like Harry Houdini was this feller. He did something with his shoulders and wrists and the rope popped off, just like that. He was wily, this one. There's no fault. No blame, just bad luck of this feller being another Houdini. Gents, I am truly sorry for your loss. Had I been a second quicker, then maybe the great Flynn O'Conner would still be alive. That's the burden I take from this room, chaps, and 'tis a heavy one in my heart."

"You can't blame yourself," two of the men said at the same time.

Their leader nodded, adding, "It's just one of those things, you know? Fate, they call it."

"Yes, fate," Riordan said in a whisper, and then snapped out of wherever his faked reverie had taken him. "Well, I don't know how you need to handle this, but I best be on my way."

The diminutive figure practically scooted from the room and across the warehouse, cash-stuffed suitcase in hand. Outside, he had a car waiting, a small French-built Renault with gas, brake, and clutch pedals he could reach.

As he went through the complex starting ritual of a modern

automobile, he felt confident that his ruse would never be discovered. No one was going to autopsy a thug like Flynn O'Conner or his driver, so the real killing shots would never be discovered. Their bodies would be at a mortician by evening and in the ground the following day.

Charley Briggs, bless his duplicitous soul, would be weighted with chains and dumped halfway down the Chesapeake. Michaleen would make sure that word got back to his wife that he'd run off with the mistress she knew existed, but whose identity she didn't. For her part, the mistress would never report Charley missing without compromising herself and so her silence was guaranteed. All very neat and tidy.

"Fine piece of work, Michaleen," he said to himself. "Yes sirree, a fine piece of work."

10

Philadelphia, Pennsylvania

MICHALEEN RIORDAN ARRIVED IN PHILADELPHIA AT SUN-set. It was too late to visit his next mark, so he found a hotel that could valet his car, ate a simple dinner, and enjoyed a couple of whiskeys. The following morning, he left his car parked at the hotel and took a taxi to a street corner several blocks from his actual destination. For this particular job, he'd ditched the suit in favor of a plain white shirt with leather suspenders to hold up his pants, and his cap.

Riordan wasn't particularly youthful looking—he was now closer to fifty than forty—but his shortness gave the passing impression he wasn't more than fifteen or sixteen years old. By dressing as a teen would dress, like a newsie or delivery page, he made people think they saw a young lad and not a middle-aged man. And by people, Michaleen Riordan meant potential witnesses.

He sorted humanity into three categories. There were witnesses, marks, and temporary allies. The line between the three groups was as fluid as the Irish Sea. Allies became marks or witnesses with deceptive ease. And witnesses made easy marks. To last long in America's underworld, he had developed a keen sense of when people were about to turn on him. The skill allowed him to either disappear or betray them first.

On this job, it made sense to eliminate witnesses as early as possible because once it was over there would be precious little opportunity to clean up afterward. His job was to ensure there wasn't anyone left around to identify him or anyone else in the crew and especially the man he called the Marquess. Flynn O'Conner had some pull in and around Washington, D.C., even though there was little by way of organized crime in the nation's capital. They used his contacts to tag and eventually bribe Charley Briggs into sabotaging the Bureau of Engraving building. Both men had outlived their usefulness and were now dead.

And now onto the next.

Michaleen loitered outside the lock shop for twenty minutes, observing the comings and goings from down the block, where he leaned against a wall at the entrance of an alley. At one point the shop door was blocked by a vehicle delivering a safe that took three men to lower off the Mack truck's bed and manhandle into the store. At around ten he sensed a lull in the shop's business. The landlords and homeowners needing duplicate keys had all come and gone. It was now the midmorning slowdown.

He pushed himself off the wall and settled his hat down low over his eyes. The street crawled with traffic, mostly motorcars and only a handful of horse-drawn carts. The sidewalks were busy but navigable. Riordan moved effortlessly through the crowds, and no one gave him a second's consideration.

He slowed for a moment when it looked like a pair of men in

workers' clothes were going to enter the shop, but they did not. One stopped to tie his shoe and they moved on.

He mounted the two limestone steps in front of the locksmith's store and opened the door so slowly the little bell hung from it didn't chime. He'd been warned about it. He locked the door as silently as possible.

The front windows hadn't been washed in a while so the light coming through them was weak and watery. The floors were wood worn so smooth they were a little slick. The walls were covered in shelves containing hundreds of doorknobs of various qualities and finishes. Several safes squatted on the floor like square iron Buddhas. There was a counter near the back of the shop, but no cash register. There was a space for a Curtis key clipper machine and a wall of blank keys. A curtain separated the showroom from a back workspace. Riordan padded down the store's central aisle and past the counter. He could hear someone beyond whistling to themselves tunelessly. He drew his pistol.

A man sat on a stool hunched over a cluttered bench as he worked on a key with a set of rasps and files, his shoulders stooped from a lifetime in that position. The smith's hair was iron gray and a little wild and his shirt was wrinkled and poorly laundered. Michaleen had been told the locksmith's wife had died years earlier in childbirth, so it came as little surprise that the man had an unkempt appearance. In the corner of the workroom was a tall safe bigger than an icebox with its door ajar. The air smelled of metal.

The sole of Riordan's shoe scuffed against some grit on the floor and the locksmith looked up, annoyed that a customer had come into the back uninvited. Then he saw the gun and his eyes went wide with fear and then just as quickly relaxed in understanding. He'd been startled by the weapon, but wasn't fearful. He was no stranger to men with pistols.

Michaleen said, "I've heard it told that the best locksmiths were once thieves."

The man waited a beat before replying, "Whoever told you that should have also told you I've been out of that racket a long time. I'm retired."

"As a thief myself, I know we never really retire. It's who we are, not what we do, Mr. Wanamaker." He pulled a wallet out of his back pocket with his free hand. It was shiny black and new with a gold monogram. "I picked this myself not two hours ago. I didn't need to take it, mind you, but a leopard and his spots and all that."

"Whatever it is you want, the answer is no. I got out and plan on staying out. You want, I know a couple of guys who would at least listen to whatever it is you have planned."

Riordan ignored him. He walked over to the big safe and heaved open the inches-thick steel door. Inside were some shelves on which were several bundles. He knew they were lockpicking kits. Michaleen usually carried one himself, but these were a legitimate part of Harvey Wanamaker's trade. On the top shelf sat a small black strongbox the size of a bread loaf. Michaleen had to stretch to reach it.

He took it and set it on the counter in front of the locksmith. "I assume it's all in here?"

"Don't know what you're talking about."

The smith tried to play it cool, but there was a hint of tension in his voice, as this encounter wasn't going along its expected arc.

"Here's the thing, Harv," Michaleen said. It came out as *Ears da ting.* "Retired people can always be enticed back to work, if only for one last job, one final score or, in the case of some legitimate mook, one last deal back with his old office."

"I suppose," Wanamaker said warily.

Michaleen suddenly exploded. "'Suppose' shite. I know you made some gear for a job recently and I am pretty sure your pay is in this box. If that's the case, I'm going to take it one way or the other. I can leave you alive or dead. The choice is yours."

Real fear drained the blood from the locksmith's face. "Yeah. It's in there."

"Key, Harv. Give me the key or I put a round through both kneecaps," Riordan demanded, the barrel of his pistol jammed deep into Wanamaker's knee.

The man pulled a massive wad of keys from his pocket and carefully selected one. He inserted it into the lock and turned. He opened the lid to show the box was filled with banded twenty-dollar bills, hundreds of them.

"Get in the safe."

"What?"

Riordan shoved the pistol toward the locksmith's face. "Get in the safe or die where you sit."

Riordan stepped back as the shop owner stood on creaking knees and shuffled over to the icebox-sized safe.

"You get in the safe and before too long a customer will come, and they'll hear you screaming in there and they will call the police, who will send one of your competitors to get you out. Two hours tops and all you'll suffer is a little discomfort and a lot of embarrassment."

Reluctantly, the locksmith stepped into the big safe. There was more than enough room for him to sit under the shelves. "I could suffocate in here."

"Tell you what. I'll swing by in an hour. If there isn't a big bal-lyhoo out front, I'll call the coppers myself."

Without another word, Michaleen closed the heavy door and ratcheted the handle and turned the lock just two numbers off the combination's final number. He looked around the shop and saw some freestanding metal shelving loaded with bins of spare parts and other oddments. The topmost shelf was a foot taller than he was and so it took Riordan a few seconds to get it rocking back and forth and almost all of his strength to finally get it to topple against the safe door. After the cascade of metal junk finished crashing to the floor, he could hear the locksmith's muted cries from within the safe.

"I'm only doing my job," he said, though he doubted the lock-smith could hear him. "Nothing personal, just so ya know."

Committing murder was easy. Anyone could do it. Wanamaker would be dead of carbon dioxide poisoning in two hours. Simple as could be. But getting away with murder was an entirely differ-ent thing. Michaleen Riordan believed the best way was to always make it look like an accident. Eventually the locksmith would be missed, and someone would come to the store to investigate. When they saw the shelving leaning against the safe, they would try to open it themselves, but fail. The Good Samaritan would then in-volve the police, and as he'd told Wanamaker, another locksmith would be called in to crack the lock. They would discover the body and the new locksmith would point out that the handle appeared to have been closed by the impact and the dial jarred just enough, two places in fact, to render the safe unopenable. An unfortunate accident while the man was working on something inside the safe.

It all came down to the details. The rope left behind the chair in Flynn O'Conner's warehouse or the lock dial only slightly askew. Michaleen had two more entries on his list of people who could become problematic after the job was complete. Both in New York. One would be pretty straightforward. Once he had some information he needed he'd stage everything to look like a homeowner had discovered someone robbing their house and paid the ultimate price. Happened all the time. The second one would be the trickier death. But there was something he'd heard many years ago when he was just a kid on the streets that had always stuck with him. Kill one person and it's a murder, kill many at once and it's only a headline.

11

New York City

Isaac Bell had a spring in his step when he entered the Van Dorn office located on the second floor of the Knickerbocker Hotel. Since the Pickett case, he had been mostly working in New York and Marion was between projects, so they'd been spending more time than usual together. They'd gone up to Vermont to admire the foliage for the weekend. They'd actually played hooky and stayed an extra day.

The suite's main room of the office was like a police station bullpen, with an open layout and plenty of desks. There were also a couple of private offices. Of course, Joseph Van Dorn had one for when he was in town, as well as Bell and Archie Abbott. Past the water fountain was a hallway that led to a large conference room and other smaller offices for support staff and the Research Department run by Grady Forrer.

Archie Abbott appeared from the back offices in discussion with the intern who'd found Bell at the gym several months ago. Abbott was about the same size as Bell and even more handsome. He'd been an actor earlier in his life, but came on board as a detective when he saw how rewarding the work was for Isaac, who'd been his friend since college.

"Where the hell have you been?" roared Joseph Van Dorn, the lion of his namesake agency. He'd heard Bell's voice and had come out of his inner office. "It's Tuesday already."

"When your wife looks over her eyelashes at you from her side of a warm bed and asks you to stay for another day, what do you think any man's response would be?"

"Fine," Van Dorn growled, his balding head shining under the electric lights. "Haul your carcasses into my office so I can bring you up to speed."

Joseph Van Dorn was between his mid- and late fifties, no one was quite sure how old exactly. His once coppery hair and thick muttonchop sideburns were laced with coarse silver threads, while the bald spot atop his head had grown to include all but a monk's halo of hair ringing his scalp. His nose was large, pugnacious. Above his brown eyes were thick untamed brows that almost met in the middle. He kept himself reasonably fit, although client lunches at Delmonico's or Keens had softened his middle. He had a sharp mind for both business and investigative work and engendered loyalty from almost everyone who knew him.

"Since you're just back from D.C., anything new regarding the attack on the President's yacht in August?" Bell asked.

Van Dorn leaned back so his chair creaked ominously. "I've got my feelers out all over Washington. The Secret Service is being tight-lipped. They got caught flat-footed while someone nearly sent the President to the bottom of the Potomac. Obviously not a bright shining moment in their young history."

"What about the money I found? The uncirculated Fed bills?"

"No joy there, either, I'm afraid. They won't say where it came from, or how the pilots and whoever paid them got the cash. Nothing."

"It was obviously stolen," Bell said.

"True, but we're locked out of their investigation. They claim it's an internal affair. No one is offering even a rumor. Sorry, I know that case feels rightly personal." Van Dorn shifted gears. "Do you know Jack Morgan?"

"J. P. Morgan's son? Not really. I saw him at his dad's funeral last year. I recalled remarking to Marion how much he looked like his old man, but luckily didn't inherit that purple monstrosity of a nose."

"He's been behind the scenes on the Federal Reserve's launch, shepherding it along with both the influence of his family name and his own financial acumen."

"I see."

"I bumped into him at the Round Robin." The Round Robin Bar at the Willard Hotel in Washington was what many believed to be the true epicenter of power in the nation's capital. More deals were made there than in the halls of Congress. "He confided in me that the launch is going to be far tougher than they're making out. There is tremendous resistance from the big state banks and a genuine fear that people won't trust cash backed by an institution in Washington that they don't know or understand."

"And any hint of scandal will amplify the difficulty," Bell said to take his boss's statement to its logical conclusion. "Is there even an investigation into a connection with the airplane attack?"

"There is, but whatever they discover will likely never see the light of day, let alone the front page of a newspaper."

"I don't like it," Archie said. "The Treasury Department is essentially investigating itself with no oversight."

Van Dorn nodded. "Jack Morgan said the same thing and also warned that as the government gets bigger, that will happen more and more often. But back to the things within our control. We've been hired by two new hotels, one in St. Louis and the other in Pittsburgh, who want us as their house dicks."

"Do you want me to go and get things established?" Bell asked.

"I'm sending Dashwood."

"Good." James Dashwood, one of their younger agents, was one of Bell's protégés. "It's past time he take on more responsibility. What else has been happening in my absence?"

"The big thing for you is a member of a Staten Island Railway syndicate reached out to us. He wants to meet with you about some background work on another member of the group. He isn't sure if his potential partner is being honest about how he's representing himself. Before our new client puts a large amount of money in play, he wants to be certain he's not getting in bed with a swindler. Time is of the essence, which is why I'm upset you took yesterday off. You were supposed to meet with him then. I smoothed it over, but he insists you get together today at two in his office on Staten Island. You can get the particulars from the main desk."

"Okay."

"This could be a good way for us to get in with this consortium, railroad protection is a lucrative field. Otherwise, I wouldn't waste your time on a simple background check."

"I'll have them eating out of the palm of my hand in no time, and have them all signed up for Van Dorn services soon after." Bell said it lightly, but in his heart, he really didn't like wooing potential clients. However, he was also pragmatic enough to realize it had become part of the job.

Tragedy on the Hudson

12

NEW YORK'S BOROUGH-CLASS FERRIES WERE ESSENTIALLY
the front half of two ships that had been welded together
with propellers somehow stuck out of both ends. They were ungainly, unsightly, and ubiquitous for the past decade in the waters
of the upper bay. During rush hour the ships' passenger areas,
usually segregated by sex, were packed shoulder to shoulder, but
Bell had embarked at the Whitehall Street landing at one-fifteen
p.m. and so the ferry was only about half full.

No sooner had the approximately two-hundred-fifty-foot craft
pulled away from the dock when he felt the air begin to cool and
the industrial odor of the city fade until he could smell only the sea
and a little of the ferry's coal smoke. Indian summer was in full
swing, and it was sunny and warm. He would have liked to remove
his jacket, but he had his Browning strapped to him in a shoulder
holster. He noshed from a package of Cracker Jacks he'd bought
from a news kiosk at the ferry landing and soon had a curious gull

seemingly hovering next to him as they made the half-hour transit to Staten Island.

Its occasional cry sounded very much like the teenage boot-black crying out, "Shine. Shine."

He knew not to feed the bird or otherwise the air would fill with a flock of honking gulls thick enough to blot out the sun.

Like him, many of the passengers stood lining the rail of the white-hulled double-decker. Mostly it was men in rough work clothing finishing an oddly timed shift at some factory in the city, but there were also groups of mothers out with their infants in carriages and older children decked out in frilly little dresses or sailor suits with short pants.

He'd asked Grady Forrer to dig up what he could about the potential client, a young heir to a Maine timber and paper fortune. Granted he hadn't a lot of time for research, but there appeared to be scant information about the family, at least in New York. Bell had tasked an agent from the Boston office to see if there was anything in the *Globe*'s or *Herald*'s archives about them. There should at least be an obituary for the man's late father.

Bell idly watched the river traffic, which was particularly heavy. He counted no less than three train ferries crossing the Hudson, as well as a handful of big merchantmen heading into the city from ports foreign and domestic. When he ambled from the aft deck to look forward, he saw the Statue of Liberty, of course, but also the *Mauretania* working her way up to the Cunard docks in Midtown, black smoke pouring from her funnels.

Many people gawked at the distant ship, pointing when they first noticed her. The ship was no longer the world's largest, but remained impressive all the same.

Bell got jostled by a young man in a flat cap and immediately felt for his wallet. He recognized a pickpocket's practiced bump because he'd done it himself more times than he could count. The wallet was gone, and the lad had already vanished into the growing crowd.

"Thief," he shouted as he took up the chase. People certainly heard him, but in the jaded city New York was becoming, no one really reacted.

He could tell where the kid had run by the way the crowd seemed to part temporarily and close ranks once again like a shoal of fish.

"Stop him," he shouted as the kid reached the top of the stairs leading down to the main deck.

To his credit, one man tried to intervene. He moved away from the railing to block the fleeing thief, but the kid put a hit on him like a college linebacker. The civilian flew back with an explosion of breath and bowled over three women dressed in nurses' uniforms. All four fell to the deck in a tangle of limbs and flaring skirts and cries of surprise more than pain.

The thief vanished down the steps, his feet two blurs that barely touched the stair treads.

Bell felt his blood heat up as adrenaline began flooding his system. He was mere seconds behind the thief, but lost time going down the stairs when his feet crossed, and he had to clutch at the railing to keep from falling headlong down the iron treads. At the base of the stairs was a long corridor with interior seating to his right and more open rails to his left for people to enjoy the view. This side was the ferry's male promenade, so there were no alarmed cries from women passengers feeling threatened by the intrusion. The kid was two-thirds the way down the corridor and looked back to see that his victim hadn't given up the pursuit. He banged through a door to the sheltered seating area.

Bell took off at a full sprint, hands held rigid like blades to cut through the air, knees high with each step, and his breathing timed in perfect sync with his footfalls. Like upstairs, passengers watched them race past, but did nothing to interfere. He reached the door the thief had slipped through and would have knocked an old couple flat had he burst through without looking. He juked around the pair. The interior cabin was long and filled with hard wooden benches. Since it was such a nice day there were only thirty or so passengers inside avoiding the sun and fresh air.

Bell searched the space, his head swiveling, his eyes never resting. He noticed one woman who seemed to be searching like he was, but knew she wasn't hunting for the thief. It looked like the kid had vanished into thin air, but then he saw an interior door complete its automatic closing. He was too far to hear it click shut and yet his imagination conjured up the sound anyway. He raced for the door. Beyond was the working part of the ship. The walls and deck were painted metal with wires and conduits running overhead and along the walls in a labyrinth only an engineer could love.

The lighting was sparse and shadowy, weak bulbs in metal cages to protect them from clumsy crewmen. The noise from the ship's engine and running gear was much louder and the air was a cloying mist of heat and steam with a bitter tang of coal dust laced with machine oil.

He stood on a narrow landing above a very steep set of stairs. Over the thrum and clank of the steam plant, Bell heard footsteps descending deeper into the ship. He raced downward as fast as he could. This had gone far beyond the money or the wallet now. The pickpocket had tweaked Bell's professional pride and there was no way he would not catch him.

At the bottom of the stairs was a watertight door he had to high-step through to avoid bashing his shins. This led to a cramped, low-ceilinged room with another watertight door on the opposite wall, two regular doors to his left, and some unknown piece of equipment to the right that was behind a floor-to-ceiling wire cage. Judging by the way the hair on his arms suddenly came erect and the burnt taste of ozone in the air, he guessed the machine was part of the ferry's electrical system, a dynamo perhaps.

A thought struck him even before he hit the bottom of the stairs, but momentum carried him a few steps too far. Pickpockets made their move when the ferry had just docked and people were bunched up at the exit ramp and used to being jostled a little. They didn't strike in the middle of the river when there was no way to escape if the snatch was noticed.

He whirled around just as the thief emerged from behind the door. He dashed back through the watertight hatchway and slammed closed the heavy steel door. Bell actually got his hand on the brass dogging lever before the man could lock it, but the pickpocket had the leverage to ram the handle down and lock it tight.

Bell slapped at the indifferent metal slab, noting that the "kid" had in fact been a short, slender man in his mid-forties or so. He felt with some certainty that the door across the claustrophobic room would be locked as well.

"Can ya hear me, Mr. Bell?" The voice was muted by the intervening metal, but buoyed by a bright Irish accent.

"Who are you?"

"That is of little concern," came the reply. "I just want you to know that this isn't anything personal."

"What isn't? Locking me up on the Staten Island Ferry?"

"I'm afraid it's a wee bit worse than that."

The pit of Bell's stomach suddenly felt like it had been filled with cannonballs. "Hey," he shouted and slapped at the door again. "Hey!"

There was no answer, as he knew there wouldn't be. He ran across the room to check the other watertight door. As he suspected, the handle had been jammed so he couldn't open it. He tried with everything he had, but the brass tap felt like it had been welded in place.

The violent blast came just as he was turning to check the two other, non-watertight doors. It was well aft, in a separate compartment, but an explosion that shook the ferry hard enough to knock Bell off his feet. His first thought, even before he got up off the deck, was that a coal bunker had exploded, but even as this idea sprang up, he knew the truth was far, far worse.

This was no coincidence. With sickening dread, Bell understood that the pickpocket was going to sink the entire ship just to cover the murder of one man. Him. It was monstrous, he thought, gripped by equal measures of fear and guilt for all the other victims about to perish. As soon as the rumble of the explosion faded, Bell heard the ominous sound of water gushing into the hull.

He whirled to check the other doors. The first was solid and the other had a ventilation grille at the top, the size of a cafeteria tray. That door, like the others, was either locked or stuck closed. Bell yanked on the handle of the first door. It opened with no problem. Inside was a cramped bathroom with uncleaned porcelain fixtures. A kid was just getting up from the floor. He wore a uniform that Bell recognized belonged to the recently formed Boy Scouts. Though not as popular in the city versus rural areas, New York had several troops and one had visited his storied agency to talk to real live detectives. They'd kept the old man away, but Archie had been a natural.

"What happened, sir?"

"Explosion. What are you doing down here?"

"The bathroom upstairs became unusable, so a steward told me about this one." He was probably eleven or twelve, with dark hair and eyes, and lashes that would be the envy of any girl. "He told me it was okay because his son was also a Scout in New Jersey. I'm from Chicago. I'm here with my mother to visit my aunt and uncle."

Bell recalled the woman upstairs who appeared as if she'd been searching for someone, doubtlessly the boy when he didn't return from the head when she'd expected.

The watertight doors would prevent this room from flooding for a while, but he didn't know if the area beyond the second door, the one with the ventilation louver, was also so well protected. If not, the room would flood just like the rest of the lower decks.

The ship's siren began to wail, a modulation tone as mournful as a dirge.

"Is it bad?" the boy asked, his voice cracking with fear.

"Yeah, kid," Bell told him as he tried to find a solution to an impossible situation. "We're sinking."

13

————❦————

"W"ON'T WE BE SAFE IN HERE?" THE BOY SCOUT ASKED. "I recognize those are watertight doors. I read about them in a book about the *Titanic*. She didn't have enough of them or the right kind or something."

"They didn't go up high enough," Bell told him absent-mindedly. He was contemplating and rejecting ideas on how to save themselves. Never had his gun felt more useless in a crisis.

He ran over to the first door he'd come through and began slapping at the steel and shouting. The boy added his own sharp falsetto, but it was no use. It was then that Bell felt the ship's movement start to change. The captain would have disconnected the direct drive to the screw to slow the ferry itself and thus the ingestion of water into her hull. Without propulsion, she began to wallow in slow lumbering movements as her belly filled with a mixture of the Hudson and the Atlantic.

On the two upper decks, the scene must have been pure bed-lam. First the shock of the explosion and then the realization that the ship might sink. The pumps would be switched on to maximum, but if the blast had been close to the engines or boiler room, she'd soon lose power completely and the pumps would fail. She carried plenty of cork life jackets and survival rings, but boasted only a couple lifeboats. Bell had no idea how long they took to deploy. He suspected if the worst happened, most of the passengers of the nearly two-thousand-ton vessel would end up in the river.

He recalled there had been plenty of boat traffic around the ferry moments earlier, but that didn't mean everyone who went into the Hudson would be pulled back out alive, only that the number of dead would be somewhat reduced.

Bell felt certain the watertight doors would hold. He was also certain that he and the kid would be out of air long before the ferry was salvaged off the river bottom.

The boy asked, "What are we gonna do?"

There were all manner of pipes and conduits bolted to the ceiling and running along the walls. There was a pipe the size of a baseball bat just in front of the door that had the ventilation grate near its top. Bell didn't stand a chance of wiggling through, but if he could at least save the kid, it would mean something.

The pipe was wrapped in asbestos. He touched it with the back of his hand. Despite the insulation, the metal beneath was hot. Had to be a steam line straight out of the boilers, he surmised.

He stripped off his summer-weight suit coat.

"Whoa," the boy said upon seeing the lethal-looking pistol slung under Bell's left arm.

"It's okay, kid," Bell said and pulled the knife he carried in his boot, "I'm an investigator with the Van Dorn Detective Agency. Do you know who they are?"

"Sure. You guys are famous for always getting your man."

"That's right." It took him only a couple of seconds to slice off both of his jacket's sleeves and wrap them around his hands as extra insulation. "And right now, you're my man and I'm getting you out of here."

Bell squared himself up with the door, reached overhead to grab the pipe, and pulled himself off the deck. The insulation and extra cloth gave his hands a decent level of protection, but by no means was he not feeling the presence of the high-pressure steam coursing through the pipe. He jackknifed his knees and kicked out at the ventilation grate with both heels. The steel rattled, but held. He repeated it, aiming for the grille's lower-right corner. Again, the metal shook at the impact, but whether it was screwed or welded in place from the other side, it wasn't budging.

The heat was starting to build up in his hands and his grip was growing uncomfortable. Also, because he was holding himself off the deck, he could feel his body pendulum slightly as the ferry began to list. He noted that the sound of water pouring into the hull had grown appreciably louder.

With more urgency, Bell repeatedly kicked at the metal vent, slamming his heel into the same spot over and over. He grunted and then roared as his hands felt like they were going to blister at any moment, and yet it appeared he'd made no progress dislodging the grate.

He was about to give up and drop down to the deck, his hands now in agony, and yet he lashed out three more times in rapid-fire, jackhammer-like strikes and the metal grille snapped out of its frame and clattered against the steel deck beyond. The kid whooped and Bell dropped to his feet and gingerly unwrapped his hands.

They were red and painful, but there were no blisters and none looked like they were going to form. The ferry's list was growing exponentially worse. Bell had no point of reference to know how long they had, but it didn't feel like much time remained.

"Okay, kid, I'm going to lift you through. Think you can do it?"

"My name is Eliot."

"Eliot, huh? Eliot what?"

"Ness."

"Eliot Ness. Nice to meet you. Wish we'd met under better circumstances. Think you can make it?"

"Yes, sir."

Bell lifted the boy from under his arms and, to his credit, Eliot walked his feet up the door until he could thrust them through the tight opening. He weighed no more than eighty pounds, but Bell's hands were tender and the exertion took its toll. The boy wriggled like an eel, working himself so that the center of the door was under his backside. There was just enough room for him to roll onto his stomach, but it was a tight fit and the pain made him grimace.

"You okay?"

"Yeah. Just tight is all."

"Unlock this door as soon as you land."

"You got it."

Bell grabbed hold of Eliot's wrists and lowered him to the deck on the other side of the door. He heard the kid's feet land with a shallow splash of water. He looked down and saw river water sluice through the gap under the door. And then he heard more splashing that sounded like . . .

"Unlock the door, Eliot." He called louder than he intended, concern not yet becoming panic.

Nothing happened.

"Eliot? Eliot. Eliot!"

Fear made the kid bolt. Bell let loose a string of profanity. The boy had seemed so levelheaded and in control, but he must have been hiding his stark terror with a brave front that collapsed as soon as his feet hit the water. The reality and danger of their situation had overwhelmed him. Boy Scout or not, his instincts for self-preservation had kicked into high gear.

Bell couldn't blame him and felt a little ashamed for the number of curses he'd heaped on the lad. He prayed that the kid would find a way out and not perish down here with him on the doomed ferry.

Water was surging from under the door now, forced by the pressure of the rising water in the hallway beyond. He glanced over at the humming piece of equipment he believed help supply the ship's electrical system. It was raised off the deck less than a foot by metal stanchions. Water had already climbed up an inch in the minute since the kid vanished. The water ebbed and flowed as it lapped against the machine's support legs and yet inexorably rose with each passing moment.

He watched it in grim fascination, knowing what would happen when the water reached the charged wiring within the machine's guts. He'd heard the gruesome reports of prison guards who'd attended electrocutions up at Sing Sing. He'd been told that if the condemned weren't strapped down properly, they'd thrash hard enough to break bones. Isaac Bell stood facing perhaps the worst death he could imagine.

The ship's hull was giving off torturous moaning and creaking sounds as the dynamic forces against her steel plates shifted with each additional ton of water. The ferry's very frame was being warped as she sank. Atop that noise were various deep rumbles and belches as the coal moved and air pockets released.

Something suddenly shifted in the way she was sinking and the water in the room raced like a tsunami for the far wall. Bell knew it would swamp the dynamo and send an unknowable but certainly lethal jolt of electricity through the water.

He jumped up to grab an overhead pipe, having just a second to note it wasn't insulated and thus wasn't carrying steam. His feet cleared the surface of the shifting pool and he just managed to close his eyes and turn his head when the swirling waved slammed into the machine and it shorted in a head-splittingly loud bang and a flash of light so bright that Bell could see the red of the blood in his eyelids. He clung to the pipe for several seconds, waiting for whatever additional electricity was in the system to discharge before lowering himself back down into the dank water.

He was deaf and blind, as helpless as a kitten. He groped to find a wall to give him some orientation in the topsy-turvy room. His hand brushed against paint-scaled metal, and he quickly oriented himself. He was between the bathroom door and the door through which he'd lowered Eliot Ness. A new smell hit him just then as the ferry's sanitation system backed up and water began gushing from out of the toilet like it was a geyser.

Great.

The room was stygian black, so he couldn't tell if his vision was returning, but his hearing was vastly improved. The tormented noises the ship made as she sank would be the final sounds he heard. He thought about trying to wiggle through the broken vent, but he knew it was no use. It was so small that even young Eliot had nearly gotten stuck. When they eventually raised the sunken ferry and found his body, he wouldn't want it jammed ignobly into a vent, caught forever in a final moment of animal panic. Better he be found lying on the deck as if he'd accepted his fate and met it with dignity.

Just as soon as he had that thought, he rejected it immediately. He would fight to escape until the last bit of air in his lungs was used up and to the final beat of his heart. He decided the best way through was to wait until he could float at the level of the vent and go feetfirst. He could use the leverage of his legs against the far side of the door and keep one arm by his side and one raised high in order to alter the geometry of his shoulders. He would lose some flesh on his hips, but maybe he could pull it off.

He was sure his ears were playing tricks on him because he thought he heard a voice over the thunder of roiling water. He turned and got on his tiptoes to look out the empty vent frame, realizing at that moment there was no way he'd make it through with whatever contortion he tried. He could barely get his head through the slot by turning it sideways.

And then it didn't matter. Wading toward him from down a long hallway and carrying an electric torch was a man in the uniform of the ferry company.

"Hello!" Bell shouted.

"Hello. Is that the Van Dorn man in the dynamo room?"

"Yes." The kid had done it! He hadn't panicked at all. He must have seen there was no way for him to open the door and so he'd run off to find help.

The light swept Bell's face, blinding him, but he didn't care. A second later the porter jangled some keys and yanked the door open against the current of water pouring out of an open water-tight door at the far end of the corridor.

"The kid?" Bell asked as they sloshed like water buffaloes back up the hallway toward some distant stairs.

"He told me about you. I knew a Boy Scout wouldn't lie. His mother refused to leave without him, but I imagine they're now well away."

"How bad is it?" He followed the porter as they mounted the steps and reached dry decking.

"She's going down, that's for sure, but a lot of ships and boats are coming to our aid. I think we'll be able to rescue everyone."

They climbed up to the main deck into the same port-side salon where Bell had chased the pickpocket. He held back from stepping out to where he could be spotted by the throngs of frightened passengers waiting at the bow. He hadn't forgotten that the little Irish killer knew who he was. It was doubtful the man who set off the charge in the coal bunker had waited around to watch his handiwork sink from underneath them. But still . . .

"Why did you stop, sir?"

"I just need a moment," Bell said as if he were suddenly overwhelmed.

In all, maybe fifteen minutes had passed since the explosion. He could see the ferry was down by the stern and listing to port. The angle wasn't so severe that people were tumbling back as they waited their turn to jump off the ramp to another ferry that had pulled up to the sinking craft. The women and children were off for the most part, leaving just a crowd of men to await their turn for rescue. Because they were stepping from one ship to another, many had abandoned the life rings they'd been issued.

Looking aft, Bell saw the river slowly creeping up the open deck, black and as relentless as death. He went to peer out one of the big side windows and saw smaller boats idling around the ferry like remora around a shark. Some, however, were motoring away, their decks standing room only with survivors already safely aboard.

Without warning, something deep in the bowels of the ferry failed and her keel snapped in two. The hull gave a great lurch down and back that was like pulling the rug out from under the feet of a hundred men. The bow soared up into the air. The orderly evacuation turned into chaos as fallen men began rolling and tumbling down the steeply sloping deck toward where the river had already claimed the stern. Four automobiles that had been parked at the bows also raced aft, rolling over men with indiscriminate abandon. They hit the water in titanic gouts of froth, crushing the handful of victims who'd landed in the water before them.

The rate of the ferry sinking accelerated as though she wasn't following the laws of gravity but was being pulled down into the depths by some invisible hand.

The shouts and cries of men rolling past the salon were horrifying. The angle had grown so steep that there was nothing they could do to arrest, or even slow, their fall. When they hit the water nearly a hundred feet from where they'd been standing seconds earlier, there was no time to make room until the next man plunged into the water. And the next. And the next, until the pool of rising water was full of unconscious and broken bodies, some already dead and many more soon to be because the ferry's central deck was like a tunnel with very few exits other than the ramps at either end. One was already deeply submerged and the other impossibly out of reach high overhead.

Bell had managed to stay upright because he had paused near a wall that had suddenly become the floor. He had tried to grab the porter in that first frantic second, but the man vanished down the deck and ended up being one of the first victims to hit the water. He'd landed only seconds before the cars.

There was no further time to waste as the ship faced its death knell. Bell snatched up one of the discarded cork life rings and used it to protect his face for when he drew his Browning 9 millimeter and put two bullets through the wide plate glass window before hurling his body after them.

14

He watched the door to the gymnasium for twenty minutes. In truth, he watched the surrounding area to establish if someone else was watching the door to the gymnasium.

He took every precaution that he could think of because he now had the advantage and had no intention of giving it back. The lengths they'd gone through to eliminate him meant that they had resources and that he couldn't drop his vigilance for even a second.

Once Bell leapt through the window of the ferry's passenger salon, he managed to grab the rail across the narrow promenade before he, too, dropped from the dizzying height into the river. He twisted and turned until he could get good purchase with his feet and hands. He looked down. He was still some twenty feet above the river, but the distance was vanishing with alarming speed as the ferry sank. He looked up toward the bow. Above him, another man clung to the railing.

Surrounding the stricken vessel, the rescue boats moved about with useless vigor. Most had pulled back when the sinking catastrophically accelerated and were now going back and forth in restless circles, helpless as the ferry continued to vanish from sight.

Just then, the ferry's stern slammed into the river bottom with enough force to accordion her hull plates and decks. The grind of tearing metal grew to a shrieking scream as the bow tore free of the sunken aft portion of the vessel. The hundred-foot-long front part of the ship fell back to a more or less even keel in a ponderous splash that produced waves high enough to almost swamp the hovering rescue craft.

Bell was nearly ripped from his perch by the sudden change in direction. The guy who'd been above him hadn't been able to hold on and had fallen as the hull slapped into the river and had gone under. The remaining section of the ferry bobbed and sloshed and was soon taking on water through her torn midsection. Bell tossed his life ring into the river and leapt after it. His suit was already soaked through, so landing in the water meant nothing.

He slipped one arm through the cork ring and began kicking his legs and swimming with his remaining arm, trying to distance himself from the rapidly sinking derelict. With the current and the dynamic forces of water pouring into the ferry's hull, Bell felt like he was making no progress and feared he was actually being drawn back toward the hulk. He kicked harder, giving it his all. After a minute of full exertion, he began to put distance between himself and the sinking ferry.

A few minutes later, one of the small, gas-powered oyster boats that had backed off when the ship split in two motored toward Bell, and soon strong, rough hands were pulling him over the gunwale and onto the boat's slick deck.

"Thanks," he panted.

He was handed a coarse towel to dry his face and hair. He left it covering his head to hide his blond locks. He couldn't risk being spotted. There were a few other boats about with survivors aboard, although most of the rescue craft were heading back to Manhattan.

"Oh Lord," one of the three fishermen said and crossed himself.

The others looked in the direction the man stared, and the horror became apparent. Bodies were emerging from the depths, swept out of the rear section of the ferry now that it had torn in two. At first it was just one or two, but then there were a dozen and finally a literal raft of victims rose en masse. It was one of the most terrible things Bell had ever witnessed. Soon enough the tide and current tugged at the cluster of bodies, disentangling the knots of limbs so the dead began to drift apart. It was a macabre scene, all the more chilling because of the silence.

Two of the city's fireboats arrived just then. The water cannons affixed all over the *James Duane* and the *Thomas Willett* remained off, but the crews were as vigilant as if facing a five-alarm warehouse fire. One of them slowed to begin the gruesome task of collecting bodies, while the other sidled in close to the sinking section of the ferry and blared her horn as a warning to other river traffic while it drifted south with the current. The fireboat would mark the spot where the derelict finally sank for when it was time to raise and scrap the two pieces of hull.

The survivors were being returned to the Whitehall Street landing, where their typically banal ride had started barely an hour earlier. Most of the survivors were women and Bell could hear their sobs and wails while they were still a good distance from shore. It was a pitiful dirge.

Bell thanked the oystermen and climbed onto the dock. He kept a hand near his face to block it and hunched his shoulders and slouched deeply to hide his height. Ferry employees were passing out drinks while taking the names of the survivors and inquiring about anyone they had traveled with. The crying was worse up close. He didn't see Eliot Ness or his mother. He owed the boy his life and the kid didn't even know if he'd made it.

Best all around if the world thought him dead, he reckoned, so he left the landing as quickly as he could.

"Sir, please. Sir." An employee still sporting a summer white uniform chased after him with a clipboard in hand. "Were you on the ferry, sir?"

"No," Bell said. He indicated his wet clothing. "I was doing my laundry in the river."

He vanished before the befuddled man could say anything else.

He had no money, thanks to the Irish pickpocket, and so he had no choice but to walk the equivalent of eighty blocks in wet shoes that squelched with each step and socks that felt like they'd turned to mush. He'd developed his first blisters while still south of Houston.

Knowing he couldn't return to the office or his apartment in the Knickerbocker, he'd come to Alberto Cicchetti's gym. He seriously doubted that whoever had tried to have him killed had the resources to stake out every place he spent time other than the two most obvious ones. Yet he'd still waited to make certain there were no loiterers in the area.

The sun had long set and there were few electric lights in the neighborhood. Bell dashed from his hiding spot and into the gym as furtively as a rodent returning to its den.

The place had the welcome smell of old leather, fresh sweat, and the sawdust used to absorb whatever blood was spilled in the rings. All three of the squared circles were being used. Alberto was refereeing the center ring, where two heavyweights were sparring like a couple of dreadnoughts going toe-to-toe. He watched the pair throw a lumbering series of punches that were largely ineffective before noticing Bell standing on the wooden floor just outside the elevated ring.

"What the hell happened to you?" the bantamweight Italian called.

"Long story, Berto. I need to use your phone."

"Help yourself."

The office in the back of the gym was a glassed-in cube with too much furniture and far too much stuff left in piles atop that overabundance of furniture. The walls were covered in unframed photographs of boxers either fighting or having their arm raised by a referee signaling a victory.

Bell dialed his apartment number first and let it ring a dozen times before giving up. He'd let Marion know he was heading for Staten Island, so she had to suspect he had been on the doomed ferry. If she wasn't at home, it meant she was holding a vigil at the office with all the other staff. He needed to keep his survival as quiet as possible. Rather than call the main switchboard at the agency's New York office, he called the Chicago branch of Van Dorn. It was the second largest in the country and a good bet that he wouldn't know whoever picked up the phone at the end of their workday.

"Van Dorn Agency," an overly chipper woman answered.

"I have information about the ferry sinking today in New York that affects Joseph Van Dorn. Have him call this number right away." Bell gave the agent the number to Berto's gym, making certain the woman had it right and hung up on the string of questions she'd tried to throw at him.

Bell guessed it would take ten minutes for the young agent in Chicago to get an answer from whoever was supervising the night shift about what to do. Then it would take a minute or two to place the call, and then at least—

The phone trilled. Bell glanced at his watch, grateful it hadn't been submerged for very long and still worked. Eleven minutes.

"Don't react in any way," Bell said when he got the earpiece in place and leaned in to the microphone.

"Okay," Van Dorn said in a monotone, recognizing his lead investigator's voice.

"The ferry sinking was no accident. I was locked in a room belowdecks, and someone set off a bomb. The perpetrator told me it wasn't anything personal before he left me to die. Right now, they think they succeeded and we need to keep it that way."

"Okay," the old man repeated.

"Are you alone?"

"No. There are a dozen people in my office."

"Clear the room except for Archie, if he's there. I wish Marion could stay, but it would look too suspicious to a room full of trained investigators. I've been under observation for a while. They might keep it up and I can't risk my coworkers acting like they know I'm not dead. Archie can tell Marion later and I just hope she understands."

"I agree." A couple of moments passed before Van Dorn spoke again. "Okay, Isaac, it's just the three of us."

"How you doing, buddy?" Archie Abbott asked. Bell could picture him standing behind Van Dorn as the two shared the phone.

"Physically fine, but I'm torn up inside and mad as hell. How many died?"

Archie said, "They suspended operations at dusk, so this isn't the final tally, but there are a hundred and eight dead."

"Only two of the dead are women and all the kids got off safe," Van Dorn added.

"That's something, I suppose."

"Who did it?"

"Short wiry Irishman I thought was a teenage pickpocket at first. He lifted my wallet. I went after him, and just when I realized I might be running into a trap, I did."

"Joseph said he told you it wasn't personal?" asked Archie.

"Those exact words."

"Hired hit?"

"Obviously. And meant to look like an accident."

"Accident?" Van Dorn scoffed. "Sinking a ferry loaded with people is a damned Greek tragedy, if you ask me."

"The question is who, and why now?" Archie asked.

"Could be anyone," Bell admitted.

"We've got to be honest here," Archie said. "There is a list as long as my arm of thugs, gangsters, thieves, murderers, and every other form of ne'er-do-well that would love to see the legendary Isaac Bell down for the count, permanently."

"He makes a good point," Van Dorn said.

"I agree," said Bell. "How do we explain the timing. Why now?"

"We need to look at anyone you've arrested who's gotten out of jail in the past six months, see if any of them wanted payback," Archie said.

"And not just here in New York," Van Dorn added. "You've made arrests in every major city in the country. We need to look at a whole lot of parole sheets."

"We'll have to cable our satellite offices around the country and have them start digging," Bell said. "This has to be done quietly. Our advantage here is they think I'm dead. If the perp finds out we're digging into his life, it might be a tip-off that the assassination attempt failed."

Archie said, "Yeah, you need to lay low for a while."

"I might have something for that," Van Dorn stated. "Got a call today from Jack Morgan. He wants to meet me in the morning and hinted that they need our help after all."

"Me working out of D.C. might do the trick," Bell said.

"What about Marion?" Archie asked.

"Obviously, I'll tell her I'm fine before I leave. I doubt she's in any danger, but can she sleep in your guest room for the time being, Arch? It'll look natural enough that she's grieving at the home of her best friend. Come pick me up at Berto's gym. I'll borrow one of your suits and meet with Joseph and Jack Morgan in the morning."

"Sounds like a plan."

"I still want to talk to my people in the War Department," Van Dorn said. "If there is even a chance that this was carried out on behalf of the German government, they need to know right away."

"I agree," Bell said. "Joseph, pick me up at Archie's in the morning. Archie, come get me at the gym as soon as Marion puts a bag together for herself."

15

THE DISGUISE WAS HOT AND UNCOMFORTABLE AND BECAME even more so when Bell stepped onto the printing room floor and was struck by a blast of heat and noise that was as palpable as a shove in the chest. The room was vast, with hundreds of machines called spider presses clanking away while being tended to by printers, inkers, and myriad other workers. The air was heavy with the chemical smell of the glutinous ink that was used to produce the notes, and the smoke from the braziers at each press needed to keep the special ink pliable enough to fill even the most minute line on the special eight-note plates fitted on each machine.

"This is the heart of our operation," said C. Frederick Lawson, the chief security executive with the Bureau of Engraving and Printing. He'd been tapped as Bell's tour guide.

Bell had secured the invitation to assist in the Fed's investigation into the mystery notes found in connection to the *Mayflower* attack with Jack Morgan's help. He hoped to decipher how those brand-new Federal Reserve notes could have been obtained, and, more important, who could possibly have acquired them. In keeping with his need to remain incognito for the time being, he had presented himself at the Bureau as senior Van Dorn investigator Wes McMahon.

He wore a padded vest under his shirt to give him a paunch and a thickened waist. He wore suit pants that were tighter than normal to make his legs appear overly skinny, almost birdlike. Small silk pads pushed back up against his molars fleshed out his face. He'd shaved off his mustache, dyed his hair a mousy brown shot through with gray, and wore large, unfashionable eyeglasses.

Christoff Tamerlane, real name unknown, was Marion's go-to artist for her films and he'd help craft Bell's disguise. During the transformation he theatrically lamented that his work turning Bell into a plain nobody was like taking a hammer to Michelangelo's *David*. With the addition of a limp thanks to a pebble in his left shoe, Bell felt confident that no one outside of a close circle would ever recognize him.

"We're printing in two shifts right now," Lawson explained. "We never would have been able to in our old building because it lacked electricity."

"That's the large brick building down the street?"

"That's right. Hard to believe it's already outdated. It was built in 1880."

"In New York these days, a building's lucky to last twenty years before it's torn down and something taller goes up," Bell said, and then fell silent as he and his guide walked around the echoing hall of noisy machinery.

The process was straightforward but painstaking, as ink had

to be applied evenly on the shiny metal plates and all excess removed before the press applied the weight that stuck in a micro-thin veneer on the linen paper. He noted that the paper was wet when it went through the press. Lawson must have done this tour often because he said over the fractious din, "Once we print one side, the sheets of bills go into an oven to dry completely. Only then do we rewet it and print the other side. Once it's dried again, the sheets are inspected, cut, bundled, and stored in our vaults until we're ready for shipment to the Fed's twelve regional banks."

Besides the pressmen in their ink-smeared aprons and their attendants, Bell noted there were uniformed guards on patrol throughout the room. Surely the workers were properly vetted to work amid such temptation, but human nature was just that, human, and so the pressmen and all the others would need to be watched.

They left the printing room and found a quieter spot in a stairwell. There was really nowhere in the building one didn't hear or feel the cacophony. They talked as they climbed.

"You've sent out some money already?" It was a question to which Bell already knew the answer.

"We have. About a hundred thousand dollars' worth of bills to each of the Reserve banks as a test run for our logistics."

"Any problems?"

"No, none," Lawson said. "Every branch received their shipment within minutes of the estimated times we'd devised in advance."

They reached a door at the top of the stairway. Beyond was a rooftop terrace with tastefully arranged plants in large pots and many chairs. It was obviously a break area, since there were at least thirty men and women chatting in small groups. Many of them were enjoying a cigarette alfresco since smoking was prohibited near all the flammable, and valuable, material within the BEP building. Lawson offered Bell a cigarette, which he politely declined, and lit one for himself.

"I wanted you to see this," Lawson said, and then admitted, "Well, I really wanted a smoke, too. You see, once an employee enters the building, they aren't allowed to leave without passing through a security checkpoint."

"I can't imagine it's all that hard for someone to palm a couple of bills."

"Once the sheets are cut into individual notes, security measures become even more strict." He added, "I suppose a bill or two could make it out of the building, but these are all good-paying jobs that no one would risk losing for a couple of hundred dollars and a guaranteed conviction for a federal crime."

"What about the vaults?"

"Let me finish this"—Lawson held up his half-smoked cigarette—"and I'll show you."

While he waited for Lawson to finish his cigarette, Bell wandered over to the edge of the roof. The Potomac River was a short distance away. Closer still behind a scattered grove of trees was the Tidal Basin at the head of the shipping channel. Near its bank sat a partially capsized and obviously grounded metal barge. Buoys had been anchored near it to warn traffic away and a sign had been erected on its flat sloping deck that stated G&E Marine were to be its salvors.

Bell asked Lawson about the one-hundred-fifty-foot barge. "It ground during a storm a couple of weeks ago. It's filled with gravel. The owners came forward right away. They tried unloading by hand, but it was too slow and costly. They're waiting for a floating crane with a clamshell bucket that's on its way from Philadelphia."

"With it stuck so close to your building, did you have it investigated?"

"I went out there myself the day after it grounded," Lawson told him. "Met a representative from the owners and looked into all the holds personally. Nothing but a big metal box full of little rocks."

Minutes later they stood outside an open vault door that was easily three feet thick. There looked to be two dozen hardened steel bolts that would extend into the frame when the door was locked. Bell walked around it to see its face. The lock dials were the size of dinner plates and the rotating handle to retract the bolts as sturdy as an ocean liner's helm. As they approached, a pair of workers were moving bundles of newly printed bills stacked four feet high on a wheeled trolley. Lawson looked a little apologetic. "I'm sorry to say I can't tell you much about the vault itself. Security and all that."

"I understand. If my sense of space is correct, we are nowhere near any exterior walls, right?"

"Very good."

"And I'm going to assume the vault uses a variation of Isaiah Rogers's undrillable walls."

"I. Ah . . ."

"Relax, Mr. Lawson. Filling the cavity between two steel walls with loose metal balls is a forty-year-old technique that remains valid today. A thief's drill can penetrate the first wall of steel, but then the bit hits one of the balls, which spin freely, negating the drill's ability to auger through to the second plate wall. Behind that I assume are three-foot-thick walls of no-slump concrete reinforced with steel bars. And all of that is sitting on a ten-foot-thick cement slab."

Understanding he was dealing with a professional who lived by discretion, Lawson admitted, "Closer to twelve, actually."

A metal gate barred casual entry into the vault. Seeing Lawson approach, the guard made to undo the lock, but paused. Out of the corner of his eye, Bell saw Lawson make an "all clear" signal with his right index finger and thumb. Had he not done so, the guard wouldn't have unlocked the gate and would have likely pulled the revolver he carried holstered on his hip.

They passed through the yawning portal of the open vault door and into a room whose size couldn't easily be determined. The vault was divided into two stories of separate locked cages, like some sort of chaotic prison for the millions upon millions of dollars of new money being hoarded here before being shipped around the country. The air was rich with the aroma of newly printed bills.

Each of the separate cages that Bell could see had their own locked gates and were all filled to capacity with neat bundles of currency. Once these bills became the official currency of the United States, he would be standing amid more wealth than just about any human ever had. Just from his immediate surroundings, he guessed there was a billion dollars in the vault, more likely several billion. His mind reeled.

"Have you audited the vault?" he asked his guide.

"It's impossible. There is simply too much money to count. Once each cage is fully loaded, the door is locked and the key is kept in a secondary vault where we store the master printing plates. Like this vault, it takes two people knowing different combinations to open. The four who guard that secret do not know the combination for this vault, and vice versa, and all are among our most trusted employees."

"What about the serial numbers of the bills that were recovered? Do you have a ledger to say where they should be?"

Lawson looked a little uncomfortable, paused, and then came clean. "The one detailing the notes shipped to the regional banks as a test run was ruined by a sprinkler malfunction. It's a new building and we're working through a laundry list of issues, what the engineers call 'bugs.' But we have assurance from all twelve banks that the full one hundred thousand arrived and is secured in their vaults, all nearly as impressive as our own."

They continued their tour and finally ended up in Lawson's top-floor office with a view across and up 14th Street to the Department of Agriculture building. Unlike the Bureau of Engraving's neoclassical style, it was done in Beaux-Arts. It had a similarly colored white limestone exterior and was a story or two taller. Directly across from the Engraving building was a rather run-down neighborhood of cheap row houses and trash-strewn empty lots.

A hundred and twenty-five years after its founding, Washington, D.C., was still very much a work in progress.

"So, what do you think, Mr. McMahon? Any preliminary thoughts?"

"About where those bills came from?"

"That and your impression of our security."

Bell accepted a glass of water that had gone warm and stale in a glass carafe. The late afternoon remained warm, but the air had gone electric with the promise of a coming storm. "Obviously, the building is impenetrable with anything less subtle than an artillery barrage. And even if someone could gain access, I've seen enough armed guards to put an end to a robbery pretty quickly. How many guards are working when the building is closed?"

"Six, working in three teams. Someone is always by the vault and another is always manning the front door. The other four are roaming throughout the building."

"You're safe here, for sure," Bell said. "I would like to go over the details tomorrow about how you transport the money from here to Union Station and how each money train is guarded. As to how the attackers were paid in uncirculated bills, I can only speculate. You're absolutely certain they aren't counterfeit?"

"Yes."

"There are only three circumstances that I can think of. Number one is that the money was lifted from here inside the mint bill by bill over the past few months."

"Unlikely."

"Number two is that the money was intercepted on its way to the twelve Reserve banks during your test run."

"But all of them said they received the full hundred thousand dollars."

"Some of their notes could be counterfeit."

It was clear from his expression that Lawson hadn't considered that. "I will need for them to double-check."

"In case all of the money is fake, you'll have to courier a hundred-dollar bill you know without question is legitimate to check against."

"Good thinking. You have a knack for this."

"Mr. Van Dorn likes to say that a detective who can't outthink a criminal will never catch him."

"You mentioned a third possibility?"

"The least likely," Bell admitted, "is that someone has gotten their hands on one of the plates used to ink the notes and are printing legitimate hundred-dollar bills for themselves."

"Not possible," Lawson said. "The plates are even harder to steal than the banknotes."

"You should inventory what you have and question the men responsible for destroying the plates that have come to the end of their useful lives."

Lawson considered Bell's recommendation. "Two men work together to destroy worn-out plates. It's possible, though not likely, that a pair of them working together could try to get one out of the building somehow. I will talk to some of the others on our security team about it."

The staff in the large office outside Lawson's private office was making noise as the workday came to an end, chatting and closing filing cabinets and scraping back their chairs against the stone floor.

Bell stood and extended his hand. "I'll be back Monday morning at ten to study your transportation protocols. I am staying at the Willard while I'm in town, if you need to reach me over the weekend."

16

RICK SHEPHERD'S JOB WAS PRETTY EASY. HE SAT BEHIND A large desk at the entrance of the Department of Agriculture building all through the night and made certain that nobody entered it until employees arrived the following day. He could use the lobby bathroom for no more than fifteen minutes per his ten-hour shift and under no circumstances was he to unlock the glass and bronze doors.

In the three years since taking the job, he'd improved his reading skills so he could tackle almost any book and had whittled two dozen chess sets, though he had no idea how the game was played. A neighbor had a friend who sold them at Georgetown for a nice price.

Not much ever happened during his shift. A few times a month, he'd have to see out an employee who'd stayed far into the night, and on rare occasions some drunk passing through the area would see the light and rap on the glass. They moved on when Shepherd showed them the truncheon he kept buckled around his waist.

With a windstorm lashing the city with door-rattling gusts, there wouldn't be any drunks wandering about tonight and, it being Friday, he didn't think there were any late-night worker bees still in the hive.

Shepherd's eyes weren't what they once were and his desk lamp had a low-wattage bulb, so he had to squint to shape the mane of his equine knight. He was using black walnut, so it was especially tricky work.

Without warning something slapped against the glass door that nearly made him slice his finger. He looked up from his whittling. In the glow of the outdoor lights was a woman at the entrance, dressed well but with a face white with terror. Where she'd slapped at the glass doors, she'd left behind dark palm prints. Blood.

The doors were thick glass and the wind was a shrieking gale, but Shepherd could still hear her screams, muffled but so fear-filled it made the hairs on his arms rise. Despite himself and his orders, he got to his feet. He didn't leave his post behind the desk, but he was compelled into a more alert stance.

The woman looked to her left and her actions became even more frantic. She pounded on the glass, her bloody hands blotting out more of the pane, her screams now as high-pitched as anything Shepherd had ever heard.

Then a dark figure loomed out of the night, large and cloaked. He grabbed the woman and spun her around to face him, one hand up in a vicious slap that corkscrewed her to the ground at his feet. He bent to strike her again.

Shepherd ran from around the desk, one hand holding the key to unlock the heavy door and the other trying to draw the wooden baton from its loop on his belt. Orders be damned. He couldn't sit by while a woman was beaten a few feet from where he sat. He fumbled the key into the lock and finally got it to engage. He twisted hard and pushed against the door, angry words of warning forming at the back of his throat.

The patent for the pistol silencer was just over five years old and so they were relatively unknown. They worked with modern automatic weapons to reduce the sound and pressure of the exploding cartridge because there were no gaps between the chamber and the gun's muzzle as in a revolver.

The dark figure looming over the defenseless woman already had the silenced pistol out and held low along his thigh. The moment the Agriculture Department's door opened, he whipped the silenced pistol up into position and shot Rick Shepherd twice in the heart. Rather than echo across the National Mall and back, the two shots were no louder than a pair of polite claps.

The man in the cloak helped the woman to her feet.

"I told you, for what you're paying me, love, you could have really slapped me."

"Wouldn't dream of it, darling," he said and shot her at point-blank range.

Two large trucks arrived in front of the building just then. They'd been watching the drama from down the street. Men carrying heavy duffel bags emerged from the backs of the trucks and entered the government building with military precision. Two of the men tossed the body of Shepherd into the back of one of the trucks while the cloaked figure lifted the dead girl over the tailgate.

"You know, Marquess, I don't think I could kill a lass I'd taken to bed," said Michaleen Riordan, looking at the murdered woman's face in the murky light.

The man Michaleen referred to as royalty had long stopped asking that his little Irish friend desist. "When I hired her out of the
brothel," replied the cloaked figure, "I didn't sleep with her first."

"Either way, your plan worked. The guard unlocked the door
for us and we're in."

While one man used a bucket and soapy sponge to clean the
fake blood from the glass, all of Shepherd's possessions were taken
from his desk, his unfinished chess piece and his precision tools as
well as an old tin lunch box and a more modern thermos bottle,
all of it was thrown into the truck. The morning-shift guard would
report that his predecessor was not at his post when he arrived and
none of his belongings had been left behind. Likely conclusion,
Rick Shepherd had quit. As a lifelong bachelor, it would be days
before anyone began to miss him.

The girl was one of a hundred prostitutes who came and went
from the notorious brothels in an area of the city called Hooker's
Division. No one was ever going to miss her.

The trucks pulled away from the curb fifty seconds after their
arrival and just a few seconds later, the eighteen heavily burdened
men were on their way up to the building's roof. They'd been
forced to wait weeks for the perfect weather conditions and so
they had drilled in the intervening period like the most disciplined
army in the world.

Access to the roof was from a staircase that rose next to one of
the elevator banks. The knob had a lock that the man Michaleen
nicknamed Marquess picked with practiced ease. Six stories above
the street, the wind felt stronger, which is why they had chosen
this night. The fact that the rain held off was a bonus.

Most of the men huddled back from the roof's edge to give their compatriots room to work. From one of the duffels came a long-braided steel wire as thick around as a man's finger and weighing approximately eighty pounds. One end was snap-linked to a large airfoil made from ribbed black silk. It was six feet by four feet—its size determined by the weight of the wire it had to carry across to the Engraving building. Sewn in such a way as to mimic an airplane's wing when in flight, the airfoil inflated with a *crump* as soon as it felt the stormy wind. It took three men to keep what was essentially a giant kite from blowing away. Each side of the airfoil had thin ropes attached that could be manipulated to spill air from either the left or the right and give the contraption a measure of maneuverability.

"Ready," said one of the men.

"Do it," replied the Marquess.

With practiced caution, the men let the wind take their oversized kite over the side of the Agriculture building. It was designed to lift only slightly as it resisted the wind, giving them greater control. They played out more line and the kite was soon floating over a dead-quiet 14th Street. It wanted to twist and curl like a Chinese festival dragon, but the men paying out the main wire and the other two controlling the foil's angle of attack kept it mostly in check.

For several tense minutes they kept at their task, Michaleen and the Marquess watching intently, involuntarily swaying their bodies as if they could control the kite by bending and twisting and sucking air between their teeth when the craft dropped suddenly or veered too far off course. When the weight of the wire paying out behind the kite increased to the point the craft was slowly sinking toward the road, the two men controlling the airfoil's shape tugged sharply on their lines to untie knots that released additional material to expand the airfoil's size.

This was coordinated with a quickening of the main wire being paid out so that the kite didn't soar into the night. They had practiced and perfected this maneuver until they could do it from muscle memory alone. The original proposal was to have a man harnessed to the airfoil, but so much weight made the rig too big to control and so they had devised their current plan.

When the wind shifted and the kite sheared off, air was spilled from the foil, and it righted itself as if by magic. They steered the kite nearly a thousand feet down 14th Street until it hovered twenty feet above the Bureau of Engraving and Printing. The men working the main line held firm, while the two others watched the kite's almost hypnotic gyrations.

They had worked together enough to know the exact moment and acted in perfect accord. They dumped all the air from the foil and it collapsed onto the building's roof like a giant black ghost returning to its haunt.

This was the critical moment when their attempt to bridge the long gap between the two buildings was at its most vulnerable. But like all the moving parts of the most daring heist in history, the Marquess had everything thought through in advance. The angle from Agriculture to Engraving and Printing was relatively shallow, so the cargo carriers they attached to the wire had precision ball bearings for ease of movement. The first little car they sent flying down the wire only weighed ten pounds. Anything heavier risked dragging the airfoil from the roof. It gave off a low whining sound as it zipped along, and as soon as the sound ended, the next weight went flying through the night, this one weighing in at fifteen pounds.

Ten more weighted carriages went zipping across the void, each heavier than the last until they had nearly six hundred pounds of steel plates anchoring the far end of the line. By now they had tied off their end of the wire to a standpipe near the elevator housing; they just couldn't put on maximal tension yet.

"Moment of truth, Michaleen," the Marquess said.

"Aye, your Lordship," the little man replied as two men helped him into a harness. "I may look like a leprechaun, but watch me fly like a *bananach*."

He lay back into one of the men's arms and his feet were lifted from the roof so that when he was clipped onto the wire, his weight didn't jerk it unnecessarily. They sent him on his way as gently as a tossed paper airplane. He was a slender man, but was still double the heaviest iron weight.

Because of his size, Michaleen Riordan had worked as a successful second-story man in his twenties. He could scale nearly any building in New York and had never had vertigo. As he'd grown older, and embraced mortality, he'd lost some of his head for heights, so he didn't look down as he soared some six stories above 14th Street.

Because there was little tension in the wire, it sagged under his weight enough to slow him almost to a standstill. He supplemented his speed by pulling himself hand over hand for the final forty yards. He landed ignobly atop the Engraving building on his backside amid a jumbled mess of fluttering silk and iron plates.

In short order, bags of equipment shot out of the night as they came zipping across. Michaleen unclipped them as they arrived and set them aside. To him some felt as heavy as he did himself. Despite the wind and the cool night air, he was sweating. Ten minutes after arriving on the building, the airfoil was now anchored by more than a ton of iron weights, equipment, and one diminutive thief.

He felt more tension put on the line as his partners ratcheted back on the wire. Next came the sound of another man crossing the void between the two government buildings. By rights it should be the next smallest person on the team, but it was no surprise that the heist's mastermind wanted to be the next across. The increased tension on the line made him come in much faster than Michaleen's own journey, but not so fast that the Marquess couldn't absorb the impact when he hit the roof.

"Pretty as a picture," Michaleen told him.

Like the fabled *bananach*, night-flying wraiths out of Irish folklore, the rest of the large team zipped down 14th Street and came to rest on the single largest repository of wealth in human history. The party all wore black and so they were nearly invisible if anyone had been out this blustery night. The men were silently efficient, each shouldering the individual bags they'd been assigned.

The men were all loyal to Michaleen Riordan, just as he owed his allegiance to the man he called Marquess. The others that Riordan had killed were outsiders to one degree or another, worthy of betrayal. This crew was generally the sons of men Michaleen had run with back in his twenties and who had come up together through the ranks of Irish organized crime along the East Coast from Boston to Savannah. He was godfather to several of them and the others generally referred to him as Uncle Micky.

Still, none knew the identity of the Marquess or even knew there was another man even higher on the food chain who'd actually bankrolled the heist.

The building was shaped like a capital *E*, but with two projections in the middle. They were on the wrong one and so picked their way around various vents and fan housings and along the eave of the central section of the large building, keeping low out of instinct. Rain began to fall in cold sheets.

Two members of the team peeled off from the rest. Their mission was to establish another zip line off the back of the building. This one wouldn't be as long as their ingress line, but it was just as important. Once they had one end of the wire anchored to the building, one would rappel to the ground with the remaining line in a backpack. He would cross the street to the bank of the tidal pool, where a rowboat waited to ferry the pack out to the derelict gravel barge.

As those two were following their orders, the bulk of the team arrived in the area where the contractor, Charley Briggs, had intentionally under-reinforced the building's roof. They verified the location with precut lengths of twine and two men dropped to their knees with chisels and hammers. The blades were hardened with tungsten and cut into the roof like the concrete was a hundred years old and not freshly poured. Once the perimeter of the secret trapdoor had been chiseled completely, the inch-thick piece was hoisted out of its place and set aside. The wood underneath looked solid, but was actually balsa and succumbed to the chisel even easier.

It took just fifteen minutes in total. The last of the balsa wood dropped away into a closet below. They had only needed to bore through three inches of roofing structure in what was otherwise a two-foot-thick slab of steel-reinforced concrete.

"We're in," said the Marquess with a wicked smile.

"I can smell the money from here," added Michaleen. "And what a lovely smell it is."

17

THE PHONE IN BELL'S SUITE RANG JUST AS HE WAS ABOUT TO step into a hot bath with a tumbler of whiskey, his belly full of room service roast beef. He'd requested the long-distance wire upon his arrival at the hotel some three hours earlier and was surprised it had gone through at all. Stormy nights tended to see service go down with snapped wires or become logjammed with callers inquiring about loved ones enduring the weather.

He threw on a robe and strode out to the sitting room. The phone was on a delicate little table next to the oversized sofa. "Archie, is that you?"

"None other."

"How was the funeral?"

"Didn't happen."

"The deceased got better?"

"Funny. Actually, it's a good thing I was there."

The funeral was for one of Archie's father-in-law's top executives and close friends, Reggie Hauser. Apart from being beautiful, Lillian Abbott, née Hennessy, came from a wealthy family. Her father, Osgood, owned a railroad. In much the same way Bell's dad tried to convince him to go into banking, Osgood Hennessy couldn't convince Archie to give up being a detective and settle into a corner office at their building near Grand Central.

"What happened?"

"It was one of those corporate events for railroad wallahs wanting to pay their respects. More fat cats than at my crazy spinster aunt's house. Oz wanted Lillian there and obviously I had to accompany her. We do the whole view-the-body thing when I notice there's heavy makeup around the stiff's wrists."

"Covering up a bruise?"

"I couldn't exactly move his hands, but from what I could see the bruising looked like it went around the top of one wrist and the bottom of the other."

"Uh-oh."

"Yes, uh-oh. The widow was still pretty flibbertigibbety with grief, but I spoke with Hauser's son-in-law. Turns out the maid found the old guy dead behind his desk, his hands on his chest like the last thing he did is try to calm a heart under attack."

"Did she see any bruising?"

"The son-in-law didn't know, but the maid did notice a broken window with the glass on the floor inside the study where he'd been working. She thought little of it and just cleaned it up. The guy had been under a physician's care for about a dozen different conditions, including treatment for two previous heart attacks, so no cops were called. The funeral home sent a van and four of their biggest guys to cart him out of the house. It wasn't until the next day she mentioned the broken window to the daughter and son-in-law and only because it now needed replacing. They didn't think anything of it, either, and if they had thought it odd it was too late anyway. The dearly departed was pumped full of formaldehyde by then."

"What did you do?"

"I told them dear old Dad might have been the victim of a crime and that a pathologist needed to examine the body before he was put in the ground. The daughter fainted dead away. Her mother happened to be looking our way when the girl hit the carpet and she began to wail that her little girl was dead, too. We were at the back of the funeral home's largest receiving room and the next thing you know it's total chaos. A guy near us thought I had attacked the daughter and so he rushed over to take a swing at me. I ducked it and he hit the son-in-law. He went down. I laid out the would-be hero with a haymaker of my own. Marion could have filmed it as a farce."

"Oh boy."

"Right. Fortunately, the funeral director has seen this a thousand times and is by her side with smelling salts."

"The wife?"

"No, the daughter. The wife's sister and brother were trying to shake some sense into her. Then the guy and the son-in-law come up ready to duke it out. The director and I restrained them until they calmed down. Anyway, that was the end of the funeral. I had them close the casket and explained my suspicions to the son-in-law.

"The director didn't perform the embalming himself and the guy who did never mentioned the chafed wrists. He felt bad because, like I said, he was an old pro and would have recognized the sign of someone whose hands had been bound behind their back.

He put me in touch with a private pathologist and said he'd make the arrangements for the doc to perform a gross physical examination to look for other signs of trauma."

"Did you go to the house and check out the study?"

"Briefly," Archie said. "The family was in a tizzy and wanted me out of their hair. A glazier had already replaced the broken pane of glass. I didn't see any obvious signs of a struggle, but I only had a couple of minutes before the wife's brother threatened to call the cops on me."

"What do you think?"

"If I'm right, and I do believe the pathologist will verify that I am, someone broke into the study from an outside garden, ambushed and tied our railroad executive to his chair in order to extract information through nefarious means. As luck would have it, our boy's ticker ticks its last tock before our villain can get to work."

Bell asked, "What did the guy do for Osgood?"

"Heads the department that negotiates with other railroads who want to run trains on their track. Mundane stuff, really."

"Not something you'd get tortured over."

"I think having to listen to someone talking about it would be the torture."

"So, something else, then?"

"I'll get back into the study tomorrow once people's nerves have eased. If there's a clue in there, I'll find it. What's the latest on your end?"

"I still haven't figured out how someone got their hands on the new bills," Bell admitted. "The security chief, Lawson, insists no one can walk out of the building with any cash and that all the money sent to the Reserve banks has been accounted for. There's a slim possibility a used printing plate could have walked out the door. We're exploring that more on Monday."

"What about the attack on the yacht?"

"I've not been read in on that yet. The rumor Lawson shared is that the Secret Service has nothing. No one has reported a missing plane or pilot in this area, so they're expanding the search to pretty much the entire country."

"You flyboys like your clubs, so something is bound to turn up."

"I feel the same way, but it's going to take time."

"You feel there's some urgency?"

"The attack on the *Mayflower* feels like the opening gambit of something far bigger."

"A heist?"

"Maybe. Either the armored cars carrying the money to Union Station here in D.C. or en route aboard one of the trains." Bell paused as an idea hit him. "Train scheduling."

"Huh?"

"Archie, get into that study as quickly as possible. Your dead guy schedules railroads. In a few weeks the Bureau of Engraving is going to ship billions of dollars across the country by rail. Thousands of miles of track owned by dozens of different companies. That's a lot of coordination and it has to be done in complete secrecy."

"Why target just my father-in-law's line?"

"Maybe they didn't. Maybe they've blackmailed or bribed a lot of others, but your guy happened to die as a result."

"What are you going to do?"

"Nothing at the moment," Bell said. "There's nothing to go on. Unless or until you find evidence linking that death to the new money, this is all conjecture based on coincidence."

"I thought you said you don't believe in coincidences."

"No. I said I don't like them, I never said they don't happen. Right now, Lawson has enough on his plate with the upcoming shipments without me crying wolf."

"I suppose you're right."

"In the meantime, I will stay by a phone either here in my room or in the office downstairs. Call me the instant you have something. Wait, hold on."

"What?"

"The ferry sinking. Any leads?"

"Eddie Tobin's tried every dockside informer he's ever talked to. No one knows anything about it or about an Irishman who can pass himself off as a kid. As to the recent parolees who'd like to see you pushing up daisies, we're making progress. Most of the guys you've put away are upriver for life, so the list isn't long. So far there's no one suspicious."

Bell's voice turned speculative. "What if it wasn't a coincidence and that going after me was the second move following the attack on the *Mayflower*?" His voice then sharpened. "No, that would be far too elaborate. Criminals like to keep things simple."

"By sinking an entire ferry when they could have shivved you?"

"Overkill, I agree, but had I died in the river, would anyone have suspected anything other than a tragic accident? On the other hand, if I had been murdered, the old man would have bankrupted the agency hunting for my killer and they knew it. That incident is tied to my past, to someone who really doesn't want to get caught. Look at the softer criminals, men who I put way for things like embezzling or fraud. The hard boys would have gone the shiv route."

"Okay. We'll keep digging. Stay safe."

18

THE MARQUESS WAS THE FIRST TO LOWER HIMSELF THROUGH their ingress hatch. Dangling by his hands it was still a three-foot drop to the tile floor of a currently empty storage closet. He helped catch Michaleen, who would have had an extra twelve-inch fall due to his stature.

"Begging your Lordship's welcome."

"You're welcome."

The Marquess pulled a two-cell flashlight from a deep pocket of the coveralls he wore, but didn't turn it on. He eased open the closet door into the pitch-black space beyond. He and Michaleen stepped out so that the men could lower their equipment. They worked in near silence save for the soft squeak of wet shoes on clean ceramic tiles.

He flicked on the hand torch. The murky cone of light showed them to be in a large space where naked steel columns held up the massive roof. Already pyramids and ziggurats of cardboard boxes were being stored up in the attic, tucked along the perimeter under a shallow eave. There was also a confounding mass of cast-iron pipes running overhead and bundles of electrical wires running in hollow tubes between insulators.

About fifty feet away was a door that they knew led down to the main floors of the building. It took five minutes for the team to assemble with their gear. One of the thieves had stripped out of their dark coveralls to reveal a uniform nearly identical to the ones the guards wore. They'd been made from secretly taken photographs by the mother of one of the crew.

As a unit, the men crossed the attic and entered the stairwell. They hadn't been overly concerned about roving guards in the attic, but anything was possible on the floors below.

"Stay here until we return," the Marquess said, the flashlight back in his pocket, the silenced automatic pistol now in his hand.

He knew there were six guards, one always at the vault, one at a desk in the main entrance, and the other four either on patrol or in a break room located near the second-floor cafeteria. He and Michaleen, his little Walther .32 also silenced, left the stairwell at the bottom and found themselves in a central corridor with dozens of numbered doors running down each side. There was almost no light except for a couple of emergency bulbs that were left burning all night long. Their night vision was more than adequate.

They knew the general layout of the building, if not what was behind each and every locked door. The building was so solidly constructed they could hear nothing of the storm outside. That made it so much easier to hear approaching footsteps should they stumble on a roving guard. With the stealth and patience of stalking cats, the two men checked every corridor on every floor. The building was huge and the going slow, but they couldn't afford to be anything other than methodical. They saw no one.

The second floor was slightly better lit, but still shadowy. They moved along the very edges of the hallways, keeping as flat as possible. They came to a mezzanine outside the cafeteria. The dining hall was large, like an urban high school's, and on the walls to the left and right of its glass entry doors were bulletin boards covered in tacked-up notes about people looking for roommates or wanting to sell a bicycle or a hundred other mundane transactions. There was much more lighting on this floor.

A muted sound of a toilet flushing came from down the corridor, closer to the guards' break room. Michaleen took off like a rabbit and he reached the men's room before the occupant had finished up inside. He waited outside the heavy wooden door, his left hand up, his pistol clutched low. The door suddenly flew back as the guard prepared to leave, his hands down at his thighs as he dried them on his pants.

Michaleen hit him in the throat with his open left hand, stunning the larger man more with surprise than strength. The guard staggered back and Michaleen pressed his attack until they had cleared the door enough for the automatic hinges to close. The instant he heard the latch click, the career criminal put two bullets into the guard's chest and stepped back as the man collapsed to the floor, his heart no longer pumping.

The Irishman dropped to his haunches as the light faded from his victim's eyes. "Just so ya know, 'twas nothing personal."

He rejoined the Marquess and together they strode through the door to the break room as if they were the guard just returning from the washroom. There were two men in the room, one at a table reading the *Daily Racing Form*, the other either asleep or just resting on a couch. The two thieves fired in unison, intuiting which was their target. Michaleen shot the sleeping man three times, and the Marquess put two through the head of the would-be tout.

Had there been anyone out in the hallway, they would have heard the sound of someone wrapping their knuckles hard on a table a few times.

The Marquess knew his partner's superstition. "Nothing personal, right, Michaleen?"

"Aye. It never is."

They backed out of the room. There was only one more guard unaccounted for and they figured he was chatting with the guard outside the vault or at the duty station by the front door.

They decided to take the vault first and descended into the building's subterranean level, where the very earth itself helped protect the money being stored. Leading with their pistols, they took the main stairs down. In the center of the stairs was an oval opening about the size of a bathtub that went all the way to the top floor. Because of this the staircase echoed. They moved at a glacial pace and reached the bottom without hearing anything but the scuff of their shoes.

The door opened without warning and a guard appeared. He was closest to Michaleen and his reactions were lightning quick. He pushed Riordan's gun up and away with his right and jammed the forearm of his left into the Irishman's throat, pinning and then spinning him around to gain distance. Across the room, the guard sitting at the vault desk jumped to his feet when he saw two darkened figures wrestling in the entrance to the stairwell. He fumbled for his gun.

The Marquess couldn't get a clear shot at the man fighting Michaleen. They were grappling and twisting as they tried to gain control of the silenced .32. Instead, the team leader lowered his aim and fired a single shot through the guard's kneecap, shattering bone and shredding ligaments and tendons. The guard shrieked and seemed to lose his will to fight. Ignoring the wounded man for a moment, the Marquess raised his pistol and fired just as the second guard cleared his big revolver and fired back. The noise was deafening, a sharp blast of sound that compressed the eardrums almost to the point of rupture.

His shot missed. The Marquess's did not. The wall behind the guard's head was suddenly painted in a blotchy red stain of his blood.

Without hesitation, the Marquess raced back up the stairs. Whether the wounded guard would kill Michaleen or Riordan would prevail, he did not know. That wasn't his fight. He climbed the stairs three at a time, his legs like the pistons of a charging locomotive. He had no time, he knew that, but he had to try. At the next landing he crashed through the door and into the building's plain but large lobby.

His eyes went straight for the guard's tall desk with the expectation of the man being there with his weapon drawn. Instead, he caught movement at the edge of his vision. He turned to see a portly figure dressed as all the other guards running back from the window where he'd been watching the storm when the pistol discharged loudly enough to alert everyone in the building. His face was flush and his equipment belt rattled around his thick waist.

By some miracle he'd been away from his post and hadn't yet tripped the silent alarm that would call every cop and agent in the District. The range was workable and the target large enough, but he was moving and the Marquess was panting from the climb. He fired and missed. Fired and missed a second time.

The guard was now rounding his desk, his fingers a foot or less from blowing the entire operation.

The master thief pulled the trigger as quickly as he could, the heavy silencer preventing the pistol's natural barrel rise. He fired three rounds before the slide locked back empty. He hit all three. The guard dropped to the granite floor, his chest a mass of blood as his heart pumped his life away. Reloading as he drew closer to the guard, the Marquess saw that he was still trying to reach the electric buzzer under his desk. The Marquess administered the coup de grâce just as the stairwell door flew open.

He turned as fluidly as a matador, his arm rising by instinct until the weapon was perfectly aimed at Michaleen Riordan's chest. The Marquess dropped his aim.

"Never had a doubt, my friend," he called. "We've wasted enough time; go get the others and let's get to work."

19

WHILE HE WAITED FOR THE OTHERS TO ARRIVE DOWNSTAIRS, the Marquess checked the street outside through the windows. There was no traffic and it appeared the storm, though already slowing, was keeping pedestrians off the streets. He doubted anyone walking in front of the building would have heard the unsilenced gunshots because of how securely the Engraving building had been constructed, but there was the chance someone had witnessed him shooting the guard.

Details are where criminals go wrong. Losing a button at a crime scene or discarding a book of matches in a victim's house because tossing them feels like second nature. Leave behind even a smudged fingerprint and cops could get a conviction. For most of his crimes, he always wore coveralls and burned them as soon as he could. Shoes, too, were destroyed in case he left behind a print. After this heist they would hold a bonfire and torch everything but the money.

The guy dressed as a Bureau guard arrived and took up his station behind the duty counter. He was getting an equal share as the others just to sit on his duff in case a beat cop happened to look into the building while the robbery was underway. Details.

The Marquess went down the main stairs to the vault level. Men were already anchoring the bottom of their pulley system to the concrete floor using a pistol-like device that fired specially hardened nails into the cement using .22-caliber bulletless cartridges. Still being cautious, each time they used the nail gun, they covered it with thick sound-absorbing blankets.

The blood splattered against the wall had begun to drip macabrely. The master thief put it out of his mind and approached the vault door.

He gave no outward sign, but he was a little daunted by what he was about to attempt. The door was massive, like the breach on a battleship's main gun, only ten times the size and complexity. Michaleen was waiting for him. Even before this job was planned, both of them were master safecrackers. Since then, they had been practicing on a safe only slightly smaller than this, but made by the same Pittsburgh company.

A bag of equipment sat at the base of the enormous round door. It gleamed under the bright lights cold and unforgiving and, if he were honest, maybe a little malevolently. The two dials of the double-locking door were hidden behind a large, hinged steel box that used a scaled-down version of Isaiah Rogers's undrillable wall. The keyhole was the size of a bar of soap and the key that fit it likely weighed five pounds. The pins and tumblers inside the lock were of equally massive proportions.

By definition, lockpicking is a delicate operation requiring precision, dexterity, and an incredible sense of feel to know when the pins are aligned in the gate and the lock is ready to give. This lock's sheer size made it all but unpickable, as no one had the strength to hold the closest pins up and out of the way while manipulating the ones farther inside the mechanism to release it.

A black duffel had been left by one of the men at the base of the enormous vault door. The Marquess opened it and retrieved a heavy but intricate piece of equipment. It looked like a spidery-fingered mechanical hand mounted on a metal base. The base was magnetic and the master thief centered the odd apparatus just above the large keyhole and let it stick to the door with a dull clank.

He moved the long fingerlike probe into the lock, his four fingers inserted into thimble-like cups that were mechanically linked to what was essentially a giant tensioning tool. Through the linkage, he could extend the device into the lock and use it to hold back the heavy pins while maintaining the feel to know when each one lifted into place. The pick he used with his other hand, manipulating the pins back into the lock and holding them there with the mechanically advantaged tensioner.

He could pick most locks in just a couple of seconds, the sensitivity in his fingertips honed over many years of practice. This felt almost like picking a lock with a couple of coat hangers from two feet away with hands that were numb to the elbows, but he knew he could do it.

This was the piece of equipment the retired thief-turned-locksmith Harvey Wanamaker had made for the heist. The fact that it would be left behind and could potentially be traced back to him was a risk the Marquess couldn't take. Thus, Michaleen's earlier visit to Wanamaker's shop in Philadelphia.

The feedback from the probe to the thimbles was clunky, but

just adequate enough to perform the job at hand. By the time he was feeling for the last pin, he'd been at it for four minutes and the tensioner was holding back eight pounds of pins and pin tumblers plus the mechanical resistance of the internal springs. It didn't sound like much, but even the world's strongest man wouldn't be able to maintain the proper tension without muscle cramps and uncontrollable shaking. Thanks to the magnet and the metal armatures, the Engraving Bureau's penultimate line of defense was about to be breached.

The final pin dropped, and the Marquess rotated the tensioner and his pick using a small cranking mechanism built into the machine that twisted the wrist of the clockwork hand. The lock released and he eased open the door to reveal the two large combination dials.

"Time?" he called.

"Dawn is in six hours twenty-one minutes," replied one of the men who was preparing the bags they would fill with cash.

He grinned at Riordan. "Then let's get to it, my wee Irish friend."

Michaleen handed him a standard doctor's stethoscope and fitted the earpieces of his own into place. The lock wasn't so sophisticated that the combinations had to be entered at the same time, but the two had to be unlocked simultaneously or secondary bolts would slam in place and a representative from the manufacturer would need to be called in to unlock it. To save time, Michaleen had been learning alongside the Marquess on how to defeat the six-number combination locks.

The dials were numbered one through eighty, but the lock was so precision-crafted that the space between the numbers could be the right combination. One number might fall exactly on fifteen or seventy-two or it might fall on twenty-one-point-two or fifty-five-point-eight. Dial movement at that level of accuracy meant working in fractions of inches almost too small to measure.

With eyes and ears and the tips of their fingers, the two men began working the large dials, feeling for the instant the nose of the lock lever inside the mechanism dipped against the drive cam's contact points. They finessed the wheels, searching for that correct first number that would drop the fence attached to the nose into the gate of one of six disks that corresponded to the six numbers of the combination. The gate was a notch that when the correct numbers were spun would align and allow the nose to fall fully between the contact points. At that spot, the lock could be opened.

Both men had a piece of chalk to write down numbers they felt were close and worked the dials back and forth at times as quickly as possible and at others so slowly they appeared frozen.

The work was painstaking and inexorably frustrating to those not properly trained. Every minute they took opening the locks diminished how much money they could haul out of the vault, but neither man let that distract them. Their concentration was total. They weren't even aware that they were standing side by side. Michaleen worked with the tip of his tongue thrust out the side of his mouth. The Marquess's face was blank, impassive even. Only his wrist seemed to be working as he manipulated the dial to give up the lock's secrets. His list of potential combination numbers was down to just seven.

And then it finally happened. He felt the fence drop into the last aligned gate and the nose locked into the drive cam. He looked over at Michaleen and was startled to see the little man leaning casually against the vault door, his clay pipe between his lips, though unlit. His eyes actually twinkled.

"When?"

"Oh, a good five minutes ago, your Lordship."

"You do recall I, too, have a master participant in this little caper."

"I do. I do. 'Tis why I call him the Baron, seeing you're merely a Marquess. You're not quite at the top of the peerage pecking order."

He stepped aside to let one of the more strapping sons of Ireland have the honor of cranking the large wheel that would retract the twenty-four massive bolts. It took far more strength than Michaleen possessed. The Marquess shared a curt nod with his accomplice and together they muscled open the most secure vault in the United States, possibly the world. Once the bolts were retracted, they stepped back, and two other thieves pulled on the door's handle. Though it weighed multiple tons, the door was so well-balanced that they opened it with relative ease.

They didn't stand on ceremony to celebrate what they had just accomplished. Getting into the vault was only half the job. The Marquess moved inside, pulling a set of lockpicks from his coveralls. The lock for the iron-grilled door was of superior commercial quality, but only held him up a handful of seconds.

By now everyone was in place. The pulley system had been erected and tested. The men on the roof were ready to receive the hand-stuffed sacks of cash and pack them into larger bags for the zip-line run out to the "derelict" barge. Already ballast water was being pumped from tanks concealed under her load of gravel and when they were ready and the towboat would be back, the hidden iron hooks that anchored it to the bottom of the Tidal Basin would be released and the craft would float free.

Other members of the crew were tasked with pushing the trolleys laden with the sacks from the vault to the stairwell where the hoist was located. Other men would be inside the vault itself, raking stacks of Federal Reserve notes into the bags as fast as they could.

The only inefficiency in the plan came from the fact that the money was being stored in separate cages inside the vault, not by denomination but rather destination. As these were the first shipments to the twelve scattered Reserve banks, each load contained bills in all denominations, in a ratio devised to best serve the individual branches. That meant there were far more one-dollar bills than twenties, fifties, or hundreds.

The man who'd conceived of the heist and bankrolled all the necessary training and equipment, a man from Georgia that Michaleen didn't know but referred to as the Baron, had assured the Marquess that this was perfectly fine, but the thief in him had a hard time not maximizing this opportunity. The idea of breaking into the largest repository of cash ever amassed and leaving behind the lion's share of the loot rankled his professional sensibilities.

"Let's go, boys," he said as the four men tasked with gathering the money followed him into the vault, each taking up a trolley left by the last shift of workers transporting bundled bills from the printing area.

The locks for the cages were much easier than the main gate. Riordan opened a separate cage for each thief and they got busy filling sacks with the bundles of cash, pushing aside the ones, fives, and tens in order to get to the more valuable twenties and hundreds. Their bags, when full, were roughly the size of a five-gallon paint can.

When both decks of the double-decker pushcarts were mounded with sacks, a runner would take it out of the vault and down the hallway to the main staircase. A wooden trestle held the bottom pulley for their hoist, while the top was secured to the ceiling up on the top floor. A rope fitted with woven straw baskets looped between the two bicycle tire–sized pulley wheels.

Looking up the narrow gap between the stairs was a little like looking through a kaleidoscope, as the geometry of the countless banisters and rails tended to fool the eye.

The sacks were dumped on the floor. One of the two thieves stationed here loaded each woven basket with one of the bags of cash, while the other kept up a steady rhythm pulling on the rope so that baskets were hoisted up to the team waiting above.

Once on the top floor, two dozen sacks were stuffed into a pair of duffel bags. These in turn were run back to the attic, where they were boosted through the roof and handed up to another pair of thieves, who saw them attached to the zip line with metal C hooks. Handlers on the barge tossed the duffels into the hold as they came zooming down the line from the back of the Bureau of Engraving building.

Once they got into their groove, two bags, with an estimated value between four and eight million dollars, were zipping over to the barge every few minutes. Dawn was a little over five hours away. By the Marquess's back-of-the-envelope estimate, they'd steal the better part of six hundred million dollars this night.

Tumble through the night

20

BELL CAME AWAKE BUT DIDN'T KNOW WHY. THEN THE BED-side phone rang as if somehow he knew it would. He sat up and grabbed the instrument, pressing the Bakelite speaker to his ear, and holding the microphone below his chin.

"Bell."

"It's me," Archie Abbott said. "We've got trouble."

Archie's words and tone sent a jolt of adrenaline through his heart and stripped away the gauzy curtain of sleep. Bell kicked the blankets and sheets from his legs and set his feet on the floor. He hadn't bothered closing his suite's heavy velvet drapes when he'd crawled into bed and a quick glance toward the window told him he was deep into the night with dawn a good way off.

"What's happened?"

"After dinner last night I convinced my father-in-law to let me search Reggie Hauser's office at the railroad's headquarters. It's where I am now. Nothing of note in the office, but Hauser had a safe. I tore the place apart looking for the combo when Oz told me he didn't know it. No luck. Do you remember Giacomo Spezhattori?"

"Jacko the Hat? The safecracker that owes you?"

"The same. I tracked him down to a billiards hall under the Third Avenue El on the Bowery. He came up to Midtown with me and cracked the safe."

Bell pulled the chain on the bedside Tiffany lamp to check the time. It was two in the morning. "And?"

"One-hundred-dollar Federal Reserve notes just like you described them. Ten thousand bucks."

"Bribe money," Bell deduced, as this final clue explained why the executive died. "Hauser wasn't going to be tortured to extract information about railroad scheduling. He'd already been paid for that."

"Whoever paid him off had second thoughts about the level of loyalty he'd bought and planned to kill Hauser instead."

"I think that's it exactly. Only, Hauser died before he could be tortured for the location of the incriminating money." Bell let his voice trail off as his mind played out various scenarios.

"What does this all mean?" Archie asked to fill the silence.

"They would only go after Hauser and the money they'd given him after he'd already fulfilled whatever it was they bribed him to do, right?"

"Presumably."

"Finding the new money in his safe means this ties back in with the Reserve Board and the attack on the *Mayflower*."

"Agreed."

"If you're part of a criminal enterprise and you double-cross a partner, don't you do it after the crime has been committed?"

"Usually. Or at least after they've used whatever they needed from you."

"There was one other item with the cash. A railroad schedule for Richmond. It had a penciled note on the margin, 'For Greenback,' but no other markings."

"That must be the trade-off," Bell said, "the routing information of the money trains traveling from Washington through Richmond, or an off-the-books train and clearance to some specified location."

"Has this train made its run, do you think?"

"No way to be sure, but I don't think so," Bell said at length. "The cash doesn't ship for several weeks yet. The obvious thing here is that whatever Hauser was paid to do links to how the Reserve is using the railroads to ship their money. A hijacking of some sort."

"There's too much time between the money shipping out and whatever Hauser did for the thieves," Archie said. "Their side deal could easily come off the rails between now and then, pardon the pun."

"That's the weird thing here. Why double-cross him weeks before you need the train he's providing information about?"

"Could they have killed him for another reason? Maybe he was getting cold feet and threatened to expose them."

"The marks on his wrists meant he was tied up. If you're going to ice the guy, just shoot him and be done with it."

"They wanted to know if he'd already told someone."

"Possibly." Bell paused before springing to his feet. "We're overthinking this. We need to stick to what is most likely. Double crosses always happen after the crime or just before it."

"And?"

Bell cursed. "What if they're not going to hijack one of the money trains? What if they're going to knock over the Bureau of Engraving instead?"

"You said its practically impregnable."

"If they've paid off a railroad executive, who knows how many others have been bribed to help."

"And killed?"

"Right. First thing tomorrow I want everyone in the Research Department combing through newspaper obituaries for suspicious or unusual deaths where the victim could have skills related to a major heist."

"Like what?"

Without needing to think, Bell said, "Known thieves, locksmiths, anyone involved in the design and construction of the Bureau building, mechanical engineers, mining engineers, blasting experts, hired muscle from crime gangs, anyone owning a fleet of cars like taxis or trucks, law enforcement with an emphasis on high-stakes thefts, especially banks or any other type of vault."

"How big of an area?"

"Eastern Seaboard from Boston to D.C. and as far west as Pittsburgh, but also include Chicago. Have them go back at least two weeks."

"Done. What are you going to do?"

"Looks like the rain has let up down here. I'm going to drive over to the Engraving building."

"A Friday night would be a good time to rob a bank."

"We couldn't get that lucky. No, I just want to look around and get a feel for the area at night. I'll call Fred Lawson first thing in the morning and tell him of our suspicions. It'll be best if he beefs up security until they get the bulk of the cash out to the regional banks. I'll call you tomorrow with an update."

"'Night."

Before he dressed, Bell called down to the concierge to ask that his car be brought around. He donned dark slacks and a black sweater over a plain undershirt. Rather than dress shoes he put on a pair of low boots with a sturdy tread. He shucked on his shoulder harness and made certain that the two slots for spare magazines were full. He grabbed two more spares and put them in the pockets of a lightweight duster that hung almost to his ankles. He added a two-cell flashlight and a pair of black kid gloves.

He didn't bother with a hat.

He took the stairs down from his fourth-floor rooms, knowing it was always quicker than the elevator. Bell's mind wanted to run down a dozen scenarios concerning the case. So much of it made no sense. If the Fed was the target, why pay accomplices with their yet-to-be-circulated bills? Any slipups by the thieves prior to the heist and the Treasury Department would know they were a target and take appropriate steps. He shook his head as if to clear it when he reached the hotel's opulent lobby. He had to focus on the here and now and leave speculations for later.

The same performance-enhanced Model T he'd driven following the air raid on the Potomac came around the corner of Pennsylvania Avenue just as he reached the curb. He tipped the attendant a buck and swung behind the wheel. There was absolutely no traffic and the city remained especially dim, with low scudding clouds hiding the moon and stars.

He turned south onto 14th Street and raced across the Mall. His headlights' reflection off the still-wet asphalt gave the road an oily sheen and forced him to squint despite the surrounding darkness. He came to a halt just a few minutes later in front of the Engraving and Printing building. None of the windows were lit with the exception of the main lobby. He mounted the stairs and peered inside to see a guard sitting behind an imposing counter.

Bell rapped on the glass to get the man's attention. He looked up from whatever he was reading and made a dismissive gesture with his hand as if to push Bell away from the building. Bell pounded a little harder and called, "This is an emergency."

Again the guard waved Bell away and returned to his reading. The Van Dorn detective hit the glass door even harder and with more urgency. The guard got off his stool and crossed the lobby so that he was standing opposite Bell.

"Go away, pal," he shouted through the glass.

"This is an emergency. My name is Isaac Bell. I'm working with Fred Lawson. Please open up."

"I ain't ever heard of you and no matter who you say you work with, there ain't no way I'm opening this door."

Bell realized his gaff. No one here knew him by his real name. "Wes McMahon. Do you know that name?"

"No. Now beat it, all right? This place will be open on Monday and you can talk to anyone you like then."

Bell recognized that he would never be able to talk his way into the printing plant. He said, "Just tell me if anything unusual has happened tonight, like the power flickering on or off or suspicious vehicles driving by."

The guard looked like he was just going to turn away without replying, but said with a touch of compassion in his voice, "No, mister. Nothing like that. Typical quiet night. Okay?"

"I guess that'll have to do," Bell said. "Thanks."

He turned away and looked up to the sky, when the clouds parted and the moon's milky glow shown through. He saw the zip-line wire immediately and deduced its purpose in the blink of an eye. He spun back in time to see the guard's hand coming away from his holster with a big revolver gripped in his fist. He was no guard. He was part of a crew hitting the Bureau in real time and he'd anticipated Bell's discovering their means of egress and almost had the shot when Bell dove to the sidewalk. He rolled hard as the fake guard fired three rapid shots. The glass was double thick, but at such close range the bullets penetrated. They were severely deflected by the glass and sailed harmlessly into the night.

The thick pane had gone opaque with tight whorls and spidery forks of cracked glass. The guard couldn't see where Bell had ended up, but Bell knew where the man had been standing. He'd already drawn his pistol and arched up from the sidewalk, placed the Browning's muzzle against the glass, and worked the trigger four times. All four hit the guard in a vital spot as he collapsed to the floor.

The glass window was a ragged mess after so much abuse, but no matter how hard Bell tried to kick it in, it wouldn't budge. He emptied the rest of the clip to no avail. The glass was just too tough and there was wire mesh embedded within it.

Bell ran back to his car, changing out the magazine for one from his duster pocket. He'd left the Ford idling and so he immediately put it in gear and slowly worked it up the shallow flight of steps before the main entry. He nosed the Model T against the damaged door and gunned the motor. The steel fender bent back on itself, but also dug into the weakening glass. With a crunch and a loud pop, the pane came apart into a thousand shards that glittered and spread across the lobby floor, the embedded mesh sagging to the floor.

He backed up the Model T to give him just enough room to crawl into the building by ducking under the door's horizontal brass handle. The guard had died quickly enough, so there was very little blood except for the stain from the bullets passing through his body. Looking around the dim space, Bell took a moment to riffle the man's pockets. He found nothing but a pack of cigarettes and an unmarked book of matches.

Bell's shootout and entrance into the building were far too loud for anyone inside not to have heard. That meant he was as much the hunted as he was the hunter. He padded across the lobby toward a set of double doors. He gently pushed down on the lever and pressed one of the doors open with the palm of his hand.

The response was a hail of gunfire from inside the stairwell with the kinetic energy to slam the door closed hard, leaving his hand vibrating in its skin. Bell swore and scooted away before jumping to his feet and running behind the security desk. There was a phone, but its cords had been sliced with a knife. He had to get help.

He went back to the front door and was ducking back outside through the hole he'd created when a bullet fired from above hit a piece of glass close to his head. The fragment shattered and a chip hit his cheek. He pulled back inside as quickly as possible, feeling for his wound and needing his fingertips to pull the shard from his flesh. His cheek was hot with blood. The shot had come from the roof of one of the building's central L-shaped wings.

He tried to stay low and see if he could pinpoint the sniper. The gunman had him pinned down and sent another high-powered round through the dim square where the glass had once been. The copper-jacketed bullet sparked off the floor and vanished inside the lobby at an oblique angle. Bell was left panting with adrenaline. He looked around. There were a few tall brass doors in the lobby that led deeper into the Bureau building. He checked them and found them all locked. They were too big to shoot his way through and the lockpicks he always carried were far too small to manipulate the locking pins.

He was trapped and had no idea what was going on in other parts of the structure. He crept back across the lobby to check the stairwell again. No sooner had he thumbed the lock than a half dozen bullets from an upper floor slammed into the stout metal door.

His frustration ran at a fever pitch, hot on the back of his neck and deep into the pit of his stomach. It had been Archie's offhand humor mentioning the heist was going down tonight. How could he have been so prophetic? How could Bell not have taken the threat more seriously? He should have at least called the District police.

And told them what, exactly?

He'd had no credible threat, no concrete suspicions—nothing more than a vague uneasy feeling that barely rose above the level of idle curiosity. More than anything Bell trusted his instincts and intuition. They'd served him well over a distinguished career, but even they could sometimes be off.

The thieves would have no choice but to back out of the building. He expected their escape route would take them off the building like they'd made their penetration—from the roof. There weren't a lot of residences left in this part of the city, but the rifle fire would attract attention. He had to trust that a Good Samaritan would call the police. That meant the cavalry were coming and he could hopefully lead the charge.

He tried the stairwell door again. The hail of bullets sounded just like before. Six rapid shots. He could hear the first pair hit the door low, with the next shots rising and the third ones rising higher still. He then realized something. That wasn't the shooting pattern of a pair of gunmen. That was a lone shooter firing two pistols gunslinger-style, unable to limit the barrel rise.

Bell stood, activated the thumb latch enough to release it, and kicked open the stairwell door, his pistol already raised and his finger curling through the guard as the scene came into focus. The stairs were marble-clad with oaken rails and banisters with a central opening between the zigzagging flights. The shooter was one flight up and directly opposite Bell's position. He was re-centering himself to fire back down the stairs when Bell got his sight picture and shot him in the throat. The man was flung back while his two revolvers dropped past Bell and down into the building's subbasement levels.

Bell took off at a run, climbing the stairs with his back to the wall, his pistol swinging to cover all blind spots. Clearing a stairwell required precision tactics and timing that couldn't be rushed, but Bell pushed his pace past what was sensible. If they left only one man to cover the stairwell, it meant the thieves were in retreat. Time was slipping away.

21

———◆———

B ELL SAW NOBODY, BUT AS HE WAS ABOUT TO CLIMB UP TO THE
fourth floor, he heard a metal door slam above him. He
corkscrewed up the last flights of stairs and came to the door he'd
just heard. He stood to the side and flipped it open. Like so many
times tonight, his action drew a barrage of gunfire. He ducked low
and peeked out for a moment. The roof was too dark to see many
details, but it looked like a cluster of men were rushing for a far
corner of the building. He slid out through the open door and
moved to his right, taking a route the fleeing thieves wouldn't
expect.

The building was so big that it was hard to see what was happening when the men reached the roof's edge. It looked like they
were jumping off the building because every few seconds the group
seemed smaller. He sped up. Suddenly there was only one of the
thieves left. He raised his pistol to fire, but the man simply vanished.

Bell ran forward and reached the edge a moment later. He looked down.

The lawn below was nearly black, but there was enough light from a handful of nearby streetlamps to tell there was no one down below. He remembered the zip line running across from the Department of Agriculture. There was another one here. It was attached near the eaves of a shed-like elevator housing and ran out into the night in the direction of the grounded barge that didn't look so grounded any longer. A tugboat was standing by to haul it away, its stern fixed to the barge by thick hemp lines.

He heard the sound of a person zooming along the length of the line. It reminded him of the tearing of a long piece of paper.

Bell didn't pause. He stripped his belt from its loops, threw it over the steel wire, and with a running start leapt off the building. The strain on his arms was immediate but manageable and his grip was firm. The problem was the friction between the leather and steel kept him to little more than a snail's pace.

Bell tried shifting his body to gain more speed, raising his legs and trying to make the belt jump off the wire to go a bit faster. He had barely made a hundred feet when at the other end of the zip line, the last thief to drop off the roof reached the barge.

A distant voice called out from the gloom ahead. "I hope you know this isn't personal."

Bell recognized the voice immediately, the mass murderer from the Staten Island Ferry. And then the wire was cut and he went from a controlled descent toward the river to a nearly four-story free fall.

He dropped through space for the first ten feet, his stomach an empty hollow inside his body, and then he felt scratchy wooden fingers grabbing at his head, body, and limbs. A tree. He was falling through a leafless tree. The instant he realized what was happening, he crossed his feet at the ankles to prevent his legs from spreading and opening him up to a most ruinous injury.

The branches of the upper canopy were mere twigs that he flew through as if they weren't there. When he fell lower still, the branches grew thicker and punched at his body like he was going toe-to-toe with a prizefighter. He tried to grab one to slow his madcap descent, but they were too springy to grasp. A branch swiped across the side of his head, feeling like it had ripped off his ear, though it had merely folded it back painfully fast. The limbs grew thicker and stronger by the second. Bell took a blow to the thigh that almost made him uncross his feet. He managed to grab on to that one as it zoomed past, but couldn't hold on to it at all. The maneuver twisted him from a vertical axis and opened him up for more punishing impacts.

He tumbled through the branches, taking shot after shot, his arms and hands cut bloody. He hit the largest limb yet, a lung-emptying impact right on his diaphragm. Against the tide of agony, he clutched at the branch, realizing below him was a twenty-foot drop to the ground. He hadn't fallen through the center of the tree, but had hit out near the edge of the canopy. The branch swayed and danced and drooped dramatically. Suddenly he could hear wood fibers snapping and tearing in toward where the limb attached to the trunk. He had to move.

Careful to keep the branch from swaying any more than necessary, Bell began wriggling along the wrist-sized limb, his bruised ribs scraping against the scaly bark. As he shifted the center of gravity, the branch began to spring back to its normal position. The snapping stopped.

Once he was close enough to the trunk and relatively safe, he looked around to see what was happening with the thieves. The barge and its attending tug were already out of the Tidal Basin and well down the shipping channel. Her single funnel had a damaged spark arrester because he could see a thin trail of glowing embers rising above her deck as she vanished into the night.

He couldn't let them get away.

Bell looked down. A fall from this height was survivable but potentially very injurious. A twisted ankle or broken collarbone would put him out of commission for far too long. He had no choice but to climb down to the ground. There wasn't enough light to comprehend the snarl of branches, limbs, and twigs and so he climbed blind, feeling for sturdier handholds and trying to avoid his face getting whipped by the tree. It took ten minutes to navigate to a branch low enough that when he hung from it, his feet were just four feet from the rain-softened ground. He dropped and rolled and came up on his feet.

He stripped off the muddy duster and set off at a sprint for the other side of the building and his waiting Model T. He reached the car wedged up against the building's main door, his lungs afire and his bruised ribs burning even hotter. Cranking the starter handle gave a new definition of agony. He worked through it. The pain he was gutting through wasn't the debilitating agony of a shattered leg forcing him to stop; rather it was his body's way of asking for him to slow down. It could be ignored.

The motor turned and caught with a blast of exhaust. Bell swung around to the driver's seat and settled the transmission into reverse. Immediately, the tire rubbed against the mangled fender. He cursed and lost precious time trying to work the metal away from the vulnerable pneumatic tire. Henry Ford built them too tough. He could free the tire when it was pointing straight, but a turn to the right brought the wheel in contact with the steel and he couldn't bend it any further without a hammer heavier than the tire iron he was forced to use.

Bell took this setback as he took all others, stoic on the outside, raging within. He backed the sedan down the few steps and over the curb, turning the wheel as gently as possible. The tire made a squelching sound when it rubbed up against the fender and gave off the noxious smell of burned rubber. The hotel was straight across the Mall and so long as he didn't encounter any traffic, he'd be okay. He stomped the gas and worked the gears so the finely tuned engine was humming at top speed. He reached the Willard in record time, swung left onto Pennsylvania, and mashed the brakes at the main entrance, a slow-to-react bellboy needing to jump back onto the sidewalk to avoid being hit.

"I'm Isaac Bell of the Van Dorn Agency," he said, leaping from the car before remembering his ribs and wincing when his feet hit the ground. "Fetch our second pool car quick and there's a twenty in it for you."

He ran upstairs to the Van Dorn office. It was quiet this night with only a single first-year agent on duty and he was asleep with his feet on his desk and his hat tipped over his eyes. He startled awake when Bell came through the door with the subtlety of a bull moose.

"Mr. Bell!" he cried in startled alarm, his sleepy eyes growing as big as saucers.

"Larry, get on the horn to New York. Tell Archie Abbott that we were wrong. It was tonight."

"What was tonight?" asked the young agent.

Bell was at one of the numerous safes kept in the offices. This one was full of ammo to reload the magazines he'd depleted. "He'll know. Just tell him what I said, that we were wrong and that it happened tonight." He handed over Fred Lawson's business card. "Tell him to call this guy and explain what happened."

"Yes, sir, Mr. Bell. Anything else?"

"Rustle up the on-call agents and head over to the main entrance of the Bureau of Engraving building. Do you know it?"

"Across the Mall on Fourteenth Street."

"Stand guard there. Don't let anyone in until Fred Lawson arrives. He's their chief of security."

"What about—"

"No questions asked. This is a federal matter. The D.C. cops have no jurisdiction." Bell wasn't sure if that last statement was true, doubted it actually, but the kid believed him and that was enough. "I'm leaving you a car downstairs. It's a little beat-up, so be careful with the steering. On the jump now."

With four full magazines for the Browning and his orders being carried out, Bell rushed back downstairs just as the second Agency car came around the corner. As promised, he handed the valet a twenty-dollar bill and roared away from the Willard with a singular focus.

Deductive reasoning led him to believe the thieves would eventually make their escape through more-urbanized Virginia. Because they were going to transfer the money to a train, there were more rail lines in the commonwealth than the corresponding Maryland side of the Potomac.

Or were they? he wondered. Could the murder of rail executive Reggie Hauser have been a red herring cleverly laid to throw off the investigation? Could his murder and the placement of Federal Reserve notes in his office safe have been a ruse? Bell had to consider the possibility. He was dealing with a master thief, someone who had just planned and executed the greatest heist in history. To what lengths would he go to cover his tracks?

No, he decided almost as soon as the doubt hit him. The barge was slow and conspicuous. They would need to abandon it quickly. That left a transfer to another boat, doubtful since he imagined Lawson ordering every craft on the Potomac be searched. Or the money would be moved to a fleet of cars or trucks, or a train.

Even if he hadn't known about the railroad angle to the heist, he never thought they'd move the money in a bunch of vehicles. If he'd just stolen a billion dollars, there was no way he'd let one red cent out of his sight. The thief was going to stay with his loot. All of his loot. That meant the bags of cash were going to leave the area by rail.

Bell crossed the Potomac into Virginia and made his way south. He wasn't at all familiar with the area, so he drove by instinct, trying always to keep the river on his left. He calculated the time he'd lost versus his estimated speed of the towed barge. They were miles ahead and every time he took a wrong turn or found himself at the end of a dead-end lane, that gap widened.

Bell drove on through the night, taking roads that had the potential to lead him to the river and often having to backtrack out again when they came up short of where he needed to be. It soon felt hopeless. He came across a couple of sleepy towns clinging to the Potomac's bank. The railroads so dominated freight and passenger transportation that the docks were all but abandoned. He stared out across the black shining water from a gravel parking lot next to a pier with a single workboat at anchor. There was no way of knowing how long ago the barge had been led past this spot. He knew for certain, though, that he hadn't gotten ahead of it.

He continued south, not driving with the urgency that saw him fly out of the nation's capital two hours earlier. The road looped through the night, passing dark farms set in the middle of open fields and cutting through forests that had once been cleared during the colonial period and now looked like old growth once again.

The landscape was rising in elevation and he felt himself more disconnected from the river than ever. He vowed to give the search fifteen more minutes and then he would turn around and aid in the investigation back at the Bureau of Engraving and Printing. Archie would have contacted Fred Lawson as soon as he got Bell's message. The building had to be crawling with T-men by now. His place was back there, he decided.

Just then he broke out of the woods and found himself riding along the crest of a bluff that overlooked the river nearly two hundred feet below. The clouds had long since been blown to the east and the moon appeared silver and bright. A set of train tracks ran along the narrow strip of land abutting the river's edge. He saw a locomotive with several freight cars behind the coal tender. Men with fiery torches and handheld flashlights were milling around the idling locomotive, looking like spectral wraiths amid the steam pouring out the expansion exhausts. Adrift in the river was the barge, freed once again from the tugboat. It appeared to be sinking for real this time.

Almost lost from sight as it chugged south for the Chesapeake Bay, the tug with its damaged spark arrester was a red ember growing too dim to see.

With neither bell nor whistle, the train started to move, its great drive wheels revolving slowly at first, but the power of the expanding and cooling steam within her boiler soon overcame the engine's massive inertia. Men scrambled up ladders to sit atop the boxcars or hung out in the wagons, sitting with their legs dangling or leaning against the open cargo doors.

Bell felt it was the first break he'd gotten this night. The road he was on looked like it paralleled the rails from a little higher up on the bluff.

The chase was on.

22

B ELL KNEW THAT HIS ABILITY TO TRACK THE TRAIN CAME
from simple geography and whatever residual luck he still
possessed. The railroad had to follow the flattest path to make
construction easier and the lines more profitable. Roads for automobiles generally followed alongside them if their destinations
were the same. However, that wasn't the case very often. Rail lines
generally ran from city to city with stations in between if a town
happened to be on the route, otherwise there was no need to stop
at all. America's roads, especially the rural ones, meandered from
town to town in a seemingly haphazard fashion, ignoring terrain if
necessary and generally with the logic of a child's scribbled scrawl.

He couldn't rely on the road and rail line remaining parallel for
very long. If he was going to foil the heist, he needed a way to get
on the train.

Below, the locomotive was picking up speed. The thieves kept the single headlamp burning brightly, as they knew they were a scheduled train, thanks to the late rail executive Reggie Hauser, and had nothing to hide. They maxed out at about thirty miles per hour, a safe speed for the conditions, and Bell had no trouble keeping pace in the tuned Ford.

The tracks stopped running along the banks of the Potomac. The river receded to Bell's left and the road and the railway tracks cut out through open country. The road was no longer above the tracks, but at the same elevation, and only about thirty feet separated the two lines. Bell slowed and proceeded to follow the train at a comfortable distance. With his own lights doused he doubted anyone could see him and the locomotive's own steaming boiler and the clatter of steel wheels on the rails meant they couldn't hear him, either.

Again he was faced with the real likelihood that the road would diverge from the railroad tracks at any time. He tried to recall a Virginia map in his mind. He believed they were heading south toward the city of Richmond and that Fredericksburg lay someplace in the middle. Would they stop there? He could only speculate.

He was not aware of the passage of time, only that the train remained tantalizingly ahead of him and yet totally out of reach. There was nothing he could do to slow the behemoth. Sacrificing the Ford by stopping it on the tracks at a crossing would be a useless gesture. The train would swat it aside the way a horse's tail swipes at flies.

The terrain soon changed again, and Bell found himself climbing up and down hills, while the train arrowed through specially dug trenches and the occasional tunnel. From the top of a particularly tall hill, Bell looked east and saw the first blush of a rising sun painting the underside of clouds far out over the Atlantic. Ahead, he saw the feeble light turning the surface of a distant river to bronze. He imagined the railroad had built a bridge to cross the river, but with no distant lights of any town in sight, Bell felt certain there would be no bridge for this rural dirt road. He was about to lose the train if he didn't think of something quick.

The car rode up onto the spine of another long hill. The train was once again below him, the top of the cars almost hidden as they trundled inside another long trench. In the blink of an eye, the locomotive and its cars vanished altogether. It took Bell a startled moment to realize it had entered another tunnel, a long one by the looks of it. He looked ahead, the approaching dawn revealing fresh details.

The road would soon turn sharply to the right, as he'd suspected, and run along the banks of this unknown river, while there was an iron bridge built on mortared stone piers to take the train across the water shortly after it emerged from the tunnel. At the bend, it appeared the road and tunnel were nearly on top of each other.

Bell pressed his foot to the floor, even as he questioned the sanity of what he was about to attempt. A moment's hesitation came and went. These men were the ones who attacked his father and the other Fed bankers and killed over a hundred people on the Staten Island Ferry. They'd left a trail of bodies in their wake, and they were about to escape.

Like hell, he thought, and practically pressed his foot through the floorboard.

The four-cylinder engine moaned. As was common on longer tunnels, there were a couple of vents that linked the subterranean passageway to the surface in order to dissipate smoke and steam. He could track the train's progress by the escaping geysers of exhaust and adjusted his speed accordingly. He had one shot, and if he blew it, his best-case scenario was probably a month in the hospital.

The locomotive emerged from the tunnel in a blast of steam and soot, followed immediately by the coal tender. Ahead of Bell was a sharp turn to the right at the top of a steep hill overlooking the river. The train was slightly to his left and below the roadway, heading straight for the bridge.

The guardrail that curved around with the road was made of rough-sawn planks supported by creosote-coated wooden posts. Bell gave the car a final correction and braced. He needn't have bothered. The old wooden rails were so dry-rotted that they turned to powder when the radiator slammed into them. The front tires hit the lip of the hill, a slight rise that lifted the nose enough so when the car left the ground, it was pitched up.

The momentum and angles involved started the car to spiral slightly, like a football, but the distance it had to cover was only about five feet. It landed atop the last railcar on its left-side wheels. Both collapsed at the impact and the car nearly flipped onto its side. It fell back onto its two remaining tires and a shaken Isaac Bell used both feet to mash the Model T's beefed-up brakes, while a shower of sparks danced to his left where the stubs of the axles scraped against the boxcar's metal roof.

Bell opened the door as soon as the car came to a stop. He found himself looking down from the top of the car all the way to the track's crossties whizzing past. The Ford had stopped precariously close to the edge and partially suspended between two of the railcars. He slid across to the passenger-side door and eased it open. Expecting the element of surprise was wearing off and that the thieves would soon open fire, he had his pistol ready.

The train entered a final curve before shooting out across the long metal bridge. As the final two cars entered the corner, the forces working to keep the Model T in place shifted dynamically and the Ford began to fall from the top of the boxcar. Bell leapt just as the car fell off the train. It hit the bed of gravel ballast the railroad's wooden crossties rested on and tumbled under the last set of wheels. The Ford was literally torn in half in a shrieking collision and then sent skittering out in a scattershot of ripped steel and loose parts.

Bell lay motionless on the train's roof, unsure why no one was firing at him. He looked around and saw no targets, no men guarding the train like he'd seen when they'd loaded it back at the Potomac. Were they all now down below in the boxcars?

The train trundled onto the bridge. There were so many stone piers that it needed no additional trusses. It was flat and utilitarian.

The guards had vanished, which led him to believe the train engineer and brakeman were also gone. Which meant? Bell looked over the side of the boxcar. The water was only fifteen feet or so below the rails and moving sluggishly. It was impossible to tell its depth, but he had a sinking feeling it was plenty deep enough to hide a stolen train. Just past halfway across the river, Bell heard a sound like a sledgehammer pounding a giant gong.

He looked ahead and saw the locomotive jerk up on its left side and come down again with its giant drive wheels outside the rail and clattering against the bridge's deck. Bell knew enough about trains to know his had just hit a derailer, a device that clamps to a rail and causes an intentional derailment. Typically used as a fail-safe device during construction to prevent a runaway car from injuring workers, he'd seen them used countless times for intentional sabotage.

The big locomotive began to roll onto its side as the wheels slid off the bridge, its tremendous weight twisting the attached coal carrier until it, too, left the rails. The train was going to flip completely before plunging into the river below.

The first car behind the coal tender was pulled up and started to topple before reaching the derailer, but when it struck the device, it was as if some force in the water yanked at it. The next car followed its brethren and the next one, too, before the engine's hot boiler and firebox hit the river in a muffled explosion of steam and steel.

Bell had seconds only. He lurched to his feet while tossing aside his pistol. Either in his hand or in its holster, the gun would likely strike him in the face when he hit the river. He began sprinting for the back of this final car and just as he reached the right rear corner he leapt as hard and as far as he could, but in such a way that he spun one hundred and eighty degrees. This got him facing forward when he slammed into the water, his ankles and knees clenched tightly together and his arms up to protect his face.

His sprint had negated about fifteen miles per hour of the train's forward speed, but still the blow was a heavy one because of the angle of impact. The breath he tried to hold exploded from his lungs. He was driven deep enough that he was giving in to panic before he clawed his way back to the weak predawn light. The final railcar crashed into the river on the other side of the bridge, throwing up titanic walls of water. Steam continued to bubble up from the submerged locomotive. Wisps of it clung to the river's surface like fog on some haunted English moor.

Panting to refill his bruised lungs, Bell let the current push him to one of the stone support piers. The mortar was old and crumbly and afforded him an easy grip. The water retained a little summer warmth and so he clung to the pier in order to catch his breath. His body ached from the abuse it had endured this night. He gave in to the pain for a few moments and shut down his brain.

With his mind blank and the natural sound of water burbling by, he felt almost at peace. He'd done everything humanly possible to stop the thieves. While normally he kept his failures fresh in his mind so that the shame of them fueled him to always do better, this time he let it go. There was no point in self-recrimination. He'd done his best and come up short. It happened.

At first he thought his ears were playing tricks on him. He could have sworn he heard singing from up on the bridge. It was faint at first, but grew steadily louder. He knew the tune.

Or when the valley's hushed and white with snow,
'Tis I'll be here in sunshine or in shadow.
Oh, Danny boy, oh Danny boy, I love you so!

One of Bell's gifts was his ability to recall faces. It's what made him such a legendary investigator. He could meet someone only twice in his life, years apart, and not only would he recognize the individual, but he also generally remembered the circumstances of their first interaction as well as personal details if any were shared.

The same could not be said for voices. He had no more recall of them than anyone else. Except on this occasion. He knew the singer above him, knew him by the impish Irish lilt that masked the heart of a monster. Bell quietly swam around the stone bridge support searching for a ladder, but there was no way up.

As Bell searched, he heard the little man grunt at some difficult task, followed by a sharp splash. He'd unhooked the diverter and tossed it into the river, after the train it had sent tumbling from the tracks. On his return trip, he whistled "Danny Boy" rather than sing it.

The little Irishman's tune faded into the night.

Unarmed, and knowing that there was no civilization for miles behind him, Bell started swimming across the river, resting at each of the stone piers because the bruising he'd endured from the fall was beginning to take its toll and cramp his body.

He hadn't yet made the far bank when another train clattered across the bridge in the opposite direction. Bell had thought his presence back in Washington had pushed the thieves into leaving the Bureau of Engraving earlier than planned. And maybe it was true, but only to a point. He realized now that the heist had been timed to precision. Had they stayed twenty minutes longer, their train and this one would have struck head-on. But that had not come to pass and now the train loaded with the money was safely in the one place no one would ever look. The thieves could come back and salvage the bags, which were surely waterproof, any time they pleased.

Something about the meticulousness of the operation niggled at the back of his mind, but he was too physically and emotionally exhausted to examine it further.

Bell emerged from the water just as the sun finally appeared over the eastern horizon. He was soaked through and cold. Without knowing how far he'd need to travel, he took a second to start a fire using sun-bleached driftwood and matches he kept in a small silver screw-top case Marion had given him years earlier.

He was just about to strip out of his wet clothes when a canoe appeared from downriver with two teenage boys at the paddles. The tips of their fishing rods poked over the canoe's gunwale.

"Hey, fellas," Bell called and startled the pair. They eyed him with suspicion, but stopped paddling. "Twenty bucks if you can row me to the closest town."

The two exchanged a glance. One said, "Prove it or no dice."

Bell pulled a soggy note from a vest pocket.

"Deal."

23

———⚮———

IT TURNED OUT THE NEAREST TOWN WAS A MILE DOWNRIVER and around a bend that had hid it from Bell's view. There was a concrete commercial dock fronting the small town and Bell left the boys there. The town was a grid of four streets, with a large park overlooked by the county courthouse. Its perimeter was bare-branched elms and in its center stood a verdigris statue of a Civil War–era horseman.

The sheriff's office was attached to the back of the courthouse. The man himself was loading something into the trunk of a marked patrol car.

"Early start for a Saturday morning," Bell said as he approached.

The sheriff closed the trunk and studied the stranger in dark wet clothing standing dripping into the street outside his office. The sheriff was in his fifties, paunchy but with thick shoulders and strong-looking hands. His eyes were a watery blue nearly hidden in pouches and his skin had the pocked scars of some childhood ailment.

"Got word of some commotion out near the railroad bridge a mile north a here."

"I can save you a trip. Five boxcars plus the locomotive and tender went off the bridge about forty minutes ago."

"Oh, Lord's sake," he exclaimed. "Anyone get out?"

"I am almost certain that I was the only one aboard when she went over. My name is Isaac Bell. I am the Van Dorn Agency's lead detective, and the derailed train is part of a far larger crime. There was a theft in Washington, D.C., last night and the thieves made their getaway on that train."

The sheriff nodded with recognition at the mention of Van Dorn, but maintained a cop's healthy skepticism. "And it just happened to derail over the river?"

"They used a derailer to send her off the tracks. I believe they planned this all out in advance. Is that spot in the river deep?"

"There's a hole in the river bottom under that bridge nearly eighty feet deep. Railroad surveyors missed it and they'd laid too much track to reroute the line once they discovered it. That bridge nearly bankrupted them. Big scandal at the time."

"I figured it would be something like that," Bell said. "The mastermind behind all this leaves no detail to chance. Eventually clues in the case would lead an investigation to believe they had used the railway system to escape Washington. Rather than hide the cars on a siding someplace they could be discovered, they sank the train in a river with plans on returning when the heat dies down. They just didn't expect a witness to be aboard."

"What was it that was stolen, Mr. Bell?"

He considered how much to tell the sheriff. This was going to be a federal case with national implications, and it wasn't up to him to read in the local law enforcement. "It was a bank heist, Sheriff . . ."

"Bill Dunham."

"Sheriff Dunham. Quite possibly the largest that's ever been pulled off. We need to get men down to the bridge to ensure no one attempts to enter the sunken railcars. Armed men at that, because these thieves have no aversion to murdering anyone who gets in their way and that includes the victims of the Staten Island Ferry that sank this past Tuesday."

"I read about that," he said.

"I experienced it firsthand." Bell gave voice to a sudden realization. "They were trying to kill me."

His earlier speculative conversation with Archie had been right. They wanted to kill him before the theft because they feared he would get assigned the case. He was considered the best detective in the country and he had a connection to the Federal Reserve through his father. It would make sense he'd be called in to assist the government. This time his notoriety had become a lead weight in his gut.

"I'd best call my deputies," the sheriff said.

"And I need to get to Washington to tell the powers that be everything that transpired last night. Anyplace in town I can rent a car?"

"Not at this hour," Dunham said, and paused as if considering something. "You really with Van Dorn?" Bell showed him his re-issued company identification. "All right. You can borrow my car so long as you come back by this afternoon."

"I appreciate that, Sheriff. I'll make sure the tank is full when I return. That said, I will need directions. I have no idea where I am."

Two hours later, Bell found a parking spot two blocks from the Bureau of Engraving and Printing building. As he approached, he saw little out of the ordinary. He noted that the wire that had stretched from the Department of Agriculture building had been removed and he assumed the one that had run out to the barge was also gone. The building looked sealed up like it would be for any other Saturday morning. As he neared the imposing structure, he saw that the window he'd crashed through had already been replaced with a piece of flat steel. He turned to mount the low steps and was startled by a man who'd been lurking just out of view.

"Sir, this is a restricted government building. You are not allowed to be here." Bell noted two other agents had emerged from the shadows, hands resting on guns hidden under their suit coats.

"My name is Isaac Bell. I'm a Van Dorn agent known to Fred Lawson as Wes McMahon." That made no impression on the man's stony face. "I was here last night at the tail end of the break-in. I am responsible for the Van Dorn agents guarding the building until you guys arrived."

"Sir, there was no break-in. Just some vandals smashed a window."

Bell realized either they didn't know or they had their cover story and were sticking to it. "Fred is here, correct?"

"I'm not at liberty to say. Sir, please move on. I'm not going to tell you again." With that veiled warning, the other T-men closed ranks a little tighter.

Bell understood that he would need to go through channels by returning to the Willard and calling the number Fred gave him. At most a half hour wasted, but it was a frustration he didn't need.

He turned on his heel to leave, when one of the undamaged doors opened and Fred Lawson popped his head out.

"It's okay, fellas," he called in a voice dripping with exhaustion. "I know this man."

Still playing the part of tough guys, the government agents didn't exactly clear a path for Bell. He shouldered past them and climbed up to the door. He shook Lawson's hand. "For the record, you don't know me. I'm here in D.C. undercover. I am a Van Dorn agent, but my name is Isaac Bell and not Wes McMahon."

"What? Why?"

"The thieves who knocked this place over last night tried to have me killed in New York last week and I thought it's better if they believed they'd succeeded. Now it doesn't matter."

"I guess not. Bell?"

"Yes, Isaac Bell."

"Nice to meet you for a second time. I was just on my way down to the vault when I saw you outside. This is an unmitigated disaster."

"It's not as bad as you think. The money is sunk inside a railcar two hours' drive from here. It's being guarded by local sheriff's deputies as we speak."

Lawson nearly tripped at hearing the news. "What?"

"You heard me. I managed to follow the thieves last night. They first loaded the money onto the barge—"

"I figured that when I saw it was gone," Lawson interrupted.

"Right. Then they transferred it onto a train. I was able to follow the train and eventually get aboard, but that was just before they derailed it on a bridge over a particularly deep river."

"Why would they do that? Why transfer it to a train? They were getting away."

"The barge was too slow and conspicuous. They had to ditch it and then ditch the train because they left a trail that led to a particular railway executive, and some digging into his work would reveal the serial numbers of the cars he'd arranged for their benefit. They understood that those cars wouldn't make it past the next jerkwater town once the government alerted the nation's rail network. Better to hide them where no one would look and go back later to retrieve the money."

"Seems like a big risk."

"It's a fairly common technique, though admittedly this is on a grand scale. You see, thieves will often stash loot near the scene of a crime because they can't risk being seen with it right away. I once saw a thief snatch a diamond necklace from a lady whose husband I was guarding. He tossed it into a public trash can almost immediately. He was only caught because I happened to be there."

"Huh."

"Another trick is to hand an item off to an accomplice. The thief might get noticed and frisked, but since he no longer has the loot, he's set free."

"If you say so."

"How much did they get?" Bell asked.

"I was heading down to the vault to get the running tally. Last I checked it was four hundred and twenty million dollars."

Bell gave a low whistle.

"Trust me, it'll be more. Lots more."

Lawson invited Bell to come in and tell him exactly what had transpired the night before. Halfway through the tale, they reached the vault. Bell took some time examining the device the thieves had left attached to the door that allowed them to pick the enormous lock protecting the main vault dials. He'd never seen anything like it. Inside the vault, grim-faced men with sleeve garters on their arms were going over the tallies of what should be in the cages versus what had been left behind.

"Mr. Lawson," the supervisor holding a clipboard greeted his boss when they entered.

"How bad, Bruce?"

"Eight sixty and we have at least another twenty minutes of work."

"So near enough to a billion dollars?"

"Afraid so."

"This is Isaac Bell. He's a Van Dorn man. He gave me some amazing news just now. The money is on a submerged train about a hundred miles from here."

"Really, sir? Why, that's wonderful news. The best of news, in fact. Just wow. Did you hear that boys? The thieves didn't get away with the money after all."

The men gave a throaty roar.

BELL FINISHED HIS STORY IN LAWSON'S OFFICE.
"That's a hell of a thing you did. On behalf of the United States Department of Treasury, I want to say how grateful I am for your quick thinking and bravery."

"I appreciate that," Bell said simply and turned the conversation away from himself. "How do you want to proceed?"

"What do you mean?"

"Right now, a couple of sheriff's deputies are watching the money. In the minds of the thieves who might be watching over the river, their presence can be explained away because someone heard a loud noise last night out that way. We can pull them off the site and watch the bridge from a covered position and wait for the thieves to show themselves. We get the money and the bad guys all at once."

"This will be decided by the President and Secretary McAdoo, but I don't think that's the way to go."

"Why not?"

"Because the nation can never know the robbery even took place. Banking is built on trust. People trust their bank with their money and as long as the bank remains a good, honest steward, everything is fine. But if there is a whiff of scandal, a hint at something off, real or imagined, people want their money back right away and it turns into a stampede."

"Bank runs. They happen pretty often."

"The problem is that once people run on one bank that *could* be in trouble, other folks will want to withdraw from their bank as well, even if there is no issue with it. This causes massive recessions like the one we had back in '07.

"Now we're asking folks to put their trust in a brand-new monetary system and currency. Most people have never dealt with the government on the federal level. They have no idea who we are or what we do. Washington seems like a foreign country to them. So in order to make the Fed system work, the rollout has to be flawless. People must believe in our operation or they won't give up the millions and millions of dollars they have hidden in basement mason jars or stored under mattresses."

"I think I see your problem," Bell remarked.

"If word gets out that we couldn't protect our money here, at its source, no one is going to rely on it for their day-to-day needs. The Reserve system dies before it's even born."

"The last thing you want is for the thieves to go on trial and the details of the robbery to become public."

Lawson nodded. "Even at the cost of the money they stole, if I was being honest here. The fact that we can recover it is a bonus, really."

Bell was a little stunned by that admission. "If I hadn't found the money, you'd have let them get away with it and done nothing?"

"I'm not saying that," Lawson said quickly. "Certainly, we would do everything in our power to hunt them down, but if the cost of that was exposing our vulnerabilities to the public, then other factors would need to be considered, other avenues explored."

Bell had in his head the image of an Old West posse shooting first and asking questions much, much later.

Someone knocked on Lawson's door. It was the counting supervisor from the vault.

"Got a final tally, Bruce?"

"Yes, Mr. Lawson. Nine hundred and forty-five million, give or take."

That number hung in the air for several long seconds. The supervisor backed from the office and closed the door.

"To think," Lawson said at last, "that when the new currency goes into circulation, whoever masterminded this heist could rival John Rockefeller as the richest man in America."

24

ISAAC BELL WASN'T FORMALLY HIRED AS PART OF THE RECOVERY operation, but nonetheless he was on hand twenty-four hours later when a diver in a three-window bronze helmet, lead-soled shoes, and a waterproof canvas suit was ready to be lowered into the river. He was a civilian contractor on loan from the Washington Navy Yard. The dive team was working off a Chesapeake trawler that had been brought upriver and anchored upstream from the sunken train. Its derrick had to be lowered to pass under the bridge, but was now re-stepped and ready to lift the diver over the gunwale on a special cradle trucked down from D.C.

It was an overcast morning, chilly and raw with rain in the forecast. Bell wore a thick peacoat over wool pants and a soft denim shirt. Engineers from the railroad had already inspected and certified that the bridge hadn't been damaged by the derailing and the line remained open. As a result, onlookers were resigned to watching the proceedings from the distant riverbanks. Bell had gotten himself a coveted spot on the trawler with Fred Lawson and Treasury Secretary McAdoo. Archie Abbott was there, too, having arrived from New York earlier that morning.

A grizzled petty officer acted as divemaster and stood next to the bleating air compressor while the trawler's owner stood by at the derrick controls. The diver and his gear had already been triple-checked. Another member of the dive team stood ready to pay out the vulnerable hose that supplied the diver with life-giving air. They were upriver of the derailed train so that they had better control over the hose and could make certain it didn't get snagged or, more dangerously, cut by the debris on the riverbed.

The diver made a gesture that he was ready and the petty officer threw a curt nod to the trawlerman. He eased back on the crane controls and the cradle, called a dive stage, lifted from the deck. He paused so that the platform fully stabilized before raising it up over the gunwale and then lowered it into the river. The assistant was letting the hose pay out through his hands.

It took several minutes to lower the diver standing in the cradle all the way to the bottom. Judging by the angle of the line entering the water, the current had pushed the man a good twenty feet downriver by the time he got settled.

There was no communication with the diver, though experiments were underway for a telephone connection to run alongside the air hose. The observers could only speculate on what the man was doing down below by watching the hose move one way and then another as he walked along the length of the submerged locomotive and her equally sunken string of cars.

Twenty minutes crawled by. A light rain started to fall. The guards watching over the site and the authorized employees of the Bureau of Engraving and Printing had grown bored and returned to their cars.

Another fifteen minutes passed and even Bell's patience was wearing a little thin. He was sore and stiff from the beating he'd taken falling through the tree and again when he jumped from the road over to the train in his car. The cold was seeping into his bones and his mind conjured up dreams of a steaming bath and a snifter of brandy the size of a fishbowl.

"He's back," cried the assistant paying out the air hose. The flexible line was jumping in his hands as the diver down below gave it several hard tugs.

"You watch that line as you haul it back, ya hear?" warned the petty officer, the gnawed stub of a cigar tucked into the corner of his mouth.

"Aye, Chief."

Once again at the controls, the trawler captain slowly raised the platform from the depths while the dive assistant pulled up air hose and coiled it expertly at his feet. The chief called for a decompression stop during the ascent, which slowed the procedure.

The water was so dark there was scant warning to know the dive stage had reached the surface. It came up in a rush of white water. The diver stood with his hands clutching the stanchions, his body fighting the tremendous number of weights he'd been forced to carry to counter the buoyancy of his air-filled suit. Once he was high enough, a deckhand pulled in the outstretched derrick arm and centered it over the trawler's open aft deck.

The captain lowered the diver to allow the platform to touch down as lightly as possible. The assistant was already there with a stout wooden stool. The diver sat gratefully with his help. The petty officer came over to help remove the fifty-five-pound helmet from the man's sweaty head. He was handed a towel to wipe his face.

Even with the water being chilly at that depth, diving against the current looked to Bell to be tougher than an hour sparring at Cicchetti's gym.

"Well?" asked Secretary McAdoo quickly.

"Train's there all right. The engine is a mess. The boiler burst when it went in, and the firebox, too, came apart on account of the cold water hitting the hot iron. The coal tender's right behind it and still attached."

"What about the boxcars?"

"They opened the side doors so that they sank right away. Two landed on their wheels and I could tell they were empty. The other two came down on their sides. It's too risky to try and climb them without another diver watching my line, so I don't know what's in them."

"Five," said Bell.

"Huh?"

"There were five cars in that train, plus the engine and coal car."

"Wait, what?" McAdoo cried, thoughts of an easy resolution to this nightmare evaporating.

"When I saw them loading the train from the barge, there were five cars."

"There are only four cars down there," the diver countered. "They were all still in a row, as pretty as you please. But just to make sure I swept back toward the far bank for a good hundred feet. Nothing there."

"Bell, are you sure what you saw?" Fred Lawson asked, just as concerned as the treasury secretary. "Could you have mistaken the coal car or something?"

"I know what I saw," Bell replied with utter conviction. "My job depends on my observational skills. I'm not mistak . . ."

His voice trailed off.

Archie knew the look that settled on his friend's face. He gave Bell a moment to order his thoughts and said, "What have you got?"

"I thought I miscalculated when I jumped my car onto the train. I had planned to land on the fourth boxcar, to give me a margin of safety, but I landed on the last car instead, what I assumed at the time was the fifth. My timing was right all along. I did land on the fourth car. It's just that the fifth was no longer with the train."

Bell paused again as he remembered another detail from the night before. A second train had passed over the bridge minutes after the derailment, which meant the missing car, the one loaded with nearly a billion dollars in cash, had to have been uncoupled not long after it had been loaded.

"It's long gone," he said. "When I was following the train, there were plenty of times it was out of my sight. Furthermore, I'd stopped paying attention to the number of cars the engine was hauling. I was just satisfied keeping up with it."

That didn't ring true even as he said it. Bell hadn't consciously kept counting the number of freight cars, but he knew how his mind worked. Had one gone missing during the trip from the Potomac to here, he would have noticed. Full stop.

Bell turned his attention to the diver. They'd removed the weights that had hung on his chest and peeled the suit down to his waist. A thick towel had been draped over his shoulders. "You're absolutely certain there are only four cars down there?"

"Rivers are usually murky, but this one isn't too bad. The

visibility was fine and my dive light is one of the brightest ones made. There are only four cars. I'd stake my professional reputation on that."

Bell looked at the trawler captain and said, "Take me to the far shore."

"Water gets too shallow," the man replied.

"Just get me as close as you can."

"What's going on, Bell?" McAdoo asked, a fresh glimmer of hope in his voice.

"There are four boxcars in the river and I'm almost certain that five cars entered the tunnel. Therefore . . ."

Archie said, "Little bit of sleight of hand with a twenty-ton train car. Impressive."

WORKING THE WHEEL AND THROTTLES, THE TRAWLER'S captain edged his boat as closely as possible to the grassy riverbank, while his deckhand rustled up a D-cell flashlight.

"We should wait," Fred Lawson said. "That's an active rail line. What happens if a train comes and you're in the tunnel?"

"We haven't seen a single train since we got here," Bell replied. "It's a risk we're willing to take."

Once they were in position, Bell made certain the locks were off the derrick's boom and the dive stage was disconnected. Holding the hook in both hands, Bell stepped up onto the rail on the starboard side of the boat, away from shore. He judged the distance and set off at a run along the rail, rounding the side and onto the transom and then threw himself into space. The boom swung him out over the water, while the rope he clutched swung him over the shoreline. At the perfect moment, he let go of the hook and landed with an acrobat's ease. A stunned silence was followed by raucous cheering at such an unexpected and athletic feat.

"Show off," Archie called across, a tinge of reluctance in his baritone.

The deckhand used a rope to retrieve the out-swung boom, and Archie took up position on the gunwale just as Bell had. He retraced his friend's movement, rounding onto the transom and then leaping for the shore. He landed just in front of Bell, but awkwardly. He started to fall back, his arms windmilling wildly to keep him from falling into the water. Bell was there to grab Archie by his belt and pull him to a more stable posture.

"Thanks, old boy," Abbott said with a nervous grin.

"Just trying to keep your laundry bill down."

The bank was steep, forcing both men to use their hands as they climbed up to the level of the train tracks and the tunnel entrance a short distance away. They passed the ruined husk of Bell's Model T laying next to the rails. The passenger compartment was crushed flat, and the engine had been torn from its mounts. Amid the thorny weeds growing along the railway's verge the ground was littered with glass chips from the Ford's shattered windows.

They reached the tunnel moments later. Because the day was so overcast, the far opening was a dim circle that wasn't exactly light, but not complete darkness, either. The tunnel had to be a thousand feet long, its walls and ceiling sheathed in mortared bricks.

Bell switched on the borrowed flashlight. "Shall we?"

"Let's," Archie replied. Twenty feet into the tunnel he asked, "What exactly are we looking for?"

"A secret spur, is my guess."

"You think the thieves took the time to excavate a siding inside this tunnel? In total secrecy?"

"No. I think the thieves learned about an existing siding from your father-in-law's trusted executive."

"Ah, the great and now late Reggie Hauser."

"That's the man. His involvement might have been deeper than providing a train and clearing the tracks for the thieves."

"And he got double-crossed before the deed was even done," Archie remarked. "On that front, the Research Department came up with a suspicious death. A Philadelphia locksmith named Harvey Wanamaker was found suffocated in a large safe in his workroom. It appeared some shelves had collapsed and locked him in while he was working."

"Odd, but possible."

"But not likely. Here's what our guys dug up. Harvey T. Wanamaker was a safecracker from the old school. A real yegg. Did two years back in '79 and a fiver in '88. He's been clean, so far as we could tell, but who knows."

"Any chance he was a toolmaker?"

Archie replied immediately. "The obit said he was a master craftsman."

"There were some bespoke precision tools that the thieves needed to even reach the vault's dials. Could be your yegg made them and got whacked for his trouble."

"Seems likely. Think your Irish friend offed him and made it look like an accident?"

"He's no friend," Bell growled.

"Noted. Also, from the D.C. police blotter we got word that a Charles Briggs has been reported missing by his wife."

"Who is he?"

"He just happens to be one of the contractors working on the Bureau of Engraving building," Archie said with a self-satisfied look.

Bell grunted. "Now we're getting somewhere. Fred Lawson told me the spot where they got through the roof was woefully under spec."

"Intentionally, do you think?"

"If Charles Briggs remains missing or if he's found as remains, I'd say yes. He could have been paid to sabotage that section of the roof during construction and make it weak enough for the thieves to bust through."

"When we get back to the Willard, let's put some guys on it and tear his life apart."

Bell agreed. "Same with the locksmith."

Archie said, "I know the old man likes doing favors for the government, but we're talking a lot of shoe leather. Who's going to pay for this?"

"I imagine the finder's fee on a billion dollars will more than cover . . ." Bell paused.

"What is it?"

"Fred Lawson indicated that they are more interested in keeping this whole thing quiet rather than actually catching the thieves. Maybe we don't need to tear anyone's life apart if my hunch here is correct."

"If you'll notice, we only have another hundred feet of tunnel to go."

"I know," Bell said with concern darkening his voice.

They reached the far end and discovered precisely nothing.

There was no spur or siding off this main line. Bell's theory was wrong.

"If the facts don't fit your theory," he said, "change your theory."

"Quoting the boss?" Archie teased.

"I'm adding a corollary: 'or find better facts.'" He turned around. "Let's do this again, but no chin-wagging this time. We missed something. I'm sure of it."

25

THIS TIME THROUGH, THEY WERE MUCH MORE DELIBERATE and attentive. Rather than step from tie to tie in an elongated pace, they made sure to set a foot between the ties to slow themselves. When first entering the tunnel, Bell had expected to find a yawning great tunnel splitting off from this one, with obvious switching gear and attending equipment. Now he didn't quite know what they were looking for.

Bent almost double as they returned down the tunnel, they examined the rails like bloodhounds following a scent. For a train to shunt onto a spur line, its wheels have to cut across the original set of rails. There had to be a small gap in each of the two rails, just large enough to allow each wheel's inner guide collar to slide onto the new line. That was the key.

Swinging the flashlight from side to side so they could study the parallel tracks, the two men retreated down the tunnel. Had they stepped on the ties, they would have had a chance to feel the vibration slowly building within the rails they were spiked to, but they kept to the stone ballast and had no idea what was coming.

"There!" both men said at once when the light flashed on an anomaly.

A short piece of rail was colored slightly different from the rest of the line. Bell dropped to a knee to see that it had been crudely welded in place. He set his hand on it to test the joint and that's when he felt the steel rail vibrating like they were caught in a minor earthquake. In horror he turned to look behind them.

The lamp on the front of the oncoming locomotive seemed as bright as the sun in the otherwise dark tunnel, and the whistle blast just before the train entered the underground passage was like the scream of some terrible monster. The steam engine filled the tunnel from side to side with barely inches to spare.

Bell and Abbott wasted a second looking at each other, knowing this was it. Unlike a subway, they couldn't lie between the rails because the engine's pilot, what some called its cowcatcher, scythed the air just above the tracks to clear any debris from fouling the wheels. It would be an instantaneous but gruesome death.

Bell turned his attention back to the track. He found a second disguised cut a little ways up, both on the right-hand rail. He looked at the wall on that side. It appeared to be solid brick, as old and implacable as all the rest.

He looked back. The train was moving at twenty miles per hour, devouring distance deceptively fast in the confines of the tunnel. They had seconds. He looked at the far end of the shaft, at the weak light coming from outside. Even the fastest Olympic sprinter would extend his life by only a few seconds if he ran for it.

Bell launched himself at the wall in a last desperate gamble. His shoulder smashed into the mortared brick and, rather than bounce back, he fell partially through the wall in a shower of broken plaster and faux bricks only a quarter-inch thick. It was attached to thin laths of wood that had been nailed in place against a custom wood frame.

The tunnel was full of sound, the roar of the fire in the firebox, the gush of steam, and the echoes of all that against the ceiling and walls. The train was upon them. There was no time to rear back and slam himself against the wall again.

Archie Abbott had seen what had just happened, understood the implications, and acted out of desperate instinct. He ran into Bell with everything he had, placing a hand on the side of his friend's head and using it as a battering ram to enlarge the hole enough for both men to tumble through just as the locomotive raced past, steaming and snorting like some mechanical beast.

The clatter of its trailing string of cars seemed to go on forever. But then it was gone and an eerie silence returned.

"Ow," Bell said from the floor of the hidden railroad siding. He rubbed his head. "I appreciate the save, but did you need to slam my head into the wall?"

"Had I not braced that melon of yours I would have snapped your neck when I hit you."

Bell had dropped his light when Archie tackled him and it lay on the ground nearby. Powdery dust filled the air and covered both men, so they looked like they'd come from a flour mill. From this side, they could see how the tunnel had been hidden. They'd wedged wooden studs from floor to ceiling and attached premade panels of lath covered in brick veneer. A well-practiced team could put the whole thing up in just a few minutes. Up against the wall of this side tunnel were two lengths of curved rail they'd used to shunt the last car from the main line once the train had passed.

Nearby were track tools, some rail tongs so the men could move the heavy lengths, and a gauger to make sure their temporary link to the spur was the proper width.

The two friends helped each other to their feet and they dusted themselves off as best they could. Bell poked his head out the human-shaped hole in the wall to see the train was long gone.

Archie picked up the flashlight. "Should we go back? The crew on the boat might think we're dead."

"They might think it, but will any of them really care? We're practically strangers."

Abbott nodded. "Good point. Let's see where this leads."

Their exploration took them less than a hundred feet. The tracks on the ground and the lining of bricks up the walls and across the vaulted ceiling had been installed for only half that distance. The rest was solid rock that had been blasted with dynamite and hauled away. Loose stones had been left on the ground when this side project was abandoned. Neither man was an engineer or geologist and so they had no idea what caused this spur line to be left uncompleted. And neither man supposed it mattered. What mattered in the end was that the old rails had shiny spots that showed a railcar had been shunted into this passage recently, but that it was no longer there. The thieves had stashed it here for less than twenty-four hours, and while the county sheriff was guarding the river and bridge, they'd returned, attached the car to another train, and escaped with the money.

"Well, this didn't go as planned," Archie said with his typical understatement.

"Tell that to these guys," Bell said. He had the flashlight now and stood a short distance off.

Archie walked over and grunted. Eight men dressed in black

lay dead behind a pile of mining spoil. Judging by the streaks of blood on the ground, they'd been murdered here in the side tunnel, but dragged so they all lay together in a row. Examining the corpses closer, Bell saw that some had been shot, while others stabbed. One pour soul had his throat cut so deeply his head flopped at an unnatural and unsettling angle.

Most disturbing of all was that their faces had been beaten unrecognizable after their death. A pair of baseball bats had been tossed to the ground next to them.

"No honor among thieves," Archie said as their epitaph.

"That's why they put up the wall," Bell said. "They planned on killing these guys all along, but didn't want the bodies discovered by a track inspector."

"Wouldn't the fact that a new wall had been built to hide this spur raise red flags? . . . Our buddy Reggie Hauser."

"I bet there's a work order with his signature on it in all the right filing cabinets in case anyone checked. And it's part of the Richmond line."

"I guess if you're going after the biggest score of greenbacks in history, it has to be the most meticulously planned heist."

Distracted by his own thoughts, Bell asked Archie what he'd just said.

"If you're going after the biggest score of greenbacks in history—"

A sudden look of realization swept across Bell's face and he let out a curse.

"What is it, Isaac?"

"Greenback. I should have seen it earlier."

"What, exactly?" Archie asked.

"Back in Lawson's office, he said this robbery would make the thief rival Rockefeller for being the richest man in America."

"And he's not wrong."

"I had a fleeting thought that it could be a woman rather than a man, because one of the cleverest criminals I've ever encountered was Fedora Pickett. She almost got away with framing her husband for murdering her, when in fact she took her own life."

"Okay, I suppose, but she's dead and couldn't have robbed the Treasury."

"No, it couldn't have been Fedora. But it's not what I thought. Fedora didn't actually take her own life." Bell shook his head. "It was her husband, Jackson Pickett."

"I don't follow."

"'For Greenback,'" Bell said wistfully. "It was all a test, Archie. That night in Newport. Jackson Pickett set the whole thing up to test me. To see how good I am. He was the one who staged her suicide to look like a murder, but it wasn't a suicide at all. He must have known from her doctor that she didn't have long to live. He would lose access to her wealth either way, so the ruthless cutthroat killed her and played a little cat and mouse with me to test my skills.

"When I succeeded and proved he was innocent, he knew I was a good-enough detective to track down whoever robbed the Federal Reserve when he hit it. That's why he sent his apologetic little assassin to kill me in New York while he was cleaning up all the other loose ends. Charles Briggs, Reggie Hauser, and God knows how many more. But Hauser clued us in with his note on the Richmond train schedule. Greenback wasn't a reference to the Federal Reserve notes, it was to Pickett himself. The former star quarterback of Tulane University and an old alumnus of the Olive and

Blue, where the athletic teams are known as the Greenies or Greenbacks."

"Greenback," Archie repeated. "Hauser would know that. He played baseball at Vanderbilt."

"The robbery itself was the perfect crime," Bell continued. "Had I not stumbled into it in the middle of the night through blind stupid luck, we never would have known. He'd covered every track and contingency, killing his accomplices along the way. Or sometimes even before. Just brilliant. And with so much cash stolen, there is no way the banks or the Fed system can track individual bills. A billion dollars, scot-free."

"Sounds like you almost admire the guy."

Bell grit his teeth. "I want to see him pay. For putting my father's life at risk. For the poor hapless passengers on the Staten Island Ferry. And even for the idiots he bribed or blackmailed to help him. He thinks he's smarter than me and that he got away with it, and I want him to know he's wrong."

Archie watched his friend for a second.

"I know that last bit sounded arrogant," Bell said, after regaining some of his composure, "but I'd be lying to you and myself if I didn't admit it. I got played and it's burning me up inside."

"It's what makes you so good," Archie agreed. "Without it, Isaac, you'd be a mere mortal like the rest of us."

Bell chuckled. "Thanks. Just frustrated, you know."

"I get it. No one likes being a sucker, and you more than most. So, what happens now?"

"You and I go out and prove that Jackson Pickett didn't commit the perfect crime and that whatever he can steal we can just as easily steal back."

26

THE TREASURY DEPARTMENT CONFERENCE ROOM OVER-
looked the south plaza, the Ellipse behind the White House,
and the greater National Mall beyond. There were more than a
dozen men seated at the table, while their aides leaned against the
walls, briefcases at their feet stuffed with whatever information
they thought their superiors might need. The meeting was just
getting started and already the atmosphere was choked with hazy
cigarette smoke and tension.

Secretary McAdoo sat at the head of the table. Bell had asked
the Van Dorn's Washington section chief to put together a brief
biography of the man. A southerner by birth and a lawyer by education, he'd once been arrested for his part in a deadly riot over
streetcars in Tennessee, had overseen the completion of two problematic rail tunnels under the Hudson River, been vice chair of the
Democratic Party, and spearheaded the unlikely nomination and
subsequent election of Woodrow Wilson. All by the time he was

fifty. A champion of progressive politics, his personal slogan was "Let the public be pleased."

Bell recognized a few others he'd seen from the Bureau of Engraving, including its security chief, Fred Lawson. Also present were Vic Carver and his partner, Paul Haygarth, the two T-men heading the investigation into the plane attack on the presidential yacht. Others in the room were either more Treasury people or representatives from the White House.

Vic Carver was wrapping up their meager progress on the aerial assault on the *Mayflower*. "There are just too many small airfields within the scope of our investigation to properly check. We've sent letters of inquiry to as many as we could find, but so far of the handful of responders no one has any knowledge of any missing aircraft or pilots. The body recovered near the crash, who we believe to be an accomplice to the pilots, had no identification or identifying marks.

"The Reserve notes recovered shortly after the crash by Van Dorn detective Isaac Bell are genuine, but because of the loss of the serial number ledger, there is no way to determine their origin beyond the Bureau of Engraving itself."

"You're telling me that after this much time has elapsed," Mc-Adoo said in a rebuking drawl, "you have nothing to show for your effort?"

"Well, sir, we know a lot about who didn't attack the *Mayflower*," Carver replied, employing a little Washington bureaucratese.

"But not who did?"

"Er, no."

"Fred, tell me you have more than Carver about the robbery."

Fred Lawson cleared his throat. "We're getting a clearer picture with every passing hour, Mr. Secretary. This has been in the works for quite some time, and we believe started with either the blackmail or bribery of one of the principal contractors of our new building. A man named Charles Briggs. At some point late in the construction, he removed multiple layers of the roof cladding to create a weak spot the thieves could use to access the building. He has been reported missing by his wife and his whereabouts are currently unknown."

"He's dead."

"Who said that?" McAdoo asked sharply, his eyes scanning faces.

"I did."

"And you are?"

"The aforementioned Isaac Bell, Mr. Secretary. Though we didn't formally meet, I was on the *Mayflower* with you during the attack."

"I recall your bravery and I must say your name has come up a lot recently."

"I've been busy."

"Yes, and then some. And am I to understand that you are Ebenezer Bell's son?"

"I have that honor, yes."

"How do you know that this Briggs fellow is dead?"

"First thing this morning I stopped by his house and interviewed his wife. She told me that the police were dismissive of her concerns and took no notes of their interview. Apparently, there's rumor of a mistress and a possible abandonment. I asked her what the police should have asked about and she told me that there was an item missing from her home. A dishrag that usually hangs from the handle of the oven door. She insists one is always there and that she changes it out every three days. It and her husband weren't home when she returned from Bible study. Any anomaly at a potential crime scene is important, so I asked her to inventory any linen closets. She discovered that she was missing a spare pillowcase.

"Logic tells me that Charles Briggs was abducted from his home because of the material support he gave the thieves and that the pilfered rag from the kitchen was used to gag him while the pillowcase over his head was to keep him disoriented. I've seen this happen a dozen times. Kidnappers remembered the rope but forgot the other items and have to improvise. Considering the number of bodies piled up in the wake of this robbery, including eight of their own they killed, Briggs is most certainly dead."

"That sounds tragic but reasonable," McAdoo said, and looked to Fred Lawson for confirmation. The security chief nodded.

"There is something else," Bell added.

"About Charles Briggs?"

"No. His abduction. The mastermind behind this Treasury Department robbery had planned the break-in down to the most minute detail. Nothing was too trivial for his consideration. An example, the black outfits worn by the thieves had no pockets for the men to carelessly carry something to identify themselves. Another is that they timed the derailment of their train so there were just minutes before another one came past in the opposite direction. Being that detailed and meticulous is how they got away with this crime. Keep that in mind and consider the abduction I just outlined."

Bell was met by blank stares. He finally said, "The kidnappers forgot to bring both a gag and a hood."

"So?" said an executive whose name and function Bell didn't know.

"Someone whose schedule is so tight they play chicken with locomotives wouldn't have left without bringing their own gag and hood. This tells me that our mastermind wasn't behind the abduction or at least not directly. I believe he hired another crew to do it for him. This other crew also provided some of the muscle for the actual robbery and I think it's these guys who are the dead men we found in the railroad tunnel."

Just then there was a knock, and a young page entered the room and went straight to Secretary McAdoo. The lad whispered in the man's ear, and he casually pointed over to where Bell sat. McAdoo nodded and the kid came over to hand Bell two items. One was a piece of jewelry and the other a folded piece of paper. While the aide retreated from the room, Bell took a couple of seconds to identify them both.

A smile tugged at the corners of his mouth for the first time in days.

"What is it, Bell?"

"With Fred Lawson's permission, I asked that an associate attend the preliminary examination of the dead men we found in the tunnel. Of the autopsies, I have no interest. They were either shot or stabbed, and their general state of their health, and the contents of their stomachs, etcetera, is of even less import. But these two pieces of evidence are very telling. Very telling indeed."

Bell passed the necklace with its small silver medallion in one direction around the conference table and a very detailed drawing done in the morgue in the other.

As Bell was nearly opposite where McAdoo sat, they reached him at almost the same time. He asked, "What am I looking at, here?"

"The pendant is a standard St. Nicholas medal."

"Like in Santa Claus?" someone blurted.

"Not exactly," Bell replied. "The early Dutch settlers in America celebrated St. Nicholas Day, but they called him Sinterklaas. That got anglicized to Santa Claus by the English. But I'm referring to the original fourth-century martyr who is the patron saint, among other things, of sailors, children, I believe brewers, and most importantly to us, repentant thieves."

That last bit of information caught the assembled men's attention.

"And this drawing?"

"The most famous story told about St. Nicholas is how he secretly gave sacks of gold coins to a poor father so that he could pay a dowry for his three daughters and keep them from a life of prostitution. The drawing depicts the three leather bags of coins from the story. Two are cinched tight, the third is loosened, and a single gold coin lays next to it. The loose coin is a symbol that the dowry will remain intact and none of the coins will be stolen.

"The medal and necklace were found clasped around one of the dead thieves' ankles under his sock. The drawing is of a tattoo another of the men had hidden on his hip. I know all of this stuff because I've seen this before. These men were thieves, but weren't at all repentant. Yet I've known of some Catholics, particularly Irish gangsters, who think that if they keep some talisman of St. Nicholas on them, if they die, they will be forgiven and get into heaven."

"Hedging their bets?" Fred Lawson, seated nearby, whispered wryly.

Bell replied, "I'd call it gambling their souls with loaded dice." He once again addressed the crowded room. "Our mastermind covered his tracks by destroying his hired accomplices' faces after he and his gnomish little henchman killed them. He never would have left these behind if he'd known about them. These are our second real clue in the case."

"Second?" Agent Carver repeated with a little heat in his voice. He was being upstaged by Bell and didn't like it one bit. "What the hell is the first clue?"

"I'll tell you in a minute," Bell said. "We are currently investigating the suspicious death of a Philadelphia locksmith named Harvey Wanamaker. He was an ex-con turned legit after his last stay in prison. He was known as a master craftsman, and we believe he built that mechanical device that allowed the thieves access to the vault's dials. He had the machine tools in his shop necessary to manufacture the giant lock tensioner, and I don't know what else has been found there. The Philly police are keeping tight-lipped about the case, but I'm working on them."

"Impressive amount of work in a short time," McAdoo remarked.

"That's what we do at Van Dorn, Mr. Secretary. Employ enough resources until we crack the case."

"Have you, Mr. Bell? Have you cracked the case? Because I would sure like my billion dollars back."

"Actually, I have, sir. That's our second break. I know who pulled it off. The mastermind's name is Jackson Pickett." Bell's declaration was met with a chorus of shocked noises. He raised his voice to speak over the din. "Last summer I personally investigated his wife's murder and completely exonerated him of that crime, though now I am quite certain that he killed her and painstakingly staged it as a suicide."

"You know this for a fact?" McAdoo asked.

"Near enough, Mr. Secretary. I believe his tentacles extended to the recent sinking of the Staten Island Ferry as an attempt on my life."

"Good Lord," McAdoo exclaimed. "I've read up on that tragedy. That was all about killing you?"

"One of the saboteurs called me out by name, Mr. Secretary. Jackson Pickett is smart, meticulous, and utterly ruthless."

"Do you know where he is?"

"I've reached out to his late wife's father," Bell said. "Pickett was kicked out of all their family properties soon after his wife's death. All of the locations have been sealed up. Bill Scarsworth has no forwarding address. I know Pickett has ties to New Orleans, so I have our field office there already asking around."

Bell didn't add that once he told the senior Scarsworth that his beloved daughter was in fact a victim of murder, he first threatened to kill Bell for his role in Pickett's exoneration, then to sue the Van Dorn Agency for everything it was worth. It had taken all of Bell's power of persuasion to calm the man down and get him to accept that Pickett would be brought to justice, no matter what.

"You seem to have things well in hand," another White House insider remarked.

"We're treating this like your money has been kidnapped. The first forty-eight hours after an abduction are critical. Leads need to be generated quickly or else the trail goes cold."

"What do you propose as your next step, Mr. Bell?"

"I want to explore the gang angle of the case. An Irish criminal organization made a deal with Pickett to abduct contractor Charles Briggs and then provide muscle for the actual robbery. Eight of those men are now dead. I've already reached out to a bunch of our field offices and have agents talking to police gang squads about any criminal crews undergoing recent changes. If we find one, I want to lean on them as hard as I can because whoever Pickett left alive is a loose end that I might be able to exploit."

Vic Carver caught William McAdoo's attention. "That's what I was driving at in the memo I sent you—the need for a national police force with offices spread to all the major cities. Like what the Van Dorns have now, only this would be under a government umbrella."

McAdoo made an impatient gesture. "Mr. Bell, you and your agency seem well positioned to pursue the case leads. Are you willing to continue your investigation at the behest of the Treasury Department?"

Bell was already so personally invested in this case, he would pursue it whether McAdoo wanted him to or not. He also knew his boss would back him one hundred percent in the matter.

"I'll have to cable Joseph Van Dorn for authorization," he replied with a knowing smile. "But I believe the answer will be 'Yes.'"

Hiding in plain sight

27

Baltimore, Maryland

THE NEWS ARRIVED THE NEXT MORNING FROM THE BALTI-
more office of the Van Dorn Agency. That particular office
wasn't very big because of its proximity to the larger Washington,
D.C., bureau and mostly did hotel protection and mundane investigative jobs. All of the men who worked for Van Dorn there were
former Baltimore police officers and maintained good relations
with their brothers still on the force. Archie accompanied Bell to
Charm City on an express train from Union Station. They met
with Telford Jones, the head of the Baltimore office, at the main
bar of the stylish Belvedere Hotel. The eleven-story brick building
sat in a posh neighborhood north of the main downtown business
district and inner harbor basin.

The bar was a largish room, loud and smoky and patroned only
by men. Jones was in a booth with a youthful-looking uniformed
Baltimore cop. On the table before him was a schooner of beer and
his billy club.

"Tel, how are you?" Bell said as he approached the table.

"Isaac. Good to see you. It's been a while. This is my cousin, Clarence."

"That's an espantoon," Bell said, pointing to the beat cop's wooden baton.

"You must be from Baltimore to know that," the fresh-faced officer said.

"No. Back in my college days I was visiting some buddies at Johns Hopkins. One thing led to another and, long story short, I almost got my head bashed in by one of those. The cop after me could twirl it like an airplane propeller. Good thing he just couldn't run."

"It takes some practice," Clarence said.

"This is Archie Abbott," Bell said to complete the introductions as they all shook hands. He caught the eye of the barman and ordered a pair of whiskeys.

"You are sharing one, yes?" Archie quipped.

"I can't believe you got back to me so quickly on this," Bell said to Tel Jones, ignoring his friend. "It's rather an esoteric request."

"Not to us," Jones replied. "Clarence and I have been talking about something strange going on for a few weeks. There's a gang of about twenty that works the docks run by a guy named Flynn O'Conner."

"All Irish?" Bell asked.

"To a man. Their fathers all grew up together back in the old country."

"Okay."

"The thing is, Flynn hasn't been seen in a while. Rumors are flying. Some say he was axed by a rival gang moving down from New York. Some say he took a powder with some dame from the

Follies. Others are talking about his younger brother, Sean, killed him to take over."

"What do you think?" Bell asked Telford's cousin.

"No one knows for sure. What I'm hearing, though, is that the Flynn gang isn't servicing their territory as often as usual. Protection money is going uncollected and a numbers guy has even started working out of a barbershop not four blocks from O'Conner's headquarters."

"Could be they're down eight guys," Archie said.

A look of confusion swept the young cop's face. "Huh, why eight?"

"We found eight dead men connected to a large robbery. One had a St. Nicholas medal and one had a tattoo linked to St. Nicholas."

"Patron saint of reformed thieves," Telford said, in case his cousin wasn't aware of the significance.

"Popular with Irish gangs," Clarence added to show he wasn't as wet behind the ears as his tender age implied. "I know a few of Flynn's boys. Can you describe the dead men you found?"

Archie said, "Their heads looked like melons that had been dropped off the top of this hotel."

"Whoever killed them used a baseball bat to erase their identities," Bell added with a bit more tact. "Where do they hang out?"

"Down by the waterfront. Flynn O'Conner worked out of a bar he owns with his brother. They also have a, well, a warehouse I guess you'd call it, but it's more like a fortress in the middle of the city."

"Why do you say that?"

"It's this old armory building near the waterfront that survived the Great Baltimore Fire. O'Conner bought it after a minor local issue and turned it into a warehouse for a lot of the bootleg stuff he boosts off freighters coming into the harbor. Place is built to withstand artillery barrages, or so it's claimed. Big, ugly, and squat, with only two ways in, a back door controlled from the inside and a regular door down an alley between some other buildings."

"Can you take us there?"

"Sure." The kid took a slow sip of his beer. Bell eyed him until he got the message. "Oh, now?"

"On the jump, Patrolman Clarence Jones."

With one of the Van Dorn Model Ts littering the Virginia countryside and the other in a body shop having its fenders beaten back into shape, Bell had reached out through the Willard Hotel for another car. He would have preferred another ubiquitous Ford, but ended up with the hotel manager's new Chevrolet Classic Six. It was a large four-door tourer with plenty under the hood and some interesting, European-inspired design. Fortunately, this model was painted in an understated dark blue and not some garish color to draw attention.

The valet had yet to park the car around the corner, so it still sat in front of the hotel. Bell gave the valet a dollar for essentially doing nothing and got behind the wheel. The car had a Gray & Davis electric starter that fired up the six-cylinder with little fanfare. Archie took the seat next to him and the two Jones cousins sat in back, but both leaned forward between the seats, as eager as St. Bernard dogs.

"Let's look at the bar first," Bell said, and eased them into traffic.

Because of the massive fire that had destroyed half of downtown Baltimore only ten years earlier, the rebuilt city core remained new and vibrant, and bustling with people who seemed proud of their home. Sidewalks were broad and storefronts enticing. Many of the row houses they passed on the way to the waterfront had freshly swept front stoops and pretty curtains in their windows, signs of proud ownership.

Closer to the harbor, the tenor of the city changed, as it did in all port cities. There had been a great deal of rebuilding to be sure, but the quality was shabbier and the materials cheaper. Ten years on and the blocks of buildings nearest the busy piers looked run-down or hadn't been rebuilt at all. There were still vacant lots heaped with trash and construction debris punctuated by thorny vegetation that somehow grew out of the hard urban soil.

The people, too, lacked the vim and vigor seen just a few blocks north. There were drunks passed out near the entrances to saloons that catered to seamen, fancy girls dressed in garish costumes to attract clients, and dirt-streaked urchins who lived as ferally as wild dogs.

A few people they passed eyed the Chevrolet. But Bell didn't get a sense of menace from them. Down here, a car like this meant someone important was behind the wheel and important people always brought trouble. So as quickly as someone took note of the automobile, their gaze was averted.

"Okay, it's on the left at the end of this block," Clarence announced from the rear seat. "It's called the Kraken's Cleat."

Bell slowed as they passed by. The entrance was broad and the angle of the light was just right to allow him to look deeply into the seedy interior. For midafternoon it seemed to be doing all right. The main bar ran along one wall and it looked like all the stools were taken. Along the opposite wall were several tables of men hunched over their drinks. A pianist of some talent was playing an instrument that was in dire need of tuning.

Bell chuckled at the sign over the establishment's entrance. It showed a purple octopus tugging to free a tentacle that had been wrapped around a nautical cleat.

Clarence said, "It's rumored that Flynn O'Conner forced the bar's previous owner to sell it to him for a song and then ran him out of town. Oh, look at that!"

"What is it?" Bell and Archie Abbott asked in one voice.

"Those two who just walked out. Those are the Pats. Patrick Rourke and Patrick Murphy. They're a couple of Flynn's enforcers."

"They look the part," Bell remarked. "That one's got to be six foot six."

"Pat Murphy," Clarence said. "I heard he stopped a man's heart with a single punch."

"You said they weren't making their regular collections," Archie said. "Sure looks like they're on the prowl to me."

"Mind if we follow them?" Patrolman Jones asked.

Bell thought for a moment. "I don't want to interfere with whatever they're up to. I've got bigger game in my sights."

"I completely understand. I'm just curious as to what their game is."

Bell pulled the car to the curb and waited for the two toughs to get ahead of him and to allow a couple of cars in between their vehicle and their quarry. Once he felt the situation was right, he pulled out into traffic. The stream of cars was moving faster than the pair of goons, so Bell had to pull over and wait several times as the men walked four zigzagging blocks into a better neighborhood. Bell noted that pedestrians gave the men a wide berth, like fish shoaling around apex predators. A couple of shopkeepers stuck their heads out of their establishments once the men had passed, puzzled that the enforcers hadn't demanded their monthly protection money.

"I think I know where they're heading," Clarence said.

"Where?"

"Remember I mentioned a numbers guy had set up in a barbershop in O'Conner territory?"

"Yes," Bell said.

"That's it near the corner."

On the corner sat a woman's haberdashery with stylishly dressed wax mannequins in its windows. Next to it was a storefront so narrow that the interior could only have room for a single rank of barber chairs and perhaps a narrow counter. Outside its glass door a candy-striped barber pole spun lazily at just above head height. The two gorillas ducked inside as Bell pulled abreast. A handful of seconds later a man still wearing a barber cape raced from the shop, his face pale and his eyes wide. He didn't look back.

There was no place for Bell to park the Chevrolet so he circled the block as quickly as he could. O'Conner's enforcers were already leaving the barbershop by the time they returned. A spot had opened a couple of stores shy of the barber and Bell nosed the luxury car in.

"Wait here," he said and jumped out.

He rushed to the little shop. A bell chimed when he opened the door. The barber was sitting on the floor, clutching his right wrist with his left hand to keep the mutilated remains of his right hand elevated. It looked like they'd worked over his hand with a hammer and left most of the twenty-seven bones in broken fragments.

The man gawped soundlessly at the agony radiating from his ruined member. There was a curtain at the back of the shop. The barber didn't even register Bell's presence when he stepped over him.

Behind the curtain was a storeroom/break area with a gramophone sitting on a desk and jars of homemade blue germicide on a shelf. The numbers guy was also on the floor. They'd used the same hammer on his face and it looked like they'd broken everything there just as thoroughly as the barber's hand. It was impossible to guess the man's age or how he once looked. They'd left his face a bloody lumpen mask that would never properly heal.

At least they'd left both men alive. The barber had his livelihood taken from him for letting the bookie use his back room and the bookie himself would spend the rest of his life resembling Frankenstein's monster. Bell left them and ran for the clothing store on the corner. Two salesgirls were gossiping behind the counter while a pair of ladies looked at dresses. All four were mildly scandalized that a man had entered such a bastion of femininity.

"Do you have a phone?" Bell asked of the employees.

"We do, but we aren't allowed to let anyone use it."

"Please call the police and have them send an ambulance. There are two seriously injured people in the barbershop next door."

"Mr. White?"

"If he's the barber, yes, and the guy working out of his back room, too. Make the call."

Bell strode from the shop and got back into the car.

"Well?" Archie asked.

"They're alive. The barber's gonna have to learn to cut with his left hand and the bookie's face is going to scare children until his dying day."

"You went into the women's store to have them call the cops?"

"Yeah, and for them to send a meat wagon."

Bell was no stranger to violence, and in the world these people ran in, the punishment might have been seen as fitting, but the casualness of it left him a little shaken. He knew they had to do it to send a message to the rest of the gang's territory that the past few weeks of inattention were coming to an end.

"Show me their headquarters," Bell said, his voice hardening at the prospect of taking on these thugs.

A SHORT WHILE LATER THEY CRUISED DOWN AN EVEN SEEDIER street. The businesses were mostly cheap restaurants, cut-rate bars, and flophouses advertising beds in dormitory-style housing. There were more men loitering about, rawboned and haggard, their eyes bloodshot by last night's excesses. The prostitutes looked cheaper than their uptown sisters.

The armory building sat back from the street, so enterprising store owners had built cement-block walls roofed with corrugated tin that butted up to the imposing three-story brick building. From these illegal stalls they sold all manner of goods, mostly second- and even thirdhand items that they had reconditioned, things like electric fans with new motors, mauls and axes with new handles, clocks whose guts had been reworked. One of the stalls had a wood-burning stove for making meat pies, and judging by the line of people waiting, they were quite good.

Between two of the stalls was an alley barely five feet wide, and at its end was a stout metal door. Bell could just make out that it had no handle on the outside and a viewing slit at head height that could be closed up tight. There was some trash in the alley, but not as much as would be normal. The gangsters kept it clean to allow them to see out clearly, and it was such a natural choke point that a frontal assault would be about as successful as Pickett's charge at Gettysburg.

"You said there are two ways in?" Bell asked. He'd slowed as they passed the alley, but now accelerated away.

"Yes. Out back," Clarence said. "A little local history, if you'll allow me. The loading docks facing the harbor out back were bricked up years ago. After the fire a guy ran an illegal sawmill in the building in the early years of the city's reconstruction. The authorities turned a blind eye for a while because so much wood was needed. But then legitimate lumber companies complained about being undercut in price and the city closed it down and had it bricked up. It remained like that until Flynn O'Conner bought it. He installed a metal door out back that he uses to bring in truckloads of boosted goods. I've got some informants in the area. No one has seen any activity in or out of that door since Flynn vanished. O'Conner's boys only enter or leave via that alley."

Just to be thorough, Bell had Clarence direct him around the building off a different cross street. Heavy gates with thick locks prevented anyone from accessing the dockland area behind the old armory. Bell was still afforded a view across a barren lot of the big brick structure. The door the mobsters had installed was visible, and judging by the height of the weeds growing in front of it, hadn't been used in weeks.

"Like we said, damn near impregnable," Telford remarked.

"Clarence, could any of your informers get them to open the door at the end of the alley?"

"I suppose if they had something the guys inside want, but what's the point? They'd cut us down the moment we started rushing down the alley or just close the door and wait us out."

"Leave that to me."

Archie groaned theatrically. "How did I know you were going to say that?"

28

I T WASN'T YET TEN O'CLOCK AND THE STREETWALKER ALREADY smelled faintly of gin under the cloying sweetness of her perfume. Her customer had an air of smarmy desperation as he leered at the pearlescent décolletage she had on display while they found an alleyway to consummate their commercial transaction.

When they reached the end of the alley next to a shuttered steel door, they paused to look back and see if anyone was paying attention.

Satisfied, the prostitute said, "All right, love, two dollars and I'll send you to heaven."

In a whisper, the man said, "If I had a dollar for every—"

The slit in the metal door suddenly crashed open with a metallic clang and a raspy voice shouted, "You two get the hell outta here if you know what's good for you."

"Come on," said the woman. "Won't take me but a minute."

The angry eyes glaring at them from the other side of the solid door were replaced with the barrel of a large revolver. "Now!"

Upon seeing the gun, the john lost all interest in carnal delights and practically sprinted out of the alley.

The thug gave one last warning. "You ever try working this alley again and we'll bust you up so bad your face will scare a bull-dog outta a butcher shop."

Not intimidated in the least, she threw him a sassy little curtsy and twitched her hips all the way back to the street. The thug inside the O'Conner gang's hideout didn't close the viewing slit until the last of her vanished around the corner.

Her would-be customer was waiting just out of view of the alleyway, a freshly lit cigarette smoldering in a theatrical ivory holder. He handed her his jacket.

Marion Bell slipped her arms into the coat and clutched the lapels closed so she no longer showed herself off like the harlot she was pretending to be. She gave a little laugh. "You should have seen your face when he flashed that gun."

"Darling," said Christoff Tamerlane in a breezy voice, "I am many, many things, but brave is not one of them."

"You were brave enough to take this job."

"Only because I know that Adonis of a husband of yours would come to my rescue."

On cue, Bell pulled up to the curb in the Chevy with Archie riding shotgun. Tamerlane opened the door for Marion and followed her into the car's rear seat. As they pulled away, Bell asked, "Did you get it?"

Tamerlane pulled a little Vest Pocket Kodak camera from his jacket and held it like a trophy. "Mission accomplished, *guapo*."

"Any problems?"

"They shooed us away as soon as they heard my voice," Marion replied. She was using a compact mirror to remove the garish makeup Christoff had applied to tart her up for their performance.

"Not quite," her artist friend countered. "Didn't you feel the pressure plate on the walk down the alley?"

"Pressure plate?" Bell asked.

"There's a piece of metal about halfway down the alley that looks like it was placed there to cover crumbled asphalt. It gave a little when we walked on it. My feet are very sensitive, by the way. Ticklish, too. Anyway, I think that triggers an alert inside and he only reached the door to kick us out when your lady of the evening mentioned sending me to heaven."

"Okay. Good to know. You just upgraded the bottle of champagne to accompany tonight's dinner. How long do you think you'll need for the painting?"

Christoff thought for a moment or two. "I already have several pictures of the buildings across the street and have matched all the colors. Painting the alley walls is a cinch. Once we develop the snaps on this camera, I'll have the proper perspective. I'd say five hours."

"For a picture that big?" Archie asked in a dubious voice.

"Honey, when you work for Marion Bell for as long as I have, you learn quickly that there are two modes, breakneck or breakdown. Nothing in between."

To the best of Bell's recollection, no man had ever called Archie "honey." He said, "Okay, Mr. Tamerlane. You're the boss."

"No, I'm the painter, makeup artist, prop master, and all-around boy Friday." He jabbed a thumb toward Marion. "She's the boss."

Marion snapped closed her compact, her face now scrubbed clean and glowing. "Isaac, I'd better hear an amen out of you."

His grin in the rearview mirror was both boyish and infectious. "Yes, ma'am. Amen."

BELL'S PLAN TO BREAK INTO FLYNN O'CONNER'S WAREHOUSE was delayed by two days of overcast and rain. True to his word, Christoff Tamerlane painted the backdrop in record time, but had made the sky portion of the artwork blue and cloudless. They had to wait until Mother Nature cooperated and matched Tamerlane's artistic vision. Clarence Jones's snitch, a twitchy little gutter rat named Portnow, was kept on ice in a room next to the one Bell and Marion shared. It was costing Bell a fortune in room service and the informer expected him to shell out for the nocturnal guest he entertained as well.

The third day broke clear and the city glistened following its thorough soaking. It was time. Bell was to be accompanied on the raid by Archie Abbott and Telford Jones. Clarence wanted to join them, but if things went badly, he'd surely lose his badge. To round out the team, Bell had sent for James Dashwood from the New York office and another marksman from Philly named Clint Slocomb.

Dashwood was one of Bell's protégés, now promoted to full detective. He was an ace with any kind of firearm and as cool a customer as Bell had ever known. Clint was older than Bell, a mustered-out Army master sergeant and a veteran of the Spanish War who could make sense of the chaos of battle on an intuitive level. His hair and beard were shot through with coils of silver and his eyes were ringed in wrinkles, but the old dog had a lot of fight left in him.

Young Mr. Dashwood was trying to pull off a mustache similar to Isaac's, but it wasn't quite there yet.

The Chevrolet was too small for their needs, so Bell rented a commercial truck from one of Tel Jones's contacts. Dashwood had raided the New York office's extensive armory for the weapons they would need, though Clint Slocomb came down on the train with his own duffel of personal weapons. These included four match-grade Colt Model 1911 pistols that he wore in a custom harness that held two of the automatics near his kidneys and the other two low across his stomach.

Bell had seen him fire all thirty-two rounds in a handful of the loudest seconds he'd ever endured and place all but three bullets on target.

They chose two in the afternoon for their raid for a couple of reasons. Generally, retail businesses slow between two and four, so there would be fewer pedestrians on the street near the alley. Also, whatever business the mobsters needed to accomplish would likely be finished and they'd all be lazy and complacent while waiting to go out carousing for the night.

Christoff Tamerlane had been paid for his artistic services, but had become caught up in the intrigue of it all and volunteered to drive the truck. Marion insisted on riding shotgun. Bell saw no real harm since the two of them would be blocks away by the time the trap was sprung.

Clarence Jones had been watching the street for the better part of two hours. When Christoff eased the truck to a stop near the head of the alley he walked past and gave Marion a casual nod that everything was clear. She in turn rapped her knuckles against the dividing partition between the truck's cab and cargo bed.

"Showtime," Bell said, and lowered the gate. He and Dash-wood slid out the large painting and held it in front of themselves like some sort of giant medieval shield. It was held rigid by a breakaway balsa wood frame that was only visible from the rear. The snitch, Portnow, looked nervous and sweaty despite the chill air. He finished one cigarette and lit another from its dying ember. His eyes never fixed on a subject for more than a second.

"I'm not so sure about this," he wheedled.

"Knock it off," Tel Jones said with menace in his voice. He knew his rat was about to ask for more money. "You've been paid. All you need to do is get them to open the door and then get the hell out of our way."

"If this goes sideways, they're gonna know I was involved. No one defies the O'Conner gang and lives to talk about it."

Bell caught his full attention and said, "If this goes sideways, no matter what happens to us, the first guy to die is the one who opens the door and the only one who can identify you. We clear?"

Portnow couldn't hold Bell's glacial stare. He blinked hard and turned away, pretending smoke got in his eye rather than admit-ting he was thoroughly intimidated. "Okay, okay, we're clear. Take it easy."

Portnow entered the alley first, followed by Bell and James Dashwood carrying the painting. Tel Jones and Clint Slocomb crowded right behind them. As soon as they were in the alley and away from prying eyes, the men slipped off long jackets that hid the guns they carried strapped to their bodies. Slocomb drew his first pair of Colt 1911s. They were chambered and ready for action.

Bell had already warned Portnow about the pressure plate span-ning the width of the alley and he dutifully stepped around it. They didn't dare alert the men inside until the painting was in position. The men following behind did likewise. They finally stopped just shy of the steel armory door with its vision slit. Portnow had managed to smoke an entire cigarette in the few seconds it took them to walk the length of the alley. He didn't light another.

Bell and Dashwood set the painting on its bottom edge, perfectly perpendicular to the alley walls and straight up and down in the exact spot where Christoff had taken his perspective picture. Bell nodded to Slocomb, who rushed back to step on the pressure plate. Somewhere deep inside the armory, a bell must have sounded because a few moments later the cover over the vision slit rattled open and a pair of wary eyes peered out.

The guard saw Portnow. Behind him stood the lifelike painting done to mimic exactly the view of the alley he'd looked down a thousand times. He could see that blue had returned to the sky and the puddles on the crumbling asphalt had already dried up. The street at the end of the alley appeared quiet—no cars or pedestrians—but that wasn't unusual for this time of day.

"What do you want?" he sneered at Portnow in both recognition and annoyance.

"I need to talk to Flynn."

"He ain't here. Beat it, Portnow, before I beat you."

"No, Tommy. Ya gotta listen. Those guys of yours who went missing. I know what happened to 'em."

There was a pause while the doorman thought about what the little fink was saying. There had been no word about the eight guys who went on the job with Michaleen Riordan and that had everyone on edge. He decided this was above his rank and quite frankly his intelligence.

The goon called Tommy closed the vision slit and threw three sets of bolts to unlock the door. He opened it and beckoned Port-now to enter the gang's fortified urban lair. His brain couldn't process what happened next. Four men appeared out of thin air as the alley behind them twisted and shriveled, like he was halluci-nating on the worst drunk of his life, but then looked perfectly normal once again.

When the steel door opened on its rusty hinges, Bell and James snapped the flimsy sides of the big painting's balsa frame so that the entire thing collapsed into an artistic heap on the ground. To the guard they must have appeared as if by magic. First you don't see them, now you do.

The four Van Dorn agents came in like a flying squad. Bell went to hit the O'Conner thug in the forehead with the butt of his sawn-off shotgun, but Portnow hadn't ducked out of the way as he'd been instructed and he missed entirely.

The guard came to his senses and made to slam the door closed. He was too late for that. Portnow was bowled aside by the inrush of Bell and his men. Tel Jones tripped over him and hit the ground just inside the door while the guard turned and fled toward the building's soaring interior.

Half of the cavernous armory was open storage space that the O'Conner gang used to store whatever they boosted off the docks. The other half was the old mill. Years of accumulated grime on the high windowpanes left the entire interior gloomy and oppressive.

The sawmill operation had utilized some European company's automated system that used conveyor belts fitted with sharpened steel spikes to grasp the logs as they came in through a now sealed entry. The logs were shunted around the mill, through various machines that stripped off the bark and sliced them into various dimensions according to what a customer had ordered. The entire space was a confusing jumble of belts and hoists and saw stations with circular blades as big as wagon wheels.

When the city shut down the mill, they hadn't even been allowed to finish with the wood that had already been fed into the machines. Logs remained in the mill in various stages of being shaped just as they had been on that fateful day.

"Police," Bell shouted at the top of his lungs as they exited a narrow hallway into the main part of the armory. "Nobody move!"

29

B ELL'S ALERT HAD THE SAME EFFECT AS TURNING ON A LIGHT in a room full of cockroaches.

It looked like a half dozen men had been in a space on the storage side of the armory where tables, chairs, and couches had been set up as a living area. There were partitions to create bedrooms, a makeshift kitchen with an icebox over a floor drain, and a wood-burning stove with a haphazard tin chimney venting out a hole hammered through an exterior brick wall. Pilfered Oriental rugs covered the concrete under the furniture. A gramophone on a pedestal table played Irish folk music.

The men reacted like sprinters at the starter pistol. A table where two had been playing cards was upended in a cascade of chips and spades and all their chairs fell back when they leapt to their feet and started running. One guy who'd been reading the paper on the couch threw himself over it in a startling display of agility and speed. Others sought cover where they could find it.

The two men in the kitchen tending a stewpot ducked around the potbellied stove, while the original guard who knew he'd screwed up by letting the raiding party through decided to do something about it.

He slowed in a loose-legged deceleration that saw his size twelves slap at the concrete floor as he pulled a big revolver from his holster.

"Gun," James Dashwood shouted. Like Bell he carried a shotgun, but his hadn't been as shortened as his former mentor's. And unlike Bell's loads of buckshot, his fired twelve-gauge slugs with the kinetic force of a charging elephant.

The range was only thirty feet, and such was Dashwood's skill that he didn't bother raising the weapon from his hip. As he watched the doorman swing his aim toward the Van Dorns with obvious intent, he pulled the trigger and had the weapon racked at almost the same time the slug found its mark.

The guard was lifted off his feet by the impact and his body thrown against a wire-mesh door that blocked access to a small utility room crammed with wiring and a pair of industrial-scale power switches. The wire door gave way under his weight, and he hit the room's back wall hard enough to shake the brick. His corpse immediately sagged, and as it dropped to the ground, his coat caught on the two switches. They managed to hold him somewhat upright for a beat and then they both lowered, and the body hit the ground. Circuits that had been closed for years were suddenly open.

All at once, the two sawmill production lines swung into motion. Saws spun up in devilish whines, the conveyor belts made of bolted-together steel plates came to life, their steel teeth glinting, and logs were once again feeling the sting of the blades. The noise was ferocious, but the building was so overbuilt that one could fire off the cannonade of the "1812 Overture" and a person on the street would be none the wiser.

"Clarence Jones gave a pretty generic description of the O'Conner brothers," Bell shouted over the din. "We need one of them alive, so go easy on the guns."

"I doubt either O'Conner was on guard duty," Dashwood countered, to which Bell nodded, conceding the point.

By now, the gang members had all found cover and shots began to ring out over the sound of commercial-sized saws cutting wooden logs into dimensioned lumber. Sawdust came cascading down the chutes from the upper mill and soon grew like dunes under the lower-level machines.

While Tel Jones maneuvered to flank the guy who'd dived over the couch, Bell moved to get an angle on the two men in the kitchen behind the stove. Dashwood and Slocomb also went off hunting.

The two goons behind the stove fired revolvers without exposing their heads to take proper aim. It was one thing to terrorize innocent shopkeepers and lean on gamblers to repay their debts, but it was a whole different proposition going after men who were firing back.

Bell felt the rush of adrenaline as he moved closer to the mills, where there was ample cover and the confusion of moving machinery disguised any movement he had to make to get a bead. He felt more than heard someone come after him from deeper inside the machinery spaces. One of O'Conner's men, who didn't have a pistol, lunged at Bell's midriff with a length of two-by-four. Bell moved aside just enough so the butt end of board missed the middle of his stomach, and instead grazed his side with the same feeling as if he'd been sliced with a sword. The board collided with his hands, knocking the shotgun free and sending it flying across the room.

He involuntarily grimaced at his reddened hands, giving his opponent a chance to riposte and try again. Bell jumped aside and managed to pull his Browing automatic, firing a wild, unaimed shot to force his attacker to back off. The man was fearless and charged yet again, this time throwing the two-by-four like a spear. Bell ducked and held up an arm to protect his head. This was what the gangster had anticipated. He broke into Bell's personal space as the wood clattered to the floor. He threw his arms around Bell, pinning his arms to his sides, and began squeezing with unimaginable strength.

It was then that Bell realized he was fighting the bruiser who'd beaten the barber and the numbers guy half to death. Three-quarters to death, really. Patrick Murphy, the guy who could stop a man's heart with a single punch.

Considering he was still alive, Bell felt the fight was going better than expected.

He tilted his head back and rammed it forward as hard as he could, tucking his chin at the last second. Murphy was so tall that Bell managed to headbutt his cleft chin and probably did more damage to himself than the Irish enforcer. His next trick was to pull his feet off the floor and hope to get gravity to break Murphy's grip. The man held him aloft as easily as a principal dancer holds a ballerina and somehow increased his boa-like constriction.

Unable to aim because of how he was being held, Bell hadn't dared fire his automatic toward the floor in fear of hitting his own foot, but now in the clear, he cycled through a magazine, catching a break when the last bullet struck Murphy and blew off the baby toe on his right foot.

He immediately released Bell, who hadn't yet got his feet set under him and stumbled forward into the giant. Murphy's pain and shock of losing the digit lasted only an instant. He grabbed Bell by the front of his shirt and threw a straight left, which Bell managed to turn aside with his forearm. Bell then brought the butt of his Browning down on the crown of the thug's head in a multi-blow attack that finally gained him his freedom. Murphy staggered back as blood started to wash down his face from the half dozen scalp lacerations.

Bell threw his empty pistol at him as a distraction and charged at the big man with everything he had. In all his life, no one had ever thrown themselves at Big Pat Murphy. It just wasn't done, and he had no defense against it. Bell's shoulder went deep into Murphy's gut, blowing the air from his lungs in a massive explosion. Bell wrapped his arms around the man's torso and drove him back with his legs working like pistons.

The two staggered backward and Bell let go just as they reached his target. The hoist was a continuous belt of chains studded with spikes to hold logs and carry them up to the second-tier mill. Designed to grasp and lift four-hundred-pound logs, the spikes were more than sharp enough to impale Patrick Murphy. This time the pain made him roar aloud, a sound that even managed to drown out some of the gunfire echoing throughout the armory. He instantly tried to pull away, but the chain drive was already lifting him off the floor, the spikes tearing ever deeper into his body.

He squirmed and screamed as he was hauled up to the upper deck, blood raining freely to the floor. In seconds, the chains had lifted him all the way up and he was pulled deeper into the clanking machine. Then came a scream that would haunt Bell to his dying days. Murphy at last realized he was being drawn into one of the furiously spinning saw blades. His wail was a high-pitched keen of terror that ended with an abruptness that made Bell wince.

Blood soon glazed the mound of sawdust under the saw's waste chute.

Bell retrieved his pistol and reloaded. He went to find his people and quickly located Clint Slocomb taking cover behind a mass of logs that had yet to be fed into the mills' hungry mouths.

"Status."

"There's too much damn cover in here. It's hard to get a clean shot on these boys. Though, I can see why they're called the Fighting Irish."

"How's your ammunition?"

"If I can't take a clean shot, I won't waste it for a bad one. I'm okay. I hear young Tel firing off like he's the last man at Custer's stand. He's covering the alleyway exit and they're all trying like hell to leave this sinking ship."

Bell moved on. The two guys from the kitchen had left their position behind the stove, and he saw one of them loping up the metal stairs to reach the catwalks surrounding the upper-tier mill. As no new logs were being fed into it, the twin systems were running out of wood to cut, and the sound levels were diminishing somewhat.

He took off after the fleeing man, drawing a hasty shot from someone hiding amid the cargo boxes stacked in the other section of the armory building. That shot was met by a barrage from Clint Slocomb's .45s as he laid down his own cover fire to advance on the gang member.

Bell reached the open steel steps, seeing no sign of his quarry. He climbed slowly, his gun held tight to his body so that it couldn't be yanked away by someone hiding around a blind corner. The mill was pretty open-planned with little full concealment, but his stance was a result of muscle memory. The walkways ran parallel to the moving conveyor belts with no safety rails to separate them. He tried to avert his gaze when he spotted what remained of Pat Murphy.

He continued to search around the mill, his feet just a couple of inches from the conveyor belt whooshing by like a metal river. Bell's feet were suddenly yanked out from under him by a pair of hands that had been hidden under a workbench strewn with tools for sharpening the various saws and blades. He crashed down hard and the guy who'd ambushed him rammed his feet into Bell's gut. Bell rolled onto the conveyor belt, taking one of its spikes in the shoulder, though not too deeply.

The belts didn't move all that quickly, but it felt like he accelerated from zero to twenty in an instant. The system was designed in such a way that the belts delivered logs to various stations and continued on after dropping them in the arms of autoloaders that then fed them into the different cutting machines. Bell quickly found himself coming up onto a platform where a chain saw cut each log into various lengths depending on the setting. When the mill had been shuttered, they were filling a fence installer's order for four-foot lengths of wood. Bell scrambled back when he entered the cutting box, but his feet still hit a pressure bar that normally a log would butt up against. This caused the conveyor to stop and the electric-powered chain saw to swing down on its mechanical arm.

Bell had to crunch his stomach and do the hardest, fastest sit-up of his life to avoid the whirring blade as it sliced downward just inches from his spine.

Once the saw reset itself, the pressure bar swung open and the conveyor started up again. When he cleared the enclosed trough-like saw station, Bell managed to roll off the mechanical belt and regain his feet. The guy who he'd been following was just vanishing around a large piece of the mill that ground up the bark stripped from the log for use as landscape mulch.

He had a moment to fire at the fleeing figure, but didn't know if it was one of the O'Conners in his sights. He started after the man, his footfalls rattling the ironworks' catwalks.

The other man was ahead, but not by much, and as they approached a ninety-degree bend in the walkway, Bell saw his chance to catch the man in an instant. There was a chain fall hanging from a swivel crane derrick mounted to the armory's soaring ceiling. As the man reached the corner, he turned briefly and fired two shots from a snub-nosed revolver. Bell leapt over the rail and grabbed the dangling chains on the fly. His momentum caused the derrick arm to rotate and Bell swooped around the turn well outside the catwalk, but then the rotation brought him around so that he was now in front of the gang member.

The man raised his gun to fire again as Bell jackknifed his legs and kicked him in the chest far harder than he'd intended. The impact threw the man against the scaffold's outside railing and then up and over it. He fell, screaming, and landed in the debarking machine for the lower-level mill.

Two long revolving drums studded with hundreds of iron fingers designed to remove bark without damaging the log caught him up. The drums rotated too fast for him to even try to climb free, and while the metal projections weren't that big, the battering they gave him was unrelenting.

Bell worked the chain fall to lower it down so the thug could haul himself out of the death trap, but by the time he got it hovering just above the drums, the man had been beaten unconscious. The machine was built with the rotating cylinders at a slight angle so the logs it removed the bark from eventually were dumped out of one end and onto another conveyor belt. That's what happened to this guy, who Bell knew wasn't one of the O'Conners based on his small size and bright orange hair. Where the Irish mobster went after that, Bell didn't want to contemplate.

He saw someone running from a back area he hadn't noted before, wondering if there were old offices in one corner of the building as well as restrooms. The man fit Clarence Jones's description of Sean O'Conner. From his vantage atop the upper mill, Bell couldn't see his men other than Tel still guarding the only working exit out of the building. He was just opening his mouth to shout a warning that O'Conner was coming when the gangster pulled a sawed-off shotgun out from under his long coat.

He wasn't close enough to guarantee a kill, so when he fired, and the buckshot spread in a widening cone, only one of the lead pellets struck the Van Dorn man. It hit him high on his right shoulder, breaking his collarbone and nicking the subclavian artery. His shirt was instantly awash in bright blood. His arm was all but useless. His deadened fingers let his shotgun clatter to the floor.

O'Conner didn't get to his other barrel. Instead, he put on a burst of speed now that his way out was clear. Bell shouted to his men that their target was escaping. He couldn't fire because Telford was in his line of fire as O'Conner ran for the exit. Bell gave

Jones credit. He tried to retrieve his weapon with his left hand and was just getting it up when the Irishman plowed into him with the force of a charging bear.

Jones went flying, screaming at the fresh pain in his already battered shoulder. Bell threw himself headfirst down one of the sawdust chutes, hit the pile on the first floor, and somersaulted to his feet. Another of O'Conner's men broke cover at that moment, seeing that he, too, could escape what they all believed to be an attack by a rival gang.

Fearing that the man would escape, Bell didn't want to slow to take a wild shot at him. He needn't have worried. From across the vast space James Dashwood fired his rifle and the gangster went down.

Bell had too much ground to cover to reach O'Conner before he made the exit, and he hated the prospect of trying to capture him on a busy street. He would never fire into a crowd to get his man, but he doubted the mob boss would be so hesitant. He could imagine the carnage left behind from a couple of blasts from O'Conner's shotgun.

Over his own frantic breathing and the echo of Dashwood's rifle shot that still bounced around the brick building, Bell heard the alleyway door fly open. Bell estimated that O'Conner would be out of the alley and down half a block by the time he reached the door. He was still struggling with all the abuse his body had taken over the past days. O'Conner would be at least a block away if he were being honest with himself, and increasing that lead by the second.

Bell finally made it to the door. He wrenched it open and nearly fell flat on his face.

Sean O'Conner lay unconscious on the alley's crumbling asphalt. Standing a few steps away was Marion Bell holding a field hockey stick over her shoulder and Christoff Tamerlane with, of all things, a cricket bat over his. The bat's sweet spot had a smear of blood from O'Conner's forehead.

"Turns out," the artist said while giving his bat a carefree twirl, "I have a bit of courage after all."

30

Forty-five minutes later, Telford Jones was being tended to by a physician the Van Dorn Agency kept on retainer, as was their practice in any city where they maintained offices. His cousin was by his side. A disappointed Marion and a relieved Christoff were on the train back to Washington, D.C., congratulating themselves on their forethought to return to the alley armed with some used sporting equipment they'd bought from one of the vender stalls adjoining the armory. In a garage under the building where the Van Dorns kept their office, Bell, Archie, Dashwood, and Clint Slocomb stood in a loose circle around a chair where Sean O'Conner sat bound and gagged. A trickle of blood had dried above his eyebrow and he had a splitting headache after being struck with what he thought was a coal shovel.

He'd been conscious for enough time to realize he was in the back of an enclosed truck and that he was in severe trouble.

Bell let some time pass so that O'Conner's imagination would start to conjure up the things he feared most. It was a classic interrogation technique—make the subject start torturing themselves before you ever ask a question. This was a critical point in the case. Everything hung in the balance and Bell knew he had one chance to do this right and a couple dozen that would end the investigation here and now.

He stood in front of the mobster. "You lost at least eight of your men working for Jackson Pickett." Bell noted O'Conner's eyes. He had recognized the name and was confused as to how Bell knew it. "Three more are dead today and a couple more pretty badly injured. The rest the cops have now. Don't know if any charges will stick, but that doesn't really matter. With your brother missing and all that I just said, it's clear to anyone that the O'Conner gang is no more. With me so far?"

Sean remained still, trying to project defiance.

"You have no idea the forces at work right now as a result of the theft at the Bureau of Engraving and Printing. This wasn't some two-bit holdup of a rural bank in Hind-end, Kansas. The future of the nation's banking system is at risk because of what they did. We're talking a financial panic unlike anything we've seen before. Millions out of work. Families destroyed. Children starving to death. Those are the stakes, the way the government sees it. And entire government agencies have been mobilized in an effort to find the money and those who stole it.

"In other words, you and Pickett have kicked a monumental hornet's nest, and right now every one of their stingers is pointed at you."

Bell knew he had O'Conner's full attention. He could see the gears turning in the man's head as he tried to find a way out of this situation.

"Do you know the key to catching criminals? No? Everyone assumes it's that you must outsmart them. You have to look at how clever they are and find a way of being more clever. That does work, but not always. No, the real way you catch a criminal is to be more ruthless than he is. Pickett and his sidekick stabbed or shot eight of your guys after you lent them out for the job as muscle. Pretty ruthless, I'd say. So today we raided your warehouse and I personally fed one of your men into the log debarking machine. I pressed another against the lift carrying logs to one of the big saws."

He paused to let O'Conner contemplate the manner of death of two of his friends.

"I know how to be ruthless, too, and I have something even more spectacular in store for you if things don't go my way in the next few minutes."

By now Sean O'Conner was nodding his head and moaning into his gag in his eagerness to talk.

"I have two questions," Bell said. "If you tell me you don't know the answers, I will believe you. I will also kill you and bury you in a hole so deep you'll turn into petroleum before anyone finds your body.

"In order for Pickett and his other safecracker to get into the vault so quickly, they had to have had access to a similar safe on which to practice. They knew the vault's defenses and how to defeat them long before they zip-lined into that building. He also knew the scale of the thing so as to have custom tools made for the heist. He was able to practice on this other safe dozens, if not hundreds, of times, meaning he had open and easy access to it. Now, when the Fed system was launched and the vault in Washington upgraded, twelve similar vaults were installed at the twelve new

Reserve banks. I have no doubt that Pickett had been granted access to one of these vaults with permission from that local Fed chief."

Archie gave Bell a look that was equal parts astonishment and respect, a look that told him his friend hadn't thought of that, but that it made perfect sense.

"My first question," Bell continued, holding up a finger, "is which Fed chair gave them access to his safe and lied to the Treasury Department about having possession of all one hundred thousand dollars in new bills since the very same man doled them out to various coconspirators?"

Bell put up a second finger. "My other question is the name of the leprechaun-looking psychopath who's doing all of Pickett's dirty work and I suspect clawing back much of the money I just mentioned."

Bell nodded to Clint Slocomb, who loosened O'Conner's gag enough for him to speak.

His words spilled out in a tumbling rush. "Michaleen Riordan. He's as crazy as they come. My brother had a deal with those two and Riordan gunned him down anyways. Tried to lie about it, but I know the truth. My guys working with 'em on the heist, they were already off training and had no idea what betrayal was coming for them. I wasn't even supposed to know his name, but Flynn told me one night over too much whiskey. I thought you and your men were with Riordan when you came busting into our place, there to finish off the rest of the gang, seeing as we were more loose ends.

"I see now that you're not part of Riordan's crew," O'Conner added. "You're a government man, ain't ya? From one of those agencies you mentioned?"

"Our identities are meaningless to you. What do you know about Riordan?"

"Not much, I swear," O'Conner said quickly. "Flynn dealt with him mostly. Flynn told me Riordan came from County Cork, but he never said anything beyond that."

"How about Pickett?"

"He's from New Orleans, I know that. He and Riordan were the ones to open the vault. I only met Pickett a couple of times. Real charmer, that one. Has a way of talking a lot without saying much a'tall. He's the kind of guy you check to make sure your wallet's still in your pocket when you take your leave of him. I also felt he'd likely kill for no other reason than he could."

Bell thought back to his time with Pickett in his Rhode Island mansion and the portrait of the wife he murdered above the mantel in her private chambers. He couldn't imagine a more apt description than O'Conner's.

"As to my first question," Bell said. "What is the name of the Federal Reserve banker who betrayed his nation?"

"His name is Philip Findley. He's the head of the Atlanta branch."

"Wrong," Bell shot back. "I sat across from the Atlanta guy not two weeks ago and his name is, ah, Weldon Burdett."

"No. It's Findley. I'm sure of it," O'Conner insisted. "Flynn needed convincing that this job was feasible when Pickett came to him for muscle."

Archie interrupted. "Back up for a second. How did Pickett know about you and your brother and your gang?"

"He said we've got a reputation of being good at boosting stuff. He needed a crew that knew how to work together and were smarter than regular street hoods. Most of us can read, which

Pickett said was important 'cause it showed we could follow instructions."

Bell suspected just the opposite was true. Pickett wanted someone he could easily dupe, and he imagined with his sophisticated charm and an Irishman as his chief lieutenant that Flynn O'Conner lapped up the flattery and never saw what fate really had in store for him.

"Get back to your brother needing to be convinced about the heist," he said.

"Right. So Flynn knew this would take a lot of time and loads of cash. He wasn't going to take Pickett's word for it even when he showed him ten grand of the new money. Flynn made Pickett introduce him to the backers. That's Philip Findley. Flynn and Pickett and Riordan went down to Atlanta together to meet with him. Late one night, Findley showed him the vault that the two would be practicing on and all the rest of the money. It turns out Findley owns a bank, too. One of the largest in Georgia. The guy was loaded. More than rich enough to bankroll a heist of that size."

Bell gave Archie a nod. The two men pushed aside the canvas covering the truck's rear gate and jumped to the garage's oiled dirt floor. The soil still had embedded lengths of straw from when the space had been an underground stable.

"A Fed banker being in on it?" Archie said while unscrewing the cap of a small hip flask. "Brilliant piece of intuitive logic."

"Deductive, but thanks." Bell took the flask from him after Arch had taken a sip. It was Napoleon brandy, so smooth it slid down like melted caramel.

"What do you think?" Arch asked.

"I knew I was right about one of the twelve bankers being involved, but for the life of me I can't imagine why. What does

Findley or Burdett, or whoever is the real head of the Atlanta Fed, gain by robbing the very institution he represents? I can see Pickett wanting to score big. He loved the high life he'd had with his wife, and we confirmed his story that with her out of the picture he gets to keep the clothes on his back and little else. But why would a deep-pocket banker get involved?"

"You told me there was some resentment that Atlanta was chosen over New Orleans for the southern regional Fed. Could that be a factor?"

"Possibly. My dad told me some of the other Fed chairs said Atlanta was selected because of Wilson and Secretary McAdoo having deep Georgia roots." He paused. "Actually, there's no use speculating."

Archie grinned. "I assume we're going to Atlanta to have a conversation with him in much the same manner we're talking to this sack of manure?"

"Same manure. Bigger sack. But before we leave, I want to know what was found in that locksmith's shop in Philadelphia."

"Why?"

"Call it a hunch," Bell said, the gears grinding behind his clear blue eyes.

31

Washington, D.C.

THE NAME OF THE ATLANTA CHAIR FOR THE FEDERAL RE-
serve was Philip Findley and he hadn't been to his office for
a week. No one knew where he was or how to reach him.

Bell said to Marion, "This means my investigation has ground
to a halt."

They were in a suite of rooms at the Willard with a spectacular
view down Pennsylvania Avenue of the Capitol Building. Currently Marion was soaking in a bubble bath that was rapidly losing
its opaque coating of soap bubbles, much to Bell's delight. Her
blond hair was piled atop her head in a messy heap and the water
had been so hot that her skin remained pink and still glistened like
the finest alabaster. Bell sat on a teak towel cabinet filled with
rolled towels as thick around as birthday cakes. A glass of wine sat
within Marion's reach, while Bell enjoyed a whiskey as his predin-
ner drink.

"Who was the guy you thought was Findley on the President's

yacht?" Marion asked, scooping bubbles from one strategic area at the sacrifice of another. She saw in his demeanor, despite his attempt to hide it from her, that he was hitting a dead end in the case. Her little show was her way of cutting through some of the gloom.

"McAdoo told me he's a Treasury Department employee who filled out the meeting on the *Mayflower*, so Wilson didn't know one of the board members had canceled at the last minute. Remember, Wilson hadn't met these guys. He'd just rubber-stamped the commission recommendations and moved on to other business."

"Why did Findley not appear?"

Bell saluted her with his drink. "The very question I posed to McAdoo."

"See," she said with a bright grin. "I do pay attention."

"Never in doubt. He told me that Findley claimed some family emergency. I followed up with a call to his bank. I got as high as an assistant vice president. All he knew was that Findley took off for a few days around the time of the meeting on the Potomac. Came back as if nothing had happened, and then vamoosed last week."

"If he had to cancel out of the meeting, why didn't he send someone else from his bank?"

"His bank and the Atlanta Fed have completely different staffs and I don't know if he's appointed a second-in-command for the Reserve bank yet."

"Ah." There was more moving of bubbles, but it was obvious her modesty was being thwarted. "Are you going to track him?"

"I'll try, but he's got a week's head start. McAdoo thinks he can keep this whole affair from the American public. I have my doubts. I'm afraid that by the time I have him, the lid will be blown off the story and the robbery will be on every front page in the country."

"Oof. Sad trombone."

"Huh?"

"Vaudeville. You know, when something goes wrong for the actor onstage, and they play those three notes on a trombone. *Womp, womp, woooomph.* Sad trombone."

"This is far worse than a pratfall or a pie in the face. Not only will that be the end of the whole Reserve system, but McAdoo had mentioned earlier that there will be bank runs in every city and town in America. The financial ruin heading our way will be unprecedented."

Marion gave up on the bubbles and used her oddly dexterous toes to pull the claw-footed tub's rubber stopper. She stood, proud and sleek and beautiful, and Bell couldn't have loved her more. He plucked one of the rolled-up towels from the open cabinet and handed it over.

"What else did McAdoo have to say?" she asked, drying herself in a deliberately provocative way, bending far deeper and far longer than was strictly necessary.

Bell had to clear his throat to speak in his normal voice. "Not McAdoo, but Vic Carver, the treasury agent in charge of the investigation into the attack on the President's yacht. I'll give the big guy credit, he's tenacious and thorough. His team found four more bombs not far from the Potomac River that had been jettisoned from the plane. They hadn't been armed, which is why they hadn't gone off. Two of them were incendiary and the others filled with high explosives and ball bearings."

"Sounds ghastly."

"I think their strategy was to get everyone on deck and try to burn the ship, tossing in some shrapnel for good measure. They wouldn't have killed all of the Reserve heads, but a good chunk of them."

"Seems a bit random to me," Marion opined with a coquettish glance over her shoulder.

Her antics continued to distract Bell. "Huh?"

"Trying to kill twelve specific passengers on a boat by blowing it up with bombs tossed from an airplane? That leaves a great deal to chance, don't you think?"

Bell suddenly realized the glaring contradiction of it all, and just like that, his case was thrown wide open again. He laughed and grabbed his wife by the bare shoulders. He gave her a strong kiss on the lips that left her a little weak-kneed. "You genius of a woman. That's what's been bothering me about this whole thing. Jackson Pickett is a criminal mastermind, right?"

"If you say so."

"I do. His planning, timing, and execution of the heist was utterly flawless. And he covered his tracks mercilessly, but also with perfect aforethought. If I hadn't happened to walk by that night it would have been the perfect crime. But I didn't just happen to walk by that night."

"No?"

"No. I was on alert because of the airplane attack on the *Mayflower*."

"But that was so long ago."

"It was," Bell agreed, "but because of it, the Federal Reserve system has stayed in the back of my mind. The night of the heist, Archie told me about finding some of the new notes used to bribe one of his father-in-law's railroad executives. I felt the railroads were where the money was the most vulnerable, but I couldn't stop thinking about the mountain of cash sitting in a vault just a couple of miles away. Next thing I know, I'm driving over to the Bureau of Engraving and Printing. I had no real reason to go, other than to satisfy my own curiosity."

"It was like the attack focused you on the money, like a tip-off," Marion said.

"Like that, yes. But it made no sense. Why would Pickett bring attention to the Fed in the months prior to his big night robbing them blind? He wouldn't. He wouldn't want anyone thinking there was something amiss."

"Or something afoot," Marion said quickly.

"That's it. And the answer is he didn't."

"Didn't what?"

"Didn't send that plane to attack the President's yacht. It was a sloppy plan from the beginning. Like you said—too much left to chance. Pickett is far too clever to have come up with that."

"It was Findley," Marion said, suddenly seeing what her husband had.

"That's why he didn't show. He knew the yacht was going to be attacked. Also why he didn't send someone in his stead. I assume his deputy will be a close friend who he didn't want to place in danger. I need to get to Atlanta."

"What? Now?"

"I've had Agent Carver investigating airfields in an ever-widening circle, looking for a missing pilot and plane that matches the attackers. Waste of time. The airfield is someplace close to Atlanta because Philip Findley knew and trusted the pilot enough to take him into his confidence and get him to agree to bomb the *Mayflower*."

"Why?"

"Betrayal and a change of heart is all I can figure. This whole case is rife with betrayal. Pickett betrayed his wife, a building contractor, a locksmith, a railroad executive, and a crime lord, along with a handful of his thugs. Findley started out the whole thing by betraying the very partner he instigated the theft with—Jackson Pickett. At some point, Findley must have gotten nervous about the robbery and backed out or tried to preempt it. Maybe he no longer trusted Pickett to do him right. By sabotaging the Federal Reserve system through the murder of its head bankers with the attack on the *Mayflower*, there wouldn't be any need for Pickett to rob the Engraving Bureau. But for Pickett, no robbery meant no money. And no money would mean no independent lavish lifestyle he was accustomed to, along with the fact that he would have murdered his wife for no reason whatsoever."

"That's why Findley's in hiding?"

A grimmer thought occurred to Bell. "I have to consider that Michaleen Riordan has gotten to him already." No sooner had he said it, he shook his head. "I can't even think that way. Findley is my only link to Pickett. I need him alive if I'm to recover the money in time."

"I'm sure it'll all work out," Marion said breezily. "By the way, what happened to that gangster that Christoff bashed over the head?"

"Yeah. About that. Why a cricket bat?"

"The man did have some baseball bats for sale, but Christoff said they lacked style. If you're going to brain someone, he told me, do it with a little panache. So, what happened to him?"

"After we finished questioning him, we couldn't risk him going to the police with our descriptions, so Clint and James poured half a bottle of whiskey down his throat and press-ganged him onto a cargo schooner bound for Rio. If the winds are favorable, he'll get there in about two months."

Marion laughed. "Now that's what I call panache."

THEY WERE CROSSING THE WILLARD'S LOBBY HEADING FOR AN after-dinner cocktail at the Round Robin Bar when Bell saw a large man push through the hotel's brass and glass door. The man was stone-faced and wearing what was likely a Treasury Department–issued dark suit and tie. Bell didn't recognize the agent, but he knew that he was there for him. That supposition was confirmed when Paul Haygarth, Agent Vic Carver's dim-witted partner, strode through behind him, his arms stiff like a child's windup toy.

They weren't here for a conversation about the case. They were scut-work errand boys sent to fetch Bell.

Haygarth scanned the lobby, missed Bell on the first pass, but then realized his mistake and zeroed in on the Van Dorn detective. He came over as subtly as a charging bull.

"Boss wants to see you," Haygarth said, like he'd rehearsed the line so he sounded tough.

"Nice to see you, Agent Haygarth," Bell replied with a big smile that told the T-man he wasn't intimidated in the slightest. "I don't believe you've met my wife. Marion, this is Paul Haygarth of the Treasury Department."

His stoic-to-the-point-of-dourness act blown, Haygarth muttered a greeting and shook her proffered hand.

"Isaac has told me all about you," Marion said in such a way that Haygarth couldn't quite tell if that was good or bad. Bell could have kissed her for reading the man so perfectly.

"We have a car outside," Haygarth told Bell.

"Give me a moment to escort my wife to our room. I'll be right down."

Marion was more than capable of seeing herself up, but Bell didn't like men who hid their lack of intelligence and imagination by bullying others.

He was back downstairs after making the agents wait an extra few minutes while he helped Marion out of the elaborate dress she'd worn for him. Their car, a glossy black Packard Twin-Six idled just outside the hotel. Bell and Haygarth took the spacious rear seats, while the unnamed agent on escort duty sat next to the driver. The luxury car eased from the curb with the dignity of an ocean liner.

Since the Treasury building was literally right next door to the Willard, Bell was surprised they had a car at all. His next surprise came when they drove past the mammoth limestone building and instead paused at the White House's main gate for two guards to vet them and let them in. The driver pulled up to the entrance portico.

Bell had never been to the White House and, although impressed, he gave no outward sign as Haygarth lead him to the front door and a servant in a morning coat escorted him upstairs to what were the President's private quarters. Bell noted the furniture looked like it had been around for several administrations. He was ushered into a private dining room across a wide hall from what looked like the President's master bedroom.

Wilson and his son-in-law, Treasury Secretary William McAdoo, were sitting together at one end of the six-person table. A bottle of scotch sat between them, and each man had a full tumbler in easy reach. The atmosphere was one of sorrow.

"Mr. President, Isaac Bell," the aide said and padded silently from the room.

"Mr. President," Bell said, "I know some time has passed, but I would like to add my condolences on the passing of your wife."

She had died the day after the attack on the *Mayflower* and Wilson had been at her side.

No one made a move to shake hands, but Wilson gestured for Bell to sit and grabbed a third tumbler off a sideboard. "Thank you, Mr. Bell. Three months this very night. I was feeling a little maudlin, so I asked Bill over. We've been discussing the robbery."

McAdoo said, "We've reached a decision about the case. Or about how to handle it going forward. I knew you were staying at the Willard so I chanced you could come over to hear our thoughts. When I met with him about all this, Joseph Van Dorn mentioned how you like to have information as soon as it's available."

"And to act on it on the jump," Bell said.

"We have managed to hide the theft from all but a handful of Engraving Bureau employees. We've told the remaining personnel a cover story of some of the money being shipped early. We're sure that news of the theft will never get out."

Bell silently doubted McAdoo's assertion. Of the many lessons he'd learned over the course of his storied career, the main one was that people talked. Always.

"You have a suspect, right?" President Wilson asked.

"I do, sir. Yes. A man named Jackson Pickett."

"But you have no proof?"

"That is also correct, Mr. President," Bell replied. "The only way to definitively prove Pickett is the mastermind is for me to find him with the money."

"Therein lies the rub," McAdoo said. "We can't prosecute him for a robbery we've maintained never happened."

"We've decided," the President said, "that it's best for the country if Pickett and the money are never found. The scoundrel performed such an audacious feat that we are left having to pretend it never happened at all."

Bell had been warned this could happen as the date of the official Federal Reserve launch drew closer. Though embittered by the decision, he kept his tone casual. "And you've accepted allowing a murderer to get away with a billion dollars?"

"What choice do we have?" McAdoo snapped. "We can't just kill the man."

"He's an American citizen with rights, no matter how reprehensible his character," Wilson said, with some force in his voice.

"In the grand scheme of things, Mr. Bell, what is losing a billion dollars when we have fifty times that invested in this federal-level banking system? If it fails, we will have bankrupted the country."

It wasn't to Bell's way of thinking, but he could appreciate the magnitude of the problem at hand. Losing a billion dollars surely stung, but it was a sacrifice to the greater good Wilson and McAdoo were willing to make. He said, "Pickett murdered his wife a few months before the heist. What if we ignore the robbery and charge him with that?"

Wilson visibly brightened. "Is there proof?"

"Not at this time," Bell told them, and the President's newfound optimism faded. "But I have agents actively working that case and I have a suspicion that if proven right will send him to the electric chair."

"Do you know where he is?" McAdoo asked.

Bell shook his head. "No, but I have a lead. The strongest one since this whole case fell into my lap."

"Not good enough," McAdoo said. "Today is Monday. I'll give you till the end of this week, Mr. Bell, to find Pickett and proof of his guilt in the murder of his wife. If you have one without the other it does us no good. If you are unsuccessful in this task, the government's interest in pursuing Jackson Pickett is at an end and you are expressly forbidden to continue your investigation privately or in any other capacity. Is that understood?"

Bell remained silent.

McAdoo continued. "First thing in the morning I will have a letter drafted stipulating what I just said and the penalties for ignoring it. You and Mr. Van Dorn will sign it. Understood?"

"With all due respect, I wholly disagree with your decision tonight, yet I understand your reasoning and I will abide by your conditions. That said, I will be on a train heading south long before your letter reaches the Willard, but my word is as secure a bond as my signature. Good night, Mr. President, Mr. Secretary."

Back at the Willard, he made a call to Newport, Rhode Island, and left a police duty sergeant some detailed if baffling instructions. Bell would have preferred to wait, but there was now a clock over his shoulder ticking ever louder.

32

New Orleans, Louisiana

T HEY WERE SO DEEP IN THE BAYOU THAT THE ONLY CREATURES
to hear the shot were alligators and mosquitoes. The engineer was the last of the men working the heist who wasn't part of Michaleen Riordan's crew. Everyone else were outsiders brought in for their various skills. Now the locomotive driver lay slumped over the controls of the train in which they'd fled south from the defunct tunnel in rural Virginia. The coal shoveler was dead in the adjacent coal car with a knife wound through the heart. Neither man had any idea that the Irish assassin had stowed away on the train.

The train had five cars, the money car, a sleeper for the men, and three others just to make it look more legitimate. With the driver dead, Michaleen pushed the corpse to the coal-coated floor and applied the brakes at the same time bleeding off steam until the boiler was nearly empty. The engine and wagons clanked to a halt, effectively blocking an abandoned private spur that cut through the swamplands off a main line that barely ever saw traffic.

It was the mile walk back to the cannery that Michaleen dreaded. The tracks were laid on an earthen levee that had been covered in a layer of gravel and so it was raised high enough to prevent any animals that called the muddy water home from climbing up. But the sun was slowly setting and he knew from his years of living in Louisiana that this was when the bugs came out, and he detested insects more than he feared the gators, snapping turtles, and venomous snakes.

His short stature and gait meant it took him nearly thirty minutes to make it back to the fish factory. The rambling facility was perched along a canal off a tidal estuary that had been dug two generations ago, only to be left to nature after the business venture failed long before the Marquess was born. Michaleen had given Jackson Pickett that teasing moniker the day they'd met at the shop of a fence they both used in the French Quarter nearly two decades earlier. Pickett had been so nattily dressed and was so debonair that Michaleen couldn't help but think of him as a titled gentleman. The two men had recognized in each other the same larcenous spirit and had partnered on and off ever since.

Of course, after he and Pickett had been hired by Philip Findley to tank the Federal Reserve before it even started, he'd dubbed the Atlanta banker the Baron, since that was a higher-order royal rank. Pickett was even less amused by that.

He finally made it back to the abandoned factory. They had done nothing to clean up the facility except hire a couple locals to clear a channel of vegetation from the mouth of the old canal to the cannery's dock. Michaleen had wanted to kill those men once the task was finished, but Pickett overruled him, knowing that their deaths would raise too many questions. The high wages paid to them, along with a promised bonus to come, ensured those men wouldn't talk.

The main building looked like something out of a Gothic horror story; its two-story facade of white clapboard was scabrous with mold and choked by English ivy and liana vines. The dock upon which it sat was in better condition than it had any right to be, but still had numerous patches of rot. There were two old cranes on the dock as well and they reminded Michaleen of the spindly trunks of dead trees.

An old tugboat was tied to the dock, a coil of smoke rising from its funnel. Also tied to the pier was a barge designed to move train cars on tracks laid down its spine. This particular barge could carry three cars, but would only transport the single money car out once Pickett felt it was safe to move on.

Nearby was the shed where they had uncoupled the boxcar full of cash. The doors were still open and Michaleen could see several men inside. Other men were organizing the provisions that would sustain them here in the middle of the bayou until the Federal Reserve system was officially launched and they were all multimillionaires.

He ambled over to hear Jackson curse. "Problem then, squire?"

Pickett turned to look at him. "All done?"

"The train is blocking the tracks and the bodies are in the swamp. Glad I got to push them down rather than pull them up. That stoker was a monster. What's going on here?"

"There's something wrong with the scale. It won't stop bouncing, so I can't set the alarm. And now we don't have enough light to go under the floor and fix the problem."

"Easy enough," Michaleen said. "We've got nothing but time

on our hands. I can lock myself in here tonight with a couple of loaded guns and you can fix the scale in the morning."

Pickett trusted Michaleen, but even that trust went only so far. "All right, but I'll be joining you for the evening."

"Fine, fine, I welcome the company. Has to be some furniture in the cannery's main office. We'll boil up some coffee and play cards till I take the first shift and wake you early dark o'clock for your turn."

"I suppose that'll work," Pickett conceded. The floor of the shed was an enormous scale for weighing cargo that was sensitive enough to detect the weight of a child. Once it was fixed, any deviation would send an alert to the tugboat, where the men were quartered. "We need to talk about Findley. Once he realizes we're not going to give away the money like we'd promised, he's going to become a liability."

"I felt he was a liability all along," Michaleen said. "Once we'd mastered opening the locks in his vault, I should have put him out of his misery."

"I told you then we didn't want to draw attention to anything about the Federal Reserve. Killing one of their twelve directors would have sparked an investigation that could have led in the wrong direction at the wrong time. But Findley knows too much. Once we're safely clear of here, I'd like you to make him disappear. It will add another layer of confusion to the robbery."

"Good thinking. I'll plan an excursion to Atlanta when you think the time is right and pay an 'impersonal' visit to our former banking comrade," Michaleen replied with a wink.

Later that night, after the two men had been locked in with the railcar stuffed with money and they'd played countless games of gin, whist, and truc, Michaleen said, "I know it's bad luck to think about what to do with the money after a score, but we're sitting next to our billion dollars, so now it's okay. What are you going to do with your wealth?"

"I intend to restore my family's holdings," Pickett said without giving it a thought. "There is a plantation about eighty miles from New Orleans, as well as a twenty-bedroom house in the city. I don't know who owns them now, but I'm going to make them offers they won't be able to decline. Of course, I can't use my real name. After this, Jackson Pickett is no more. Our name when my great-grandfather came from Tours was Piquet. I think I'll be John Piquet from now on. What about you? Going back to Ireland?"

"I've still got so many enemies on both the Loyalist and the Republican sides that I can never go back. I'm not even all that safe in many parts of America. Haven't you ever wondered why I'm practically the only Irishman in New Orleans? It certainly isn't the god-awful half-French slop you eat. Lord, what I would do with some black pudding and boxty.

"Truth is I wouldn't last a week in any city here with a lot of my countrymen. Place like Boston or New York? The Republicans especially have agents there raising money and recruits for the war they want to start. Someone's bound to recognize me and get word to the wrong ear. I'd be a dead man soon after."

"So, what will you do?"

"The writing is on the wall here. Sooner or later, they're going to ban alcohol, and when they do, Cuba is going to be the place for rich Americans looking to wet their beaks. I'm going to open the biggest, swankiest nightclub that island has ever seen. First-class all the way. Men in tuxes, ladies in gowns, and serving girls in as little as possible."

"Sounds like a place I'd like to come and visit."

"And you'll be more than welcome, Marquess de Piquet."

In mock anger, Pickett said, "To hell with you, you little gnome. With a half a billion in my pocket you'd better start calling me Viscount."

33

Atlanta, Georgia

T HE TREASURY DEPARTMENT TEAMS SCOURING THE COUN-
tryside for airfields where a plane and pilot had gone missing
were working in an ever-widening circle with Washington, D.C.,
at its center. So far, they had only reached as far south as Columbia, South Carolina. Bell leapfrogged ahead and took the train to
Georgia with Archie Abbott and Clint Slocomb. James Dashwood
remained in Baltimore to cover the office until Telford Jones was
back on his feet.

After checking in at the Georgian Terrace Hotel, Archie and
Clint went off to check out Philip Findley's bank and his home.
Van Dorn hadn't yet opened an office in Atlanta, so the three were
on their own. Bell took a taxi to the Five Points district, where the
Atlanta Constitution newspaper had its headquarters. The building was five stories tall, brick, and somehow managed to look like
a prison.

The newsroom, like newsrooms all over the country, was a bee-hive of activity with phones ringing, typewriters clacking away, and two dozen conversations all going at once. The printing presses got cranking every night at the exact same time, and so the men and women who fed it content lived under an onerous dead-line every single day. Windows had been thrown open, but it was a windless day. Cigar and cigarette smoke was a dense fog.

"Help you?" a harried receptionist asked without looking up from her typewriter.

"I hope so. My name is Bell. I'm down from Washington, D.C., looking into aviation in various cities in the South and I wonder if anyone here has done stories on local pilots?"

"Bill Scutter, science and technology desk. Left corner."

Bell thanked her for her terse directions and weaved his way through the sea of desks and people, dodging rushing reporters with the grace of a toreador avoiding the bull's horns. Scutter was at his desk on the phone. He was a youngish guy with his jacket hanging off the back of his chair to show off bright red suspenders that matched his tie.

"I'm sorry, but everyone tells me their product will be bigger than Coke. I'm not doing a story about presliced bread." He hung up the phone and noticed Bell. "Everyone with a crazy idea wants me to run a story about it for some free publicity. Can I help you?"

"Hope so. My name is Isaac Bell. I'm the chief detective for the Van Dorn Agency. You've heard of us?"

"By reputation. There aren't any of you guys in Atlanta."

"I hadn't realized how much the city has grown. I am defi-nitely going to recommend to Mr. Van Dorn we open a branch here soon."

"What can I do for you, Mr. Bell?"

"I'm searching for a plane that crashed outside of Washington, D.C."

"And you're looking for it in Atlanta?"

"What I mean is that I'm trying to find where it came from. I have reason to believe it is from this area. I know there's no municipal airport or anything, but I wonder if there are some private fields."

"Is there a story in this for me?" he asked eagerly.

"I don't believe so," Bell said quickly, to dash his hopes. The last thing he needed was the press snooping around. "We were hired by the family on whose land the plane crashed. They want the body of the pilot and passenger returned to the family for a proper burial."

The young reporter looked a little crestfallen. "I suppose someone could do a human-interest angle, but that's not my thing. I'm all about science and inventions. You were right to come to me. I've interviewed a few local pilots and have gone up once myself. There are three private fields in the area, though I've only been to one. It's on a farm. The farmer leases the land to a couple guys with planes. He let them reroof an old barn for storage. I don't recall the farmer's name, but the place is due north of Decatur. If you can give me a minute, I can rustle up the address and the pilot's name."

"I do appreciate that, Mr. Scutter. It's been my experience with aviators that once you find one, he'll know all the others in the area. This is a huge help."

"Smart of you to come here and ask," the reporter said as he sifted through a bunch of files in a drawer.

"You want to know something specific about an area, talk to a reporter. I've saved a lot of shoe leather doing just that. It usually costs me the price of a couple of drinks. Not sure how long I'll be in town, but I'd make good if you're interested."

"Fair offer. Where are you staying?"

"Georgian Terrace."

Scutter gave a low whistle. "Nice place. Maybe you can spare a meal while you're at it."

Bell smiled. "My only other option to find a pilot was to drive around and hope to spot a plane and try to keep up when it returns to its airport. I think I can spring for dinner, too."

"Here we go." Scutter scribbled the farm's address and the pilot's name on a piece of paper and handed it to Bell.

"Payton Hyde," Bell read aloud. "Any chance you have a number for him?"

"Sorry, I don't. That article was a year ago. I'm not sure if he's still in the area."

"No matter. I can talk to the farmer just as easily."

The three detectives met up for lunch. They had nothing to report about Findley's bank and saw very little activity at his Victorian mansion just off Peachtree Street. Bell figured those would be dead ends and tasked the other two with scouting out a location for a future Atlanta office for the Agency. He arranged to rent a car through the hotel, a plain old Ford this time, and he drove north.

Founded as a rail hub and mostly destroyed during the Civil War, the city of Atlanta was one of the fastest growing in the country. Much of the cargo heading into the Midwest from the busy port of Savannah passed through Atlanta. There was a sense of vitality even stronger than Baltimore's. Like so many expanding cities, the streets and buildings ended rather abruptly at the city limits and the landscape gave way to forestland or farms. Bell had to stop for directions several times in order to find the farm with its own private runway.

The setup was much like he imagined. The farmhouse itself was relatively close to an unpaved road, with a large barn behind it, and a short ways off was an open-sided structure with a newer corrugated metal roof. A single biplane was parked under the roof in a spot that Bill Scutter said usually contained two. Fields beyond were thick with cotton plants already picked clean of their white puffy bolls. Along a hedge that likely delineated the property line, a strip had been left unplanted for the runway.

Hopeful he'd found the right airfield on the first try, Bell approached the farmhouse, hat in hand.

A woman answered the door, wary, the way rural folks can be with someone obviously from some place very different. She was in her fifties, wrinkles etched deep around her eyes and hair the color of tarnished pewter. She dripped with the South's famous hospitality and was politely informative when Bell inquired about any missing pilots.

"Hunter Sloane. He was the pilot, and his best friend, Jimmer Clovins, was the mechanic. They left about a month ago and said they'd be back in a couple of weeks. Dan and I feared the worst."

"Dan is your husband?"

"Yes. Dear me. I am so sorry." She tried to give him a welcoming smile, but her heart simply wasn't in it. "I'm Carol-Ann Chubb. Can I get you something? Sweet tea perhaps?"

"I don't want to bother you."

"No bother. I was about to bring a pitcher out to Dan in the barn."

She poured him a glass and together they crossed the yard,

avoiding a clutch of chickens pecking at the earth that hadn't been around when Bell had driven up. The tea was cool but so sweet it made Bell wince.

"Dan," she called as she opened a judas door set in the barn's main door. "We've got the worst news possible about Hunter and Jimmer."

Dan Chubb was a farmer out of central casting, wearing denim overalls, gum rubber boots, and a straw hat that should have been replaced at least three seasons back. All he lacked was a long piece of grass in the corner of his mouth or a golf ball–sized plug of tobacco bulging one cheek. He had a piece of farm equipment torn apart atop a workbench. Carol-Ann made the introductions and Bell spun his story for the third time.

"I don't know much about Jimmer's family," Carol-Ann admitted. "He's from Tennessee. Hunter, too, but he married into a prominent local family."

Bell forced himself to remain passive even though his heart was racing. He'd been right. Findley had gone to someone he trusted, his son-in-law, to carry out the attack.

"And would that be the Findleys?"

"Why, yes," she replied with mild surprise. "How did you know?"

"Oh, there were some papers found at the crash site, I believe. That name was mentioned. Do you have an address for Hunter Sloane?"

"Sure, up at the house."

"If you don't mind. I won't take up any more of your day and I have grim news to report to a grieving family."

The address was downtown, not too far from the Findleys' mansion. Bell knew that wasn't what he wanted, so the next day he and his two companions went to the county seat office and poured over tedious land records, looking for another property owned by Hunter Sloane. This was all open to the public, but was such a chore few ever bothered to find someone in this manner. The office was stuffy. The ceiling fan barely moved the humid air and soon the three men were sweating through their shirts. The two clerks that worked in the office seemed immune to the heat, but they were southern by birth and used to it.

They hit pay dirt an hour after a hasty meal at a nearby diner. Hunter Sloane owned a cabin along the banks of the Chattahoochee River. Checking the address against a map tacked to the wall, Bell knew he was right again. The house was in a rural stretch of the county and Sloane had bought up a fair amount of acreage. The nearest neighbor he could see was four miles away.

"That's it," he told his companions. "That's where Philip Findley is holed up."

"Think that Michaleen Riordan figured this out, too?" Clint Slocomb asked.

"No way. One, he doesn't even know there was an attack on the *Mayflower*, because it's never been reported. Two, even if it had, there's no way Philip Findley is going to advertise the fact he was behind it in an act of betrayal against Riordan and Jackson, so three, there's no need for him to look for a house belonging to the pilot."

"Four," Archie said, "if he had put everything together, he wouldn't have left this deed filing behind."

"Good point," Bell said. "Fetch that man a cigar. That all being the case, let's get out there now and be prepared for anything."

34

HUNTER SLOANE'S PROPERTY WAS MORE AN ISOLATED HUNT-
ing and fishing cabin than a proper house. It was in a
thickly wooded area backed up against the banks of the river just
where there was a bend, so the view was spectacular.

They had parked a mile up the road from the cabin's driveway
and hiked in through the woods. The sun was still high in the sky
and sent dappling rays through the trees to spotlight patches of the
forest floor. Birds sang and flit from branch to branch, and once
close enough the swoosh of water was a relaxing murmur. The
only blemish on this otherwise ideal spot were the insects that created halos around the men's heads and no amount of swatting at
them made the slightest difference.

"I'm going to be down a pint of blood when this is all over,"
Archie said in a whisper as they watched the cabin from behind an
uprooted tree.

The cabin was one story, likely single-bedroomed, with a tin roof and cedar shingle siding that had turned ash gray over the years. A coil of smoke rose from the river rock chimney, telling the men that the place was occupied.

Bell made a gesture to his men for them to wait. He approached the house from the side with the chimney because it was the width of the building, so there were no windows. He crawled around the corner, keeping his movements slow and deliberate—soundless. He moved to just below the big back window overlooking the river.

He tilted his head as he raised himself up so that he showed just a sliver of his cheek before he could peer into the room. A heavyset man had his back to the window as he worked a cast-iron skillet atop a small woodstove. Bell watched him as he prepared his dinner. He had no physical description of Philip Findley, but the man before him had the same look as most of the other eleven bankers he'd seen back aboard the presidential yacht—out of shape, self-assured, and entitled.

After watching for half a minute, Bell felt certain Findley was alone. He noted there was a shotgun propped next to the front door and that a new lock had been installed up near the top of the door. Whoever told him to do that knew how security worked. A regular door can be kicked in with relative ease. Adding a lock on top ensures the door remains unbreachable long enough for the person inside to arm themselves.

He crawled back to his men and explained the situation. Archie snatched up a two-foot log that had been split for the woodstove. "I've got the top lock."

"I'll breach the door," Bell said. "Clint, you cover us."

"You got it, Chief."

They moved in, careful not to show themselves to the windows flanking the front door. Once in place, Archie held the piece of wood over his head like a battering ram. Bell stood next to him, ready to take out the main lock with his right foot. Clint Slocomb had two of his .45s in hand, standing right behind them.

In a whisper Bell counted, "One . . . two . . . three."

On three, Arch slammed the butt of the log in the upper corner. of the door at the same time Bell's boot shattered the wooden jamb and the door flew open hard against its hinges. Their movements had left both men in awkward positions, but that was why Clint was there to cover them.

"Don't move!" Bell shouted as Philip Findley spun away from the stove.

The blood drained from the banker's face as his eyes appeared to grow as large as the skillet he'd been cooking with.

Bell and Abbott both regained their proper footing and rushed into the cabin, Bell grabbing up the shotgun to prevent his quarry from trying anything heroic.

Findley tried to stammer something, but Archie grabbed him by his arm and slammed him down onto one of the two wooden chairs near the plain dining table. The chair slid six inches with the impact. Clint Slocomb had come in right behind them and entered the cabin's sole bedroom, his pistols at the ready.

"Who are you?" the banker finally muttered, his voice quivery and dry. "Are you . . . ?"

"Sent by Michaleen Riordan or Jackson Pickett? If we were, you'd already be dead," Bell told him. "We're here to offer you a way out of the mess you're in, Mr. Findley."

Realizing he wasn't about to be tortured and killed, the fire of fear in the man's eyes dimmed to no more than a flicker. His shoulders squared. His hands unclenched. Bell knew that, in the circles Findley ran in, he was the alpha, the leader to whom everyone else deferred. Every second passing saw his demeanor return to its normal smugness.

"You've got no right barging in here. Get out."

Findley got to his feet, but Archie was there to shove him back down again with enough of a push to empty the banker's lungs in a convulsive whoosh that left him gasping. "That's not how this works, Phil."

Bell still had the shotgun cradled in his arms. It was an English-made Purdey side-by-side with probably a full ounce of gold leaf and cost more than a Rolls-Royce. "We know your involvement with the theft from the Bureau of Engraving and Printing. We know about your son-in-law and his mission to attack the meeting of the first board of the Federal Reserve. We know that Jackson Pickett is having all who have assisted him on the heist systematically killed, which is why you're hiding in Hunter Sloane's house and why your home downtown is so quiet. I assume you sent your wife and daughter away."

"Florida, with my in-laws," Findley admitted, and then turned defiant. "You can't prove anything."

"I don't need proof," Bell said. "I'm not a prosecutor and this isn't a court of law. We're men with guns who've been told that any obstacle preventing us from recovering the money can be steamrolled without so much as a second thought.

"Now, I don't exactly understand your plan. Did you think hiding in your son-in-law's cabin for a week or two was going to stop Pickett from having you killed? You're the only person on earth who can prove he stole that money. He is going to use some of his ill-gotten gains to hunt you to the ends of the earth, your wife and daughter, too, since he can't be sure you didn't tell them about him. For good measure he's going to burn your house to the ground and your bank, as well, in case you've left behind any evidence. Hiding is not an option."

"You don't . . . I mean, he might . . ."

"Were you aware that Michaleen Riordan sank a boatload of innocent men, women, and children just to try and kill me and make it look like a tragic accident? You are already a dead man, Mr. Findley, and there's nothing you can do about it. We are your only chance of survival."

Bell knew he had the banker's interest. He knew how ruthless Pickett and Riordan were and how they really would hunt him down no matter the cost or how long it took.

Archie hunkered down so he could look Findley straight in the eye. "Don't you get it? You're prey now. You'll have a target on your back until the second they pull the trigger and end your life."

They weren't telling him anything he hadn't already known, but just hadn't acknowledged. It's why he fled here. It gave the illusion of safety, like a child hiding from imaginary monsters under a blanket. But Findley's monsters were not imaginary at all and they had him terrified.

"Let us help you," Bell said, tossing him a lifeline.

He looked from Archie to Bell and back again. Clint Slocomb leaned negligently against the wall, picking at a cuticle with a folding knife. Findley understood his position. He was out of options and would die at the whim of Jackson Pickett. He nodded slowly, and then again with more resolve. "What . . . What do you want from me?"

"I need to know your plan for the money, so we can intercept it."

"Ha," Findley barked. "That rat Pickett double-crossed me like I knew he would."

"Tell me."

"He was supposed to split the proceeds, and then we'd start spreading the money around as soon as we got it. Exchange it for gold, farm commodities, real estate, and other hard assets. Even loan it out at discount rates."

"Wait. What? Why?"

"To flood the market with the new notes. I wanted to destroy the Federal Reserve and the best way to do that was to get a lot of their money into the hands of people before the official launch. It would instantly devalue the currency and the whole scheme would collapse even before it started."

Archie was back on his feet. "Hold on a second. You do know you're part of the system, right? You're the chairman of the Atlanta Federal Reserve Bank. Why would you want to destroy it?"

"To save the control and profits of my own bank here in Georgia. The federal government has no business launching its own currency. That was left to state charters. It's a gross overreach that will allow the government to put its hand on every wallet and into every purse in America. We are a federation of states, not a central power emanating from Washington, D.C. Why the hell do you think we fought the Civil War?"

"To end slavery once and for all," Archie said.

"That's what you in the North tell yourselves. We fought to prevent the federal government from interfering in what had always been a state-governed practice. We understood back then that, well beyond slavery, they would take away our other rights, too. This new banking system gives them control of the nation's money and once they have that they can do anything they want. Gun rights, speech rights, policing rights. Nothing will be safe.

"We're already seeing it. For more than a hundred years, personal income tax was deemed illegal by the Supreme Court, but now they have the new income tax amendment. At the moment, it only affects a small handful of people, so no one really cares. But you mark my word, they will lower the requirements of who pays until everyone is sending money to Washington. There's no way to revolt against this because the feds already control the money. It's theirs, don't you see, not yours. They are the issuers, and they will determine how much of it they'll get to claw back."

"Really?" Archie said dismissively.

"You trust your government not to write itself a blank check? Washington only cares about Washington. The federal government must not be allowed to grow or it will ruin our founding principles in ways far more destructive than a civil war."

Archie was getting hot. "It was fought for a lot more than property."

Bell didn't want this to turn into a debate about the Civil War. Findley looked too young to have fought in it, but he surely was alive when General Sherman and the Union Army put the torch to his native Atlanta. "Gentlemen, let's stay focused. Jackson Pickett was supposed to help spread around a billion dollars in order to ruin the Federal Reserve, but didn't."

"That is correct."

"In that case he's keeping the money, knowing that the Treasury Department has no choice but to plow ahead with their plans to roll out the new currency. He's just biding his time until he becomes one of the wealthiest men in America. My question to you is, where is he holed up? The authorities have been scouring every rail yard in the country for that car. Even if he emptied it, the location he abandoned it is a clue."

Bell's only hope of catching the thieves collapsed with Findley's reply. "I haven't the faintest idea."

"I can't accept that," Bell shot back. "You were partners in the biggest heist in history. To pull that off you had to have built a rapport. I know from personal experience how much Pickett likes to talk."

"I don't know about a rapport," Findley countered. "We did end up betraying one another."

"You snuck him into the Atlanta federal bank, presumably at night, and you would have stuck around to make certain he and Riordan weren't spotted leaving before dawn. You must have talked."

"I was there," he admitted, "but I mostly slept. I had my own bank to run during the day, so I needed to rest while they practiced on the vault."

"I can't accept that," Bell snapped. "Think!"

Philip Findley's mouth worked soundlessly as his mind tried to bring up details of conversations he'd only half listened to. The man in front of him holding his prized shotgun was right about Pickett. The man never seemed to shut up, and yet he rarely said anything of substance. It was odd. He remembered having talks with the Louisiana native over the course of the three weeks he and his savage little friend practiced opening the big vault, but none of the words stuck with him. He gave up.

"I don't—"

"Come up with something or we're leaving you here like a staked goat for Michaleen Riordan."

Findley gulped. "He, ah, he was from New Orleans."

"I know that already," Bell said with visible frustration. "He told me that his family had once been wealthy, but the money had all run out by the time he was born."

"Yes, he shared that with me as well. He told me they used to have all kinds of business ventures that all went bankrupt or were destroyed by fires or storms. But I remember him telling me one night that there was one last property that had been abandoned, but was still owned by his parents when he was a boy. It was a fish-processing plant deep in some swamp."

Bell and Archie swapped an encouraged glance.

"Yes. It's coming back. He said it was practically a ruin when his father took him out there by boat one time. It was about an hour from New Orleans. He told me that going there was his one fond memory of his dad. That's why he told me about it. I'd asked him how he had gotten into crime, and he said that even though he'd gone to college on a scholarship, he received no support from his father. His mother had died by then and so he resorted to robbery in order to keep up the proper appearances."

Bell could see an amoral egoist like Pickett feeling entitled to the property of others in order to maintain the appearance of wealth. And rather than get a job after school, he'd continued in a life of crime, learning and honing new skills along the way. He'd conned his way into a pretty good place with his marriage to Fedora Scarsworth, but then Philip Findley dangled an even sweeter deal, and now he was sitting atop a railcar stuffed with a billion dollars in cash.

Bell nodded to Archie and they stepped out of earshot. Clint came a few paces closer to Findley to let him know that he wasn't going anyplace.

"What do you think?" Archie asked.

"Pickett will hide someplace he feels safe but that doesn't have a connection back to him directly. It also needs to be a place no one would think to look. A derelict factory in the middle of a swamp sounds about right."

"Think they transferred the money to a boat and sank the rail-car in the bayou?"

"That or they left the money in the car and barged it to the factory."

"What's our play?"

"Soon as we're done here, I'll telephone the New Orleans office and put the entire crew on the trail of that piece of property and we get ourselves on the next train to the Crescent City."

"Let's make it happen," Archie said. "I have a question for Findley."

"Fire away."

Archie moved back to be closer to the banker. "How did you find Pickett in the first place?"

"He robbed my house," Findley said matter-of-factly. "Seven years ago, he came to Atlanta and quickly ingratiated himself in our society scene. The wives were particularly charmed, my wife included, so he was our guest on several occasions. After one particular evening when I went to place some jewelry she'd worn in our safe, I discovered someone had been in it and removed about five hundred dollars in cash.

"When I confronted him the next day, he denied it, and since I had no proof, there was nothing I could do. Later, in private talks with others in our group, I discovered I wasn't the only victim. It wasn't long after that incident that he left Atlanta to prey on some other city. When I came up with the scheme to rob the Bureau of Engraving, I hired a private detective service to track him down. Given his circumstances at the time, I was surprised he agreed. It seemed he had found the perfect mark for his confidence games."

"His was a gilded cage and you offered him freedom," Bell

remarked. "Can you tell me anything else about this processing plant?"

"No. I swear. It was a passing comment only."

"No matter. We will find it."

"What happens to me now? How will you protect me?"

"That's easy. My partner over there with the .45s and hard eyes is going to escort you to Washington, D.C., where you will give a full confession to Secretary McAdoo and Attorney General Gregory."

Findley's eyes bulged and his one-word reply came out as an angry screech. "What?"

"You heard me. I told you your options were limited. Put your faith in us or get hunted down by Michaleen Riordan."

"But I'll be safe once you stop Pickett. I don't even care if you get the money back to the Reserve and they have a successful launch. I'll resign and no one will ever hear from me again."

Archie laughed. "You've committed a list of crimes as long as my arm and you think we're not going to make you answer for every last one of them?"

Bell had been through this so many times he knew that this was the exact moment when Findley was going to start bargaining for his freedom.

"Listen, fellas, I'm a man of means. I can pay you anything you want. I can set you up for life."

"I'm not going to tell you our identities, but all three of us are Van Dorn men." The crestfallen look on Findley's face was price-less, like a child who'd dropped an ice cream cone before the first lick. Bell added unnecessarily, "You can't bargain with us, and you certainly can't bribe us."

Findley gaped like a fish for a few seconds longer, looking from man to man to man and receiving nothing but stony silence. He then slumped in his seat when he realized he had no choice other than to accept the inevitable.

Clint Slocomb holstered his guns and pulled out a pair of cuffs with a metallic rattle. He approached Philip Findley, his voice coming out in a gravely rasp. "You're fat and out of shape, so I'm gonna trust you're not going to give me much bother. I'll cuff your hands in front. However, you give me any guff, I'll put you down hard and cinch 'em behind your back so tight you'll think your hands are going to fall off. We clear?"

Findley gulped. Clint could have that effect on people.

"Was that an answer?" Clint asked, tightening his already narrowed eyes.

"Yes, sir. I won't be any trouble at all. You have my word."

Clint just nodded and slapped on the cuffs.

Because there was no active arrest warrant for Philip Findley and seeing as he was a prominent member of the Atlanta community, Bell couldn't chance him making a scene at the train station if there were any cops around. He went alone to check schedules and they brought the disgraced banker into the city moments before a Seaboard Air Line Railway train pulled clear of Terminal Station on its way north. The three men bundled him into a private sleeper room and Clint cuffed him to a safety grab rail firmly fastened to the carriage's wall.

Archie and Bell jumped from the train at the conductor's last whistle and had time to return the Ford to the hotel, pack up their belongings, and return to the large central train station for their overnight to New Orleans.

35

New Orleans, Louisiana

THEY MET AT ANTOINE'S ON RUE ST. LOUIS IN THE FRENCH Quarter. The fabled restaurant was celebrating its seventy-fourth year in business. The dining room wasn't open yet and the place was overrun with the din of the kitchen staff prepping for the day and the waitstaff setting the tables. When Bell and Archie Abbott entered the restaurant, they saw a man in a booth wave them over.

"Bernard Arseneaux, good to see you," Bell said as the man stood. They shook hands warmly.

"Bernie, how are you doing?" Archie said by way of greeting.

"I would be so much better if you used my full name, Archibald." His accent was thicker than Jackson Pickett's and lacked his buttery smoothness.

"I'm just messing with you." They, too, shook hands.

Arseneaux headed the small cadre of Van Dorn agents in New Orleans. He'd been hired away from a rival agency by Joseph Van

Dorn himself. Bell and Abbott had worked with him when a fugitive they had tracked onto a riverboat coming down the Mississippi had jumped ship when the craft passed New Orleans and disappeared into the city. Such were Bernard's connections in the city that they had the fugitive in custody in under twelve hours.

He was a slim, dapper man who, though born in Louisiana, kept the European manners of his French-born parents. He smoked using an ivory holder and wore his dark hair slicked back with a subtly perfumed pomade.

"Great idea meeting in a restaurant," Archie said, sliding next to Bell in the booth. "The kitchen on our train down was out of order. I'm starving."

"Sorry to disappoint, but the kitchen won't open until this evening. Here."

Arseneaux slid across a wax paper sack. "We can get coffee, though."

He ordered from a passing waiter and asked that a man named Keith be sent out.

Archie pulled a piece of fried dough covered in sugar from the bag. It was still warm. "What is this?"

"You two weren't here long enough to enjoy a New Orleans staple. That is called a beignet, our local version of a doughnut. These are from Café du Monde and are the best in the city."

Archie took a bite and his eyes went wide with delight. Bell helped himself to one as well.

Two men approached the table, an older white man in a suit and a young Black man wearing a chef's apron wrapped around his waist.

"Do not keep him for too long, Bernard. Keith is my best oysterman and we have a full house tonight."

"We'll keep it brief, Jules." The suited man stepped away. Bernard said to Bell and Abbott, "That's Jules Alciatore. His parents founded this place and he's the chef that invented oysters Rockefeller. They sell thousands of them a week."

"You don't say," Archie said with another bite of beignet in his mouth.

"Gentlemen, this is Keith Hill. Keith's grandfather knows the waters around New Orleans better than any man ever has. He's named every tree and befriended every gator within a hundred miles. Keith, this is Isaac Bell, my boss's lead investigator, and his general partner in crime, Archibald Abbott."

Bell stood to shake his hand and Archie, stuck in the booth, sort of raised himself off the seat a little to do likewise. Hill slid into the booth next to Bernard. The waiter came with the coffees and they doctored them to taste. Keith Hill helped himself to one of the beignets.

Bernard said, "When I got your call about an abandoned fish-packing plant I reached out to Keith because of his grandfather's knowledge of the swamps."

Bell interrupted. "The owner said you're an oysterman. Do you go out and harvest them yourself?"

"Oh, no, sir," he said with respect rather than deference. "I work here preparing them for the dinner service. I'm a great disappointment to my grandfather. I never much cared for the outdoor life."

"So, you turned to cooking?"

"A means to an end, Mr. Bell. I'm studying business at Straight University."

"That's a wise move."

"The only way to effect positive change is through education."

Bell gave a nod of understanding. "I can't agree more."

"Thank you."

"Back to business before Jules shanghais Keith back to the kitchen," Bernard said, sipping at his coffee.

"Right," said Hill. "So I went to see my grandfather after Bernard asked me to. He knew exactly what I was talking about. He'd landed on the pier there a few times to explore the place a handful of years ago. He remembered when it was open for business and recalled that it didn't last long. He told me they didn't build their own ice factory and had to rely on one that was too far away. They brought it in on railcars and the melt was so bad that they were half empty."

"Wait." Bell held up a hand, his instincts twitching. "The place had rail service?"

"That's what my grandfather said. He said other than the water, the train was the only way in. It's very isolated out near Brown Creek."

"You were right," Archie told Bell.

"By God, I think I am. What else does he remember?"

"He recalled that the owners had a big dispute with the icehouse because of all the ice melting on the trip in. He said they installed a big scale to weigh the cars and insisted on paying only for the amount of ice that survived the journey and not for the water that dripped onto the tracks. He believes the negotiations failed and it wasn't long after that the place shut down and was abandoned."

"Can your grandfather take us there?"

Hill shook his head. "He doesn't know how old he is, but he thinks he was at least forty when he was freed. His days of poling through the bayous are long over."

"We can find it through the railroad," Bernard suggested. "I know a retired engineer who knows every inch of track in the state. He'll pinpoint where the spur to the docks comes off a main line."

"We can find it that way," Bell said, "but we can't get to it that way. If I were Pickett, I'd have men watching that line at all times. We need to approach from the water."

"We'll need a small powerboat."

"You won't get within five miles of the factory," Keith told them. "The place was weeded in pretty bad the last time Grandpappy was there. It'll be even worse now. Prop would get fouled the first two yards in. The swamp's taking it back, like it does everything down here if you let it. You'll need to pole your way in on a pirogue."

"A what?" This from Archie.

"Native boat," Bell told him. "That takes weeks to master, I would imagine."

"Months," said Keith. "And you learn when you're young so you have a shorter fall into the water."

"Think we should hire some boatmen to take us in?" Archie asked.

"No, I won't risk anyone else. Pickett is too dangerous. All we need to do is verify the train car's still loaded. Once we know that, we turn this case over to the Treasury and they see it through to the end."

Keith Hill spotted one of the other kitchen staffers looking out across the dining room, presumably for him. He stood. "If you gentlemen are done, I need to get back to work before the head chef tans my hide."

Bernard quickly agreed. "Yes, thank you, my friend. You've sent us in the right direction." He reached into a pocket to pay the young man, but Hill stopped him with a hand gesture.

"Any excuse to see my grandpappy and eat my nana's crawfish is payment enough. I'll see you around. Mr. Bell, Mr. Abbott, a pleasure."

"Likewise," said Bell. "Thanks for your help."

"What's in this train car that's so important?" Bernard Arseneaux asked.

"Sorry, Bern," Archie replied. "This case is really hush-hush."

Bell usually didn't like keeping fellow agents in the dark about the cases they were working on, but he had to agree with Archie on this one. So far, the secret of the theft had been kept. "It's a government job and they have a strict nondisclosure policy on this one."

"No matter," Bernard dismissed breezily. "A good detective is always curious, while a good agent is always loyal. Since curiosity can't buy the beignets, I will accept your explanation."

"Thank you," Bell said.

"Alas," he said in a teasing voice, "it means I have to keep a secret from you as well."

"Secret?"

"I know how you can get to that factory without poling a skiff miles across the swamp."

"Spill."

"It will be easier to show you than to tell you."

Airboat on the bayou

36

⚜

I T'S CALLED AN AIRBOAT," BERNARD SAID AN HOUR AND A HALF later and a world away from the Gothic charms of New Orleans's French Quarter. "Invented about ten years ago by Alexander Graham Bell. Hey, any relation?"

"No," Isaac Bell said, eyeing the odd contraption with growing appreciation.

They were at a ramshackle marina on Delacroix Island, deep in the swamps and bayous that stretched from New Orleans all the way to the mouth of the Mississippi River. The buildings were dilapidated, with broken windows and rust-streaked iron roofs, and built on pilings that were rotting under their crust of dead barnacles and mussel shells. The narrow channel the marina fronted was dotted with rainbow-hued patches of spilled fuel that sat stagnant, as there was no current.

The few fishing boats tied along the pier didn't look seaworthy at all, but men were aboard them, preparing for their next expedition into the Gulf of Mexico.

Though it was fall, the heat was oppressive and the humidity so thick, it felt like breathing through wet gauze. The air smelled of standing water, brackish mud, and rotten fish. While Bell, Archie, and Arseneaux mopped at their faces with already limp handkerchiefs and swatted at the legions of bugs that swarmed the group, their host didn't seem to mind at all.

They had already been introduced to the proprietor in the marina's office/bait shop/general store and explained what they were after. He only went by the name of Jose and was a descendent of the Canary Islanders the Spanish brought into the area while the American Revolution raged to the north and Louisiana was still a Spanish territory. Jose was anywhere between forty and seventy, it was impossible to tell, wearing rubber fishing boots and denim overalls without a shirt. His chest, shoulders, and back were covered in dense coils of hair, like an animal's pelt. His smile was half gaps and half teeth.

"Jose built it from an article he read in *Popular Mechanics*."

"Like the magazine says." Jose spoke with an accent almost undecipherable, but he was by no means an uneducated man. "Written so you can understand it."

Tied to a leaning wooden jetty, the airboat was a wide, flat-bottomed aluminum craft with a raised platform built over the stern. On the platform was a bench seat for a pilot and passenger, rudimentary controls, and a small gasoline-powered engine attached to an aircraft propeller facing aft. A safety cage of thin metal rods had been erected around the propeller to prevent a limb accidently getting severed between the prop's blades. Behind the propeller was a steering vane similar to an aircraft's vertical stabilizer and rudder.

Like the marina, and the airboat's builder himself, the craft looked cobbled together from spare parts, patched and repatched until whatever was original seemed buried, and yet still looked ready to work despite itself.

"With the propeller in the air rather than under the water, it can't get fouled by all the marsh grass and creeper vine," Jose pointed out proudly. "She glides right through it all. Alexander Bell said he ran his on the ice and snow around his lab in Nova Scotia."

"Jose's taken me out a couple of times," Bernard said. "Exhilarating feeling, like I imagine what it's like to be up in an aeroplane."

"I have to know," said Archie, "how do you two know each other? We are literally in the middle of nowhere."

"Jose's daughter left here to find work in New Orleans. She's my maid. When I learned she was *isleño*, I begged her to take me out here to try some of the local food. It's a mix of Spanish, French, Acadian, and Creole that puts what you can get in the city to shame, in my opinion. I've been invited back whenever there's a big celebration."

Bell wasn't paying particular attention. He was spellbound by the airboat. He easily saw through the improvisation Jose had been forced to use to bring the craft to life and recognized its brilliance right away.

"I get how it steers," he said to Jose, "and cutting the power would slow it, but how do you stop in an emergency?"

"That there is the right question to ask. The wheel links to the steering vane. Gentle rotation, gentle turn, yes?"

"Yes."

"You chop the power and crank the wheel hard over, the boat does a spin, but she digs her side into the water. That slows you enough that you don't hit whatever it is you no wanna hit."

Bell imagined a flat spin in a plane, but with the added drag of water. "Smart."

"Trial and error," Jose said with his gap-toothed smile. "This boat been upside down more than once and I've had to pound out her bow a fair number of times from when I run into trees and things. I've built a second boat from what I learned with this one. Bigger boat, bigger engine and prop, and two rudders working side by side. Much smoother and easier to control."

Thinking he'd rather have a better boat, Bell asked, "Where's that one?"

"Sold it a few months back. Didn't know the guy and no one around here has seen it since. Some reckon he took it to Florida to head into the Everglades. Be perfect for that."

"Do you know the abandoned fish factory near Brown Creek?"

"Dropped off a few catches there back when I fished."

"Could your airboat reach it today?"

"I've not been out that way in a long time. They were the ones keeping Brown Creek open. Overgrown bad now, I reckon."

"But could it?"

He thought for a moment. "Cedars likely blocking the creek now. If they ain't too tight you should be able to, just not too fast, mind ya."

Bell liked that Jose didn't ask about his interest in either the boat or the old fish factory. In all the rural places he'd visited in his life, locals tend not to care about others' business unless it affected their own. He asked, "Could you draw me a map from here to there?"

"Wouldn't do you much good. There's about ten thousand

square miles of bayou out there. It changes every day. New channels shift, islands dissolve and new ones form. Lest you know what you're doing, a man could go in there and never find his way back out."

"The problem is that I can't risk anyone but us."

"You a stubborn man, Mr. Bell?"

"My wife would say that I am, yes."

"Stubborn men die 'cause they don't know what's best for them and they don't know when to quit. A stubborn man goes into the delta by hisself, he ain't coming back. That's fact."

"I'm willing to pay anything to use your boat, Jose, and a couple of hours of lessons, but I won't risk your life on our mission."

"Bernard treat my Maria good," Jose said, as if he was shocked there was decency in the world beyond the surrounding bayou. "He work for you, so the favor I do you is really a favor I do him. I'll tow the airboat close to Brown Creek in my seiner. You do whatever it is you have to do and then I'll wait for you to come back and tow you home. This way I know I get my boat back, eh?"

Bell considered the offer for a few seconds. "Deal. But if you hear gunfire or anything else out of the ordinary, you pull anchor and go."

"Fair enough."

They settled on a price and time and shook hands.

37

After three hours of towing the airboat behind Jose's small fishing boat, Bell recognized that he never would have found Pickett's abandoned fish-packing factory by just using a map. He actually knew that after just a few minutes. The mouth of the Mississippi River was a vast area of interconnecting channels, mangrove islands, tidal flats, and just about every other coastal geographical feature nature had dreamed up. It was a constantly shifting maze that took a lifetime to master and he was grateful for the local mariner's help.

Weather was another factor for which he was grateful for Jose's assistance. Menacing dark clouds crowded the sky, lowering it so it felt oppressively cramped under the fast-approaching storm. The wind had yet to pick up on the ground level, but the speed of the scudding clouds foretold of high gales. To make matters worse, the air temperature had dropped below that of the water and tendrils of fog wafted out of the swamps, obscuring details already made blurry by the twilit atmosphere. Thunder rolled up from over the horizon like the pealing of ancient bells.

Jose chopped his boat's throttles and it quickly fell off plane. "We're about eight miles from the entrance of Brown Creek," he said, taking the opportunity to light a cigarette from a match he sparked off his thumb. "This channel runs right to it and has been stable for quite a while."

A day had passed since they had made their deal, a day for Bell and Abbott to buy or borrow the equipment they thought they would need for the mission. Bell had also taken airboat driving lessons from Jose.

The man had been impressed with how quickly Bell mastered the tricky craft. "I grew up sailing all around Cape Cod," Bell told him. "So I know how water reacts, and I've got a pilot's license and fly whenever I get the chance. Your amazing boat is a nifty combination of two of my passions."

"Mind ya now the channel oxbows . . . You know what an oxbow is?"

"Big looping turn in a river caused by erosion on the inside of the curve depositing soil on the outside."

The native chuckled. "Smart guy. So, Brown Creek's entrance is on the left at the end of the seventh oxbow. Ya hear?"

"Seven oxbows and we're at the entrance to Brown," Bell said. "Got it."

"Them bows is mostly grass and some trees. My boat can cut through them okay, but it's best you stick to the main channel."

"Stick to the main channel," Bell repeated.

The party moved aft as Jose's deckhand, a gawky teenager who the captain didn't bother to introduce, tied the boat off against some mangrove roots. Jose pulled in the painter attached to the airboat and hopped aboard for a final check. Bell opened a canvas bag he'd brought and removed Clint Slocomb's four-gun holster rig.

"I was wondering what was in there," Archie said as he slid on his own shoulder holster.

"Clint let me borrow it. I gave him my Browning." Bell shrugged into the leather suspenders and closed the belt with an *oomph*. With its four Colt .45s and extra ammo, the harness weighed close to twenty pounds. "Not exactly for everyday use, but certainly for special occasions."

Jose seemed satisfied that the airboat was ready for action. "Once you get to Brown, you're gonna have to kill the engine. The old packing plant is only a mile or so up the creek. It's going to be tough going with poles, but there ain't no other way."

"We understand."

"One last thing, watch yourselves. This area is infested with gators and water moccasins."

"That's a snake, right?" Archie asked.

"Bad one," the teen deckhand replied. "They mostly leave folks alone, but if you get bit, you in trouble."

"Trouble?"

"He means dead," Jose said.

Bell and Archie grabbed up the pair of pump twelve-gauges from the New Orleans field office armory and stepped over to the bobbing airboat. A flutter of wind rattled the skeletal stalks of the mangrove and ruffled Bell's blond hair.

Once they were settled onto the tall bench seat at the rear of the craft, Jose handed them each a leather helmet with extra padding around the ears. This was to protect their hearing from the sound of the propeller thrashing the air. He also had goggles for them both.

"Won't need these until the rain hits, I reckon," he said. "You ready?"

"Yes."

The procedure for starting the airboat was little different than with an automobile. Once the choke was set and the cylinders primed with gas, Jose gave the engine a hard crank and it roared to life in a puff of oily smoke. The deckhand held the airboat against the thrust of its wooden prop shrieking over the hybrid craft's flat fantail. Once Jose was back aboard the seiner, the teen let go and Bell opened the throttle to half speed.

With so little drag, the airboat was quickly skimming across the river's surface like a dragonfly, deft and graceful under Bell's capable control. Despite knowing they were hurtling into mortal danger, he still couldn't suppress a boyish grin at the thrill of piloting such a remarkable machine.

He slalomed them through the broad oxbow bends as Jose suggested. He could see weed-choked channels that cut through the lazy loops that would have given them a more direct heading, but he heeded the local man's advice. There was little flow to the channel this close to the ocean. The water appeared dead calm, and was as dark as over-steeped tea.

As they swept through the sixth oxbow, Bell cut the power to barely above idle in order to quiet the craft for the final leg of the journey. Even at a low speed the contraption remained hellishly loud and both men were grateful for the padded helmets.

The storm still hadn't broken. The sky was a roiling dome of clouds, pearlescent in some places and impenetrably gray in others, with crackling tines of lightning forking across it all. The overall effect was disconcerting, as the illumination appeared more supernatural than anything either Bell or Arch had seen before.

Finally coming through the seventh and final sweeping river bend, Bell cut the power entirely. The silence lasted for only the few moments it took for their hearing to adjust. The wind had picked up, though it had been at their backs for the most part and barely noticed. Now it whistled through the cedars and mangroves and made the sedge grasses hiss against each other. Unaccustomed to such gloom during the day, birds were squawking from branches in confusion and frogs croaked out a basso chorus.

Now that they'd slowed, Arch took the time to scan the banks for any alligators. He saw none, but he did point out a mudflat that had their distinctive splayed footprints with the drag mark of their heavy tails in between.

They climbed down off the airboat's raised platform and each man took up a paddle, Bell on the right, Arch on the left, and without a word, they dug the blades into the brackish water. They hadn't paddled a boat together on very many occasions and yet they had worked so closely together since first meeting in college that they settled into an immediate rhythm as synchronized as any Olympic double-scull crew. Both men's eyes never rested on an object for more than a second. Their heads swiveled like gimbals, checking what lay ahead as well as anything that might be coming up behind them.

What Bell took for a log rotting away on the shore suddenly launched itself into the channel in a froth of white water and green hide as thick as armor plate. The gator showed them no interest and moved downriver with lazy undulations of its tail. Bell put its length at ten feet, at least.

"Make a nice pair of boots," Archie said in a low voice. "Appears to be waterproof, too."

"You want to jump in there to skin him, you be my guest."

"That's okay. I saw a pair in his color at Saks on Broadway."

Keeping close to shore, but not too close in case there were more alligators ready to surge into the river, they rounded out of the final oxbow and began scanning for the choked-off entrance to Brown Creek.

"Uh-oh," both men said at the same time.

Expecting to see a wall of jungle as thick and tall as the swampland bordering the channel that they would need to thread their way through using the stout poles Jose had provided, what greeted them was a neatly trimmed tunnel hacked through the trees and vines and creepers that ran inland as though it had been cut back that very morning. The canal through the swamp was maybe fifteen feet wide.

Bell pointed. "If you look carefully at the variations in the background vegetation, the original Brown Creek was a lot wider than what has been recently cleared."

Archie nodded. "And I'd say that cut looks just wide enough for a barge loaded with a standard boxcar."

"One more layer of Pickett's subterfuge. Bring the car in on rails and take it out again by barge."

"Think we're too late?" Arch asked.

"Only one way to find out."

Once they crossed the channel and entered the mouth of Brown Creek, they laid aside the oars and Bell took first shift with the long pole while Archie watched the darkening surroundings over the sights of his shotgun. Unlike a native canoe, the airboat's flat bottom kept them stable enough for Bell to stand in the stern and thrust the pole against the muddy bottom to propel them silently forward. The only noise was a faint ripple of water as he maneuvered the pole and the occasional pop of a malodorous methane bubble that had been dislodged from the creek bed. Overhead the canopy of trees met as though there was no canal below them.

The sky continued to grow darker still, but the men's eyes were well adjusted, and while the bayou beyond the freshly cut channel was murky and indistinct, they could see clearly enough to press onward. Twenty minutes after entering the creek, the tight confines of the canal opened into a freshly cleared lagoon. To the right was an impenetrable wall of snarled mangroves, cedars, and brambles as dense as an English hedgerow.

To the left was a three-hundred-foot-long dock resting on pilings driven into the silt. Behind it was solid ground. On the pier sat a two-story building sheathed in rotting clapboard and roofed with corrugated iron sheets. Two spindly derricks were built into the pier that had once dipped nets into the holds of trawlers to haul out their cargoes. There were several outbuildings whose function the men could only guess at.

Though there was one structure in particular that caught their attention. It was a story and a half tall and not particularly broad, but looked long enough to contain two boxcars at the same time. It had to be the weigh station for when the plant imported blocks of ice. Being down in the water, their vantage didn't let them see if train tracks ran through the building, but both Bell and Archie were pretty certain they did. Most heartening of all was seeing a plain barge tied up to the pier and a bulldog-bow tugboat with a faint glow coming from a porthole under the stubby pilothouse.

Archie was manning the pole at this point. Bell pointed to a spit of land fifty yards shy of the dock and the defunct fish-processing plant. They couldn't chance a sharp-eyed lookout spotting them poling the airboat past the tug like Venetian gondoliers headed for St. Mark's Square. They pressed it against the shore and Bell tied it off with a painter line affixed to the bow. A few nearby branches had been dislodged by the wind and Archie draped them over the airboat to mask its silhouette.

"What do you think?" Arch whispered in Bell's ear.

"On a case where we've been one step behind the whole time, I think we're finally pulling even."

38

⁓ ⚘ ⁓

T HEY MOVED IN A HALF CROUCH, ARCHIE COVERING THEM
with the shotgun while Bell carried a duffel bag of gear. Bell
had left his shotgun in the boat. If they needed that much firepower, the night was lost.

They paused before stepping onto the dock. As remote and isolated as the factory was, they couldn't assume Pickett wouldn't
have men out on roving patrols and not just watching over the rail
spur that vanished into the jungle behind the facility. They strained
to hear the creak of footfalls on the old wooden pier or whispered
conversation between bored guards. They were too far from the
squat tug to hear anything coming from it, like laughter or melo-
dies played on a gramophone. All they really heard was the sound
of insects, which had grown to be a toneless symphony behind the
steady push of wind through the bayou, and various croaks, chirps,
and honks from the local fauna.

After pausing several minutes, Bell and Archie continued on. The dock was slick with mold and in poor condition, not to mention that it still smelled of rotting fish half a generation since it had last been used. They moved from cover to cover, hiding behind old oak barrels left to rot away or handcarts whose wheels had rusted solid.

When they finally got close enough, they confirmed that a set of train tracks did cross the facility, running through a large building and exiting in back at the edge of the dock. They could see the door facing the river was chained and padlocked. The lock would be easy enough to pick, but removing the chain, no matter how careful, was bound to make noise.

A sudden sound came from the tugboat. A metal door clanged closed. They crouched behind a stack of pallets covered in old canvas that had become home to a rat colony. They could hear the creatures' tiny claws and muted squeaks. A few rats eyed them from recesses within the folds of mildewed cloth, bold and unafraid after so long of not seeing humans in their territory.

Bell's heart pumped a little faster as they waited to see if anything else happened. Five more minutes trickled by and all was quiet.

"We're wasting daylight," Archie noted.

Jose had been adamant that if they were still out once it became fully dark, they were to tie up the airboat and wait until dawn. Under no circumstances should they try to navigate at night. The airboat wasn't built for any abrupt moves like one would need if an unseen tree suddenly loomed out of the darkness.

"Come on."

They covered the last seventy feet to the train shed. The tug and flat barge were another fifty feet away. The chain and lock

Bell had noted earlier were brand-new. Not a speck of rust on them. Small brass bells had been wired to several of the links to make additional noise should someone try to take them off. Wordlessly, Bell led Archie around the corner and along the long side of the building, testing the wooden boards as he went. Though in rough shape, the structure remained solid.

On the side of the building where the tracks entered the shed from the spur, there were two doors identical in size and shape as the others. The padlock and chain setup were identical as well. Bell looked up. The peak of the roof was about fifteen feet over his head. Just below that was a wooden beam sticking out of the building with a hook on it that once supported a pulley. Below the beam was another set of doors so that material could be hoisted up into the rafters of the train shed.

Bell set the duffel on the dock and opened it while Archie stood watch over him. From within, Bell pulled out a coil of climbing rope. Half of its length had knots placed every couple of feet for easy climbing. At one end was tied a commercial lead sinker borrowed from one of Jose's fishing nets. Bell sorted out how he wanted to hold the rope and set the sinker twirling. It sounded like the wind as he spun it faster and faster. He let go with an underhand throw and the rope sailed true. When the sinker started falling back to earth, the line was draped over the beam.

"Every move a picture," Archie whispered in approbation.

Bell had to whipsaw the rope a little to snake the knots over the beam so that the weight of the sinker dropped that end of the rope back to the ground. Bell tied the two ends together, plucked a slender pry bar from the bag, and climbed until he was level with the doors. He looped the rope tails around his feet and legs in such a way that he could free up one hand to check the doors. They were loose and wobbly, but wouldn't open. He worked the pry bar into the gap between the two doors and felt around for a latch inside. The metal bar tapped against something metallic. He finessed the tool by feel, almost like a lockpick, and the latch popped open.

Bell slipped the pry bar into a pocket and eased open one of the doors. The hinges were rusty, so he took his time.

Voices.

Two men talking loudly from the direction of the tug. With the train shed in between Bell and the men, he couldn't make out what they were saying, nor did it matter. He loosened his legs from the rope and began to swing himself in a lengthening arc, like a clock's pendulum, until he could kick out and get his feet through the partially opened door. He let go of the rope with his right hand and clutched the door, pulling himself fully into the shed. He was on a small platform that looked out over the skeletal roof rafters and joists. From here he could also see the top of a single boxcar sitting on old iron rails.

Archie finished tying their equipment bag to the rope and with his shotgun slung over his shoulder, he went up the rope just as quickly as Bell. When he was level with the doors, Bell reached out and hauled him inside by the belt. The voices were growing nearer. They had no idea if this was a security sweep or just some guys taking a brief walk after supper.

They hauled up the duffel bag. The men were definitely coming around to the far side of the shed. Bell pulled up the rope as fast as he could, with Archie behind him coiling its length on the platform so it wouldn't fall to the open floor below. Bell looked out. Two men smoking cigarettes rounded the corner of the shed. Neither looked up as he eased the door shut as quietly as possible.

A sliver of light shown through the gap between the two doors, though not enough to illuminate the building's large interior. The slit did allow Bell to listen as the two men continued on their walk, their voices fading eventually to nothing and all he could hear was the wind and the insects.

After another minute passed, Bell pulled a flashlight from the bag and flicked it on. He had masked half the lens to reduce the amount of light it threw, but it was still enough to see the layout of the building. The platform set above the joists wasn't even ten feet deep, while the shed itself was just under a hundred feet in length, but only twenty feet wide. Spare timbers had been stacked on the platform as well as two small barrels of nails. The planks that made up the platform were riddled with dry rot and punky, forcing the men to keep their weight over the rafters rather than the space in between.

The single railcar sat in the middle of the shed and looked like the one Bell had seen on the night of the heist. Archie removed the heavy lead sinker from the rope and tied it off to one of the overhead trusses, and was about to toss it over the edge when Bell stopped him with a hand to his throwing arm.

"I just had a thought," he said. "What if the scales still worked and are set up with an alarm of some kind?"

"This whole facility is a shambles," Archie countered. "Do you really think Pickett went that far?"

"Other than the dry rot up here, this building is pretty solid," Bell replied. "It might have stayed in working order all along."

Bell got down on his belly and moved so his upper torso was over the open space. He looked back at the wall under the platform and shined his light over it until he spotted the scale's display. It was a brass plaque with a slot in it for an arrow attached to the scale to be able to move up and down as weight was applied or removed. It showed the single car weighed in at thirty-eight thousand pounds.

What caught Bell's interest more than the display was the pair of wires that appeared to almost touch the metal arrow. The wires looked like a new addition. He understood that the wires were part of an open circuit and that any movement by the arrow would close the circuit and trigger an alarm.

With the mechanism located under the platform, there was no way to reach it without setting foot on the scale and Bell had no idea how sensitive the device was. Just because it currently supported a nineteen-ton railcar didn't mean that the weight of a man wouldn't tip it just that extra fraction of an inch to set off the alert.

Bell pulled back from the awkward position. "The scale is rigged to an alarm that probably runs to the tug. We can't risk blundering around outside looking for the wires. Let's just make the best of it."

The roof trusses were close enough together for Bell and Abbott to safely leave the platform and crawl out over the open floor until they were just above the railcar's sliding door. Archie had the knotted rope coiled around his shoulder like an Alpine climber. Bell worked the flashlight back and forth so each man could see where to move their feet.

Once in position, Archie tied a loop into the end of the rope and lowered it so that it was about a foot off the floor. It was then that he noticed a heavy table had been left in front of the boxcar's door, but thought nothing of it. He wound the other end of the rope around the truss and knotted it off so it wouldn't slip. Bell tucked the D-cell flashlight into the deep front pocket of his pants with the lens pointing up to give him some light and double-checked that his lockpick kit was buttoned in his back pocket.

He lowered himself down the rope with careful deliberation and when he reached the bottom, he slipped a boot into the loop Archie had made and let that leg take his full weight.

The problem was apparent immediately.

The table was too wide for Bell to reach across and pick the padlock securing the car's roller door. He tried every contortion possible and while he could brush his fingers against the lock, he couldn't hold himself steady enough to use the picks. He climbed back up to the perch where Archie waited.

"No dice," he announced.

"What about moving the table? You're not changing the weight on the scale."

"I'd really like to avoid shaking the scale at all. I've got an idea. Wait here."

Bell scampered across the trusses back to the platform, and from the pile of boards left behind all those years ago, he selected one of the right length and width that didn't show signs of decay. He also grabbed a pair of heavy leather gloves from the duffel.

It took him a little longer to return to Archie's position because he could only use one hand, as the other clutched the board. He slipped the loop he'd used earlier around one side of the wide plank and knotted the trailing rope to the opposite end of the board. He then wound the length of rope around a joist and handed the remainder to Archie along with the gloves. He made certain that the line was perfectly centered between the board, the joist, and Archie's hands.

"Ah," said Abbott. "The board becomes a sling, the joist is a tensioning pulley, and I'm your safety brake."

"And every idea a gem," Bell said, referencing Arch's earlier compliment.

He lay down on the plank and slipped the loop down his body so that it was under his chest, balancing his center of gravity. He crossed his ankles over the other end of the line as a way to maintain his stability once he was floating over the table.

"When I roll the board off the joist you've got all one hundred and eighty pounds of me."

"You'll be as safe as a babe in its mother's arms."

"Here we go."

Bell shifted his body from side to side, which slid the plank nearer and nearer to a tipping point. He made each movement smaller and smaller so he had some kind of control. If the board fell too quickly it could easily buck him off. At last, the board teetered on the edge. He could feel the ropes holding it steady and imagined Archie's grip tightening.

Then he rolled clear. The board remained suspended in the air for a fraction of a second before it began to plummet toward the floor. Bell was powerless and completely out of control. He was free-falling from fifteen feet in the air and was about to slam into the table with no way to break his fall. He cared nothing for alarms at that point because he was about to have his rib cage crushed.

And then the line came up short with a jerk that made the plank bounce just low enough to kiss the table's surface like a feather's caress. The brutal stop exploded the air from his lungs. Bell was left gasping like a fish out of water trying to fill them back up again. Had he not been holding the rope loop, the sudden stop would have slammed his arms against the table and triggered the alarm for sure. He couldn't believe how close they'd come to disaster.

"Sorry about that," Archie whispered from the darkness above. "Gloves had less grip than I expected."

Bell didn't reply for a moment. He needed to give his heart another few seconds to slow before saying, "It's okay. I need you to raise me about a foot so I can reach the lock."

Archie heaved back on the line. Pulling the rope tightened it around the joist, so he had both Bell's weight and friction to overcome. Undaunted, he fought against both and started gaining ground inch by inch. A testament to both strength and determination, Archie made up for his earlier gaff and lifted Bell until he was even with the padlock securing the boxcar's door.

"Good," Bell called quietly.

He adjusted the flashlight so it was on the plank next to him and shining against the side of the car. He pulled his lockpick kit from his back pocket, unzipped it, and removed two appropriately sized picks.

The lock itself wasn't particularly challenging, but working on his belly on a plank that swayed and rolled with every movement was frustrating. Evey time he tried to add pressure to his tensioning tool, he would push himself away from the lock and got no leverage against the tumblers. He would relax, swing closer, and try again to no avail. He needed a third arm to hold himself steady.

In a desperate move, he yanked the tensioner from the lock and used that hand to pull his face right up to the lock. He then bit down on the side of the lock to give himself a modicum of stability and reinserted the tensioner. By feel, his jaws straining and his teeth in real danger of cracking, he manipulated the tumblers until the lock gave with a muted click. He released his bite and swung back a couple of inches, the muscles at the base of his jaw aching.

Satisfied with a crazy but inspired bit of improvisation, Bell pulled the lock from the hasp. With one hand braced against the side of the car for leverage, he gently rolled the big door open a couple of inches. He grabbed up the flashlight and swept the inside of the car.

It was empty.

A string of curses echoed across Bell's brain as defeat more bitter than bile scalded the back of his throat. In that first second of realizing his failure, he wanted to scream to the heavens, to tear his hair from his head, and to burn the world to the ground. And then, as the next second ticked by, he let all of that go.

Rather than give in to unnecessary emotion he finished his search by slowly opening the roller door another couple of inches. Bell gripped it tightly in order to pull himself forward and stick his head into the boxcar. He looked left and saw nothing but empty space. And then he looked right. Piled in the back half of the boxcar was a mountain of identical black sacks that reached the car's ten-foot ceiling. There were hundreds, perhaps more than a thousand of them. Many of the bags sat within easy reach. Bell went for one. He didn't lift it free, but merely uncinched the cord holding it closed and shown the light into it. Inside the sack were several million dollars' worth of the distinctive pale green Federal Reserve notes.

Bell cracked a smile. "Jackpot."

39

BELL CLOSED THE DOOR AS GENTLY AS ONE WOULD CLOSE THE door to a nursery full of sleeping children and secured it once again with the padlock. Rather than have Archie struggle to haul him up to the rafters, Bell grabbed the rope to slowly pull himself up from a prone position. Just as he got his knees under him, the plank snapped without warning.

The fall was only a foot, but all of Bell's weight crashed down onto the table. He hit the wooden table at its very edge and ended up tumbling to the floor. He looked toward the front of the shed in time to see a blue spark wink out of existence as the circuit was completed and juice flowed to the alarm.

Bell scrambled to his feet and picked up the flashlight that had rolled free when he fell. Jamming it into a pocket, he thrust the half of the plank not tied to the rope down the back of his pants and climbed the rope as fast as he'd climbed anything in his life. Archie helped pull him onto one of the joists and immediately uncoiled the rope from the truss. Bell secured the other piece of the plank so it didn't slip free from the knot.

Together the two detectives scrambled across the joists, heedless of the fifteen foot fall they would take if they slipped. They reached the platform twenty-six seconds after the alarm had been set off. Bell estimated they had less than twenty more. He tossed the broken plank onto the pile of boards already there, while Archie took a few seconds to stuff the rope into their duffel.

Bell found the floorboard with the most amount of dry rot and slammed his boot against it so that it broke in two and part of it clattered to the floor. He then dropped one of the five-gallon casks of nails through the hole. Archie gave him a questioning look.

"They've got to find something in here that could have tipped the scales." He set the other barrel next to the hole as if it had been there for decades.

"Better than finding us, that's for sure."

Bell eased open the upper-story door. Logically, Pickett and his henchmen would open the main door on the other side of the shed, as it was closest to the tug, but still he moved with upmost caution. He heard distant voices raised in alarm. With the duffel over his shoulder, he grabbed onto the post sticking out of the side of the building and lifted himself until he could hook a leg over it. A moment later he was astride the beam. From there it was a single step to reach the metal roof.

He lay flat while Archie climbed out of the barn, closed the door by swinging a leg against it, and retraced Bell's moves. They didn't dare risk moving too much because of the noise it would generate in the metal roof panels. No sooner had they settled in to wait out the thieves, the chain and its attached bells was removed from the main doors in an inharmonious racket that carried clear across the lagoon.

The big door was swung open, and the timbre of the men's voices changed as they cautiously entered the train shed. Bell could imagine them armed with pistols and carrying flashlights. They would be tense, jumpy. The potential for an accident was high.

There weren't many places a person could hide and yet the men stayed inside the shed for the better part of fifteen minutes. They would have searched in, under, and atop the train car and likely opened it up and riffled through the stack of money bags for someone hiding under them. Bell didn't recall a ladder, so the best view of the platform they would get was from the railcar's roof. It was too far and a little too low for anyone to note the fresh footprints in the dust.

Finally, the main door closed, and the noisy chain was wrapped in place and padlocked. There was no conversation while the men made their way back to the tug.

"How long do we wait?" Archie asked.

The sky was darkening, but nowhere near full dark yet. To the south, it actually looked a little brighter than overhead, as though the storm clouds were passing without disgorging their rain. "Ten minutes."

At the prescribed time, Bell pulled the rope back out of the duffel bag and draped it evenly over the beam. It was awkward transferring his weight to the rope because he needed to hold on to both lengths at once, but once he got it right, it was an easy descent to the ground. Archie came down a second later. Bell pulled on one end of the rope, and as it fell, Arch was there to coil it and stuff it into the duffel. The rope's end whipped around the beam and tumbled to the ground in a heap.

Bell picked up the duffel while Archie pulled his twelve-gauge off his shoulder and held it at the ready. They would need just a couple of minutes to reach the airboat and be out of the lagoon a few minutes after that.

And that was when a man appeared from around the corner. He was as surprised to see Bell and Abbott as they were at seeing him. A moment of confusion passed. It wasn't even a full second, but it felt much, much longer and then the man shouted at the top of his lungs while at the same time reaching for the revolver stuffed in the waistband of his pants.

The detectives were too far to rush him before he could level the gun at them, so Archie did the only logical thing. The blast of light and sound from his shotgun shattered the evening and sent whole flocks of birds into the sky. The full load of buckshot hit the thief dead center and exited as though he were made of straw. His body was thrown back several feet. Bell and Archie were already running before he landed on the pier.

"Knew it was too good to last," Archie said, racking another shell into his weapon's chamber.

Bell looked around the corner and saw three more men approaching. They were already reaching for their guns. He and Archie backtracked and ran down the length of the train shed on its other side, although the act exposed them to the men rushing out from the tugboat. Even in the twilight, Bell recognized the diminutive silhouette of Michaleen Riordan and the elegant movement of Jackson Pickett. Bell felt a flash of rage the instant he recognized the man. He wanted to turn and fight him here and now, but he had to keep the greater good in mind. He kept running. The men rushing alongside Pickett and Riordan saw the two fleeing figures and started baying like a pack of hunting dogs.

Archie fired the twelve-gauge in their direction. He had no chance of hitting anything at that range, but it did cut down on the thieves' eagerness to run headlong into a gunfight.

One of Pickett's men didn't flinch, sprinting into the fire at a fast clip. As Archie and Bell started running down the length of the dock toward their stashed airboat, Pickett's accomplice closed to within a couple of paces. He struggled to remove a holstered revolver and aim it at the fleeing detectives.

The dock's planking was in rough shape, rotting and in some cases missing. Bell and Archie ran along the seams where the boards were nailed into the docks underframe rather than trust their weight on the wood in between the joists. The guy chasing at their heels was so intent on his quarry that he wasn't watching where he was going.

His foot hit a particularly rotted patch that gave way with virtually no resistance. He fell, but momentum kept him going forward. His lower ribs slammed into the solid edge of the next set of planks, snapping several. With his breath exploding in a hoarse gasp, his body whipsawed horizontally and he vanished into the brackish waters under the dock.

Bell and Archie might as well have never known the man was there, they ran with such single-minded focus. They had a healthy lead on the remaining pack of criminals chasing them, but would lose precious time starting the airboat once they scampered aboard. They reached the end of the dock and leapt down to the finger of land where they'd stashed the boat. Archie dropped to a knee and raised the shotgun while Bell ran the last fifty yards to the boat. He immediately went to work starting the motor.

Just before he pulled on the crank to turn it over, a bellow filled the lagoon that sounded like a continuous peal of thunder. It was the other airboat Jose had built. The one he said was bigger, faster, and more maneuverable than theirs. Pickett had bought it to scout out his family's property and used it to clear out the channel. He must have figured the intruders arrived by boat and was going to catch them in the fastest watercraft within a hundred miles.

The men chasing the detectives on foot reached the edge of the dock a second later and were met by a blast from Archie's scatter-gun as soon as their heads appeared. One man went down with a pellet in his shoulder and the others dropped flat. Abbott got off a second round to keep them pinned and rushed to the airboat.

Because the motor was still warm from the trip upriver on Jose's fishing boat, it fired on the first crank, the propeller thrashing the air and the craft eager to rush out into the channel. Archie dove over the airboat's gunwale and ripped free in midair the painter line that Bell had tied to a shrub. Bell opened the throttle and they burst from cover in a full-throated roar.

Bell immediately put the rudder hard over and pointed the boat back down the channel, toward the main river. The sky was grow-ing ominously dark. Archie climbed up onto the rear bench, set-tled his helmet over his head, and fitted Bell's over his. Their ears would ring for a while because of their proximity to the propeller, but now they were protected. Bell made a couple of hand gestures that Arch interpreted as *Keep an eye out behind us and tell me when the other boat gets close.*

Arch nodded. He fed more shells into his shotgun because this was far from over.

They made it to the river without seeing their pursuers. Rather than head south, and potentially put Jose and his teenage deckhand in danger, Bell threw the airboat to the left and headed north. He knew they wouldn't be so lucky that their wake would dissipate before the other airboat reached the junction.

From all the times he'd raced cars and motorcycles, Bell had an innate sense of any turn's apex, the sweet spot on the inside of the curve where you lose the least amount of speed before getting to the next straightaway. He slewed the airboat across the narrow river, just nicking the grass patches growing along each bend, straightening the craft a second or two early in order to shave another half second from the clock running in his head.

The controls felt comfortable in his hands. Not as responsive as an airplane's, but more than a regular boat's, and he felt he had a pretty good handle on the craft. But he had no delusions about the man chasing them. He'd had months to practice on his boat, knew its strengths and weaknesses and any quirks in its use. Bell was a dilettante compared to the hunter in his wake and he had to keep that reality in the forefront of his mind to avoid overconfidence.

The swamps along each bank tended to look uniform, yet Bell kept an eye out for distinctive landmarks: an oddly shaped tree, a large dead branch hanging over the water, anything to help him navigate back south again. They whooshed through a total of five sweeping corners before Archie urgently tapped Bell on the shoulder and pointed behind them.

Careful not to shift the sensitive rudder control, Bell twisted his torso and neck to peer through the whirling propeller at his back. The fast-approaching airboat was half again as wide as theirs, with a fifty percent bigger fan, and as Jose had mentioned, a larger motor. It also had a pair of side-by-side rudders placed in the prop's slipstream. There were two men hunkered down in the bow, a driver up on the high bench and what looked like a child next to him, but had to be the murderous Michaleen Riordan. Bell double-checked the pilot to see if it was Pickett and was disappointed when he realized it wasn't.

Bell grunted and redoubled his concentration. He cut the corners even tighter, whipping the airboat through tall grasses and as close to the riverbank as possible. The bigger craft pursuing them stayed closer to mid-channel, but was still eating into Bell's lead with alarming rapidity. Archie kept watch and when he saw the muzzle flashes of guns in the hands of the two men in the bow, he tapped Bell on the shoulder and made like he was firing a finger gun. Bell nodded that he understood they were under fire.

The motor and propeller were too loud to hear even something as concussive as close-in pistol shots.

Shooting from a moving boat at another moving boat in diminishing light was a doubtful prospect. However, that didn't mean that luck couldn't factor into the ballistic trajectories of the rounds being fired at them. Bell made tiny back-and-forth motions with his hand on the rudder as randomly as he could, slewing the craft ever so gently. Too much and he risked scrubbing off much-needed speed.

Archie was about to fire back at the thieves when Bell elbowed him sharply. Arch needed a second to understand his mistake. He was about to fire through the propeller and could have shredded the wooden blades with a single shot. Bell pulled his shotgun from a scabbard Jose used when hunting duck from the airboat. He handed it to his partner and mimicked firing through the propeller. Arch raised a questioning eyebrow and Bell hit him with an okay sign. He held up a finger and showed Abbott that he was about to chop the throttle to draw the pursuers in.

They swept through a curve and entered a straight stretch of the river. Bell glanced back and saw that the other airboat was in a direct line behind them. He tapped Archie's leg as a signal, and pulled the throttle lever back until the motor was just above idle. Their slowing was nowhere near as dramatic had this been a regular boat, but the hull settled into the water enough to bleed off their speed. The other boat came at them at full power.

Arch waited a beat and fired. Rather than a traditional spread of lead pellets, these shells fired an incendiary combination of phosphorus and magnesium. As the fiery blast passed through the propeller, it mushroomed out in an explosive wave that engulfed the other watercraft. Bell hit the gas again and veered them out of the path of Riordan's airboat.

The two gunmen caught the full burst of white-hot chemicals and fire. Neither even had the time to raise a protective arm as they were engulfed in the brief conflagration. The micro-sized bits of magnesium burned their way through skin and deep into flesh, as well as igniting the men's clothes, so the gunmen began to burn in wind-driven pyres. The pilot and Riordan were sitting above the blazing shot and had been spared, but the fire from the burning men threatened to ignite them, too.

The pilot whipped the boat around in a flat spin. The move bled off most of their speed, while the wild centrifugal force tossed both gunmen into the river, dousing the flames. The few remaining microdots of magnesium stayed lit even in the water. These men were trusted assets, unlike Flynn O'Conner's crew, and so they weren't expendable. Michaleen jumped down off the platform and leaned over the gunwale to heave both men back into the boat. He needn't have bothered. They were already dead from massive shock.

Riordan turned to the fleeing airboat. "You're a hard man to kill, Mr. Bell," he shouted. "But the day has not seen its end."

Once the pilot realized there would be no rescue, he put the hammer down and continued the chase. Even without the additional shooters, they still had plenty of firepower.

40

By the dumbfounded look on Archie's face, it was clear he'd never seen anything like that in his life. Bell hadn't either, but he'd had an inkling of what to expect. As much as he'd have loved to have taken Philip Findley's beautiful Purdey shotgun, he'd left it in the cabin. What he did take was a package of twelve-gauge shells mysteriously labeled GREEK FIRE. He'd taken one of the cartridges apart on the train from Atlanta to New Orleans and figured out its purpose.

Bell pointed at the gun in Arch's hands and held up a finger and then pressed all five fingertips to his chest. Archie nodded. Next in the chamber was a regular buckshot round. Bell held up two fingers and then wiggled all his digits to simulate a fire burning. Again, Archie nodded.

They had bought some time, but Bell wasn't sure what good that would do them. There were numerous side channels and rills spilling into the river, but to take any of them risked getting lost in the featureless bayou. He guided them through yet another looping oxbow. At its end was a slender sandbar with a large dead tree laying atop it, some of its branches crushed under it, some still thrusting up into the air.

The instant they were past it, Bell threw the airboat into a three-hundred-sixty-degree spin to shed their speed at the same time he cut the engine back to idle. Behind the sandbar was a placid-looking lagoon, with trees draped in Spanish moss like gauzy curtains. It appeared to be an idyllic little grotto until he spotted the massive number of glowing malevolent eyes staring back from the water's edge.

Bell guided the airboat until its nose grounded gently against the sandbar. Their once unstable craft was now a stationary firing platform. With the prop barely spinning, it was possible to hold a shouted conversation. "Fire from under the engine," Bell yelled. "I'll fire over it."

Archie climbed off the platform and laid himself in the aft under the bench and to the port side so he had a sight picture under the blade and its protective cage. Bell drew two of the .45s and stood on the seat so he could aim over the propeller. In the distance, they could hear the other boat pounding its way through the swamp, its engine pushing with everything it had. At that speed, Bell and Abbott would have only a few seconds to put out as much lead as they possibly could.

The noise rose until it seemed to rend the very air itself. Bell had his two guns up. Archie had both shotguns so he could get off three shots but only have to rack the slide of just one weapon. Michaleen and his pilot were running into the ambush practically blind and deaf.

Reaching a crescendo, the pursuing airboat exploded into view.

It would transverse their position and reach a safe distance in seconds. Bell and Archie had no idea the shotgun blast of "Greek fire" had taken out Riordan's two shooters and that they'd evened the odds.

Bell fired as fast as he could pull the triggers. The range was acceptable and so he was pretty certain his first bullet had hit the pilot, who was closer than Riordan. Below him, lying prone over the aft, Archie fired the first shotgun, then let it fall from his hands to snatch up the second one and let out another blast of buckshot. He racked the gun just as the airboat was passing by them and making its escape and he fired another round. Unlike before, when the burning chemicals from the Greek fire cartridge were disbursed passing through the airboat's prop, this time he fired into clean air and a shaft of fire erupted from the gun and covered the hundred feet to the other boat in the blink of an eye.

The rear of the fleeing airboat was briefly engulfed in flames. When it emerged, the pilot was slumped across the bench, dead and on fire. The little Irishman had leapt from the platform and taken cover in the bottom of the craft. The fire had overwhelmed the engine's spark or carburetor because it died and the propeller juddered to a stop.

Bell reloaded his pistols while Archie used the pole to push them off the sandbar. The other boat slowed entering the secluded lagoon. Once the Van Dorn men were far enough back from the shoal, Bell gave a little more gas and cranked the rudders hard over.

Archie covered the other boat with the shotgun as they approached. The clothing worn by the pilot continued to burn and the odor of roasting grew stronger. Onshore, the dozens of big alligators watched the scene unfold with unblinking eyes. They were growing agitated by the smell, snapping at each other in mindless saurian fury.

Bell cut the motor entirely and jumped down from the controls to be in position when the two boats came together. He tied them off with a quick knot, Arch standing watch behind him. Riordan was lying flat on the bottom of the boat. It was difficult to tell if he was injured, as his clothes were dark and the lighting uneven.

Bell cautiously stepped over onto the larger airboat. He kicked at Michaleen's leg with the toe of his boot, but got no response. He kicked a little harder. He reached down to slap the man's face. He checked for a pulse. Riordan was alive. He flicked open one of the man's eyelids. All he saw was the white sclera.

Just as he turned to tell Archie that Riordan was out cold, the killer suddenly sprang up, a knife he'd had hidden under his leg in his hand and aimed at Bell's ribs. Bell's reaction was perfectly timed and measured, as if he'd expected the ruse all along. In a modified judo throw, he used Riordan's momentum against him. As the Irishman reared up, Bell grabbed the arm with the knife and threw himself down. His own body acted as a fulcrum to flip the assassin over the airboat's low gunwale and into the bayou.

Michaleen came up sputtering.

"Now, that wasn't very sporting," he called. "Be a gent and give a lad a hand, would ye?"

The splash the assassin made when he hit the warm water wasn't much, but it was enough. There was a collective pause on-shore, as if the creatures couldn't believe the bounty they'd just been given. And then as one, the gators exploded into motion, turning the waters of the little grotto into a frothing maelstrom.

It took a few seconds for Riordan to fully comprehend what he was hearing and feeling through the water. He turned to see the gators rushing toward him, tails thrusting with single-minded purpose.

"Mr. Bell," he yelled, realizing in a panic that the current had carried the boat far out of reach. Jaws began to open as they streaked in for their prey, ranks of teeth numbering more than six dozen ready to slash and tear in a frenzy of evolutionary dominance. Riordan tried to swim for the airboat, but he couldn't outrun the gators.

On his knees in the airboat, Bell shouted out into the darkness, "Just so you know, this is personal for me. Very personal."

Michaleen Riordan's screams were choked off when a twelve-foot alpha male closed its mouth around his thighs, pulled him under the surface, and began to rotate his entire body in order to rip his meal in two.

There were six tons of alligators thrashing the water, trying to get a piece of the dead man. They churned up the surface in a frothing boil of white water and writhing bodies with flashes of teeth as long as thumbs. The frenzy was so much that the waves pushed the two rafted airboats out of the lagoon and back into the river. Bell and Abbott were both physically relieved at being away from the murderous reptiles.

Bell found a gas can with a spigot attached by a chain. He handed it over to Arch. He also came across a handheld spotlight attached to a large dry-cell battery. "Perfect."

"I figured you'd want to take their boat. It's faster."

Bell passed over the lamp and climbed back into their boat. "I've gotten used to this one. No sense relearning what I already know. Besides, even if we ditched the pilot into the water, that smell is going to linger."

"Even with a lamp, it's getting too dark," Arch said.

"Can't be helped." Bell began refilling the boat's tank by the fire's flickering light. "I've counted the oxbows between us and the cannery and memorized some distinguishing landmarks. If we keep close to the western bank, we should be okay."

"Consider me reassured," Arch said in a tone that said he wasn't.

"If we get lost, we've got plenty of ammunition and I don't think this place will ever run out of gators to hunt."

"Lovely."

They lost time because the airboat's motor refused to fire, and Bell had to partially disassemble it to clean out a clogged fuel filter. It would have been an impossible job without the jacklight. Once the engine was back together again, it fired on the first crank. Bell set the throttle to quarter speed, and with Archie holding the lamp up on the bow and casting its beam along the western riverbank, they set off back downriver.

It was a far more sedate trip than their mad dash north, but in many ways, far more nerve-racking. There was the very real potential of getting lost despite Bell's assurances, as he well knew. However, the thing that preyed on his mind the most was what Jackson Pickett had done in the time since realizing his lair had been discovered.

If he had enough men, they could have emptied the railcar of cash and stowed it aboard the tug and already been halfway to the Mississippi River. Since he and Archie hadn't fully explored the facility before being discovered, it was possible they had a small shunting locomotive and had already moved the boxcar out onto the main north-south line. If that was the case, they would be long gone by the time the two detectives reached civilization and a working telephone.

Bell felt the case slipping through his fingers once again. When he spotted a particular forked stump that he recognized from their earlier high-speed race, he dared bump the throttle a little more and eked out and additional spurt of speed.

They motored past a half dozen channels that looked similar to the cannery's entrance, but Bell kept true. He knew they weren't yet there. He felt certain they had two more long sweeping curves to go. At the end of the second oxbow, Bell studied the bank, looking for anything familiar. Nothing caught his eye. It was all just ordinary swamp.

He realized he hadn't recognized anything for the past twenty minutes and was suddenly struck by the horrifying thought that they had somehow blundered into a split in the river they hadn't seen when they were heading north.

Without conscious thought, his hand went for the throttle to slow their speed in an effort to not compound his navigation mistake. He stopped himself. He knew he was on the right path. He kept going through one more turn. He was certain that the first oxbow when they turned out of the cleared channel had been to the left. He ignored the bank on this one because it twisted the wrong way. Halfway through the next, there was an opening in the thick jungle as neatly tended as an English garden.

Bell grinned and pointed the airboat down this new channel. Pickett would expect Michaleen's return, so there was no need to be stealthy. They blasted through the waters they had so stealthily poled earlier in the evening. The white clapboard cannery building loomed out of the night, appearing more haunting and foreboding and shrouded by darkness, like some Gothic house of horrors.

Bell finally eased off the throttle. Archie looked back at him, his face ashen. They both saw that the barge and tug were gone.

As they got closer, Archie flashed the light across the dock until he found the train shed. Its doors gaped open and even from a distance they saw that it was empty. Pickett either had a small shunting motor on-site that they hadn't seen or the tug was able to winch the boxcar onto the barge.

Without wasting another second, Bell poured on the power and whipped the airboat back around, its stern carving a crescent wake in the inky black waters as they started to give chase.

41

LIKE MOST EVERYONE, ISAAC BELL HATED TO LOSE. WHAT DIF-
ferentiated him from others were the lengths he was willing
to go, and the risks he was willing to take, in order to win.

They came screaming out of the old fish factory's shipping
channel with Bell giving the airboat everything it had. If he could
have spurred it to greater speed by whipping the seat as though
this were a horse, he surely would have done it. Archie clung one-
handed to the bow, holding the light in the other to illuminate
their path.

They were doing what Jose had expressly warned against. The
light was bright enough to see only a few dozen yards ahead, giving Bell barely enough time to react if they came upon a sunken
log or any of the floating debris that appeared with frightening
frequency. Earlier Bell could've used a subtle touch on the rudder
because he could spot an obstacle well in the distance. Now they
sprang out of the night without warning, forcing him to slew the

airboat around them with only a few feet of clearance. Occasionally some unseen branch laying submerged just under the surface would scrape against the bottom with a screech like nails on a chalkboard.

As before, Bell cut as close to the riverbank as he could coming around the corners, the airboat skimming through water barely deep enough to float in and mowing over areas of seagrass and marsh scrub. Occasionally he'd have to duck under low-hanging branches that came out of the gloom as deadly as scythes.

The light would often reflect the glow of countless reptilian eyes lining the shore, a further reminder that if they crashed and the wreck didn't kill them, the gators would be on them before they'd swum more than a stroke. What had happened to Michaleen Riordan made Bell hope that if the worst did happen, his neck would snap in the crash.

Southward they raced. Archie kept the light perfectly focused despite the erratic ride, and Bell's level of concentration never wavered. Through the seventh oxbow, Bell eased off the throttle to prepare to stop the airboat so he could get a report from Jose. The fishing boat wasn't there. Bell was sure this was the place he and Archie had left from. He recognized two dead cypress trees rising out of the water and how their branches interlocked in places.

Archie cast the light back and forth as he, too, recognized the rendezvous location. There was no debris in the water or wreckage of any kind, no rainbow slicks of spilled gasoline or oil, and nothing onshore to indicate anyone had gotten off the fishing boat.

Archie set the light down and moved aft. Bell idled the engine and put the stick hard over so the boat made lazy circles in the river.

"I think Jose saw the barge and tug." Arch still had to shout to be heard. "He must have figured it was important to us and took off to shadow it."

"I think so, too," Bell replied. "We shouldn't be too far behind at the pace we're going."

"What's the plan when we reach the barge?"

"I'm going to come up behind it and if we don't see any guards, you're going to jump aboard. Make your way to the tug while I distract Pickett's men. When you make your move, I'll come in with everything I've got."

"I like it."

"Then let's go."

Once Archie was back in position, and their way well-lit again, Bell advanced the throttle. With an acceleration rivaling a thoroughbred, the airboat launched back down the river, the forest along each bank whipping by in a blur of muted color rather than individual trees. He guessed their speed at around thirty miles per hour.

The race south almost ended in total disaster. Archie pointed at a log floating in their path. Bell put the rudder over and it looked like they were going to clear it with plenty of room. The log ended up being longer with an extra eight feet of it submerged. They hit hard enough to heel the airboat over onto its gunwale. Arch dropped the light so he could use both hands to hold on. Bell kept his right hand on the stick and grabbed the opposite bench with his left, his shoulder taking most of his weight as the airboat continued to plane long with only a slice of its starboard hull in the water.

They teetered on a knife-edge for what felt like eternity but was only a few seconds before Bell realized he had control of the situation even if it felt like he didn't. A tiny adjustment to the rudder deflected the airflow around the boat and its port side dipped and then fell back into the river, hydroplaning along like nothing had happened.

No water entered the boat, so the collision hadn't holed her thin aluminum skin. Feeling they were getting close, Bell conceded a little of their speed for prudence's sake. From the bow, Archie flashed a thumbs-up of approval.

A short while later, they shot out of a long curve, and up ahead was Jose's fishing vessel. It ran without lights and barely cut a wake because it was going so slowly. Bell throttled back. Archie shone the light on himself and then at Bell as they came abreast of the fisherman. From the little pilothouse, Jose waved in recognition and pointed ahead. He held up his right hand with his fingers splayed and then touched his left wrist.

Bell understood immediately. He'd seen Jose looking at the square-face Cartier Santos watch Marion had bought him a few years back. The *isleño*'s pantomime meant they were only five minutes behind Pickett and the barge.

Bell waved in acknowledgment and sped up once again, adrenaline starting to pump through his system at the thought of confronting Jackson Pickett and making him answer for every one of the crimes he'd committed in the commission of his theft.

He knew they were close when the water sluicing under the airboat's hull grew choppy. It was the fat barge's wake through the river. Archie sensed it, too, and made a gesture for Bell to slow the boat.

A moment later, the barge came into view. Atop its back was the boxcar loaded with a billion dollars' worth of Federal Reserve notes. Archie scanned the light back and forth. There was nobody on the barge.

Bell crept in on it, his fingers adjusting the throttle to match pace with the ponderous flatboat. He judged the tugboat's speed at around five knots. Archie was in the bow ready to leap up. He had his twelve-guage slung over his shoulder and a big .44-caliber revolver in a holster at his hip. The barge's deck was a good four feet higher than the airboat and Arch bent his knees to coil tension into the muscles of his legs. As the two crafts came inches apart, he leapt.

It wasn't the most graceful of jumps. His shifting weight depressed the airboat's bow and absorbed some of the energy, but he managed to get both arms over the edge and then swung a leg up so he could roll fully onto the barge. He scrambled to his feet, gave Bell a brief bow, and started forward. Bell remained hidden behind the barge to allow Archie to get into position.

He counted down two minutes in his head and pulled out along the barge's starboard side because there was more room to maneuver there than on the port. When he was opposite the fifty feet of tow cable separating the tug from the barge, he saw Archie hanging underneath it. Upside down, he had hooked a leg over the rope and was pulling himself toward the tug with just his arms.

A lot safer bet than trying to do a tightrope act, Bell thought.

The tug had an open aft deck with a heavy steel bollard in its center. There were windows high up in the wheelhouse for the crew to glance back at their tow, and a door below it to give them access to the stern section from the stumpy superstructure. The boat was all function and no form.

Once Arch was over the tug's flat fantail, he dropped from the towrope and hid himself behind the bollard. He shot Bell a wave. Bell increased speed, racing down the length of the tug with only a couple of feet separating them. The bridge's wing door opened and out stepped a shadowy figure no more than a silhouette. Looking over his shoulder, Bell recognized the lithe slouch of Jackson Pickett leaning in the doorframe. He cut across the river in order to turn around. Another door opened and Pickett's men came out onto the small forward deck, crowding the rail to watch the airboat.

The river was too dark, and the tug too well lit for them to really see much other than the white waves left in the airboat's wake. They couldn't tell who was piloting the craft or even how many people were aboard. Bell did a couple of fast turns, carving an *S* shape in the water just to keep their interest while Archie was coming up behind them through the superstructure.

Enough, Bell thought. It was time.

He raced at the tug's starboard rail as if he were going to veer away at the last second and perhaps splash the men. Instead, he idled the engine and threw the airboat into a spin with plenty of room to spare. As it whipped around, he used his strength and the momentum to hurl the half-empty gas can high up over the tug. The container gushed fuel as it arced in a perfect parabola. The men aboard the towboat didn't even know it was coming.

Because the airboat was still bobbing, Bell remained sitting rather than get to his feet. He pulled his shotgun to his shoulder, waited a fraction of a second, and pulled the trigger.

The luminous column of flames from the Greek fire round jetted from the gun in a throaty roar. The fire found the droplets of gas trailing the can and lit them up in a mushrooming conflagration that expanded in the blink of an eye. The heat ignited the fumes inside the metal container in a percussive whoosh that split the can like a grenade and showered flaming gasoline onto Pickett's coconspirators.

Night became day with the entire bow section alight. Some of the gas had fallen to the water and there it still burned. The fireball rose higher than the superstructure so that for several seconds the bridge was engulfed in flames. The gasoline quickly burned away, and when it did, it revealed the tightly packed group of men had been turned into human torches. Bell was grateful for the loud motor so he couldn't hear the curdling screams of men burning alive. Most jumped into the river to extinguish the flames, while others were too far gone and dropped to the deck, curling into fetal positions as the fire consumed them.

A second later came a single shotgun blast from the bridge that lit it up in a blinding strobe. That would be Archie securing the pilothouse. Bell nudged the throttle to pull alongside the tug. When the speeds matched, he killed the engine and vaulted over the tug's low rail. The moment his ears stopped echoing the drone of the airboat's engine, he heard the sobs and moans of the men bobbing alongside the barge as the tug continued its southward run.

He imagined their fate with a shudder of revulsion, as so many wounded men would attract that many more alligators.

Just inside the door of the superstructure was a canister fire extinguisher mounted to a bulkhead. He unclipped it from the wall and went back to the forward deck to put out the last of the flames. For the second time that night the smell clung to the back of his throat like a viscous gel.

Gun in hand, he checked out the lower spaces and found no one. The cramped engine compartment under a hatch in the deck was also empty. Bell climbed to the bridge. While normally kept very dark while operating at night, a couple of additional lamps had been lit. The captain and mate looked like they were bayou people like Jose, swarthy and poorly dressed. The mate had his hands pointing toward the ceiling, while the captain kept his on the wheel.

Archie stood in a corner, the empty shotgun leaning against the wall behind him, the heavy .44 held at the ready. Stuffed into another corner was a figure wearing all black. Bell saw the blood on his forehead and shot Arch a questioning look.

"Idiot rushed me from the wing, so I clobbered him with the shotgun."

"Is he alive?"

"Didn't check."

Bell bent to place two fingers against the side of Jackson Pickett's neck. His pulse was strong. Bell stood. "Captain, do you mind telling me your side of this story?"

The middle-aged man looked into Bell's eyes and apparently felt the need to clear his conscience. "Name's Rufus Duquesnel. Mate's name is Wilbur. He's my nephew."

"Wilber," Bell said, "you can lower your hands, but don't try anything foolish. At this range Archie can choose which nostril to shoot. Captain, please continue."

"Me and my boat were hired to tow a train barge up to the old cannery and wait for further instructions. We been holed up there better part of five days. Then tonight all hell breaks loose. Assume that was your doing."

"It was."

"As soon as you took off in the airboat with that little devil man chasing after you, Mr. Pickett there ordered us to winch the railcar hidden at the factory onto the barge and we took it under tow."

"Do you know what's in the boxcar?"

"Nope."

"Do you know where you are heading?"

"Also, nope. Pickett said he'd give me instructions along the way."

A horn suddenly sounded from across the waters. Bell went out to the wing bridge. In their wake and overtaking them at a good clip was Jose in his fishing boat. Behind it he was towing the airboat Bell had abandoned. He pulled alongside and slowed to match speed.

He called up to Bell, "When I heard the explosion, I thought maybe you could use some help. Is that Rufus I see?"

"It is and your timing is perfect. Hold on a second." Bell ducked back onto the bridge. "Captain, where is the nearest pier where I can off-load that railcar?"

"Belle Chasse," he said without hesitation.

"And how long to get us there?"

"Twelve hours or so. My *Myrtle Mae* isn't only ugly, she's slow."

Back outside, Bell said, "Jose, can you get word to an agent named Vic Carver at the Hotel Monteleone in New Orleans that I will have the car at the Bell Chasse rail landing in twelve hours? Then there is someone else who should be at the Hotel Desoto by now that I'd like you to get. His name is Ray Burns."

"Sure, no problem."

"Thanks. Oh, hey. Your other airboat is about twenty or so miles upstream. Its owner won't be coming back to lay claim, so it's yours again, minus a little fire damage."

"Okay. Thank you, I will get it tomorrow."

Back on the bridge Archie said, "When did you tell Carver to come to New Orleans?"

"Before we left Atlanta. Let's just say I had a hunch about finding Pickett and the . . ." He was about to say money in front of Dequesnel. ". . . boxcar at the cannery after Philip Findley's story.

I want to turn over custody as soon as we possibly can, so I made the call."

"Nice one, buddy."

"Actually, I made another call even before we left D.C.," Bell said cryptically, "but it'll be a little while before I know if that hunch pans out, too."

42

THE TUGBOAT *MYRTLE MAE* PULLED INTO THE RAIL DOCK AT Belle Chasse a few hours late, but when she arrived, she had a greeting party as big as any of the notorious transatlantic express liners. Treasury agents Vic Carver and Paul Haygarth stood at the head of a pack of law enforcement officers, some in plain clothes, others in uniform. They were a mix of local, parish, and state men, cobbled together by Carver on short notice. It was doubtful they knew what they were here to protect.

The dockworkers waiting to secure the barge in its long slip looked more than a little uncomfortable with such a formidable and also unexplained police presence.

Captain Dequesnel had already cast aside the towrope and was using his tug's blunt prow to push the barge into its slip. Before it reached the dock, a pair of ropes attached to the front of the barge were fed into two windlasses on the pier. The barge was winched in the last few yards so that the rail embedded on its deck aligned exactly with the rails leading inland.

A small shunting locomotive sat huffing on the dock. Beyond that were a gravelly rail yard with a dozen spurs, a three-bay round-house with a turntable, and a few repair sheds and warehouses. There were also at least fifty railcars of various types sitting idle on some of the tracks. A separate elevated trestle system was off on the side of the yard, which was used for unloading coal cars. Heaps of coal were piled nearby.

Once the barge was in place, Archie and Bell thanked Dequesnel. They yanked Jackson Pickett out of the phone booth–sized head they'd locked him in the night before. He'd been forced to sit on the commode for hours and now his legs were completely numb and practically useless. He yelled into the gag they'd placed in his mouth, his eyes blazing with righteous fury. They each took an arm, ignoring his muted howls of pain as feeling began to return to his limbs, and lugged him off the tug and onto the dock.

Yard workers had already released the boxcar's safety chains and were running a heavy cable between it and the 0-4-0 locomotive. Rather than ballast the barge in order to compensate for the engine's weight, it was far easier to just tow the railcar off the flat-boat and then couple it normally.

Vic Carver came forward to shake hands. "Mr. Bell, that is one hell of a thing you pulled off."

"Not exactly what we had planned," Bell admitted. "We just wanted to verify the money was at the cannery and call you guys in to do the heavy lifting."

"I consider you even finding the, er, merchandise a miracle." He turned his attention to Jackson Pickett. The gag was still in place and his hands were bound behind his back. He swayed on unsteady legs. "We need to figure out what to do with you."

They stepped aside when the boxcar was pulled off the barge and connected to the yard engine. The gaggle of law enforcement walked beside it as it was moved to a lone warehouse on the far end of the depot. There, the engine was uncoupled, and it was left for its next job of the morning.

No one but the Van Dorn men, their prisoner, and the Treasury agents went inside the building. The cops set themselves into a defensive perimeter around the warehouse that would be maintained until the railcar left Belle Chasse.

Because of its many skylights, the empty warehouse was bright enough to see all the soot particles from the little locomotive's brief stay floating around. There were some boxes of cargo stacked in one corner that appeared to have been there for a long time. Bell guessed the Treasury Department had rented out the space for privacy until they shunted the money out again.

He picked the lock securing the boxcar's door and muscled it all the way open. Carver and Haygarth both climbed up and each loosened the drawstring on separate bags. Carver grinned as he pulled out a banded bundle of twenty-dollar bills. "I just can't believe you did it," he said again in admiration.

Bell replied, "Our motto about how we always get our man needs to be changed so it includes stolen fortunes, too. And I even still have a few hours left on McAdoo's deadline."

The T-men put the money back and leapt to the ground. This time Carver locked the boxcar with a new padlock he'd bought at a hardware store in town. "What about Pickett's men and that Irish murderer of his . . . ?"

"Michaleen Riordan," Bell said. "I have no idea how fast alligators digest their meals, so I can't say their precise location . . ."

"Seriously?" Haygarth gaped. "All of them?"

"We had a running gun battle for what seemed like hours," Archie told him. "Any time one of them went into the water, the gators were practically circling. It was something that'll give me nightmares for years."

Bell watched Pickett's reaction at hearing this for the first time. A shadow had passed behind his eyes at the thought of Riordan's gruesome death. However the unlikely pair had met, he really did have a strong affinity to the little Irish murderer. Birds of a feather, he supposed. Bell opined their fate should be the same.

"I had hoped to see another lawman here," Bell said. "A young detective out of Newport, Rhode Island."

"Sorry," Carver said with a shrug. "Just us and the locals we picked up."

"Vic, what happens next?"

"I called Washington last night when word of your success reached us. They're sending down a big team from the Bureau of Engraving. The plan is to organize the cash into the proper amounts to be delivered to the twelve Reserve bank branches straight from here. Our cover is that this was how we planned on disbursing the money all along, by sneaking it out of the Engraving building in the middle of the night and taking it out of D.C. by rail. No one will be the wiser."

"Security?" Bell asked.

"Tighter than Paul's hatband. I've got agents coming down to replace the local boys outside and we're borrowing an armored boxcar from the Army. It's the type they use to move explosives, so it should be more than safe."

Bell nodded his approval at the arrangements. He sidled over to where Pickett sat on the floor handcuffed to a column. He removed the gag. "That just leaves you as the last detail that needs to be taken care of."

"You can't touch me, Bell. The government can't let the people know how I made off with a billion dollars. It shows just how incompetent they are. They have no choice but to grant me a pardon in exchange for my silence. Sometimes the more outrageous the event, the more it has to be kept secret."

"Suppose they lock you in solitary at Leavenworth?"

"Not without a trial. It's already too late to make me disappear. Fifty lawmen saw me get off the tug just now."

Bell glanced in Vic Carver's direction. The agent's expression told him that Pickett wasn't wrong. "I suppose I could just shoot you myself."

"I know you better than that, Mr. Bell. Hell, I probably know you better than you know yourself. You've never killed a prisoner or anyone else in cold blood. You have a code, Mr. Bell, a rigid one that makes you have to be the good guy, no matter what it costs you. You'd see me walk free before breaking your precious moral superiority."

Bell pulled one of the .45s from his shoulder rig's kidney holster and pointed it at Pickett's head. A faint smile played across the thief's lips. He knew it was a bluff. Several seconds slipped by, time moving slower in the warehouse at that moment. Pickett's smile faded under the onslaught of Bell's unrelenting stare.

And still Bell held the pose. Sweat appeared on Pickett's lip and he swallowed reflexively. Carver and Haygarth tensed. It seemed no one knew what was going to happen next, especially Jackson Pickett.

"Bell," Carver said as a warning. "Bell, put it away. Secretary McAdoo is working with the justice people. We'll figure something out."

Bell pulled the trigger.

The hammer fell on an empty chamber. Bell smiled ruefully and reholstered the gun. "Looks like I miscounted when I was using this last night. I could have sworn there was one bullet left."

Pickett looked like he'd seen his own ghost.

Bell continued. "You're right. I could no more shoot a prisoner than I would murder my own wife. I do have a code, Pickett, a set of rules that I never break, no matter how much I want to. If I did that, I'd never be able to look at myself in a mirror again. But what you don't know is that I have, and will continue to, bend those rules every chance I get.

"You used me in Rhode Island in order to test me. To see if you could outfox Van Dorn's best detective. And I will admit that you got me. Lock, stock, and barrel, you had me convinced that your wife committed suicide in such a bizarre manner that you'd be framed for her death."

"You are very good at what you do," Pickett conceded. "It's why Michaleen tried to kill you in New York. After your master class at the mansion, you deemed yourself a risk at being around to investigate the heist."

"But I survived," Bell said. "And after that I saw through your ruse on the bridge, investigated the murders of all your accomplices, and finally deduced who on the Fed board helped you. You beat me in Rhode Island, Pickett, but I bested you when it really counted."

"A victory that'll turn to ash on your tongue when the government lets me walk."

Just then there was a knock on the warehouse's personnel door. Bell turned away from Pickett and strode over to the door. He kept his hand on a pistol he knew was loaded, out of an abundance of caution, and opened the door a crack. A uniformed cop at least two inches taller than the towering Vic Carver blocked out the view behind him.

"Couple of fellers from up north say they got business with Isaac Bell."

"I'm Bell."

The cop moved aside to reveal Detective Thomas Lassiter of the Newport Police Department and his protégé, Ray Burns.

Bell was only anticipating the arrival of Burns. "Detective Lassiter, I didn't expect you'd make the trip with Detective Burns."

"I wouldn't have missed it for the world."

Bell shook both men's hands and pointed at the black briefcase Lassiter carried. "Was I right?" Then he said quickly, "Of course I was right. Otherwise, you wouldn't have come all the way to Belle Chasse, Louisiana."

"Let me show you."

Bell led them across the warehouse to where the Treasury agents stood with Archie, well out of Pickett's line of sight. Introductions were made all around. For Carver and Haygarth's sake, Bell recounted the story of the death of Jackson Pickett's wife and his role in proving it was a suicide and not a murder.

"It was in the train tunnel that I realized I was on the trail of the most methodical criminal I had ever encountered," Bell said. "The tip-off was a clue Archie found in the safe of Hauser, the murdered railroad executive. It tied Pickett to the new Federal Reserve notes. It made me think about how meticulous Mrs. Pickett had been in trying to frame her husband for her death, when it occurred to me that both crimes, the heist and what I now was convinced was murder, were carried out by the same man.

"Only problem was I had no proof, and the county coroner in Rhode Island had already ruled her death a suicide. To get that changed I needed something ironclad, but again I had nothing but my own instincts. That is until Pickett sent Riordan to clean up some loose ends by killing anyone outside of their own crew who'd helped them."

"That was the building contractor, the railway guy, and the others you'd mentioned back in Washington?" Carver asked.

"Yes. One of them was an ex-con turned locksmith named Harvey Wanamaker, who we believe made the tools that Pickett used to force the vault lock in the Engraving building. On a hunch, I asked the Newport Police Department to send someone to Philly to see the inventory of everything in the locksmith's shop and his home. I thought Detective Lassiter would have sent Burns on his own, but he came as well."

"Any chance to put away a murderer operating in my town and I'm going to take it," Lassiter said gruffly.

Bell continued. "I'd instructed their duty sergeant that they were to go to Pickett's home and collect samples of all the stationary they could find and bring it with them."

"Why?" asked Haygarth.

"To design the tools needed to break into the vault, Pickett would have handed the locksmith a detailed set of plans with all the proper measurements taken from the identical vault in the Atlanta Reserve branch."

"Did you find those plans in the locksmith's possession?" Vic asked, not sure yet what Bell was getting on about.

"No," Lassiter said, "and we weren't looking for them."

"Pickett likely took them when he picked up the tools," Bell said. "But he made an omission when he had asked Wanamaker to create another device for him prior to the break-in. The mechanical windless device that pulled the gun he used to kill his wife. The one that yanked it across the room and up into the vent. Pickett had tasked the locksmith with its creation and forgot to ask for his blueprint back."

Lassiter had set his case on a desk-high wooden cargo crate. He popped the locks and removed a couple of flat envelopes. From one he carefully removed two sheets of paper that had once been crumpled flat, but had been smoothed out again. Sprawled across both sheets were simple sketches of the spring-tensioned winding device, as well as designs for modifying the gun used.

"Ah," said Bell upon seeing them for the first time. "Pickett must have crushed them up and thrown them away in the shop, but the locksmith plucked them from the trash and kept them for his records."

"Why?" Carver asked.

"Who knows? Leverage over Pickett comes to mind, but I suspect professional pride."

"It's just that," Lassiter said. "Wanamaker had filing cabinets full of blueprints and spec sheets on everything he'd custom made over the years."

"Do we have him?" Haygarth asked. "This means we have him for the murder, right?"

"Not at first blush," Carver said. "We have a locksmith supplying the device, but nothing linking Pickett to him."

Bell nodded. "Which is why I asked that samples of stationary from the Pickett mansion be brought along."

Thomas Lassiter pulled a slender notepad from another of the envelopes. "This was removed from the top right drawer of Jackson Pickett's desk in his private office."

A quick visual inspection showed the drawings and the blank pages were of identical paper weight and color. It was circumstantial evidence, but Bell knew a good prosecutor could get a conviction from it.

"It gets better," Lassiter said. He pointed to how one of the drawings hadn't torn evenly from the pad when it had been removed, a little bit of the top right corner had torn and had been left behind. He pushed the drawing up to the top of the notepad, where a small triangle of paper was still stuck to the spine. It was a perfect match for the chunk missing from the drawing.

"On top of that, we've got notes written on the blueprint margin that match Pickett's handwriting, and we even pulled a partial fingerprint that is dead-on."

"Got him," Bell said with a grin. "Vic, this is an independent investigation totally separate from yours. I even had these two stay in a different hotel than yours so there would be no possibility of cross contamination that a defense attorney could use to muddle the case. I didn't use any of my people, so everything was carried out by true law enforcement. The case is ironclad, airtight, and so obvious that the jury will take minutes rather than hours for their deliberation. Pickett might skate free for the theft of a billion dollars and a murderous rampage along the way, but he's going to hang after all. For the homicide of his dying wife."

"Rhode Island did away with the death penalty sixty years ago," young Ray Burns said.

"Pickett and his wife are New York residents," Archie pointed out. "I'm sure we can get a change of venue and see he gets a seat in the electric chair up at Sing Sing."

"Done and done," Bell said with a theatrical swipe of his hands.

There was another round of handshakes and backslapping. The Rhode Island detectives didn't know what the feds wanted with Pickett or what he'd done, but their relief that he was going to pay for Fedora's murder was palpable.

Bell finally said, "Let's go tell Pickett the good news."

The six of them walked the length of the warehouse to where their prisoner remained on the floor and cuffed to the column. He paid no attention to anyone other than Bell. His arrogant little smile was back at the corners of his mouth. "Here to release me?"

"I am," he replied and pointed over to Thomas Lassiter. "Into his custody."

Pickett took a moment to study the dour detective. His eyes widened when he recognized the man and remembered from when and where. He maintained an air of aloof indifference. "You've got nothing. A greenhorn public defender could beat whatever you charge me with."

Lassiter casually held up the technical drawing. Pickett recognized it at once, but he couldn't get around how it came to be in police custody. His eyes darted from face to face, searching for an answer none of the men would give.

Bell finally gave a low, mirthless chuckle. "So much for you being a criminal mastermind, Pickett. You got caught for robbery and capital murder on the same day."

While Lassiter carefully stowed the evidence, Ray Burns, with Archie's help, put Pickett in a set of manacles with leg irons that only allowed him about a six-inch step. The arrogance was gone, replaced for the time being with resigned acceptance. He'd rail and wail before too long, but for the moment, Jackson Pickett was a shadow of himself, a captured animal with no control over its fate.

"I'm sure we'll see each other again," Detective Lassiter said, shaking Bell's hand.

"I don't think either of us are going to miss his trial."

"Or execution."

"Or that."

The two detectives left with their prisoner. The warehouse door shut with an echoing clang more ominous than any jail cell gate.

A few moments of silence passed before Archie said, "I think that wraps this up for us. What do you say, Isaac?"

"I guess it does." He turned and gave a last look at the boxcar full of Federal Reserve notes, then said farewell to Carver and Haygarth.

Out in the sunshine, Archie remarked, "This was a tough one."

"It was," Bell replied. "And they just keep getting tougher."

"What's next?"

"I don't know about the next case, but I have to confess to making one more phone call I didn't tell you about."

"Who to?"

"I called Marion. She and Lillian are on their way to New Orleans and should arrive in time for dinner. Tomorrow morning, we're booked into a couple of suites on a real stern-wheeler, heading up to St. Louis. I figured the old man owes us a few days off."

Arch clapped his hands in delight. "Now we're talking."

"The best part," Bell said with a wide grin, "is that Lillian insisted you pay."

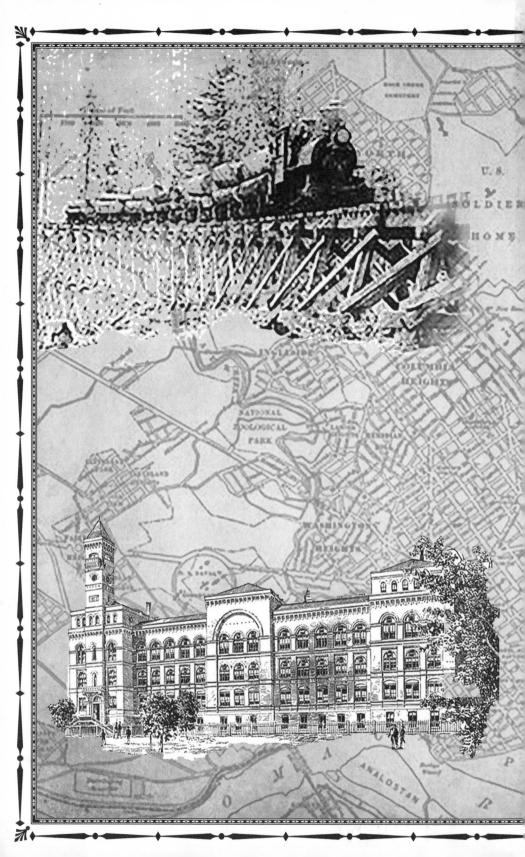